## PRAISE FOR *TH*

MW00474033

"[An] exceptional psychological thriller . . . White does a superb job keeping the reader guessing as she peels back the layers of a seemingly perfect family to reveal the shocking truth. Suspense fans will want to see more from this talented author."

—*Publishers Weekly* (starred review)

"*The Patient's Secret* is an intensely moving reading experience . . . Loreth Anne White is a writer at the top of her game, and it's never been more evident than with this piece of work."

—*Mystery & Suspense Magazine*

## PRAISE FOR *BENEATH DEVIL'S BRIDGE*

"The suspenseful, multilayered plot is matched by fully realized characters. White consistently entertains."

—*Publishers Weekly*

"If I'm lucky, maybe once in a blue moon, I read a book that leaves my mind reeling, heart aching, and soul searching. One that haunts me long after The End. *Beneath Devil's Bridge* is one of those books."

—*Mystery & Suspense Magazine*

## PRAISE FOR *IN THE DEEP*

"Convincing character development and a denouement worthy of Agatha Christie make this a winner. White has outdone herself."

—*Publishers Weekly* (starred review)

"This page-turner is tightly written with a moody sense of place in the small coastal community, but it is the numerous twists that will keep readers thoroughly absorbed. A satisfyingly creepy psychological thriller."

—*Kirkus Reviews*

## PRAISE FOR *IN THE DARK*

"White (*The Dark Bones*) employs kaleidoscopic perspectives in this tense modern adaptation of Agatha Christie's *And Then There Were None*. White's structural sleight of hand as she shifts between narrators and timelines keeps the suspense high . . . Christie fans will find this taut, clever thriller to be a worthy homage to the original."

—*Publishers Weekly*

"White excels at the chilling romantic thriller."

—The Amazon Book Review

"*In the Dark* is a brilliantly constructed Swiss watch of a thriller, containing both a chilling locked-room mystery reminiscent of Agatha Christie and *The Girl with the Dragon Tattoo* and a detective story that would make Harry Bosch proud. Do yourself a favor and find some uninterrupted reading time, because you won't want to put this book down."

—Jason Pinter, bestselling author of the Henry Parker series

## PRAISE FOR LORETH ANNE WHITE

"A masterfully written, gritty, suspenseful thriller with a tough, resourceful protagonist that hooked me and kept me guessing until the very end. Think C. J. Box and Craig Johnson. Loreth Anne White's *The Dark Bones* is that good."

—Robert Dugoni, *New York Times* bestselling author of *The Eighth Sister*

"Secrets, lies, and betrayal converge in this heart-pounding thriller that features a love story as fascinating as the mystery itself."

—Iris Johansen, *New York Times* bestselling author of *Smokescreen*

"A riveting, atmospheric suspense novel about the cost of betrayal and the power of redemption, *The Dark Bones* grips the reader from the first page to the pulse-pounding conclusion."

—Kylie Brant, Amazon Charts bestselling author of *Pretty Girls Dancing*

"Loreth Anne White has set the gold standard for the genre."

—Debra Webb, *USA Today* bestselling author

"Loreth Anne White has a talent for setting and mood. *The Dark Bones* hooked me from the start. A chilling and emotional read."

—T. R. Ragan, author of *Her Last Day*

"A must-read, *A Dark Lure* is gritty, dark romantic suspense at its best. A damaged yet resilient heroine, a deeply conflicted cop, and a truly terrifying villain collide in a stunning conclusion that will leave you breathless."

—Melinda Leigh, *Wall Street Journal* and Amazon Charts bestselling author

# THE UNQUIET BONES

## OTHER TITLES BY LORETH ANNE WHITE

*The Maid's Diary*

*The Patient's Secret*

*Beneath Devil's Bridge*

*In the Deep*

*In the Dark*

*The Dark Bones*

*In the Barren Ground*

*In the Waning Light*

*A Dark Lure*

*The Slow Burn of Silence*

### Angie Pallorino Novels

*The Drowned Girls*

*The Lullaby Girl*

*The Girl in the Moss*

# THE UNQUIET BONES

A NOVEL

LORETH ANNE
WHITE

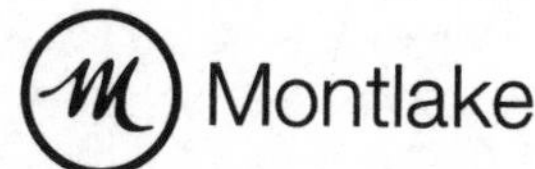

This is a work of fiction. Names, characters, organizations, places, events, and incidents are either products of the author's imagination or are used fictitiously. Otherwise, any resemblance to actual persons, living or dead, is purely coincidental.

Text copyright © 2024 by Cheakamus House Publishing
All rights reserved.

No part of this book may be reproduced, or stored in a retrieval system, or transmitted in any form or by any means, electronic, mechanical, photocopying, recording, or otherwise, without express written permission of the publisher.

Published by Montlake, Seattle

www.apub.com

Amazon, the Amazon logo, and Montlake are trademarks of Amazon.com, Inc., or its affiliates.

ISBN-13: 9781662518003 (hardcover)
ISBN-13: 9781542038577 (paperback)
ISBN-13: 9781542038560 (digital)

Cover design by Caroline Teagle Johnson
Cover image: © Stephen Mulcahey / ArcAngel; © Mehul Patel / ArcAngel

Printed in the United States of America

First edition

*For my mom.*

Evil is unspectacular and always human, and shares our bed and eats at our own table.

—W. H. Auden

# NOTE TO THE READER

*The Unquiet Bones* touches on themes around generational trauma that might be triggering for some readers.

# THE UNEARTHING

***April 2023***

A steady rain falls as Benjamin and Raphael Duvalier work their excavator alongside a dark lake on the misted flanks of Hemlock Mountain. The brothers are digging up the concrete foundations of an old and tiny wooden A-frame chapel. The chapel is located at the Hemlock Ski Resort area base and is being moved higher into the alpine to make way for an expansion. It's barely dawn, and the temperature hovers around freezing. Behind them the forest creeps down the mountain and wraiths of mist finger between the trees. Empty lift chairs hang motionless on cables that disappear into the low clouds.

Benjamin claps his gloved hands together, trying to get blood to flow into his frozen fingers. This wet cold is far worse than dryer temperatures well below freezing. His brother is at least warmer inside the excavator cab. Raphael pulls the hydraulic control and scoops up another load of concrete and damp earth. He swivels the bucket out over the bed of a waiting truck and dumps its contents inside. The big vehicle sinks a little under the fresh weight.

Using the back of his glove, Benjamin swipes rain from his face and then points to the ground, showing his brother where to dig next. The excavator bucket swings back. Raphael moves the lever. The bucket lowers to the ground, and the teeth dig into black soil. He moves his controls again and begins to scoop.

The bucket's teeth hook something and jerk it free of the earth. Benjamin's heart jumps. He hurriedly steps forward in an effort to process what he's seeing.

"Whoa! Whoa. Stop!" he screams, shooting his hand into the air and making a slicing motion across his neck.

Raphael halts the excavator arm. He hops down from the cab and runs over to where Benjamin has crouched. Benjamin carefully brushes damp soil off the long object that has been pulled up in the dirt. His heart hammers. He glances at Raphael.

They have hooked two big, long bones.

Benjamin knows they are not from a large animal because the thing hanging off the end of them is a boot.

A woman's boot with a platform heel.

# JANE

Sergeant Jane Munro forces herself to concentrate on the words coming out the mouth of the emaciated blonde seated across from her in the church basement semicircle.

"I'm exhausted," the woman laments. "To the core of my bones. All. Of. The. Time."

Her name is Stephanie. She's a mom. Or was. *What do you call a mother whose child is missing, simply gone?*

"My friends say I should return to work, but I can't." Stephanie fidgets with a tattered tissue in her lap. Her body matches her voice: ragged, reedy, broken. Her eyes are red-rimmed and puffy. That's the thing about support groups: lots of crying. It makes Jane tense. She's a cop. Not just any cop—a veteran homicide investigator. She's trained her entire adult life to *not* cry, or at least not in public, and her body and mind are at war in this church basement because while she is sympathetic to Stephanie's plight, feeling too much empathy threatens Jane's grip on her own emotions. She can't afford to crack. She'd split open, and her guts would spill all over the place—she's not sure she'd ever be able to gather the parts back into her skin if she did.

"I'm afraid to leave the house because what if Jason comes home?" Stephanie asks. "He won't know where to find me." She blows her nose with that damp, ragged tissue while the group murmurs in agreement.

Jason is Stephanie's eight-year-old son. He vanished one afternoon fourteen months ago, never to be seen or heard from again.

There are seven other similarly afflicted souls seated with Jane on orange plastic chairs that have been arranged in a semicircle to face a therapist who volunteers her time. They're gathered downstairs in the community center attached to the Our Lady of the Bay Church. A chill spring rain falls outside, and the sky is low with gunmetal-gray clouds. But down here, beneath overly bright and institutional fluorescent lights, it's too warm and the room stinks of stale coffee and the sugary smell of deep-fried donuts. The group members come from different walks of life and vary in age, but they all have one terrible thing in common. They're all struggling to cope with the strange grief that attaches when a loved one goes missing.

Not dead.

Simply *gone*.

One day they are going about ordinary life, the next they are absent. Vanished as if into thin air, leaving a thrumming, pulsing, living, breathing hole that won't die. Or live. It's a hellish kind of limbo, this not knowing. This waiting with no fixed end point. Most people who have not gone through this trauma find it impossible to understand.

"I totally get you," says a father seated to Stephanie's right. His name is Christopher—the members are on first-name terms only, sharing just as much as they are comfortable with. Jane is not comfortable. Not with any of it. Christopher has clearly come straight from some kind of construction or road work. He wears heavy-weight jeans, and his steel-toed boots are covered with mud. His hands are rough and chapped. Like Jane, he's probably taken a late lunch in order to attend group. Christopher mentioned earlier that he recently turned fifty-five, but to Jane he looks at least ten years older. Two years ago, his eighteen-year-old daughter went to a nightclub downtown with friends. She never came home. Christopher and his wife still have no answers. They've since divorced. As Stephanie has. This purgatory takes a toll in so many subversive ways. It sparks fissures through even the most solid of families. It carves off friends. Erodes confidence. Shatters a sense of self. Sabotages one's job.

Jane is intimate with the job-sabotage aspect. After a recent "episode" at work that almost cost a high-profile homicide case, she has been temporarily relegated to a cold case—or "special investigations"—unit of essentially one. Her boss at first suggested taking time off work, or perhaps starting her maternity leave early. But Jane can't take time off. She's terrified of being home alone with her thoughts. She *needs* to work. Her boss then suggested counseling. Which is why she's here now, sitting against her will in an orange plastic chair in an overly hot church basement listening to people like Stephanie and Christopher who have not managed to solve anything and will be of no help to her.

"It's like you can't even grieve," Christopher says. "Grieving feels like a betrayal, like you've given up. Meanwhile the whole world just starts to move on without you." He glances down at his chapped hands and says quietly, "Sometimes I feel like a glob of old blue toothpaste stuck in the basin that just won't wash down the drain. Stuck there and drying out."

Jane swallows. She knows the stats. She's keenly aware that the odds of him ever seeing his daughter again are nil. Christopher and his ex-wife will be lucky to just locate her remains one day, to have a chance to say a proper goodbye via a burial or cremation. Same with Stephanie and her little boy. Same with all of them. Her eyes suddenly burn, and her gaze darts to the basement window, seeking escape. She clenches her fists, fixates on the grimy pane streaked with rain and mud as she fights to hold in tears. *Just get through this. Survive one meeting. Preferably without saying anything. Don't cry. Get angry. Angry is easier. Stay angry.*

"I just want to know what happened to my baby. That's all. Even if I can't have him back." Stephanie dabs her red nose with the snotted tissue.

Jane's blood pressure peaks. There's a whole goddamn box of fresh Kleenex on the low table in front of Stephanie. Why in heaven's name can't the miserable woman take a clean tissue? Can't she *see* them? Perspiration prickles above Jane's lip. Panic tickles in her stomach. It's the start of a claustrophobia attack—she's going to be buried alive. She's never going to escape this hot basement, these sorry people, the stink of stale coffee.

"Closure," says someone else. "We all just need closure. Either a license to properly grieve, or to have them come home."

Stephanie nods and tries to reopen her tattered tissue.

The therapist leans forward and shoves the Kleenex box closer to Stephanie, who finally—thank heaven—takes a fresh tissue.

The therapist says, "This physical and psychological exhaustion is completely normal. When a loved one disappears, either in body or—in some cases, as with dementia—in mind, it can be the most stressful type of loss. A type that lacks answers. Unclear, indeterminate. No boundaries or resolution. It manifests in ways similar to post-traumatic stress disorder. And you're all correct, it's not properly acknowledged by society in general. As you've all noted, there's this perception that the world is moving on, yet you are unable to move with it, and this creates feelings of dissonance and isolation. Which is why groups like this are important. To share. To know we are not alone. It really does help to identify with others who understand what you're going through. And it's important to know this type of loss has a name. Ambiguous loss. Or grief limbo." The facilitator looks directly at Jane. "Would anyone else like to share today?"

Jane casts her eyes down and focuses on a spot on her knee. She feels the heat of everyone's attention turn to her.

"Jane?" asks the therapist.

Jane clears her throat but continues to stare intently at her knee.

"Jane?"

She glances up sharply. "Look, we all know the stats. We have the highest number of missing persons reports per capita in our province. In BC alone, well over thirteen thousand adults and five thousand kids go missing each year. To be realistic, most of those are never—"

"Jane," the facilitator says in a warning tone. "Perhaps you'd like to start with what brought you here?"

"No, I—I'm good. Thanks."

They all stare at her.

She failed.

She planned to sit through one session and not say a thing. Now she's opened her damn mouth, and her emotions are already simmering right at the surface. Her sinuses are thick with it. Her throat aches from the tension of holding it in. Her head pounds. She knows that if she dares to speak Matt's name out loud, she'll crumple into a sodden heap like Stephanie's tissue.

She draws in a deep, slow, steadying breath, and very quietly, she says, "I'm not quite ready."

"That's fine. Perfectly fine," says the therapist.

The slender and well-dressed dark-haired man sitting to Jane's right leans forward. He meets Jane's gaze with a gentle but commanding presence. The kind of presence Jane can relate to.

"It took me a while to be able to voice my loss," he says. "It's been fourteen months now, since my wife vanished. I still shop for her at the grocery store. I'm always searching for her in crowds. Sometimes I even think I see her on the SkyTrain, and my heart races before my brain can even engage. I still jump like a live wire every time my cell rings. And—" He heaves out a big sigh. "Anger. I am so quick to enrage, and I take it out on people who are only trying to help. But no one can ever say the right thing, can they?" He pauses, holding Jane's attention. "Because there is no right thing to say."

"Closure," Stephanie murmurs again. "We all just need some closure."

*I don't need closure. I'm going to find Matt. Alive. He's not gone, he can't be. I'm not prepared to capitulate. I believe with all my heart he's out there somewhere.*

The therapist says, "We need to bear in mind that in the context of ambiguous loss, 'closure' is a myth. It's easy to succumb to intense societal pressure to 'find closure,' and this message is drummed home by the media, reinforced in movies and in novels. It's echoed in comments from friends and family. We live in a society that places high value on resolving problems, on finding solutions, on 'getting over' things quickly. But when society is faced with people who are missing, there's a disconnect, a discomfort. They don't know how to cope with people who are missing loved ones, or with situations that actually have no answers or resolutions. We should not be forced to chase closure," she warns. "What we need to find are ways to coexist with our complex feelings, and to always remember that our reactions are completely normal." She glances at Jane. "They're not a sign of personal weakness."

This does not sit at all well with Jane. She's a fixer. She solves and resolves. Takes action. Gets answers. Finds bad guys. Closes cases. Punishes perpetrators.

Her phone vibrates on silent in her pocket. She considers ignoring it. The group rule states no phones. It vibrates again. It promises escape. Jane opens her blazer pocket and awkwardly peers at her mobile's screen. Her pulse quickens. It's a text from her boss.

Call me. Human remains located. Historic. Suspicious circumstances.

She immediately surges to her feet with a rush of almost gleeful energy. "I need to make a call."

"We have a strict no-phone rule," Stephanie snaps.

Jane ignores her and makes quickly for the coatrack near the exit door. She feels the eyes of the group burning into her back. She moves faster, trying to outrun an irrational feeling they might claw her back into the circle. She grabs her coat off the hook, then hesitates as guilt rises in her chest. She turns to face them. "I'm sorry. It's an emergency."

"Like what?" Stephanie's tone is mocking and angry now. "Did someone *die*?"

Jane pushes her arms into her coat. "Yeah, actually. Someone did." She reaches for the door handle, but their miserable faces make her waver. "I really am sorry," she says quietly, then pushes out the door.

Jane makes her way up the stairs and out the church building's doors. The cold, damp air hits her like lifeblood. She stands for a moment under the portico and sucks it deep into her lungs. Once she's composed herself, she calls her superior in the homicide unit at the Royal Canadian Mounted Police headquarters in Surrey.

He answers immediately.

"Jane. Human remains were unearthed early this morning at the Hemlock Ski Resort base during some construction. Likely historical. Anthropologist and coroner are on site. How do you feel about taking the lead on this one?"

Her hand tightens on the phone as excitement tingles through her body. She also hears the caution in his tone. He's wary of how she will handle this. Jane modulates her response.

"Are the remains suspicious?"

"It's a crime scene until we have evidence to the contrary. How soon can you be there?"

She glances at her watch. "Give me twenty." It's a lie. It'll probably take longer, but she's desperate for this diversion.

"Take Murtagh to assist. You'll be based out of the North Van detachment for this one. Ramp up as you see fit, and keep me apprised." The line goes dead.

Jane closes her eyes and places her hand on her pregnant belly.

*Thank you, thank you, thank you. This I can control.*

She pulls her hood over her head, steps into the pouring rain, and strides purposefully to her car as her mind races ahead. She needs to pick up boots at her apartment. It'll be muddy, possibly even snowy, on Hemlock. Her apartment is on the way. She beeps her lock, climbs into her vehicle, starts the engine. While waiting for the windows to defog, she calls Corporal Duncan Murtagh and tells him to meet her at the Hemlock Ski Resort base. She flips down her sun visor, where she keeps a photo of her fiancé, Matt Rossi. He smiles back at her. Tanned and fit and strong and so full of life. Jane's chest tightens. She touches her fingertips gently to his face, then flips the visor back up. She pulls out of the parking space and feeds into busy city traffic, aiming for the bridge that will take her over to the North Shore. From there she will head east and drive up the snaking switchbacks of Hemlock Mountain. As she drives, she hopes to hell this turns out to be a homicide, because she needs this.

# JANE

Jane begins to climb the switchbacks into the old-growth forests of Hemlock Provincial Park. Mist sifts through the moss-covered trees and veils the road. Rain drums down steadily. She turns on her fog lights.

As she drives higher, the late afternoon grows darker and temperatures plummet. She turns up the heater, but a chill seems to invade her bones. There's a brooding quietness, a loneliness, about this wilderness that presses in around her vehicle and makes the nearby bustling city seem a million miles away. Her thoughts turn to Matt, lost and hurt in a wild place like this. She tightens her fists around the wheel.

He went missing at the end of September, failing to return from a solo hiking trip in the Cayoosh Mountains. That was just over six months ago now, and every day of his absence, their baby grows a little more. Matt doesn't even know she is pregnant. Jane only found out after he vanished, and her tummy is like a visible clock ticking up the days he's been gone. Everyone can see by the size of her bump just how long her fiancé has been missing, and it makes for awkward conversations she'd rather avoid. Part of Jane wonders whether Matt might have fought harder to come home had he known they were pregnant—he always said he wanted kids, a big family. She regrets with all her heart suggesting to him that they wait some years. And now look at her. Pregnant by some cosmic design despite her best efforts otherwise. He'd have laughed so hard. He'd be so happy. Emotion balls sharply in her throat.

*Focus.*

A yellow sign materializes in the fog—Hemlock Ski Resort Boundary. A few moments later, Jane arrives at the first ski area parking lot. Rain beats down harder. Wipers clacking, she continues to the upper lot outside the Three Cedars Lodge. The windows in the heavy wooden lodge building glow with warm light. She notices a construction site trailer next to the building. Parked in front of the trailer are several trucks, all with Duvalier Bros & Sons logos, along with three marked RCMP cruisers, the coroner's SUV, and a white van displaying the logo from the Seymour Hills University Forensic Institute. Jane parks beside the coroner's vehicle. She spies a little hula doll on the dash that tells her the coroner attending today is Darby Williams.

Jane kills her engine and takes a moment to corral her work persona. But before she can fully gather her thoughts, a sharp knock sounds on her window.

She squints through the rain-speckled glass. Duncan Murtagh. Already being overeager.

Jane mutters a soft curse, unbuckles her seatbelt, reaches for her cap, pulls it on, and grabs her crossbody bag that contains her mobile, notebooks and pens, spare crime scene gloves, and other kit. She swings open her door and maneuvers her pregnant body out from behind the steering wheel.

Duncan is tall, buff. He's a gym rat and low-carb zealot who continually tries to convert everyone to his keto-style eating. As usual he's attired in all-black technical gear, which gives him that particular Pacific Northwest urban-alpine look. Droplets bead and roll off his well-cut GORE-TEX jacket like little silver jewels. He wears a Raptors ball cap over his dark-red hair. His skin is so pale it's almost translucent against his neatly trimmed red beard. He gives her a big grin that reveals a gap between his front teeth and shoves a travel mug toward her before she's even properly out of her car.

"Coffee," he says.

Jane's bolt of irritation is instantly tempered. She takes the mug from him, sips, then glances up into his pale-gray eyes. "It's still hot."

"Right? I brought a spare travel mug for you. Filled it at the gas station near the turnoff. Wasn't sure if there'd be anything warm up here in the offseason."

She takes another sip. Just the right amount of sugar, too, despite the fact he doesn't touch the "poison" himself.

"Thanks," she says. And means it, because damn, this feels welcome right now.

"I've spoken to the first responders," he says. "The remains were found in a shallow grave up that trail over there that starts at the far end of the parking lot. The remains are beneath where the old skiers' chapel was." He points.

Jane can see a white privacy tent that has been erected over the find. It's beside a small lake, about one hundred meters up a gravel trail from the parking lot. Yellow crime scene tape has been strung across the trailhead.

"What happened to the chapel building?" she asks.

"Being relocated for the base area expansion. Apparently it's been in that location by the lake since the midsixties. Right now it's up on wooden blocks behind the tent. They need to wait for enough snow to melt in the alpine before they can heli-lift it to the new location. Two of the Duvalier brothers were busy demolishing the concrete crawl space under the chapel early this morning when they dug up what looked to them like human leg bones with a boot still on. They halted work right away, called it in. Coroner and North Van RCMP attended, followed by the forensic anthropology team from the SHU institute."

Jane surveys the rest of the area as she listens to Duncan, taking in the chairlifts, the heavy mist obscuring the mountains, the two uniformed officers conversing in the rain beside one of the RCMP vehicles. As she turns her attention to the lower parking lot, she notices a white SUV with a circular red logo on the side crawling slowly into the lot. Jane curses. She calls the two uniforms over.

"Get that media vehicle out of here." She points at the SUV. "No press or unauthorized civilians are to access this upper lot. This entire area is a crime scene until we know what we're dealing with. Tape it all off."

The cops hurry to head off the SUV.

"Probably that Angela Sheldrick monster with her cameraman sidekick," she snaps as she begins to stride toward the trailhead, coffee in hand. Duncan hurries after her and quickly falls in step.

"Where are the two brothers now?" Jane asks.

"Got them waiting in the lodge for statements."

As they climb the trail toward the tent site, they're greeted by the hum of a generator. The lake reflects the gloomy sky, and the surface is pocked with rain. A yellow excavator is parked beside a heavy-duty truck partially filled with damp soil, and behind the tent, Jane can see the tiny wooden A-frame chapel standing on pallets waiting to be moved.

Duncan says, "They left the excavator and truck just as they were when they discovered the bones."

"Small mercies," Jane says quietly as she regards the A-frame. "It's seen better days—I remember that chapel." She tilts her chin toward the structure. "I came up here with my dad a couple of times back in the day." Somewhere in her mother's old albums is a faded Polaroid of ten-year-old Jane dressed in bright ski gear feeding peanuts to the whisky jacks. It was a blindingly beautiful, sunny morning. She recalls clearly the stained glass panel that still runs the length of the A-frame at the rear, and how the sun that day exploded the light in the vivid blues, reds, greens, and golds of the design: a Madonna and child.

Before she allows her mind to turn to her own unborn child, Jane swivels abruptly and heads for the privacy tent erected over the area where the chapel once stood. Outside the tent, a uniformed officer shelters beneath an extended awning. Rain drips everywhere. Beside the uniform is a table with plastic storage bins that contain white crime scene suits, booties, and blue nitrile gloves.

Jane and Duncan show the uniform their IDs. He notes the time and their names, then signs them in. They set down their coffees and begin pulling the Tyvek boiler suits and booties over their clothing. The gear is tighter over Jane's stomach than usual. She notices Duncan noticing, and tension is suddenly tangible in the air between them.

Duncan quickly clears his throat. "The forensic anthropologist has confirmed the remains are definitely human," he says in an effort to deflect awkwardness. As he speaks, the tent flap opens and a stocky woman in a boiler suit steps out.

"Jane! I thought I heard you out here. Hey, Murtagh."

Darby "Darb" Williams is a coroner Jane knows well and is fond of. In her early sixties, she sports a trademark grin, a weather-beaten complexion, and a crop of light-brown hair streaked with silver. Darb is unfailingly warm, friendly, and infinitely knowledgeable. She's earned the respect of homicide units and the communities she has served.

"Darb," Jane says. "Good to see you."

The coroner's gaze flicks briefly to Jane's belly, and her toothy grin fades ever so slightly. "How are you, Jane?"

The question is loaded. Jane becomes acutely aware of Duncan standing behind her, of voices inside the tent falling quieter, of the uniform listening. Tension bands across her chest.

"Fine." She nods toward the tent. "What've we got in there?"

Darb opens the flap and leads Jane and Duncan into a blindingly bright interior lit with generator-powered light towers. The damp and loamy scent of recently turned soil is heavy, musky.

Jane has, over the years, developed her personal approach to crime scenes. On arrival she prefers to zero in on the body—or bodies—and then expand her attention slowly outward from there, mentally cataloging details as she goes. It's what works for her. The first thing she notices is the bones protruding from a shallow pit of freshly turned dark soil. The bones are stained brown and caked with dirt. Large. They protrude at about a thirty-degree angle from the earth. Tibia and fibula. Hanging on the end of them is clearly a women's knee-high boot with a high platform heel. Part of a torso has been exposed by the team of anthropologists. Embedded in dirt at the top of the torso is a partially revealed skull.

A frisson of energy quivers through her body. She quiets her mind, focusing.

While the tibia and fibula are most definitely skeletonized, the torso by contrast is a puzzling and bloated-looking shape caked with earth and covered by what appears to be darkened bits of fabric that have gone a deep, rusty orange. The skull, however, is devoid of soft tissue. The jaw is open, exposing intact teeth in a wide scream that has been silenced with a mouthful of suffocating soil. The eye sockets are also packed with dirt. A sightless witness screaming some silent truth.

Three people in white suits work around the grave area, which has been outlined and gridded with twine and little pegs. At the edge of the shallow pit, a woman sits on an upturned bucket. She marks coordinates on graph paper, mapping the scene, while a younger woman crouches inside the pit, measuring distances between pegs and calling out measurements. On the far end of the grave, a young man works on hands and knees. He holds his ear close to the ground as he gently taps the back of his trowel onto the earth along the perimeter of the depression. He seems to be listening for changes in sound that might indicate differences in soil density that, in turn, might define the grave perimeter.

The woman on the bucket glances up. Her eyes are green and bright, her skin pale and freckled. Her dark hair is pulled back into an untidy knot. Jane guesses her to be in her early fifties.

Darb says, "This is Dr. Ella Quinn from the SHU Forensic Institute. Previously from the University of Dundee. And her grad students, Hakim Akhtar and Susan Freimont."

Jane nods. "What are we looking at, Dr. Quinn?"

A camera flashes as Duncan begins to take photos.

"Call me Ella, please. It's still early, but so far we've seen evidence of only one set of human remains." The professor's voice is husky, assured, but gentle. Jane detects a slight accent.

Ella points her pencil toward the leg bones. "The excavator teeth caught and lifted those long bones of the leg—tibia and fibula—and disturbed the boot, which appears to be a women's size seven." She meets Jane's gaze. "It's a platform boot."

"I see," Jane says, and her heart beats a little faster. She'll never admit it, but a new case, a fresh body, always hits with a thrill. She'd wager that any good homicide cop would be lying if they claimed to not feel the same anticipation. And she really *needs* this right now. She's desperate for this to be a suspicious death—a murder—something that calls for her expertise, that begs to be solved, that will get her out of the basement room where she's been going through boxes of cold case files, searching for ones that might be reopened and solved using new DNA tech.

"Definitely a female?" Jane asks.

"Well, a woman's boots. And given the shoe size, plus the length of the tibia and fibula, plus looking at the features of the skull and jaw, and from what we can see from the state of the bones and the teeth so far, this person is young. Very likely female. Likely Caucasian ancestral background. Slight in stature—possibly around five feet six at a conservative, very early guess."

"So we likely have a young, healthy woman buried in what appears to be a fairly shallow grave in the basement area beneath a chapel."

"Might not be a shallow grave," Duncan says. "I mean, she could have been buried much deeper in the earth before they started digging down toward her to lay the foundations."

Darb says, "The chapel was constructed in 1966. If our decedent was interred in this location before it was built, she would have been buried here for fifty-seven years or more. Over half a century."

Jane says, "But the torso doesn't even look skeletonized yet."

"It's not," Ella says. "It's saponified." She gets off her bucket and crouches down in the pit. She points at the torso with her pencil. "See this waxy, chalky-looking substance here? And these whiter striations there, and there?"

Jane crouches beside the professor, maneuvering around her burgeoning belly. "What is that?"

"Adipocere. Also known as grave or mortuary wax."

Hakim says, "As soon as we started to excavate around the body, groundwater started seeping up. This burial site is very damp, probably due to the lake proximity and a seasonal rising water table with the melt-freeze cycle. This moisture, combined with alkaline soil and certain anaerobic conditions, can over a period of time turn fatty human tissue into this waxy substance."

"How long does it take to form?" Jane asks. Duncan shoots more photos. The flash flares brightly.

Ella says, "We don't yet know all the specifics of saponification, but it does take an extended period of time." Her eyes gleam, and Jane realizes the professor is excited, too. "But once adipocere is formed, it can preserve a body and even soft tissue and some organic materials around it for decades, sometimes hundreds of years."

A silence hangs as Jane stares at the remains. "But the boot—a platform heel—did people wear those in the early sixties?"

"I think they did," Susan says, glancing up from her measuring. "But platform soles really took off and became the rage in the seventies." She smiles. "I'm a vintage clothing and thrift store addict—I know these things."

Jane regards the boot for a few moments, imagining it on a leg, walking. Belonging to someone alive, young. "How long to get her remains out of here and into a lab?" she asks.

Ella makes a moue. "Maybe another day or two just to brush and scrape away all the soil and fully expose her. It's a slow process. The very act of excavation destroys the context, so we really need to take the time to record, document, and preserve all trace evidence as we go. Our goal is to attempt to reconstruct the moment in time she was placed in the grave. So far we can see from soil markings that a rounded shovel—rather than a flat-ended spade—was used to dig the grave. And she was positioned in the hole on her back and fully laid out, rather than rolled in, or doubled over onto her side. As you can see, her arms were folded over her chest."

"Like a mummy," says Duncan.

"Like someone took care with her," offers Jane.

"Possibly," Ella says. "Once we have her fully exposed, and once we've examined and recorded everything about her in situ, we'll try to get her into a body bag in one lump mass." Ella addresses her students now, as much as the investigators. "At no point will we try to remove clothing or reach into a pocket to get a wallet or anything. Our job is to solely recover the remains along with artifacts, take it all to the morgue, and it's there where the relationships of any artifacts relative to the body can be further explored."

"CSI, history style," says Duncan as he snaps another photo.

Susan suddenly makes a noise of exclamation. "Oh, Professor, take a look at this." She points her brush at the side of the skull farthest from them all, which she has just cleared of soil.

Ella moves swiftly around to the other side of the grave and drops to her haunches to see what her student is pointing at. She glances up sharply. "Detective, you'll want to see this."

Jane pushes to her feet. Her knees crick. She places her hand at the small of her back as she moves around to join Ella. She crouches down awkwardly again.

Ella gently brushes away more soil with her gloved hand, exposing an irregularly shaped hole in the left side of the skull. It's about the size of a golf ball. A starburst of fracture lines radiates out from it.

"This is some significant trauma," the professor whispers as she leans closer for a better look. "I'm guessing this happened perimortem." She glances up and her gaze pins Jane's. "This is a blow that would have killed her."

# ANGELA

Angela Sheldrick and Rahoul Basra sit in their CBCN-TV vehicle at the far edge of the lower parking lot. They watch the cops stringing crime scene tape across the upper lot, barring access to the lodge. Rain hammers on the roof of their car, and water squiggles down the windows. They keep the engine and heater running.

Angela rubs a hole in the fog forming on her window. “That’s the same homicide cop who was in the news last fall,” she says quietly. “The one whose fiancé went missing in the Cayoosh Mountains.”

“Are you sure?” asks Rahoul.

“Sure I’m sure. Sergeant Jane Munro. She’s pregnant with the missing guy’s kid.”

“Crap,” Rahoul says softly. “That’s gotta be rough.”

Angela faces him. “You know what this means?” She points at the white tent in the darkening mist. “They’ve got a suspicious death up there under that tent. Something that warrants the attention of homicide.”

“What do you want to do?”

Angela mulls over the possibilities as she watches the cops moving outside the tent in the distance. They’ve put on white boiler suits and look like aliens visiting from another planet. They disappear into the tent. Rain drums down harder, bordering on slush now.

“Did you see those two construction guys entering the lodge when we arrived?” she asks.

"Yeah."

"The message we picked up on the scanner said a construction crew unearthed human remains, right? I'm going into the lodge. I want to talk to those men—it could be them who found the remains."

"You can't go in there. It's—"

"Wait here." Before her cameraman can answer, Angela exits the car and pulls her rain hood over her head. She runs through the rain toward two uniformed officers near the marked vehicles. As she nears, one steps forward.

"You need to leave, ma'am. This area is off-limits due to an ongoing police investigation."

"You mean this *whole* place is a crime scene?"

"Yes, ma'am. If you—"

"Is the lodge building a crime scene, too?" She moves from leg to leg as though uncomfortable. The yellow tape flutters. It's getting dark. Wind gusts and mist rolls down the mountain, enveloping the Three Cedars Lodge.

"You need to leave, or stay behind the tape."

"Okay, fine, sure, but if the actual lodge building is not off-limits, I really need to use the bathroom."

He glances over his shoulder at the lodge. From his reaction, Angela judges it's definitely not part of the crime scene. She doubles down.

"It's a long drive back down the mountain, and then there's going to be bridge traffic backed all the way up along the highway. It'll be hours before I can get to a bathroom. I mean, you guys can pee anywhere, but I *need* a bathroom. Do you mind if I go in quickly? The lodge is a public facility."

The cop is young. Practically baby-faced. He looks sympathetic to her plight.

She presses. "My cameraman and equipment are all in my car back there. I'll be real quick." She holds the cop's gaze with eyes she knows are her most arresting feature. Her TV trademark. Angela can draw viewers in simply with her gaze, and she uses this ability to play people, men especially. She feels no qualms doing so. If they want to be driven by their dicks and hormones, that's their problem. She isn't going to be young forever—*use it before you lose it* is her motto.

"Make it quick. Don't cross the lot. Stay along the side of the building."

"Thank you, thank you," she says breathily. That's her other marketable asset—her assured, low-timbre, slightly husky voice.

Angela slips under the tape that the officer holds up for her. She hurries through the rain and ducks into the covered portico area of the lodge. She enters through the massive double doors.

Inside it's warm but institutional with bright lighting. She assesses the scene as she pushes her dripping hood off her hair. Rows of melamine tables with benches line a wall beneath grimy windows in need of a spring wash. Cafeteria counters are gleaming and empty. A giant fireplace stands cold and barren at the far end of the hall. The flooring is scuffed after a season of skiers clumping through with heavy boots as they carry trays with burgers, fries, bowls of steaming chili. Vending machines stand along the far wall near washroom doors.

The place is empty of people apart from two men in construction gear sitting at one of the tables in the rear.

Angela draws in a breath, straightens her spine, and strides purposefully over to their table.

The men glance up and watch her approaching. She smiles as she nears.

"Hi, are you the guys who found it?"

They exchange a quick, puzzled glance.

"Who's asking?" says one.

*Bingo.*

"Angela Sheldrick." She takes a seat at their table. "Do you mind if I join you for a moment?"

"Do we have a choice?" asks the older guy.

She deepens her smile. "I'm the crime reporter for CBCN-TV." She moves a fall of damp hair off her shoulder as she speaks, and she notices the flare of interest in the eyes of the younger guy. The one not wearing a wedding band. Angela directs the heat of her attention on him. "You guys are with Duvalier Bros & Sons construction, right?" She gestures over her shoulder. "I saw the sign on the site trailer outside. You were relocating that old chapel when you made the find."

For a moment the men regard her in silence.

"Look." She digs in her pocket, fishes out two business cards, slides one over to each of them. "It's no crime to talk to the media, and this is such an intriguing story. We picked it up on our scanner. We follow fire, police, other emergency services, and we can also pick up chatter from the Hemlock Mountain staff using radios. That chapel was constructed in the sixties, right? So fascinating to think that all these years there has been a body beneath the feet of worshippers. And you were the guys to find it." She pauses, giving them a beat to process. "I was hoping you could tell me a little bit about what you saw, what you noticed first, and what that felt like. What made you think the remains were human?"

Angela is using her tried-and-true technique. If they don't refute anything, she'll assume she's generally on the right track.

"My brother saw the bones first," the older man says. "I was operating the excavator."

"You're brothers?" She grins. "The Duvalier brothers, right? I should have seen that right away—I can totally see that now."

"Benjamin Duvalier," says the younger one.

"Raphael," says the married one.

She shakes their hands. Big, rough, working hands that feel strong and warm and appealing. She likes these guys. Angela works a lot from her gut.

Raphael says, "We haven't given official statements to the detectives yet. We were asked to wait here. I'm not sure what we're permitted to tell you."

She feels the clock ticking. "The homicide cops? Oh, they can take a while. And like I said, it's not a crime to talk to the media. This is a real human interest story. Depending on what you saw, we could bring you guys on our show, interview you on air, maybe even reenact something later if we go more in depth."

"It was nothing much, really," Benjamin says. "I was spotting for Rafe, and when his bucket raked back earth and caught what looked like human bones, I yelled for him to stop."

"So you knew right away the bones were human and not from a large animal?"

"I'm a hunter. I know the bones of big animals. And animals don't wear boots."

Angela's pulse kicks. "Boots?"

Benjamin nods. "We just saw the one."

"What kind of boot? How old? What did it look like?"

As Benjamin opens his mouth, a tall, redheaded cop with a trimmed beard enters the building. He halts at the entrance, sees them, and immediately starts their way. Her pulse beats faster.

She leans forward and says quietly, urgently, "Can you describe the boot?"

Benjamin says, "It was all browned and caked with dirt, but it was long, like a knee-high."

Raphael says, "And it definitely had a heel."

The detective is almost at their table. Angela's heart races. "What kind of heel?"

Raphael glances at Benjamin. "One of those . . . wedge things, what are they called?"

"Platform heels," says his brother.

"So it was definitely a woman's boot?" Angela asks.

"Hey!" the redheaded Viking of a cop calls out to her.

"Here's your detective. I should go." She meets their gazes. "Thank you both. I'll contact you later," she whispers as she pushes off the bench.

"Hey, you," the cop calls after her.

Angela doesn't turn and doesn't wait to hear him out. She hastens for the rear exit near the washrooms, adrenaline pumping. She steps out into the rain and yanks her hood back over her head. She's amped. She scored enough for a breaking news segment on tonight's broadcast. She'll get Rahoul to film her near the Hemlock Ski Resort sign. She's also got an idea. She can use this piece to pitch her news-based reality crime show concept to Mason Gordon, the CBCN-TV program director. She'll do it as soon as her segment has aired.

She makes for the car, where Rahoul is waiting, feeling a rush through her blood. There's nothing quite like the hot thrill that comes with landing a fresh story—especially one with a body—and Angela's gut tells her this one is going to have all the feels.

# JANE

It's dark when Jane climbs the metal stairs to the site office trailer, rain glinting silver in her flashlight beam. Duncan has gone into the lodge to interview the Duvalier brothers, and Dr. Ella Quinn and her team continue their work under the tent. Ella will call when she is ready to move the remains to her lab at the institute. Jane reaches the door and is about to knock when she catches sight of the white CBCN-TV vehicle still parked beneath towering conifers at the far edge of the lower parking lot. She pauses, watches. The engine is running, and the vehicle's headlights poke hazy yellow tunnels into the foggy darkness. She sees a hooded figure cut through the beams. The figure goes around to the passenger-side door of the SUV and climbs in. Jane frowns, then raps on the trailer door.

She is warmly welcomed by the foreman, who introduces himself as Fred Duvalier. Duvalier Bros & Sons is clearly a family-run business. Fred is a burly, thick-necked man in his late fifties or early sixties with a ruddy complexion and blue-black hair. He wears a checked flannel shirt over a T-shirt and jeans. His sleeves are rolled back to expose muscled and hairy forearms.

"Sergeant, please, take a seat." He gestures toward a chair at the small table. His accent is heavily French Canadian. "Can I get you something to drink? Coffee, tea, water. We have cola?"

"I'm good." It's warm inside but she keeps her coat on. She's reluctant to draw attention to her pregnancy. It's an irrational impulse and

Jane knows it, but every well-meaning question or word of congratulations threatens her composure. She'd rather keep everyone's mind firmly on the investigation and away from the fact her fiancé is missing. She glances at plans pinned on the wall as she sits.

"The expansion for the ski area base?" she asks, gesturing to the diagrams.

"Yeah." He takes a seat on the other side of the table. "We're on a supertight schedule, and the clock is ticking on this project. We need to complete groundwork before it snows again, and every delay is costing us. Any idea when we can get back to clearing that chapel site?"

"It could take several days to fully process the scene before I can give the go-ahead. I'm sorry."

"So it's suspicious? A murder?"

"We'll conduct a full investigation." She takes out her notebook and pen, flips open a page. She records his name and the time. "From what I recall, the chapel itself is not the property of Hemlock Ski Resort but is managed by a foundation. Who contracted you to relocate the building?"

"It was part of an agreement with both Hemlock and the Skiers' Chapel Society. Hemlock needed space for the base expansion, and the chapel society wanted to preserve it. They came to an agreement to relocate it up in the high alpine along a hut-to-hut skiing and hiking loop." He rakes his fingers through his hair and mutters a soft French curse. "The mountain staff did say the A-frame was haunted."

She glances up. "Who said that?"

"The story was apparently passed down by one of the security guards who worked night shifts up here for years. Hemlock staff told a couple of my guys that the guard used to see a spirit that appeared in certain conditions at night. Some say she still occasionally hovers around the chapel."

"She?"

He gives a half shrug. "It's what the night watchman apparently said. He claimed to have seen her—the ghost—on several occasions over the years that he worked here. Apparently she manifests like a soft white light, sometimes with flowing robes, especially when it's foggy. And she materializes over the water when there's a full moon. Her appearance apparently comes with a strange sound in the trees."

Jane regards him. In her experience, most hearsay or lore is generally sparked by some small kernel of truth in origin. Given what has now been found beneath the chapel, these ghost stories might actually have some genesis in an element of truth from decades ago.

"Do you know the name of this guard?"

"I think someone mentioned his name was Horace . . . or Harvey someone, I think. No, wait, it's Hugo . . . Hugo Glucklich. Older guy. Retired."

"Do you know where I can find him?"

"Not a clue."

Jane makes a note. If her team can trace the provenance of the rumor, it could spark an additional investigative angle.

"Who heads up the chapel society?"

"Members of the Walker family. The chapel was built as an ecumenical place of worship to honor a young ski patroller who worked for Hemlock in the sixties. She went missing in an alpine avalanche while snowmobiling in the backcountry."

Jane's stomach tightens. She clears her throat. "What was her name?"

"Wendy Walker. The rest of her party was apparently dug out and survived. But her body was never recovered. Plenty of crevasses up there. They figure the avalanche washed her down one. Her father, Gerald Walker, also worked for Hemlock. He was the resort's financial officer, and he formed the Skiers' Chapel Foundation. Hemlock donated the land for them to build."

"Do you know why that parcel in particular was selected for the chapel?" Jane asks. "Did it hold any particular significance for anyone?"

"You'd have to speak to the Walkers. They're local. Live in Vancouver."

"And the chapel was constructed in 1966?"

"Yeah, over the summer of '66."

"You're certain?"

He nods. "But that's about all I know about the actual construction. If there were any building plans on file, they went up in the lodge fire back in the eighties. The south wing that housed the Hemlock admin offices was completely destroyed, along with all pre-eighties company records."

"What can you tell me about the space beneath the chapel?"

"It was basically a crawl space, or basement, under the A-frame. Maybe five feet in height. The chapel itself is tiny—just eighteen by thirty-two feet. Enough for some small pews, a little altar, and then that beautiful stained glass window with the Madonna and child."

"Was this basement area accessible from the outside of the building?"

"Yeah. It could be accessed via a door and down some steps from the outside."

"So if you went into the basement, you'd be able to walk around."

"You'd have to bend over unless you were super short, but yeah. There was also a sump pump down there. The pump was activated whenever the seasonal groundwater seeped up to a certain level."

This is consistent with Dr. Quinn's explanation of how and why the adipocere might have formed, Jane thinks as she makes a note. "And this sump pump—surely it would have been replaced or serviced a couple of times over the years since the midsixties?"

"For sure. But it wasn't there from the sixties. It came much later."

Jane's interest level ticks up. "When?"

"I imagine the chapel society might have records as to exactly when. My sense is the concrete floor was poured in at the same time the pump was installed. The flooring and the pump would both have been part of an overall moisture mitigation strategy."

"So it was a dirt floor before?"

"I reckon."

"And you don't know when exactly the concrete floor was laid?"

"We were never given those details. If the concrete was poured post 1980, there should be a record—the society would have funded it. But any pre-1980 financial records would have gone in the fire, since they were kept in Wendy Walker's father's office, which was in the south wing that burned."

Jane jots down the information. "And before you began demolishing the concrete floor, did you notice if any sections of concrete had been dug up and replaced?"

"All looked pretty smooth and consistent to me."

Jane's energy sharpens. If there was no sign the concrete had been disturbed, the shallow grave could have been dug directly into the earth at some point before the floor was laid and the pump installed. If she can nail the date the new floor went in, it could narrow the potential window for the postmortem interval.

Jane thanks Fred Duvalier and exits the trailer. As she makes her way back to her vehicle, she sees the tent up on the slope glowing with light like a strange luminous balloon. The SHU team will likely be busy well into the night. She climbs into her car, flips down the visor, touches her fingers to Matt's face, and says a quick and silent thanks to whoever left the bones lying in black earth under that tent. If Jane can't find closure for herself, she can at least try to close this—she'll find out who that deceased young woman is, give her back her name, and bring her home to her family.

# THE SHOREVIEW SIX

## Mary

Mary Metcalfe is in her office at her garden and landscaping center on Marine Drive in North Vancouver. She's checking her standing orders for spring hanging baskets. Her basket clients include hotels, restaurants, and two small municipalities, and they all want lush, blooming creations to install on patios and along walkways the instant the weather warms. It's her top seasonal pleasure. Spring is Mary's time to shine, and her heart always feels light at this time of year. She gets to meet her clients, too, as she assists hands-on with the truck deliveries. The feel of the baskets, the scents, the greenery, the color, the delight on her clients' faces when they first see the baskets—it makes life worth living.

Her two dogs, Bo and Jefferson, sleep at her feet. On her office wall are images of her company's handiwork: landscaping installments for both private and commercial clients, including a re-wilded garden and a Bavarian-style ski lodge property in the mountains. It's all a pleasure to Mary, and she doesn't mind late hours finishing up admin. Her work defines her. She wouldn't know who—or how—to be without it, especially since her beloved partner passed from breast cancer four years ago. And her daughter, Heather, long since moved away from home. She lifts her head as she thinks of Heather, and smiles.

"Soon," she says softly to Bo and Jefferson. They raise their doggie heads in unison, eyes expectant. "Soon we'll all have a new little human in our lives." Bo thumps her tail, and Jefferson gives a sigh and flops back into sleeping position.

Heather has been through a two-year-long adoption application process, and the news that she's been approved is fresh. Mary's daughter worried that being a single, working mom would be a stumbling block to adoption, but she's been given the all clear. Anyone over nineteen in this province technically has a right to adopt as long as they meet a few other basic requirements, but Heather—a worrywart—fretted nevertheless. This heartwarming news landed right after Heather learned she is the top contender for a job as principal at the exclusive Brockton House, a private university-preparatory school for girls. Mary has her own reservations about single-sex education, but Heather is ecstatic. If her references check out, as Mary knows they will, and if the parent council gives its rubber stamp of approval, Heather will start in the fall.

It means a top income, housing, status. Heather will also be able to afford an excellent live-in nanny. And Mary has made clear she will also be available to help 100 percent. She's already trained two excellent managers almost as devoted to the craft and art of gardening as she is.

It's taken a lifetime to reach this place of contentment, of self-acceptance. It almost makes up for her traumatizing teen years and her ensuing shambles of a marriage.

As Mary works, she keeps an ear out for the arrival of her takeout delivery. A small TV in the corner of her office is tuned to a local news channel, but muted. Jazz music plays softly. An ornamental water feature burbles, and her room is full with the scent of jasmine.

A knock sounds on the door that opens into a rear alley. Her food has arrived. Her stomach grumbles almost instantly. Mary gets up to answer the door just as a chyron flashes across the bottom of the television screen.

> Breaking news: woman's remains wearing platform boots found in shallow grave under old skiers' chapel on Hemlock Mountain.

Mary's brain hiccups. For a moment she can't move. She rereads the chyron. A crime reporter appears on screen. She has dark-brown hair, thick bangs, and big eyes. Angela Sheldrick. Mary can't hear what Angela is saying into her mike because the sound is muted, but images of the little chapel on Hemlock come on the screen. Historic images. The camera zeroes in on the big wooden cross at the apex of the A-frame structure.

Banging sounds again at her door. Louder. Insistent. Mary's heart thuds. She goes to open the door while still looking at the TV. Distractedly she takes her package from the DoorDash guy, almost forgetting his tip. She ferrets clumsily in her pocket, finds a ten-dollar note, thrusts it at him, and shuts the door in his face. She dumps her bag of warm pad thai onto a table and lunges for the TV remote. She bumps up the sound, rewinds the segment, hits PLAY.

Slowly, Mary seats herself on the sofa in her office used mostly by the dogs. She stares at the TV.

The CBCN-TV anchor says, "The human remains were unearthed early this morning by a construction crew preparing for the relocation of the historic chapel. Our crime reporter, Angela Sheldrick, was on scene late this afternoon."

The footage cuts to Angela Sheldrick with her mike. It's dark, misty. She stands beneath the Hemlock Ski Resort sign illuminated by camera lighting. Rain sparkles silver.

"What can you tell us, Angela?" the anchor asks.

"Construction workers Benjamin and Raphael Duvalier made the grisly grave-site find in the dark dawn hours on Hemlock Mountain today. The brothers were demolishing the chapel foundations when Raphael's excavator hooked what appeared to his brother, Benjamin, to be the lower bones of a human leg. The Duvalier brothers halted work immediately and contacted authorities," Angela says. "The local coroner and North Vancouver RCMP responded, and they were followed shortly thereafter by a forensic anthropology team from the Seymour Hills University Forensic Institute. This group was later joined by two

RCMP investigators, one—notably—from the homicide division. And the area behind me"—she gestures with her arm—"has now been cordoned off and declared a crime scene. The RCMP and the BC Coroners Service have not yet released any official statements, but it's clear this is a serious crimes investigation. Our CBCN-TV team was barred from entering, but we did manage to speak to the two brothers who made the discovery."

The anchor on one half of the split screen says, "And the Duvalier brothers were certain the bones were human?"

"Benjamin Duvalier says he is a hunter and knows his large-animal bones, and this was definitely no animal. While the leg bones had been skeletonized, they were still encased in a knee-high platform boot."

"A woman's boot?"

"With a high heel, yes. It's what the brothers described. I must stress, though, that there has been no official confirmation yet from the RCMP or the coroner's office that the body belongs to a woman."

"Do we know when the skiers' chapel was built?" asks the anchor.

Angela checks her notes as wind gusts hair across her face. "It was constructed over the summer of 1966 in memory of a local ski patroller who went missing in these mountains behind me."

The anchor says, "So these remains could date back to the summer of 1966, when the chapel was first built, or perhaps even earlier?"

"At this point nothing has been confirmed. However, the area does remain a crime scene. We will bring viewers more breaking news as soon as we have additional details."

Mary blinks. She replays the clip, listens again.

*It can't be her.*

The timing is wrong. But her best friend *was* wearing platform boots the night she vanished. Mary's mind blurs inward, narrowing down to a memory long buried, and suddenly, it's like she's right there again, on that clear, cool autumn night when she was sixteen.

*It's Friday night on Labour Day weekend, September 1976. Mary is walking home from a party with her best friend since kindergarten. It's around 11:00 p.m. The air is chilly and a half moon shines among the stars. Mary's friend is wearing her new knee-high platform boots, bought with money she earned working at the Donut Diner down on Marine Drive.*

*They chatter about how excited they are to start grade eleven on Tuesday, and what they're going to wear on the first day back at school. They circle back to discussing the exciting event of the night: the crowd of drunk older teens who came up from Ambleside Beach and crashed the dance party, overrunning the place. The young hostess, sixteen-year-old Rose Tuttle, couldn't control them. Terrified her house was being trashed and her parents would kill her when they got home the following day, Rose called the police. The cops arrived and busted up the party, scattering everyone off into the night. Some of the kids made plans to find more booze and regroup elsewhere, like the rest of Mary's close-knit group of school friends, but Mary insisted on walking her friend home. Something darker had happened at the party, and she needed to find a way to broach it, to get it off her chest.*

*"I reckon it was mostly Zane's crowd that came up from the beach," Mary says. "He knew about Rose's party from Rocco. I bet it was him who spread the word."*

*Wind gusts, scattering autumn leaves across the streets. An owl hoots. Mary hears the low growl of a slowly approaching motorbike again. She tenses as the helmeted rider rumbles past. It's the third time on their walk home that the biker has crawled by, clearly watching them. She picks up the pace.*

*"What's the rush?" her friend calls out, hastening to catch up, stumbling a little because she's had too much to drink.*

*"That biker is following us. I told you. I saw him two blocks up and one street across."*

*Her friend giggles.*

*"What's so funny?" Mary snaps.*

*"You. Big ol' Mary being frightened."*

*That cuts. Mary hates her bulk. She's been mocked about being* big *since she was in kindergarten.*

*"Mary Mary Quite Contrary, who's a wrestling champ, is really Scaredy Mary."*

*"You're drunk." Mary walks even faster. It's not like her best friend to be mean like this. It hurts. She just wants to get home now.*

*"Are you jealous, Mary?" her friend calls out behind her.*

*Mary keeps going, no longer willing to confront her friend about the issue at the party. No longer feeling charitable.*

*"I should have stayed with the others instead of walking home with loser Scaredy Mary!"*

*Mary whirls around. "What in the hell has gotten into you these past months? You're, like, determined to crash and burn up all your friendships and push everyone away, including me." Tears sting in Mary's eyes and emotion thickens her voice. "I don't know what I've done to you, and I don't know what you're trying to prove, but it's like you* want *me to hate you. That's why Darryl came up to me at the party. He's the one who said I should take you home. He was worried you were drinking too much and he saw you having sex behind the pool house and it wasn't with Robbie."*

*Her friend goes dead still. Wind blows her long, shiny blonde hair over her face, and leaves scatter and clatter over the paving. Somewhere a dog barks and a garbage can lid clatters.*

*"Darryl said this?"*

*"Yeah. He's a good guy. He's concerned about you."*

*"Fuck you. Fuck him!"*

*"What?"*

*"You heard me. I can sleep with whoever the hell I want. It's not his business."*

*"He's your friend. He's just—"*

*"He's just my fucking math tutor."*

*"Listen—"*

*"No, you listen to me." She waves a drunken finger as she comes forward, swaying. "I don't need your friendship, Scaredy Mary. I'm moving*

*on. In fact, I might even just leave town. Real soon. Get out of this shithole dump. And you know who I fucked at the party? It was Claude. And it wasn't the first time."*

*Mary's jaw drops. She can't think. Can't move. She tries to speak, but her voice comes out a hoarse croak. "Claude?"*

*"Yes, your boyfriend. Still want to be my friend now, Mary Mary Quite Contrary?"*

*"You're lying." Tears pool in her eyes.*

*Her friend comes closer. "I know why you're with Claude, Mary. I know why you do it with him all the time. You're a lesbian, that's why. You're gay and you are too scared to admit it. And you think if everyone knows you're having sex with Claude Betancourt, they won't see the truth. Even Claude says so."*

*Mary starts to shake. "That's not true. It's a lie. All lies."*

*Her friend laughs in her face.*

*Mary goes blind with rage. She lunges for her friend, grabbing her blonde hair.*

◆ ◆ ◆

Guilt rises hot in Mary's chest.

That was Friday night. By Monday night, everyone knew Mary's best friend since kindergarten was missing. And Mary's life spun out of control.

# THE SHOREVIEW SIX

## Mason

Mason Gordon, director of programming at CBCN-TV, is in his office at the station downtown. It's late evening, and he's just watched Angela's breaking news segment about the remains unearthed at Hemlock. He feels queasy. He tells himself it's nothing. Angela noted on air that the chapel was built in 1966. The remains were surely buried before it was built? Maybe the little church was put there expressly to hide the grave in the first place, and its whole raison d'être was to cover a dark deed. Maybe it wasn't even a dark deed, just a sanctioned burial in a crypt-like grave below the little building of worship. But then, why is homicide involved? His stomach cramps.

He gets up from his desk, goes to his cabinet, reaches for his bottle of bourbon. Mason has been triggered. He's suddenly desperate to temper the strange paranoia curdling in him. As he pours a couple of hefty shots into his glass, a loud knock on his office door makes him jump. Liquor spills over his hand. He curses and hurriedly sets the bottle down. The room now smells of booze. He takes a rapid swig, then another. He grabs a piece of paper towel and wipes his hand.

The knocking sounds again. Insistent.

Mason moves quickly toward the sofa and seats himself in front of his television screens, holding his drink.

"Come."

The door opens. Angela in a figure-hugging, bloodred dress peeps in. She has a file folder in her hand.

"Got a minute?" she asks.

He checks his watch. "Yeah. Come in. Close the door. Want a drink?"

She enters, and her gaze flicks from his glass to the bottle on the cabinet. She shuts the door and smiles. Angela is very beautiful. Young. Sharp. Ambitious. Way out of Mason's league. But he's still a full-throated male. He can enjoy the sights.

"No, I'm good. I'm glad you're still here. I've got something I'd like to bounce off you."

Of course he's still here. Fresh off his third divorce, Mason has zero impetus to go home to his cold, empty new apartment. It's gotten so bad he's taken to occasionally sleeping on the sofa in his office. He needs to get ahold of himself, get back into the gym, keep regular hours, eat properly, cut back on the drink. Or he'll end up in a bad place again. God knows it took him years to dig out of that pit.

"You saw my segment?" she asks as she takes a seat across from him.

"Good job scooping that one." He raises his glass in a slight toast and takes a sip. His mind races. *What does she want? Why is she asking? Does she suspect something?*

She crosses her legs in a slow and elaborate way. His eyes follow the movement. Angela notices and waits for his gaze to lift and meet hers again.

"This one's got legs, Mason."

His cheeks warm.

She grins. "Seriously. My gut tells me this story is going to go the distance." She leans forward, her eyes brightening as she speaks. "I want to use this chapel case to kick off the news-based reality show we discussed. We—"

"You discussed, I listened. We have no—"

"It's the *perfect* case, Mason. Picture it: I keep on top of the investigation as it unfolds, updating viewers on the nightly news as breaking information comes in, but at the same time we also direct viewers to a limited series program that we start streaming concurrently via our CBCN-TV app. It would be the station's first news-based, true-crime reality series. We can call it something like, *Someone Always Knows*, or *Silent Witness*, and we can use it to offer a far more in-depth, feature-style examination of the case. I'll interview forensic experts, investigators, psychologists, criminologists, true-crime writers, family members, friends, legal experts. And when the victim is identified, I'll walk viewers through that process, and we can hit the very real and emotional human angles, showing how the effects of an old crime can still ripple down new generations for years. We open up a comment area, ask for tips. People can either identify themselves or leave their tips anonymously. Tell me you don't love the idea."

Mason feels the infectious pull of Angela's barely bridled enthusiasm. But it slams hard against the unease swirling deeper and deeper into his stomach. He's got a real bad feeling about this case.

Angela presses him. "It will bring in new subscribers, Mason. The higher-ups will be on board financially," she says. "And it won't take a huge budget. It's basically low risk and a no-brainer."

"The case might be nothing but an ordinary burial beneath a church."

"I seriously doubt it's anything *ordinary*." Angela begins to check points off her fingers as she speaks. "The remains are human, and likely belong to a woman. She was found beneath a tiny ecumenical chapel built to honor another woman who died many years ago. This alone has vibes. I mean, the victim's body was beneath a floor on which people have stood for decades to worship and marry and hold memorial services and christen their babies. It's a family ski resort. Generations of kids from the North Shore learned to ski up there. Hemlock and that old chapel are part of the historical fabric of the North Shore community. Plus we have Sergeant Jane Munro, a veteran homicide cop, working the case. She was all over the news this past fall when her fiancé, Matt Rossi—a local mountaineer, search and rescue volunteer, and beloved North Shore baker—vanished in the Cayoosh Mountains north of Mount Currie." Angela checks off a last finger. "Plus, Munro is about six months pregnant, presumably with Rossi's child. Seriously, Mason, this already has all the feels."

Mason rubs his jaw. A sharp slice of memory cuts into him like a hot knife through butter.

*He grips a heavy bar in his hand. It's dark. He can't remember where he is, but it feels industrial. He recalls the sensation of raising the weight of the bar high above his head, bringing it down hard. He feels metal meeting flesh, the wet crunch of bone, splitting flesh. He swings the bar up again, hears screams. The terrible, gut-wrenching screams of a human. He smells blood. Sees blood. So much blood. He's covered in it when he wakes in his bed the next morning.*

Bile surges into Mason's throat, and sweat pools under his arms. Not clean sweat. The kind that smells acrid. The stink of fear. The rest is a black void in his teenage memory, punctuated only by these fragmented images and sensations he can never quite string into a coherent narrative. He prefers to believe his drug- and drink-addled brain conjured the images from feverish nightmares. Just imagined things. Not really real. Another part of Mason knows something very real and terrible did actually happen.

He clears his throat. "You—ah—you said the leg was wearing a boot?"

"Yes, I mentioned it in the segment—the Duvalier brothers saw a boot."

"And they're sure it had a platform heel? It was a woman's boot?"

"Well, I suppose a male could have been wearing platform heels."

He stares at her.

She smiles slyly. "See? It's hooked even you. You're asking all the questions. This is going to reel in subscribers. I promise you."

Mason tries to think of the times he's been at the chapel. He skied up there often as a teen. They all hiked there several times over the summer of that fateful year. Bob and Cara got married at the chapel. He went to their wedding. They all did.

Except for her.

Because she was gone.

"I think we should go with *Someone Always Knows*," Angela says. "Because someone out there always does. That's the attraction of these shows—they can actually solve crimes decades later. Time changes people and circumstances. Witnesses might suddenly want to talk and finally get things off their chests."

Mason gulps down the rest of his bourbon. He lurches up and goes to his cabinet. As he pours himself another, his brain races. He was hoping this news cycle would just pass and things would move on. Now Angela wants to dig deeper. She wants to shine a fucking magnifying glass on it.

He faces her. "Your 'news-based reality show' is just a tag for yet another true-crime show, and there's a glut out there. Why would yours even stand out?"

"True crime is whatever we need it to be, Mason. It's what *I* can bring to it, and what viewers can take from it."

"And what, exactly, will they take from it?"

She studies him. "Resolution," she says softly. "Closure. We all need it. One way or another."

Mason holds her gaze. He sure as hell needs resolution. He's also terrified of actually finding it, learning the full truth about what he did that night when he was sixteen. Mostly what he needs right now is to keep Angela Sheldrick and her breaking information close. He wants to hear it first. He needs to be in a position to control this narrative if at all possible. Or kill it.

"Let's see what you can do."

She frowns. "What do you mean?"

"Keep working on it. Gather your sources, information. Submit a proposal in writing. Keep me tightly in the loop with any and all new developments in the investigation, and I'll work on the money guys upstairs."

Her mouth flattens. "We need to move faster, Mason. This is going to be all over social media in seconds. By tomorrow, stations with bigger budgets will be controlling this narrative. We'll lose our window."

"I'll speak with upstairs. You go do your best out there."

"At least give me the green light to have a comment section launched on our web page, and to activate a tip line."

"Fine. Fine."

She gets up. "Thanks," she says coolly. But when she leaves, she shuts the door a little too firmly behind her.

Mason waits a few seconds to ensure she's not going to spin around and barge back in. He swallows the rest of his second drink, reaches for his phone, and searches for a number he has not dialed in almost ten years. He places the call.

As the phone rings, he stares at his own distorted reflection in the dark office window speckled with rain, and he wonders how in the hell he got here. The call connects. Mason's heart kicks, and he almost hangs up. He clears his throat.

"Bob? Hey. It's me. Long time no see. You got a minute? We—ah—we need to talk."

# JANE

Jane drapes her wet coat over a chair in the dining area of her tiny apartment. She glances at the clock. It's late and she's drained. After her interview with Fred Duvalier, she caught up with Duncan and he informed her Angela Sheldrick had already gotten to the brothers who found the remains. Jane is furious. Sheldrick's piece has probably already been picked up by other networks and social media, and she's anticipating a call from her superior expressing irritation at not having been looped in before learning via TV about the body being female with boots.

She opens her fridge. It's empty save for wilted lettuce, old cheese, and a bottle of expensive pinot gris Matt placed there last September. Despair sideswipes her. The plan was to crack open the wine upon his return from his solo trip. Jane shuts the fridge and puts on the kettle instead. She takes a packet of instant soup from the cupboard. As she dumps the contents into a mug, her thoughts fixate on Matt. Her fiancé has always been the chef in their relationship. He has three passions that inform his life: mountaineering, volunteering for his local search and rescue organization, and holistic nutrition geared specifically to endurance and extreme activities. She met him eighteen months ago, when his SAR team was tasked with a body recovery in a case she was investigating. The chemistry was instant, and their relationship moved fast. A baker by profession, Matt always had something delicious on the go whenever Jane scored a new case, or returned from long and difficult shifts. It's one of the things she loves about him—how he makes any place around him feel like home.

Their apartment is located above his tiny boutique bakery, the Bread Stop. After Matt hadn't come home for more than two months, Jane was forced to shutter the business and temporarily lay off his small staff. The bank is now demanding mortgage payments she can't afford, and in another month she'll default and totally lose Matt's business. She needs to do *something* before that happens. Logically, she should try to sell it, but she'd need full power of attorney to do that, and obtaining the legal right to manage her fiancé's business affairs when he's neither dead nor alive feels like an insurmountable challenge. There really is no simple solution when someone goes missing. Jane can't even begin to admit to herself that she will soon be a single mom of a baby who might never meet their father.

Her hands go still as she blinks back a fresh burn of grief.

*Damn you, Matt. How dare you do this to both of us? I'll never forgive you.*

Jane finishes making her instant soup and carries her mug to the sofa. She turns on the TV and selects from the menu the CBCN-TV news program she records every night. She rewinds until she sees Angela Sheldrick talking into her mike. She hits PLAY.

Sheldrick says, "Construction workers Benjamin and Raphael Duvalier made the grisly grave-site find in the dark dawn hours on Hemlock Mountain today. The brothers—"

"Helloooo, anyone home?"

Jane drops the remote and spins around. "Jesus, Mom. What in the hell? How did you get in?"

Her mother, sixty-four years old, is dressed in her gym gear and carrying a paper shopping bag. She dangles a key toward Jane. "With the key you gave me, remember? To water your plants when you . . ." She lets it slide, but the unspoken words hang in the air.

*When you were up north searching for Matt last fall.*

"I would have knocked, Jane," she says as she sets her bag on the kitchen counter. "I tried calling and texting several times today, and there was no answer, so I figured you were tied up with that new case." She tilts her chin toward the TV. "I was just going to leave this food on the counter for you to warm up when you got in." She removes a container of food from the bag. The scents of minced beef, curry, and fragrant spices suddenly fill the air, and Jane's stomach grumbles. Her knee-jerk reaction is to be mad at her mom and kick her out. But from the smell she knows what's in that container, and Jane can see exactly what her mother is trying to do. Her mom is acutely aware that Matt always cooked for Jane when she was working a case, and now she's trying to fill that hole.

"Why aren't you taking my calls, Jane?" her mother asks as she opens the container and fetches a plate from the cupboard. She pulls open a drawer and finds a knife and fork. She sets them on the counter.

"I've been busy. Like you said, I got a new case."

"Come, leave that soup. Sit here and eat. You need to look after that baby."

Jane suddenly feels nine years old again, and as much as her mom irritates her, the buried little girl inside also craves being held and comforted and told it will all turn out okay. She turns down the sound and sits on a stool at the counter.

"Bobotie," Jane's mother announces as she dishes a portion of a classic South African casserole onto a plate. The steam releases more of its fragrance. "Do you remember when you were little how you loved this as comfort food? Your dad discovered it at that Cape Winds place near the docks."

"Yeah, I remember." She gives a rueful smile. "Everything was always put right with bobotie or samosas from Cape Winds."

"Samoosas," her mother corrects. "The Hendrickses call them samoosas. They're different from samosas," she says. "Smaller. Crispier. More like spring roll pastry."

"Right." Jane reaches for a fork and takes a mouthful. She closes her eyes for a moment. The food is bliss. She scoops up another bite. "Is he still around, Mr. Hendricks? I haven't been down there in ages."

"Oh, he's still going. Old and totally blind now. I swear he won't kick the bucket until he finds his son, who took off back in the day. His daughter, Danielle, runs the place now. They still have a small bistro, but she also has a catering business with a bigger imported-goods outlet and industrial kitchen off Marine. All upmarket fusion cuisine."

Jane takes another mouthful and points her fork at the container. "Aren't you going to have some?"

"Book club tonight." Her mom checks her watch. "I really should get going. I just wanted to drop this off."

Jane lowers her fork. "Thanks. I . . . I really appreciate this."

Her mother locks her gaze on Jane's. "When are you going to come visit? I'd like to have Matt's parents around. Maybe a Sunday lunch, or dinner?"

"Mom, I—"

"They need to see you, Jane. They're missing Matt, too. They want to know his baby will still be a part of their lives."

Emotion pools in Jane's eyes. "I can't do this right now. Please—"

"Just think about it. When you get a break in the case. I—" Her mother hesitates and severs eye contact. For a moment she stares at the TV. She inhales deeply and faces Jane. "I've been thinking. I could convert one half of my house to a suite. Like a duplex. You and the baby—"

"No." Jane sets her fork down. "*This* is my home. Mine and Matt's."

Her mother seats herself on a stool at the counter. "Jane, you need to do something with the bakery."

"I know."

"You need a plan. For the baby, too. This is not just about you anymore. You have a little person to think of, and time isn't going to wait. Have you put in for your maternity leave?"

"I will. When I'm ready. God knows they can't wait long enough for me to do it," she snaps. "It's why they dumped me in this cold case unit in the first place. They didn't bargain on me actually landing a suspicious death out of the gate."

Her mother regards her in silence for a moment, then clears her throat. "If you come live with me, totally separate in one side of the house—just an inter-leading door—I could help with the baby if you decide to go back to work, and—"

"I am going back to work. I have to work."

Her mother nods. "I know. And I can help. It takes a community—a village, a clan—to raise a child. It's not an unusual arrangement, Jane. And heaven knows your job can be rough. I saw the toll it took on your father, and it won't be easy on you as a single mom. You need to be honest with yourself and face the truth. Take charge of that now, before it takes charge of you."

"Jesus, Mom—"

"I know you. You push people away. You hate anyone to see you vulnerable. As a child you wouldn't even let people see you learning anything and flailing, but you need friends right now. You need your family. Your baby needs them."

"I have friends," she says crisply.

"A mortician, a palliative nurse, and a death doula? All single women? It's like the dead girls club." Her mother comes to her feet, nods at the TV. "Do you have any idea how long those remains have been under the chapel?"

"Not yet."

Her mother regards the images of the chapel on the screen in silence.

"I thought you had book club," Jane says.

Her mother reaches for her bag, then hesitates. "Phone the Rossis sometime, okay? They're hurting, too."

With that, her mother leaves. And Jane feels utterly exhausted, and angry, and she also knows her mother is right. She does need to think about their baby now. She needs to make proper plans. She grabs the remote, rewinds the Sheldrick segment, bumps the sound back up, and listens to the report while she eats. Jane curses out loud when she hears Sheldrick say the body was found with a knee-high platform boot.

That woman is going to be her nemesis on this case. Jane needs to stay a constant step ahead of her.

# THE SHOREVIEW SIX

## Bob

The spring morning has dawned clear on Somersby Island, and a light ocean breeze ripples through the vineyard as Bob Davine walks with his two border collies along the rows of grapes being cultivated on a bench of land nestled between the Pacific Ocean and a majestic granite cliff. His wine farm slopes down to his and Cara's home on the water—architecturally designed in West Coast style, full of cedar and glass to maximize sea views. From their private beach, their dock stretches into sparkling water. His boat is moored there, and their kayaks are stacked in the boathouse. Across the waters of Boundary Pass—which separates the American San Juan Islands from their Canadian Gulf Island counterparts—Bob can see Waldron Island in the States.

He loves this leeward side of Somersby. The visually arresting landscape, the dry and sunny microclimate, the sea breezes, and the soil rich in clay and marine sediment—it all gives his grapes that special touch of the Salish Sea. It's this unique terroir that defines the Davine Estate varietals—including pinot noir, chardonnay, pinot gris, gewürztraminer, pinot meunier, gamay, and muscat.

His dogs run ahead of him, darting between the vines, chasing critters and the scent of wild goats. Bob and his wife, Cara, bought this estate a year ago, when he started the process of retiring from his firm as a top white-collar criminal defense lawyer. The property came with the winery, a bistro, the main house, a winemaker's cottage, outbuildings, machinery, and equipment. They kept the winemaker on, and they hired a new chef to work wonders with local lamb, cheeses, and produce farmed on the island. Everything is organic, pesticide-free, and the farming methods are environmentally sustainable. Davine Estate wines hit all the right buzz notes. Bob and Cara moved to the farm full-time just five months ago. Their son and daughter-in-law now run the Mad Goat Bistro. Bob's three young grandkids attend the local elementary school. And his daughter and her husband manage the marketing side of things from the mainland. A family affair, just the way he and Cara dreamed. And this morning Bob feels as though the spring dawn is rising on the cusp of the rest of his life. He's finally reached a place where he is content to sit back and enjoy the fruits of his life's labor. But a thorny issue niggles Bob today.

He stoops to tug a weed out of the soil, thinking it's all so damn perfect it was bound to go wrong. He stands erect, dusts his hands off on his jeans, and his mind returns to the strange phone call that came like a bolt out of the blue last night.

*Bob? Hey. It's me. Long time no see. You got a minute? We—ah—we need to talk.*

Bob has not heard from or seen Mason, a.k.a. Rocco the Roc, in maybe eight years.

He absently plucks a dead leaf from a vine as the phone call replays in his memory.

*"Did you see tonight's CBCN-TV news? About those contractors up at Hemlock?"*

*"No, why?"*

*"They were digging up the foundations of the old skiers' chapel and they found human remains."*

*"What?"*

*"Yeah. Buried under the concrete foundations. They found a body."*

Bob sucks in a chestful of air and exhales slowly, straining for calm as the rest of their phone conversation rolls through his brain.

*"Same chapel where you and Cara got married. Crazy-ass shit, eh? What are the odds?" A long pause. "Where did you put it, Bob?"*

*"What are you talking about?"*

*"You know, that night, the body . . . where did you guys hide it?"*

*"Are you fucking insane? What in the hell do you think you are getting at?"*

*"You never told me where. Is this—"*

*"Look, listen to me, Roc, listen carefully. This has nothing to do with us. Understand? Nothing. That chapel was built back in the sixties. If there's a body under there, it's probably from the early sixties. Don't lose your shit, man. Not now. Do you hear me?"*

*A long pause. Bob hears the sound of ice cubes chinking against glass. Rocco is drinking. He was a wild kid in his youth. So was his older brother, Zane. "Raised" by ridiculously wealthy but absent parents who thought throwing cash and independence at their boys absolved them of basic parental commitments. Both boys went off the rails. Zane killed himself on the Sea to Sky Highway, hitting a semi head-on while racing his bike too fast around a curve. Rocco lost his way with drugs and drinks. It took him well over a decade and several stints in rehab to sort himself out and leave his past firmly behind. He's been doing okay for a while now, or so Bob and Cara thought, having moved out of the music industry and into television programming. But Rocco's years of substance abuse messed with his neural network and left him permanently twitchy, and this has always scared Bob. It made his old school buddy a loose cannon. What Rocco did—or did not—recall about that fateful night in 1976 has been a sleeping land mine in all their lives.*

*"We made a pledge, Roc," he says quietly. "The six of us have a pact. The past is the past."*

*"Yeah, sure, we made a pact, but you guys never came clean to me about the rest of that night. And I—"*

*"There's no negotiation. No one talks about it. Not now, not ever. Got it? And the less you remember, hey, it's for the good, right? We're doing this for you. What you don't know can't hurt you."*

*"Our crime reporter wants to go in depth on this one. She's pitching a news-based reality series on—"*

*"I told you, relax, it's got nothing to do with us."*

*"Good. Good. Yeah, I—ah, I just wanted to be sure, you know? No surprises."*

*"No surprises."*

◆ ◆ ◆

But as soon as Bob ended the call, he hurried to his computer to search for the story. And while he tapped the keyboard, he noticed his fingers were trembling with adrenaline and his mouth had gone dry. He learned from online news that the remains were female and wearing platform boots. *Just like my girlfriend was wearing on the night she disappeared.*

He didn't sleep well last night, either. Violent nightmares kept waking him in a sweat. Rocco's phone call cracked open a locked vault inside Bob, releasing things, memories he'd buried deep in the murky basement of his consciousness years ago. Now they were crawling out, pale, slimy things, flashing themselves at him and squirming like grubs in sudden sunlight, before recoiling and burrowing back into dank darkness. Was Rocco right?

Was this discovery on Hemlock going to blow it all open again after all these years, one way or the other?

Bob swallows as he stares at the idyllic view over his vines. Marrying in that tiny chapel on Hemlock was Cara's idea.

Another image surfaces: Cara in bridal white. Sunlight filtering through that long stained glass window behind the tiny altar, throwing hues of blue and red and gold and green over her. A rainbow of a halo. As though she were blessed. After the ceremony, they celebrated on the flanks of Hemlock surrounded by forests with an endless view of the city and inlets sparkling far below in the distance. With them that day were family, close friends. Musicians played into the night as small bonfires shot orange sparks to the sky and they danced like medieval druids worshipping the setting of the sun, the turning of the earth, the stars moving across the heavens, and a new phase starting in their lives. He'd felt so blessed.

Her Greek parents wanted something different, of course. The Constantines had pushed for a massive highbrow event at their swanky club on Hollyburn. Big and traditional for the large and extended Constantine clan. But Cara thought the chapel was incredibly romantic, and she fought her family to have it her way. It was meaningful, she said. She and Bob both loved skiing, snowshoeing, and hiking on Hemlock. They'd been doing it together since grade eleven, when they became an item.

A darker memory snakes up suddenly: the circumstances around how he and Cara got close. It was after that fateful September night in 1976 when Bob's steady girlfriend vanished. He and Cara had found solace in each other, with her consoling him in his grief, confusion, guilt. Him finding deep comfort and safety in her nonjudgmental love and the fact she'd do anything for him, including lie.

Cara made it possible for him to go on.

Bob and Cara's bond was irrefutably forged in a black crucible. Their vow to each other came in the form of a terrible secret that the six of them guarded from the rest of the world. Him, Cara, Jill, Rocco, Mary, and Claude. Bob could no more leave his marriage than Cara could. What she knew could destroy him. What he knew could destroy her. It was the same with the others. Six friends on the cusp of grade eleven bonded that weekend for life. Each with the power to destroy the others. It would be mutually assured destruction if any one of them flipped now, *especially* now. Should the truth be revealed, it would take their respective children, grandchildren, and extended families of loved ones down with them. They all had so much more to lose now than when they were sixteen.

He shakes it off. He cannot dwell there.

Bob whistles for his dogs. He climbs back onto his ATV. One dog hops onto the small seat beside him to ride shotgun. The other takes the bucket seat behind him. He starts the engine and begins to bomb his ATV down the dirt trails to his waterfront home. He tells himself it's going to be fine.

The past is the past.

*Except when it's not.* A little voice whispers this thought up from his subconscious. It settles into his bones as a feeling. Cold. Something unstoppable has been set in motion.

# JANE

"Okay, let's get this thing going," Jane says as she sticks photos of the human remains on a large whiteboard in the incident room. It's old-school but she likes having images of the victim and potential suspects looking down on her team daily, reminding them all why they are here: To find resolution for loved ones. Hold perpetrators accountable. Protect others from similar crimes occurring again.

Jane currently has at her disposal a team of four investigators, including Duncan. They arrived at the crack of dawn and spent the first hour of the day setting up in office space at the North Vancouver RCMP detachment. While her unit is small, she has the ability to ramp up and to avail herself of a full range of RCMP resources and expertise. In addition to herself and Duncan, her team of detectives includes Tank Coker, a grizzled veteran of serious crimes; Yursa Ghait, a newly minted investigator who grew up in Egypt and speaks fluent Arabic and Farsi; and Melissa Brand, a tech and admin whiz.

A solemness presses down over the group as they study the haunting images of the skull, jaw open wide in its silent, suffocating scream.

"Our Jane Doe." Jane points to the image.

"So the decedent is confirmed to be female?" asks Tank.

"Likely female according to Dr. Ella Quinn, who is the forensic anthropologist heading up the excavation." Jane pins up another photo, this one of the dirt-encrusted boot hanging off the ends of the tibia and fibula. "And there's the women's size seven boot."

"With a platform sole. High heel," notes Yusra.

Jane adds another photo—a close-up of the blunt force trauma to the skull.

"Dr. Quinn said this trauma likely occurred perimortem. In her opinion this would have killed our Jane Doe."

Tank says, "So if she was killed by a blow to her head, the trauma either occurred by accident or she was struck intentionally and possibly murdered. Is there any record of a legitimate burial at the chapel site?"

Melissa says, "I'm chasing that up. So far we haven't found any record. I'll also be following up with the chapel society after this briefing, and going through the history of the place, learning who the key players were, and whether there is any historical significance to that site location that might explain why someone was buried there."

Jane pins up several images of the small A-frame chapel taken over the decades. She sourced them from the internet last night when—yet again—she was woken by horrific nightmares of Matt stuck in a deep crevasse with broken legs and calling for her help. She arranges the photos in order of the years that the images were captured.

One shows a hippie wedding and a group gathered outside the chapel with long hair, bare feet, Jesus sandals, flower garlands, leather waistcoats, flowing skirts, and peasant dresses, children and babies in tow. Another image was shot in winter. It shows a Christmas carol service with the bundled-up crowd spilling outside into the snow, everyone holding little candles. The next is an artsy shot capturing sunlight glowing behind the Madonna and child stained glass window. Another was taken on a New Year's Eve—skiers snaking down the mountain behind the wooden A-frame, each holding two red flares in the darkness. The devilish-red glow throws the cross above the chapel into silhouette. One shows a winter wedding, the bride wearing fur. Yet another has caught skiers feeding peanuts to whisky jacks. From the style of the ski suits and the skis propped into a snowbank in front of the A-frame, this was taken sometime in the 1980s. The final shot is of a somber memorial captured sometime in the 1990s, judging by the fashions of the people all dressed in black.

"The SHU forensic team should have the remains in the lab shortly," Jane says, glancing at her watch. "I got a call from Quinn early this morning. She and her students worked through the night. They wanted to keep going because the more they excavated, the more the groundwater rose, and they didn't want to risk compromising evidence. Once the remains and artifacts are at the institute, we'll start getting a better idea of the postmortem interval. All we know so far is that the concrete floor of the chapel basement was likely poured some years after the initial construction of the A-frame in '66. Prior to that it was probably a dirt floor. When the concrete went down, a sump pump was likely installed at the same time. The site foreman, Fred Duvalier, claims he saw no evidence that the concrete floor in the basement had been chopped up and replaced, so our decedent could have been buried directly in the dirt sometime before the concrete floor was poured over top of her grave."

"And we don't know yet exactly when the concrete went down?" Tank asks.

"Not yet. Records might be hard to come by because of a fire in the lodge where the chapel society documentation was stored pre-1980."

"That boot she's wearing," Yusra says, chewing the back of her pen. "Looks seventies to me. From what I understand, everyone from schoolgirls to disco dancers and glam rockers wore platforms in the seventies."

Duncan moves closer to the board and peers intently at the images of the chapel. "The sump pump—it runs on electricity, right?"

"Where are you going with this?" Tank asks.

Duncan points. "See these earlier photos shot at night? In these the chapel is lit by candlelight."

"Doesn't mean the building didn't have power. Maybe they wanted the mood," says Melissa.

"True. But see here? In these shots from the early eighties onward, there appears to be power." He taps one of the photos. "My bet is we're going to find the sump pump and floor went in around the time the chapel was serviced with utilities, or some time after. They wouldn't have been able to run the pump without electricity."

"They could have used a generator," Melissa says.

"Also true. But if we go with this hypothesis, and if I was a gambling man, I'd bet Jane Doe was buried pre those particular photos shot in the eighties that show evidence of hydro."

"Okay," Jane says. "Let's get to work on locating members of the chapel society and finding any records that will show us when the building was serviced with utilities and when that floor and sump pump went in, because that will help narrow our time since burial. We also need to connect with management at Hemlock to determine if they retained any pertinent records. And I want to know who was contracted to do the basement work. According to Duvalier there was a security guard who used to do night watches on the mountain—possibly named Hugo Glucklich. I need his contact details from Hemlock management if they have them. And—" Her phone rings. Jane sees it's Dr. Ella Quinn. She quickly holds up her hand, indicating a pause, and connects the call.

"Munro."

"Sergeant, Ella here. We've removed her from the burial site. She's in our lab."

Energy courses through Jane's blood. "On our way."

She kills the call and says to her team, "Our Jane Doe is at the SHU institute. Duncan, you're with me. Separate vehicles so we can split up after. Melissa, stay on the chapel society and burial records. Tank, you're on Hemlock management and contact details for Glucklich. Yusra, start taking a stab at missing persons databases."

"Do you know how extensive those databases are?" Yusra asks. "We're talking a span of decades here. You do realize how many thousands of people go missing each year—" She falls silent suddenly. Tension swells. All watch Jane.

"I'm fully aware," she says quietly.

"I'm sorry," Yusra says.

"Start midsixties," Jane says. "I'll call if anything comes up that will narrow the field." She pauses and meets their gazes one by one. "Let's do this. Let's give Jane Doe her name back, find her family, and bring her home, because someone out there might still be missing her."

# FAITH

Faith Blackburn listens to the news on her car radio as she drives home from yin yoga class. She abhors yoga, but it's better than Pilates or something that involves sweaty cardio. Her doctor said she must exercise. She needs to take better care of herself or she'll be in trouble.

She's fifty-six this year, and decades of being hunched over a computer have taken a toll. Then came the weird stress of the pandemic, a switch to working from home, a divorce from her abusive husband and the subsequent selling of their apartment, and finally—when everyone started returning to offices—she was laid off from her job, which necessitated a humiliating move back into her childhood home with her senior parents. Faith now carries a lot more weight than she's comfortable with, in more ways than one. Her blood pressure is sky high. She even looks ten or twenty years older than she is. And people are encouraging her to try a dating app? Are they nuts? Faith will never find someone. Not now. She's all used up.

She takes the highway off-ramp and enters the quieter subdivisions of North Vancouver where her childhood home sits at the end of Linden Street, a cul-de-sac bordering a park and forest.

The newscaster suddenly announces breaking news. Faith's interest piques. She turns up the radio volume.

"The human remains found in a shallow grave beneath the old skiers' chapel on Hemlock Mountain appear to belong to a woman. CBCN-TV first broke the story yesterday evening, and we have since learned that the remains are being excavated by a team of anthropologists from the Seymour Hills University Forensic Institute. An RCMP homicide detective is leading the investigation, but neither the RCMP nor the BC Coroners Service have released any official statements. The remains were found wearing knee-high platform boots."

A knot of tension coils in Faith's chest. She suddenly can't breathe. It's as though a giant anvil is pressing down on her lungs. Faith jabs the OFF button. Silence fills the car, and she fists her hands tightly around the wheel.

It happens every damn time there's news about a body being found. No matter where in the province or country. No matter whether on this side of the border or across in the US. Her mom goes into a tailspin. Starts drinking again. It's not good for her. Her mom has suffered for almost fifty years, since Faith's older sister vanished over the Labour Day weekend in 1976. And her mom's health in her late senior years is not good to begin with. Her dad, however, is immune to this kind of news. At least Faith thinks he is. He got locked inside his head once he had a stroke, and now a creeping dementia is swallowing up his comprehension of life in general. Faith resents him for it. She'd like to blot it all out, too.

She was only nine when her big sister went missing, but it shaped the rest of her childhood, her teens, her entire adult life. News like this—it rips off the old scars and tears open the big yawning chasm of loss that has defined their little family since her sister vanished. They are doomed by the unfinished, the incomplete, a lack of closure or resolution. People call it so many things.

But *this* piece of news is particularly disturbing. Faith doesn't like hearing about boots. Her sister was wearing boots when she vanished. High-heeled platforms bought with money from her part-time job at the Donut Diner.

She turns onto Linden Street and heads down toward the cul-de-sac at the bottom, praying her mom hasn't heard this yet. She pulls into their driveway and puts the car in park. She stares at the little house, stuck in the seventies and in need of repair and paint and love. And she thinks, *This must end.*

*But how?*

She exits the car and enters the house quietly. She sets her yoga bag down in the hallway and takes off her coat, hangs it neatly on a hook, then removes her boots. She pads on socked feet into the living room. Her dad is still planted in front of the television in his recliner. He's fallen asleep. Open mouth. Snoring. Drool glistening on his lips. On the screen is a rerun of *Judge Judy*. Faith turns down the sound, grabs a tissue, and gently dabs the corners of her dad's lips. She then goes into the kitchen, where she finds her mom baking muffins.

"Hey, hon." Her mom glances up. She looks tired. "How was yoga?"

"Good," Faith lies. "Everything okay?" *Have you seen the news?*

"Your dad is exhausted this morning. He burned his hand under the hot tap in the bathroom. He thought it was cold. I put ointment on, and he's sleeping the excitement off."

*Good. They haven't seen the news. Yet. Maybe it will blow past and they can stay safe.*

"I'm just going downstairs to check my email and have a shower, then I'll come up and give you a hand with the dishes, okay?"

"Thanks, love." Her mother pauses. "It really is good to have you home again."

Faith forces a smile and kisses her mom on her papery-dry cheek. She heads down the passage but hesitates at the top of the stairs to the basement. She can't help herself. Quietly, she leaves the stairs and goes farther down the passage. She opens the door to her sister's old room.

People who have never experienced a loved one going missing would not understand, but her mother has kept the room exactly as it was left that fateful weekend in September 1976. A shrine to the past, still waiting for its occupant to come home forty-seven years later.

Faith enters the room and steps back in time. She regards the posters on the walls. One shows the Bay City Rollers—the Scottish pop group and "tartan sensation" with their 1970s mullets. Over the bed is an image of teen heartthrob Shaun Cassidy looking baby faced and soft. On the back of the door is a large print of a twenty-one-year-old John Travolta, who rocketed to teen-idol stardom with the launch of the sitcom *Welcome Back, Kotter*.

A Raggedy Ann doll made by her mother is propped on a pillow at the head of the bed. Faith always wanted one, too. But her mom seemed to have only enough energy to sew one. Her sister came first in age, and it seems everything was used up on her first, too—gifts, attention, what little money they had. And when she disappeared, nine-year-old Faith simply became invisible beneath the thick layers of her parents' grief. That all changed when Faith entered her teens. She began to look so much like her missing older sister that her parents could barely look at her. The tension in the house grew stifling. The resemblance also freaked out her sister's friends—especially that tight-knit group of six the media dubbed the Shoreview Six because they all went to Shoreview High, and they were all questioned by police, and not everyone believed they told the truth.

A few faded Polaroids of her sister with the Shoreview Six are stuck to the mirror above a dresser. Faith leans in closer to study their young, smiling faces. Robbie, dark haired, tanned, tall, lithe. His bright-blue eyes shine for the camera. Busty Cara with her stiff, highlighted hair. Jill with her dimple-cheeked smile and striped tank top. Mary, large and bulky with brown hair that curled in all directions. Claude, the macho hockey jock. Rocco, wiry and gaunt-cheeked, with his long-haired mullet and black tank top. And Faith's sister shining like a perfect pearl among them. Big straight-toothed smile and shiny hair that falls in a curtain past her shoulders. All captured in the amber of time that summer of 1976, just several weeks before she disappeared.

Faith has suggested to her mom many times over the years that they clear out the room, maybe sell the house, start over.

*What if she comes back?* her mother asked. *What if she returns and can't find us? She has the house key with her. She can still let herself in.*

Her mother even kept the hall light burning day and night until the wires shorted and it all had to be replaced.

And so they've stayed. In this old house on Linden Street as the neighbors' homes were demolished and sold and rebuilt. As the city across the water began to spill over the inlet and march in the form of high-rises up the flanks of the North Shore Mountains. As the woods at the end of the cul-de-sac grew tall and thick. As memories faded—all but theirs. They are the forgotten family of the missing girl being swallowed by progress around them.

But if this news is about her sister, if it's her body under the chapel, everything will start all over again. The investigation, the media, the fresh pain. The questions. Have they not been punished enough?

Faith closes the door to her sister's room quietly and goes downstairs to her basement suite.

She gets on hands and knees, reaches under her bed, and pulls out a cardboard box. Faith sits on the floor beside the box, leaning her back against the bed. She takes off the lid and removes a tattered sock monkey, followed by a small purple backpack. She opens the backpack and slides out a hardback journal.

She smooths her hand over the cover.

**Secret Diary—1976**

She opens her sister's diary to a random page. Big cursive loops flow across the page, whimsical yet still neatly lined up. There are entries only every few days. Sometimes weeks or even months went by with nothing written, then something exciting would happen in her sister's life and a spate of regular entries would appear.

Faith begins to read, and not for the first time. She's basically memorized whole chunks of the journal word for word. As she reads, tension twists tighter and tighter in her chest. A breeze outside scratches shrub branches against her basement window, and twigs squeak against the glass. Her sister gave most of the people in her life code names. Faith has figured out some of them. "Boobs" is Cara. "Mullet" is Rocco. "Smurf" is Robbie because it rhymes with *surf*, and Robbie was originally a surfer from Southern California. Claude is dubbed "Puck" after his ice hockey. Mary is "Contrary." But Faith has never figured out who the "HC" is in this entry.

HC came into the Donut Diner after his shift again today. That's *five!!!* days in a row this week. Two more than last week. He says he likes the donuts. (Haha.)

When I told Contrary about him, she asked if he was stalking me. I just laughed, but I kinda like that he probably is. Contrary asked if he's good-looking. I admit I had to think about that. He's more hot than handsome, if you know what I mean? It's his presence. It's the way he walks, like a swagger. Something about him feels . . . *dangerous*. Off-limits. Yeah, that's it. HC has an aura. Illicit. Maybe it's the ring on his finger. Combined with what he does for a living. (So cool!) It's also the way the light shines in his eyes with a burning kind of intensity when he looks at me. It makes my heart race. Melts me inside. So f***ing hot! I kinda shake/tremble when I see him park outside the diner window now. Not that I show it. (I hope!) I think I manage to act pretty cool when I take his order.

He *always* asks for the honey dip donut (weirdly cute because he's so big and macho-rough-looking it's like he should be ordering steak or a double man burger or something), and he orders it with a bottomless cup of coffee.

I bring him extra creamer in those little tetrahedron packs.

I told him he sure drinks a lot of coffee.

He said he likes ordering it from me, and he will drink as much as it takes. I asked him as much as what takes. He just smiled and hummed a line from that song about believing in miracles, and being a sexy thing.

◆ ◆ ◆

Faith hears a noise outside her basement suite door. She freezes, listens. The dryer door slams shut. It's just her mom taking laundry out of the dryer. Faith waits until she hears her mother carrying her load up the stairs with a *shuffle thump, shuffle thump* noise, slowed by her arthritic knees. Guilt rushes through her.

She quickly closes the book, slides it back into the backpack. She places the backpack into the box, followed by her sister's tattered sock monkey. She gets back down onto her hands and knees and shoves the box deep under her bed, right up against the far wall. She'll burn the journal. But she needs to wait until her father goes for his next medical appointment. She'll drive her mom and dad to the hospital—it's not far from their house. Then she'll rush home, light a fire in the hearth, tear the pages out, and burn them one by one. This has to end once and for all. Her mom has suffered enough.

They all have.

# THE SHOREVIEW SIX

## Cara

Cara hums while making brunch for her husband, who is out inspecting the vines. She loves this new stage of their lives, these fresh rituals. She and Bob have worked hard, and she feels justified in enjoying these rewards now. This morning her kitchen is filled with buttery-gold sunlight and smells of freshly ground coffee from the local island roaster, bacon from a heritage farm, and sourdough toast from bread crafted in the old-fashioned way with a mother as a starter. She cracks organic eggs into the pan, and they sizzle in the hot bacon fat. On the kitchen counter behind her is a copper jug filled with freshly picked daffodils from her spring garden. Herbs froth in pots on their deck, and beyond, the ocean sparkles.

She hears Bob's ATV approaching on the gravel driveway outside. It's followed by the excited yips of the dogs. She quickly checks herself in the mirror and tucks a strand of blonde hair behind her ear. It's time for fresh highlights—she's leaving right after brunch to catch a ferry to the mainland, where she has a salon appointment booked, along with a mani-pedi. She'll overnight at her old school friend Jill's house. Jill is planning a big art show and fundraising auction on behalf of her pet charity—Mission Mosaic, an initiative to help refugees settle into the country in various ways—and Cara has offered to assist.

To be honest, Jill's sanctimonious charity missions irritate Cara. She's never told Jill, though. Cara prefers to feign interest. It keeps the harmony. But she is pretty sure Jill's passion is not derived from altruism. There is no such thing as true altruism in Cara's opinion. No person ever acts purely selflessly because humans are fundamentally wired to be self-interested. It's basic survival instinct. Those who do charity are self-interested in their own godly salvation. They seek to be *seen* doing good. They crave admiration from their peers. Or they want to soothe some unarticulated guilt over their own privilege or wrongdoing.

Cara hears the front door open. "Brunch is ready," she calls out. The dogs skitter into the kitchen as her husband takes off his boots in the mudroom.

Bob comes through as she sets their meal out on the kitchen counter where they like to eat on stools.

"Morning." He gives her a kiss on her cheek. "Smells good." She glances up at him and smiles.

Age sits well on some men, and her Bob is one. His head of black hair is still thick and shiny, barely a strand of silver. His eyes are the same intense, lively blue they were when he was a teen. His athletic body still supple, tanned, strong. Cara fell in love with Robbie Davine the moment she first laid eyes on him. She still recalls the day the new tanned surfer kid with longish black hair and dancing eyes walked into Mr. Hart's grade seven class and chose to sit at the desk next to hers.

He'd glanced her way and grinned. And that's all it took. She was smitten. From that moment, thirteen-year-old Cara Constantine became obsessed with making Robbie Davine hers. At any cost. Even though all the other girls lusted after him. Even though it was not Cara who Robbie wanted but Annalise Jansen with the long, shiny blonde hair.

Cara was not pretty in the way Annalise was, or cute in the way her best friend, Jill Wainwright, had always been. Her parents weren't as rich as Jill's, either, and they weren't famous like Claude's. But Cara had breasts. She matured early, and she quickly discovered the power of sex appeal in a playing field of postpubescent schoolboys wired with raging hormones. She learned fast how to leverage her assets. And one thing people always eventually learned about Cara—one way or another—she had a cunning patience. Cara didn't lose. Cara got what she wanted. And in the end, she made people think it had been their idea all along.

She'd gotten Bob.

She'd gotten this life flush with wealth and prestige and children and grandchildren, and now this wine farm with her grandkids close by.

"What's your schedule when you reach the other side?" Bob asks as he takes a seat at the counter.

"I'm heading straight to meet Jill for lunch at Pier 6 on Lonsdale Quay." She pours coffee as she speaks. "Followed by a late-afternoon salon appointment." She sets a steaming mug in front of Bob. "Then dinner at Jill's. We'll talk planning for her event. I'll stay over, and then after a mani-pedi appointment the following morning, I head home."

She glances at Bob when he doesn't say anything.

Her husband's mouth is set in a flat line, and he stares absently out the windows, a strange, distant look in his eyes. He catches her watching and quickly smiles. He reaches for his mug.

Cara takes a seat. "What is it?"

"Nothing."

"It's not nothing. You were miles away. What were you thinking?"

"Seriously, love, it's nothing, honest. Just haven't been sleeping well."

"Bob."

"What?"

"We're not that couple."

"What couple?"

"The couple who keeps secrets," she says. "The couple who lies to each other."

He holds her gaze, and suddenly Cara feels an indefinable chill rise in the space between them. They might not be *that couple*, but Cara knows her entire relationship with Bob was founded on a terrible secret.

And more. Bob doesn't know she has a secret lie of her own, and if it weren't for her lie, none of it would have happened. Her lie set it all in motion.

"Rocco called me last night," he says softly.

It hits Cara like a punch in the stomach. She lowers her fork. "Rocco? What for?"

Bob cuts into his egg and toast. "He just happened to mention some news about the skiers' chapel where we got married. They're relocating it to accommodate the resort expansion, and . . . well, they found a body—a skeleton—beneath the chapel foundations."

*"What?"*

"Yeah. Weird, eh?" He delivers egg and toast to his mouth, begins to chew. "To think of us exchanging our vows, standing on top of some old grave with a skeleton under the floor."

"God, that's terrible. Is it, like, a proper grave? Like for someone who died a natural death?"

"I looked up the news. Police aren't saying anything, but homicide detectives are handling the investigation."

"*Homicide* detectives?"

For a moment their gazes lock. Bob doesn't reply. She clears her throat. Quietly, she asks, "But why did Rocco call and 'just happen to mention' this?"

Bob cuts into his toast. "He's just worried."

"He hasn't spoken to us in almost ten years and—"

"Eight years."

"Fine. Eight years. A lot of years. And he calls *you* to 'just happen to mention' a body has been found and he's worried?"

Bob swallows but refuses to meet her gaze.

"Bob, dammit! Look at me."

He lifts his eyes. Cara does not like what she sees in them.

"This can't possibly have anything to do with us. Can it?"

"Of course not."

"So why *did* he call?"

"I think he's just scared this might be related to something he can't recall."

"But it's not. Right?"

"Of course not. Although it might raise questions that open up old wounds. You know Rocco. He's still twitchy as hell, and I think he's drinking again."

Cara feels sick. Having Rocco in their past is knowing there's a loaded and cocked gun out there all the time, and it's aimed at them. She reaches for her coffee, sips. And suddenly she is angry. Irrationally and hotly, furiously enraged that some unrelated news about some body has the power to unsettle them all in this way. To frighten them. She managed to bury that terrible thing into her unconscious decades ago. She'd almost entirely forgotten it. Cara was so effective at compartmentalizing that she'd reached a point where she was convinced that the awful event wasn't hers. It belonged to some other girl. A sixteen-year-old schoolgirl from half a century ago. The *bad thing* genuinely seemed to have happened to someone else.

Now here's idiot Rocco making this call, poking and rousing this hibernating beast, this heinous creature that was better left sleeping.

Cara and Bob try to finish brunch, but the tinkling and chinking of cutlery against china plates seems overly loud and loaded. Her gaze flicks back to Bob. She's pretty sure he never told her the full truth about that night, either. It didn't bother her, because it was past and buried. But could *that* be why Rocco called? He knows something *she* doesn't? Something Bob is still hiding from *her*?

"It's fine, Cara. It's going to be fine. It's nothing."

She sets down her knife and fork abruptly. "Is it really? Can you promise me?"

He covers her hand with his and looks deep into her eyes. "I promise."

And Cara knows it's a lie. She just knows. She can see it in his bright-blue eyes.

# JANE

Jane and Duncan regard the body lying amid dirt in the bag on the table. Dr. Ella Quinn and three of her grad students in white coats, scrub caps, gloves, and plastic aprons stand with them.

The Seymour Hills University Forensic Institute lab is a gleaming, state-of-the art facility. The brainchild of a billionaire benefactor, it's privately funded and serves as a research and teaching institute as well as contracting out to law enforcement as long as a basic mandate is met: students must be able to work hands-on alongside their science educators.

The body bag used to transport what remains of Jane Doe has been unzipped, and it contains damp soil, small stones, and other debris along with tiny artifacts. The skull sits loose at the top of the torso, the trauma on the left side clearly visible. The cranial vault is still densely packed with soil. The arms—not fully skeletonized—are folded on top of the strangely distended torso that has been preserved through the adipocere process. Remnants of decomposing textiles still wrap the torso. Her leg bones lie separate in the soil with the two boots.

"I guess this is what we're all eventually reduced to," Duncan says. "A bag of bones."

"She's a silent witness." Ella speaks for both the benefit of her students and the cops in her presence. "Our bones are the last of us to go, and even hundreds of years later they can still tell us so much about who someone was, how they lived, and in some cases, even how they died. Just like the lines in tree trunks, our lives are written into our bones. And if you know how to read them"—she glances at her students—"they speak. They tell us whether someone was healthy, muscled, strong, frail, ill. They reveal whether a person was a pescatarian, vegetarian, omnivore, carnivore, and if they were breastfed and exactly when breastfeeding stopped. They tell us if someone was abused, injured in the past, where they lived, and occasionally, what their profession was and how their life ended."

"So where do you start now that she's here?" Duncan asks as he steals a quick look at an attractive dark-haired student who smiles at him. Jane groans inwardly.

Ella says, "Well, we've weighed her as she is, in situ in the bag before physically disturbing her any further, and we've done some imaging—a series of computerized tomography, or CT, scans, and a series of magnetic resonance imaging scans, or MRIs. From the results we can now more accurately gauge her living height and age range. We also got a good look at the trauma to her skull via the imaging and now have a better understanding of the condition of the rest of her body. We've got the images up on the monitors over there. We can take a look at those in a moment. Our next step will be to continue removing and sifting through this soil around her remains, and separating out any small artifacts we might find. Some of the artifacts are already being processed at that table over there." She points to where two more students in white coats, scrub caps, and aprons work.

"Next we'll remove the boots and take samples of these textile remnants." She points with a gloved finger. "We'll then carefully remove and process the textiles. From that point, we'll cut away the adipocere, macerate the bones, and lay them all out, try to see if we are missing any." She glances at Jane and Duncan. "Or if we find extra."

"And DNA samples?" Jane asks.

"We should have a DNA profile for you to run against your databases in a few days."

Jane's attention returns to the skull. "What is she telling us thus far?"

"We can confirm that the biological sex is female." Ella glances at her students. "To be clear, in our field the term *sex* is used very specifically to denote the genetic construction of an individual—the X and Y chromosomes—and is not to be confused with *gender*, which relates to our personal, social, and cultural choices, and which may be at odds with our biological sex. We can also tell she was slight in build and stood around one hundred sixty-two centimeters, or five feet four, when alive."

The dark-haired student who has Duncan's attention asks, "Is it true our height varies throughout the day, and that we can be half an inch shorter by the time we go to bed than we woke up?"

Ella smiles. "Indeed. Within about three hours of rising, our cartilage settles and compresses and decreases our joint spaces. We end up shorter at the end of the day than when we started. When we find a body with a lot of soft tissue still present, we can simply measure height from end to end. If not, we calculate living height using measurements of the long bones—the femora, fibulae, humeri, radii, and ulnae—and we apply formulas that take into account statistical variations for sex and the ancestry of the individual. This will give us a living stature estimate that usually falls within about three to four centimeters of a person's actual living height."

"And can you tell what her ancestral heritage is?" Duncan asks.

"She's of Caucasian ancestry." Ella glances at her students. "Also something to note here: In anthropology, *ancestry* used to be referred to as *race*. But *race* is an emotive term, often with negative associations. The assignation of ancestry holds value in our scientific field, but it's not necessarily going to be of huge value to our detectives here."

"Why not?" asks a student.

"Because where our decedent's ancestors came from generations ago in a mixed society like ours is not going to tell us what language she spoke, or whether law enforcement should go looking for family or witnesses in, say, Russian, or Polish, or Iranian communities."

"But it could tell us something about what she looked like," Duncan offers.

"In some cases. But computerized forensic facial reconstruction can do a better job of that," offers the dark-haired student with a fast glance at Duncan.

"You mentioned she was likely young," Jane says, keen to get something she can start working with. "Have you narrowed her age down to a specific range?"

Ella speaks again for the benefit of her students, as per her institute's mandate. "Estimating age can be a challenge in adults. After childhood and adolescence, the correlation between chronological age and the age-related features of the bones grows increasingly weaker. We all fall apart at different rates depending on lifestyles, environmental influences, and genetics. But in the early childhood years, there's strong correlation between age, facial appearance, and size. When puberty strikes, things become less predictable." She touches her gloved hand gently to the exposed tibia. "In females between the chronological ages of twelve and sixteen, the head of the femur will fuse to the shaft. In about another year this is followed with the fusion of the greater trochanter. The last bit to fuse—to complete the adult bone structure—is the distal end of the knee, which happens around ages sixteen to eighteen in girls. At this point the individual will have reached maximum height." She pauses, looking at the remains on the table, then glances up.

Jane sees something in her eyes.

"Our decedent was between twelve and sixteen," she says.

The impact of Ella's words ripples through Jane's body. "She's just a child?"

Ella looks grave and nods. "There's more. But first I want to walk you through the skull trauma. Come this way to monitors."

Jane, Duncan, and the rest of the group follow Ella to a bank of screens showing the medical imaging, and Jane senses a shoe is about to drop. Ella is holding something back.

"Sariah," Ella says to the student waiting at the monitors. "Can you walk the detectives through the scans?"

Sariah's cheeks pink slightly. "Of course." She points to an image of the skull. "You can see there are two significant fractures to the skull, and either one of them alone would have been a major contributing factor to her death."

"There's more than one blow?" Jane asks, leaning closer.

"One impact over here." Sariah points to the left side of the skull. It's the trauma Jane has already seen in the grave and on the table. "The second blunt force impact came at the base of the back of the skull here." She points her pen at the image.

"Which came first?" Ella prompts her student.

Sariah clears her throat. "This was the primary point of impact here." She points to the hole in the skull on the left side of the head. "Whatever made this fracture likely had some angles to it," she says. "And this was followed by a much blunter blow to the base of the skull there."

"How can you tell the order?" Duncan asks.

"The first blow will crack the skull and send out fracture lines that radiate from the point of impact. As in here, and here, and there." She points to the starburst lines radiating out from the jagged hole. "Fracture lines from any subsequent blow will also radiate out, but the lines from the secondary impact will generally dissipate their force into the voids created by lines from the first blow." She glances at Jane and Duncan. "In other words, they won't cross the fracture lines of the first crack. In this way we can seriate the injuries, saying which happened first, then second, and third, and fourth, or whatever the case may be."

She points again. "The second impact opened up longitudinal fractures that terminate in the voids from the first blow, as you can see here, and here."

"Would there have been a lot of blood?" asks Duncan.

"Not necessarily. Bleeding could have been mostly internal. But she would not have survived long."

Jane studies the images closely. She returns to the body laid out on the table. As she does, a shadow of movement up in the observation deck catches her eye. She glances up. A man stands in the observation area behind a glass railing. He's looking down, watching them. Jane's heart gives a kick of recognition. Dr. Noah Gautier. The renowned "mind hunter," or criminal profiler, famous for his skill in understanding the mental workings of serial killers or individuals with deviant behaviors. Black hair. Goatee. From where Jane stands, he hasn't changed a bit in the years since she last saw him. It throws her.

He gives her a nod. Jane pins his gaze for a moment, wondering why he's here, observing this case, hands in pockets. Casual yet erudite. Enigmatic as ever.

She returns her attention to the remains on the metal autopsy table, feeling irritated. If he's interested in her case, if her decedent might be part of some serial killer investigation, she should have been looped in.

"Can you tell yet how long she was buried?" she asks.

Ella comes to her side. "Perimortem interval is far from being an exact science in cases like this. The artifacts found with her, including her clothing, will help determine her historical context. We'll also take samples for the C14 radiocarbon dating and additional isotopic analysis. Those results will begin to tell us where she lived for the last six months of her life. But this case is unique. Our imaging has revealed something rather professionally thrilling." She meets Jane's gaze. The professor's eyes gleam with barely restrained excitement.

*Here it comes. The thing Dr. Ella Quinn has been holding back.*

"The adipocere has encased and preserved soft tissue in the torso." She pauses. "Our twelve- to sixteen-year-old Jane Doe's body has been keeping a big secret. She was around three months pregnant, and the fetus is still in there."

# THE SHOREVIEW SIX

## Jill

Jill Wainwright Osman sits with Danielle Hendricks from Cape Winds Foods & Catering at a prime table on the Pier 6 patio overlooking the gentrified dockyards at the bottom of Lonsdale. Across the Burrard, Vancouver's skyscrapers sparkle in spring sun. Jill is going over her event menu with Danielle, who is handling the catering for her fundraising art show. Some of the city's top gallery owners are attending, and Jill hopes the event will also help launch her thirty-five-year-old artist daughter, Zara, into a new sphere.

"Does this budget include the wine from Davine Estate?" Jill asks. She hadn't expected to pay for the wine. She's disappointed Cara and Bob didn't step up and donate it. It's not like they can't afford it.

"It's all been worked into this bottom line." Danielle underlines the dollar figure with her pen. "We'll have various small buffet tables throughout the gallery." She points to the room layout she has sketched. "Open bars here, here, and over there to keep any lineups small." She closes the cover of her clipboard and smiles. "It's going to be great, Jill. I'm so excited to be working with you and Zara again."

Jill inhales deeply, trying to tamp down the jitters she always gets before a big event. A movement at the glass patio sliding doors snares her attention, and Jill's daughter steps through the doors. Zara grins and comes quickly through the tables toward them. She moves like a dancer.

Tall and so slender. Her brown skin is flawless—like her father's—her pitch-black hair long and wavy and impossibly shiny. Sometimes she reminds Jill of a young Iman, David Bowie's supermodel wife. Yet Zara appears completely unaffected by her beauty and solely focused on her painting. If only Jill had been half as self-assured in her youth as her daughter is, she might not have made terrible decisions just to belong to the in crowd. She might not have lied to the police all those years ago.

Zara reaches their table as Danielle gathers up her things, slides them into her carryall, and comes to her feet.

"Danielle," Zara says, "you're not leaving on my account, are you? Because I'm not staying—just dropped by on my way to the studio to say hi to my mom."

"I have another appointment waiting. So good to see you, Zara. The event is going to be amazing."

Zara glances at her mother. "Of course it is."

Jill regards the two women. They could almost be sisters in looks, apart from the age gap. Danielle is fifty-two to her daughter's thirty-five. Another movement at the patio door draws her eyes, and she spies Cara coming toward them. Her chest tightens slightly.

Zara says, "Oh, there's Cara now. I'll leave you guys to it, Mom. Just wanted to check if it's okay that I bring Armand from Pacific Gallery round for our dinner tonight? Or maybe you want some alone time with Cara?"

"No, of course, it'll be good to see him. Your dad will be doing the cooking. Cara and I will be watching. And drinking the wine."

Zara laughs, gives her mom a kiss, and says a quick hello to Cara on her way out.

"How was the ferry ride?" Jill asks as Cara shrugs out of her spring coat.

"Fine." Her speech is crisp. She drapes her coat over the back of a chair, sits, and reaches for the drinks menu without making eye contact. "Are we doing wine?"

"When are we not doing wine?"

"It's kind of early."

"It's never too early for wine."

Cara smiles tightly and keeps her gaze on the menu. Jane feels a bolt of irritation.

*Great. She's in a sulk again and she's waiting for me to say, "What's wrong, Cara, is everything okay, Cara?"*

Jill abhors it when Cara behaves like a princess. In spite of herself, she says, "What's wrong, Cara?"

Cara glances up from her menu. "Why are you using Cape Winds for catering?"

Surprise flickers through Jill. "Why not?"

"You have them cater everything."

Jill frowns. "Danielle does an amazing job, that's why. We understand each other. Plus she fits our mandate: the integration of refugees in—"

"She's not a refugee, Jill. She was born here."

"Her parents were. They fled racial classification under the emerging apartheid regime in the fifties, and—"

"I thought you were considering that new Persian place. It better fits your theme, given they are actual refugees, and newly landed at that. You could be supporting growth of a new local business."

"What do you have against Danielle and Cape Winds suddenly?"

"She's more Canadian than half the people you'll meet in BC," snaps Cara. "She doesn't need your charity."

"Christ, Cara. It's a business deal, not charity. Seriously, what's gotten up your nose?"

She slaps down the menu. "I just don't know why you have to go on and on with this social-consciousness stuff. Why don't you just set Zara up in her own gallery, relax, and enjoy the art world? And spend Isaias's money. You've earned it already."

Darkly, coolly, Jill says, "I have my own money and you know it. At least I've done more than just being a housewife."

Cara glowers at her friend. Hot spots form on her cheeks. "How dare you?"

"Look, I'm sorry. That was uncalled for. I just don't know what's gotten into you. Let's order some wine." Jill quickly summons the server over and asks for a bottle of chardonnay.

As the server leaves to fetch their drinks, Cara rubs her face. "I'm sorry. I'm so sorry. It's just that Danielle—" Her voice catches and her eyes shine suddenly. Cara clears her throat. "She's Darryl's little sister."

Jill freezes. She stares at her old friend. But before she can respond, the server arrives with a chilled bottle. Jill and Cara sit in heavy silence as the server pours their wine.

"Are you ladies ready to order?"

"Give us another minute," Jill says, her words overly tight. The moment the server leaves, she reaches for her glass and takes a long, cold swallow as memories whisper and circle her brain like tattered harpies that grow closer and louder. She counts backward from five, a trick her therapist taught her. Then very quietly she says, "Don't go there, Cara. It's the past."

"Everything you do is *about* the past, Jill. Can't you see it? You keep the past so goddamn present all the time. It's a perverse way of seeking atonement or something, isn't it? Born out of guilt. You trying to heal all the dark-skinned refugees of the world is just you trying to heal that old 'issue' in your own subconscious. Right down to falling for Isaias." Cara takes a slug of wine.

Jill's heart beats faster. Anger rises and heat floods into her cheeks. Her friend has crossed a line. There can be no going back. Not from this. She takes another big swallow of wine and opens her mouth, but Cara speaks first.

"Did you see the news?"

It throws Jill off her attack plan. "What news?"

"There was a body found—human remains."

The heat drains instantly from her face. "What body? *Where?*"

"On Hemlock Mountain. Buried under that old A-frame chapel. Homicide is now investigating."

"The chapel where you got married?"

Cara nods.

"Do they know how old the remains are? Like—are they from long ago?"

"I don't know." Emotion shimmers in her friend's eyes. This scares Jill.

"From the news it could be decades old," Cara says. "I looked it up on the ferry on the way over. They think it's a woman, and she was wearing platform boots. Knee high."

It hits Jill like a mallet. She knows exactly what has triggered Cara's outburst. Softly, she says, "Cara, it can't have anything to do with that night. It's not possible."

"Isn't it? Are you so sure? *She* was wearing platform boots that night, Jill. The night *we* were with her. Everyone knows we were among the last to see her alive."

"I don't believe it can be her. The guys said—"

"What if one of them is lying?"

Jill says, even more softly, "We *all* lied about that night, Cara."

"We all lied to the police. But what if we also lied to each other?"

# JANE

Jane stares at the pregnant torso in the bag, suddenly acutely conscious of her own little baby growing in her belly—she feels both vulnerable and fiercely protective of this long-dead tween, or teen, lying in a bag of dirt on this cold table in a shiny lab.

The revelation must have affected Duncan as well, because when he speaks, his voice is thick. "You serious? The fetus is really still in there?"

"The adipocere has preserved it," Ella says. "You might have heard of the famous Soap Lady? She was exhumed in 1875 from a cemetery in Philadelphia and is now at the Mütter Museum at the College of Physicians of Philadelphia." She pauses as she regards the remains of their Jane Doe. "The Soap Lady is on display in her glass-and-wood case like a sleeping Snow White, wisps of hair still on her head, her eyes shriveled and sunken into her face, preserved, even though she died in the 1800s."

"Like, mummified?" Duncan says quietly as he regards the remains.

"Similar, but a different chemical process that alters the body at a molecular level. The end result is a naturally preserved corpse."

"Her baby is like a little dragonfly in amber," Jane says softly. She glances at Ella. "Will we be able to obtain samples for a potential paternal DNA match?"

"We should, yes."

Jane and Duncan exchange a hot glance. This is a stunning breakthrough. Depending on when this girl died, the father of her baby could still be alive. The DNA profile of the fetus could help find him.

"How long for a profile?" Jane asks.

"A few days. We don't want to destroy any context in our rush to get in there." Ella's gaze meets Jane's. "But some of the artifacts we found in the soil might help you with an investigative start point." She shows Jane and Duncan over to the table where the two grad students are working.

Ella points to a metal evidence tray. "We found this key on a small key chain attached to what appears to be a small leather coin purse."

Jane leans forward and studies the item still stained with dirt and mold. The little zippered purse is about eight by six centimeters, or roughly three by two inches. It's embossed with a design that still remains unclear. Possibly a flower pattern.

"Once we've cleaned up the key, we might be able to get a serial number or other identifying marking," Ella says. "There were five coins in the purse. Those are over here." She shows them another tray.

Jane's pulse quickens. "Any dates on the coins?"

"Once they're fully processed, we might see more, but so far they appear to be two Canadian pennies, one Canadian dime, and that there looks like a US quarter." She points with her gloved finger. "The date on the quarter is legible with magnification: 1974. Again, we'll have more details to come."

"So midseventies," Jane says quietly, almost to herself.

Duncan says, "Doesn't mean she died in the midseventies. She might have been carrying old coins that well predated her passing."

"Maybe. But it's narrowing a window of potential for a perimortem interval," Jane replies.

"We'll be able to date the boots." Ella gives a small smile, and Jane again senses the professor is holding something back for last. It's emerging that Dr. Ella Quinn is a tease who enjoys a professional mystery as much as Jane does.

"Go on," Jane says. "Fess it up, Prof. What are you keeping from us now?"

Ella's smile breaks into a grin. "Come this way. My student Brock will walk you through what he has."

She leads them over to a guy working at a computer station. "Brock, can you take our detectives through the likely scenario for the boots?"

"Sure, yeah." Brock grins. "Obviously we'll process them further when we're ready. At that point we'll learn if they're stamped with a manufacturer's logo, but we do have a faculty member on campus—an expert in historical footwear—and she swung by right before you guys arrived and took a look at the boots in situ. If I can show you something up on the monitor here?"

He pulls up three images that display various angles of a pair of camel-brown knee-high boots with zippers on the insides of the uppers, and wood-looking platform heels.

"This is what our footwear historian is betting we will confirm these boots to be. She told us they were very common, mass-produced, lower-price-point boots likely manufactured by a company called DeeZee Inc. and sold across North America." He points. "This particular heel design, she says, was produced between 1975 and 1977. After 1977, DeeZee Inc. changed the heel shape and slightly modified the design of the uppers."

"Everything is pointing to midseventies so far," Duncan says.

Jane glances at Ella. The professor nods. "That's where our thinking is heading, yes. Midseventies."

"That would be consistent with the hypothesis that the concrete floor was poured before the eighties," Duncan says. "She could have died midseventies and been buried right before the earth floor was covered with concrete."

Jane thanks Ella and her students and asks to be called ASAP if anything new or interesting comes to light.

As they exit, she glances up to the observation gallery where she saw Noah. He's gone. It leaves her unsettled.

Duncan notices Jane looking and asks, "Who was that up there?"

"You saw him?"

"Yep."

Her partner is observant. Shrewd. Jane tends to underestimate him. That could be a mistake.

"Dr. Noah Gautier," she says as they exit the elevator and walk across the shiny floors of the institute's lobby toward the exit that leads to a glass-encased walkway bridge connecting the building to the cafeteria complex across the road.

"No way. The famous criminal profiler?"

"Or infamous. He's been hauled over the coals by an academic niche for some of his theories."

"Well shit," he whispers. "What does he want with our chapel body?"

"That's what I intend to find out."

"You didn't want to ask Ella?"

"I plan to ask him directly."

"So you know him?"

"Worked with him before." Jane does not offer more about her past with Noah.

She reaches for her mobile to call Yusra. As they push through the doors and enter the glass tunnel, Yusra picks up.

"We have new data we can use to narrow the window for cross-referencing with the missing persons database," Jane says. "Our decedent is definitely female, Caucasian ancestry, and stood around one hundred sixty-two centimeters, or nearly five feet four inches tall. She wore size seven shoes. And she was young—between the ages of twelve and sixteen. The boots she was wearing at the time of her disappearance were likely manufactured by DeeZee Inc. and sold between '75 and '77. She also had on her person a small leather coin purse attached to a key. Looks like it could be a house key. Let's start cross-referencing with missing persons entries from '75. And start local—greater Vancouver area. We can fan out from there."

"Got it. Wow, young," Yusra says.

Jane glances over her shoulder. She and Duncan are about to reach the bustling university cafeteria, but they are still alone in the concourse.

"Yusra, what I'm going to tell you I want to keep as holdback evidence, but it might have been reported in her file, if there was one. Our Jane Doe was about three months pregnant."

There's a silence on the other end of the line as Yusra absorbs the fact their decedent was still a child herself while carrying a child. "Wow," she says again, more softly.

"I don't want this getting out. Understand? There's a chance that if she was reported missing—by her family, presumably—they did not know. Whoever the father is—that individual might be our person of interest. The pregnancy might go to motive."

"Gotcha, boss. On it."

# FAITH

Faith washes dishes staring into space, her mind spinning. Her mom is doing mending in her sewing room, and her dad is sleeping. Faith should be hunting for a job, but her brain has been completely subsumed by the news of the chapel discovery.

She sets a plate into the drying rack as her thoughts return to her sister's journal.

The investigators at the time never knew about "HC," who staked out the Donut Diner on Marine. Surely no good could come out of handing the journal over to cops now. At least, no good that could possibly outweigh the stress this could put on her mom again. She really does need to get rid of the book. She rinses another plate, sets it in the drying rack. If there is a chance that the chapel body is her sister, and the cops find Faith has hidden a journal that might contain clues, she could be in trouble, too.

The words written in her sister's hand curl through her brain as she reaches for a dirty knife. Faith is so familiar with them she can virtually recite excerpts word for word.

Today HC was squeezing his little pack of creamer into his coffee while I stood at his booth, and we spoke about our favorite tv shows. He said his faves were

M*A*S*H, Baretta, and The Rockford Files. I told him I liked the Beachcombers, The Six Million Dollar Man, and Bionic Woman. I didn't tell him about Little House on the Prairie, The Waltons, The Brady Bunch, Bewitched, or Gilligan's Island. I figured he'd think I was childish. He was busy telling me that I looked a bit like Lindsay Wagner in The Bionic Woman when the opening of his creamer got stuck, and because he squeezed it harder to try and get it to work, the far corner of the tetrahedron pack split and the creamer spurted up into my face. I gasped in shock, almost dropping the hot pot of coffee. He stared at my face covered in creamer and he got this dark look in his eyes for a minute, then he got up and said he was oh so sorry and he began to gently wipe my face with his napkin. When he reached the side of my mouth, he stilled, and that dangerous look entered his eyes again. I felt hot, afraid, also excited, and a bit unwell. I could feel my cheeks burn. I pushed his hand away, embarrassed.

He sat down slowly, his eyes still pinning mine.

I caught the manager watching us from the far end of the diner counter. When she saw me looking at her, she glanced away quickly. But before I left for the day, she called me over.

She told me to be careful.

She doesn't know the half of it.

Sometimes real danger is invisible to people on the outside.

Sometimes the danger is much closer than people think.

Faith mentally flips forward a few pages as she sinks a mug into the warm, soapy water.

He was outside our house again last night. It was dark, raining, misty. I woke around 2:00 a.m. sensing something. I got up and peered out my bedroom window. The lamp at the end of the cul-de-sac wasn't working, and his brown car was parked beneath it, across the street. From his vantage point he could watch my window. I don't know if he saw me looking, but the engine started and he drove off. The day before I am sure it was him following me slowly in the car as I walked home from school. But he was a bit too far away to be certain. His car and the color is very common.

Faith places the mug in the drying rack. She was never clear whether the *he* in that entry was the same as HC from the Donut Diner. The entry that followed, though, was disturbing.

I need to find a way out. I don't know what to do. Part of me wants to tell Contrary about it, but I keep chickening out. It's easier to be angry at her and not say anything because I'm afraid if I tell her, it will change what she thinks of me forever. And I'm scared it will somehow get out because, after all, a secret is only a secret if you keep it exclusively to yourself. Or maybe I'm afraid that voicing it to Contrary will just make it seem more horribly real than it is, and I desperately don't want it to be real. But I can't do this alone. I really need someone to help me, and I don't know who I can ask if I can't tell anyone. Not one single soul. Except . . . maybe there is one person . . .

CW.

CW is different. He notices things no one else does. I think he suspects what is happening. Although he has never put it into words, I feel that somehow he comprehends. The other day he kind of obliquely said if I ever needed anything, I should just ask, and maybe he could help me. Then a few days after, he said he could take me away if I wanted. Maybe I do need to go with him. And maybe if I go, I will never come back. But I'm afraid to leave because of Pop Tart. I feel that my being here keeps Pop Tart safe.

I don't know. I don't know I don't know I don't know what to do. If HE finds out . . . I'm scared. I think HE might ***KILL me***.

It's short and it's the only entry on the page. It was dated two weeks before her disappearance. Tears fill Faith's eyes. She blinks them away and wipes her nose with her sleeve since she's wearing gloves and they're wet and covered in suds. Her mind turns to her sister's next words, near the final entry in her journal.

HATE HIM HATE HIM HATE HATE HATE HATE him HE'S A MONSTER SCARES ME ALWAYS WATCHING I NEED TO

GET AWAY HATE HIM WATCHING ALL THE TIME WISH I COULD KILL *HIM*

Faith quickly stabs a dinner knife into the drying rack, follows it with a fork. Her heart beats fast. Her breaths are shallow. She's worried she'll have a heart attack. The doctor said she needs to keep her blood pressure and cholesterol levels down, or she could have a jammer. She needs to relax. Her mom, too.

There's definitely no good in handing the journal over to the police now. It's probably not even her sister's body. She chooses to believe it's someone else buried in long boots under that chapel, and it will be best to close the book on it all. If she burns the journal, maybe then her sister's ghost and everything that is twisted up with her memory will finally leave this house in a whoosh of acrid smoke up the chimney.

# JANE

Jane and Duncan part ways in the university parking lot thick with mist and rain. Duncan heads across the lot to his vehicle. He has an appointment with the chief operating officer of Hemlock Ski Resort. As Jane nears her own car, her mobile rings.

She beeps her lock as she connects the call.

"Sarge, it's Tank. I have the contact deets that you wanted for the retired security guard. Hugo Glucklich is alive, in his seventies, and lives in an assisted living complex called Shady Ferns in Burnaby just off the Lougheed."

Jane thanks Tank and checks her watch. She can head out there now. She reaches for her door handle as a male voice calls loudly behind her.

"Jane?"

She freezes. She'd know that deep-timbred sound anywhere. Unwanted memories rush to the surface and her jaw tightens. She takes a beat to compose herself, releases the door handle, turns slowly.

Noah.

He comes closer. His stride easy yet powerful. Trademark black wool coat. Black hair. Dark eyes fixed on her face.

Noah Gautier has always possessed an imposing, almost intimidating presence. It's not just his physique and the way he consumes space. It's because of his mental prowess. And the questions he stirs in minds.

People want to know what kind of man can live in the brains and worlds of the most depraved, and hunt them for a living.

Jane thinks she might have loved him once. Or perhaps it was infatuation.

"How are you, Jane?" he says as he reaches her. The fine rain leaves little silver jewels in his hair and on his coat.

"What are you doing here, Noah?"

He regards her a moment, swallowing her, taking her in, processing. Jane knows just how much Dr. Noah Gautier can absorb from simply watching a person, how much he can read. It's unsettling when turned on her.

"If you have an interest in my case, Noah, I'd have appreciated a heads-up. If my chapel body is linked to one of yours, I need to know it from you. Not learn about it in some backhanded way by seeing you up in the observation gallery."

"I'm not here for your case. I'm in town as part of a lecture series at the SHU institute. Ella invited me. She told me what she'd brought into the lab this morning, and I stopped in to take a look out of professional curiosity." A pause. "It's good to see you, Jane. I heard your news. I'm so sorry."

The care in his eyes, in his voice, triggers a rush of emotion. It tightens Jane's throat in a way that renders her unable to respond without giving herself away. It's then that she notices Duncan standing beside his car, watching her and Noah from across the parking lot in a way that seems protective.

Not until this moment has Jane actually felt that she likes the guy. She raises her hand, giving him the "all okay." Her partner nods briefly, then gets into his vehicle and drives off into the fog.

Jane manages to say, "Thanks. I'm keeping busy, staying focused."

"I'm going to be in town for a while. If—"

"I'm really busy."

He nods. "If there is anything I can do. Please—"

"There isn't." She turns her back and opens her car door.

"Jane—"

She pauses. Not turning to face him, she says, "There's nothing anyone can do, Noah. Other than find him."

Out of the corner of her eye, she sees him raise his hand as though to touch her shoulder. She braces. But he stops short.

"Okay. I—ah, I really am so sorry."

She opens her car door wide. "How's Imogen?" she asks curtly, yanking attention back to the fact he's married, and he should leave her alone. She and Noah might have been an item once, during an intoxicating and heady affair—long before Matt—when Jane was single and Noah was separated from Imogen. But it was brief. He went back to his wife. And Jane's heart now belongs firmly to Matt.

"Imogen's doing really well," Noah says. "She remarried two months ago. A cosmetic surgeon in Houston. She lives there now."

It stalls Jane dead in her tracks. She glances up at him. "I thought—"

"We divorced right around the time you announced your engagement."

She stares.

"I would have called, Jane."

"Right. I . . . I really need to go. I'm running late for an interview."

He nods again. "I meant it—I'm in town for a while, and if I can help—"

She gets into her car and slams the door before he can complete his sentence. Jane starts her engine. She does not look at him again as she reverses, then turns and speeds out of the university lot.

As she heads down the twisting mountain road, she sees a white CBCN-TV vehicle coming up the road.

Jane curses. She quickly uses her Bluetooth and calls Dr. Ella Quinn.

"Hey, Doc," she says as soon as Ella connects the call. "A heads-up. I just saw a CBCN media vehicle heading up toward campus. Have you informed your—"

"My students are keenly aware that everything done at the institute is within a medicolegal context. They're aware that anything we do might end up being called on in court. They won't talk to the press."

"Thank you."

But as Jane kills the call, she nevertheless feels a tightening sense of urgency. Angela Sheldrick is going to dog her on this case, and students are humans. They make mistakes. They talk too much. Especially humans with young brains. The last thing Jane wants is for some family to learn details via the media that lead them to suspect the body belongs to their missing loved one. Especially not from a reporter like Sheldrick known to sensationalize things for clickbait shock value. It would utterly break Jane if she learned about Matt that way. It would break his parents, too.

# ANGELA

Angela drives up the Seymour Hills University road while Rahoul sits in the passenger seat fiddling with one of his tech gadgets. He's a camera guy and sound whiz by trade, but his spare time is consumed with a passion for spy craft, open-source intelligence, and general surveillance gadgetry. She glances at him as they enter the ring road that leads around the SHU campus.

"What are you doing?" she asks. "What is that anyway?"

"A new surveillance camera."

"It's basically the size of a pinhead."

"Basically. It's for my mini drone, which is like half the size of a hummingbird."

Angela turns off the ring road and heads into one of the outlying parking lots. She doesn't want to bring their vehicle, with its big CBCN logo, too close to the forensic institute building and risk an intervention by campus security staff. She saw the institute van at Hemlock, parked near the coroner's vehicle, so she's pretty sure the chapel remains will be brought here.

She parks the SUV and pulls a map of the campus up on her phone. She studies it for a moment. "We need to walk that way." She points north. "If we go around that set of buildings over there, we should reach the cafeteria building behind them. The cafeteria complex is linked via a covered bridge to the forensic institute buildings. Rahoul?"

"What?"

"Did you hear me?"

"I heard you." He pockets his gadget. "Let's do this."

"Try not to stand out too much, okay?"

He laughs as he gathers up his camera equipment. "C'mon, Ange. Tell me I don't look like every average student."

She grunts, takes her sling bag out of the back, exits the SUV, and pulls on a cap to protect her hair from the drizzle. They begin to walk. Mist rolls down the mountainside and sifts through the campus buildings. The SHU complex is surrounded by dense forests. It's eerie. Like it was on Hemlock.

Rahoul says, "This is what's good about living in the prairies."

"What is?"

"You freeze your nuts off, but at least it's a dry and sunny cold. Not this damp chill shit. It creeps into your skin. Your brain, too. My cousin is a pilot based out of Calgary, and he says when he comes to BC, it's like he can't see properly. His eyes are not adjusted to this perpetual low light."

Angela is focused on strategy, not Rahoul. She barely registers what he's saying. "At bare minimum we need to shoot footage of me outside the institute building, saying this is where they've taken the body," she says.

"Do we know that they have?"

"We just saw both cops driving down from SHU in their unmarked."

"I never saw them."

"Right. You were busy. They have the remains here—I don't doubt it. We snag a shot of me in front of the institute sign. Then maybe some footage inside the lobby area of me trying to talk to someone."

"And if they don't want to talk?"

"Same drill as always. It plays well on air to see them trying to shut me down, or running away, avoiding me. Looks like they have something to hide."

Angela and Rahoul climb the stairs to the cafeteria building, then make their way past the cafeteria entrance and into the glassed-in walkway bridge toward the institute buildings.

It's new. Classy. Clean lines. Ultramodern, ultrafunded.

They push through the glass doors of the institute and enter a lofty reception area. A security desk with a guy in uniform is positioned near the door. He watches them. Angela approaches the semicircular reception desk in the center of the shiny tiled floor. Rahoul hangs back, following at a short distance, ready to film Angela in action.

She's done her research and knows the head of the lab is Dr. Ella Quinn. Angela smiles sweetly at the guy behind the reception counter and says, "Hi, I'm here for Dr. Quinn."

"Do you have an appointment?"

"It's about the remains found on Hemlock."

He regards her warily. His gaze shifts to Rahoul and his camera. "Are you guys media?"

She smiles again and slides him her card. He checks it.

He picks up a phone and places a call.

"There's an Angela Sheldrick at the front desk asking to see Dr. Quinn." He reads her card. "Crime reporter for CBCN-TV." He nods, hangs up.

"I'm sorry, she's left for lunch."

"What time is she expected back?"

"You'll need to file a media request with SHU admin, for—"

"Never mind. Thank you."

She rejoins Rahoul. They go and sit on brightly colored blocks that serve as chairs near a bank of elevators. Angela's hope is to ambush Quinn when she returns from lunch and tries to enter an elevator. Perhaps they'll manage to get into an elevator car with her.

A half hour passes. The security guard regards them.

Rahoul scrolls through his phone, watching YouTube videos. Angela begins to feel edgy. She's wasting time. As she is about to suggest they leave, the elevator doors open and out steps a dark-haired woman in a lab coat with a lanyard and ID card around her neck. It's the professor. She's with a tall, black-haired man in a coat who looks vaguely familiar to Angela.

She nudges Rahoul, and he drops his phone, muttering a curse.

"It's her," she whispers. "Dr. Quinn. I recognize her from photos online. She was never at lunch."

"Maybe she's on her way now," Rahoul says as they watch the pair cross the floor, making their way to the doors. "Who's she with?"

"I don't know, but I swear I've seen his face in the news before."

They wait until the professor and the man exit the glass doors.

"Okay," she says quietly. "Let's go."

They follow the pair through the glass tunnel.

The couple enters the cafeteria.

Lunch hour has passed and the establishment is quieter. Angela and Rahoul slip into the food court area and watch from a carousel near the door as Dr. Quinn and her colleague take a seat at a booth on the far end of the room in front of floor-to-ceiling windows that overlook a treed ravine.

Angela whispers urgently to Rahoul, "I know where I've seen him—that story out of Ontario about that serial killer couple. He was also involved with the Pickton case here. That's Dr. Noah Gautier."

"Who's Noah Gautier?"

"Big shot RCMP officer and criminal profiler. Worked some of the top cases in North America and around the world. Written a couple of books." Her gaze is fixated on the couple in the booth. Her skin is hot with excitement. "Do you know what this means? The remains under the chapel could be connected to a serial killer."

"They could also not be."

"We can still use it," she whispers. "They can deny it later. But the fact is, Dr. Quinn and her institute have the remains here, and she is also with Noah Gautier. I can report this."

She notices a group departing the booth behind the couple.

"Quick. You go take that seat behind them. I'm going to get us something to eat so we blend in."

As Rahoul starts in the direction of Drs. Quinn and Gautier, Angela hisses, "Rahoul! Wait. Have you got that high-tech audio recording device with you?"

"Yeah."

"Use it. Start recording. See if you can capture anything they're saying. Hurry."

"Is that even legal?" he whispers.

"It's a public place full of students. Look at the CCTV cameras up there. It's not like we're in a washroom—they have no expectation of privacy. I mean, it'll be like us sitting in the next booth and overhearing them, but we'll pick up more sound with that equipment. Go." She ushers Rahoul off.

Angela buys two coffees and two sandwiches, and hastens over to join her cameraman. She takes a seat without glancing overtly at Quinn and Gautier. But her heart is racing. Rahoul is seated up close with his back to them. She sits opposite Rahoul and shoves a coffee and sandwich toward him.

"What's on it?" he asks, opening the sandwich.

"Don't know," she says quietly. "I just grabbed it."

"It's ham. I don't eat ham. And you forgot cream in the coffee."

"Christ, Rahoul. Just—just drink it."

They sit and eat in silence. Angela notices that Rahoul has positioned his little mike on top of his backpack on the bench beside him. He's put his camera into his pack so he doesn't attract attention.

The ambient noise of the cafeteria is fairly loud, rising and falling in waves. Quinn and Gautier have their heads bent close together and are talking very quietly. Their body language is interesting. To Angela it looks intimate. She pretends she's scrolling through her phone as she captures a few photos of the couple bent close.

From her research on Dr. Quinn and the forensic institute, Angela knows the woman is married to a fairly successful novelist who writes espionage thrillers in the vein of Daniel Silva. Angela sips her coffee, and as she feigns scrolling on her phone, she clicks a few more photos.

The cafeteria suddenly grows quieter, and she starts to hear snippets of the couple's words.

*Scientific gold . . . DNA . . . Sample . . . Fetus . . . Paternal.*

The noise of activity rises again as a rowdy group of students enters the cafeteria. Both Quinn and Gautier glance toward the disturbance. Angela casts her head down and texts Rahoul.

Recording?

He nods.

Picking up anything discernible?

He texts back.

We'll see later.

Ten minutes later, the couple gets up and leaves.

Angela's brain spins. She waits until they reach the cafeteria exit, then says to Rahoul, "Get your camera ready. We go after them. Film me trying to talk to them in the tunnel. I want you to capture both Quinn and Gautier on camera. Together."

They hurry after them. Angela's pulse pounds with excitement. Capturing footage of the two doctors entering the institute together will be enough to raise speculation about a serial killer. She'll have this on air tonight. Another breaking news segment. Another hook for her proposed series.

"Dr. Quinn! Dr. Quinn!" Angela calls out as Rahoul drops back and starts filming.

The professor in her white coat stops and turns. Her body stiffens, and she raises her chin as she sees Angela and Rahoul hurrying toward them. Defensive. Gautier comes close to the professor's side, protective.

Angela reaches them. "Dr. Quinn, I'm Angela Sheldrick from—"

"From CBCN-TV." Quinn finishes Angela's sentence. "I have no comment. And if you wish to film on campus, you need to file a request with SHU admin."

"But you do have the human remains from Hemlock at your lab?"

The couple turns and makes for the doors.

"Dr. Gautier?" Angela calls out. "How are you connected to the case?"

He tenses, then faces them.

Angela comes closer and presses. "Are the chapel remains linked to a serial killer investigation? Is that why you're here?"

"I'm here for a series of lectures. Dr. Quinn is a colleague of mine. We're catching up."

"Ms. Sheldrick," Quinn says, "you need to leave, or I'll be forced to call security." She reaches into her pocket for her phone.

Angela puts both hands up. "It's fine. It's okay. We're leaving."

Angela watches as the pair disappear through the institute doors. Rahoul keeps filming until the doors swing shut behind them.

"Way to go," he says. "Now she'll never grant you an interview."

Angela bites her lip, thinking. "Let's go see if you picked up anything on your recording device."

Back inside the CBCN-TV vehicle, as rain begins again to fall in earnest and fog creeps down through the forests, Angela and Rahoul listen to their recording through the car speaker.

The ambient noise in the cafeteria is dominant—even more noticeable than it seemed live. It fills the vehicle. But the couple's words have also been picked up more clearly and now have a bit more context.

*This is scientific gold . . . fetus preserved . . . saponification . . . soft tissue . . . be able to . . . paternal DNA . . . father . . . the adipocere . . . killed . . . blunt force trauma . . . likely midseventies . . . boots . . . house key . . . young . . . twelve to sixteen . . . just a child with a child . . .*

Angela's blood begins to thump. She can barely breathe. Quickly, she googles *adipocere* and *saponification*.

"Fuck me," she whispers as the information comes up on her screen. "They might indeed have scientific gold, Rahoul, but do you know what this is? It's effing journalistic gold."

She leans forward, starts the car. "We need this on air tonight."

"The audio?"

"The information we 'overheard' while sitting in the next booth."

"You should run this by legal. This—"

"We don't have to tell anyone, Rahoul. Not if we don't use the actual audio."

He mutters a soft curse.

Angela inhales deeply, hands tight on the wheel, her brain scheming as she drives down the mountain toward the sprawling city.

*This* will convince Mason to give her what she wants.

# JANE

Jane sits across from Hugo Glucklich in a small room at the Shady Ferns Assisted Living Care facility in Burnaby. She can hear the traffic from the freeway nearby. Glucklich has told her he is seventy-seven years old. A gray pallor tinges his wrinkled skin, and his limbs move constantly with tremors. Purple veins and bruising mark the backs of his hands.

"Parkinson's," he explains. "And low iron—anemia caused by cancer. I need a walker now, and sometimes the wheelchair to get around. I can't really manage at home alone anymore, so here I sit." He coughs. It's the sound of an old smoker's hack. She notices yellow nicotine stains on two fingers of his right hand.

"My wife passed three years ago, and my daughter is busy with her own life. She lives with her husband in Berlin." Glucklich gestures with a shaking hand to a framed photo next to his bed. "Three grandkids. Never met 'em, though."

Jane feels sad for him, that his life has come to this. She thinks of her own mom living alone at home. Her mother is only in her early sixties and still acts like she's forty half the time, but who knows where she'll be in another ten, fifteen years, or whether she will be able to manage alone. Jane's pregnancy, the loss of Matt, it's all butting her up against life issues she'd rather not think about.

"Mr. Glucklich," Jane says as she leans forward slightly, meeting the man's rheumy gaze, giving him her full attention, "you mentioned you worked as a night watchman at Hemlock Resort in the seventies."

"I suppose one might call it security these days, but back then things were so informal, different, especially up there on the mountain. I started with Hemlock in '74. I responded to an ad in the paper looking for someone to do a night shift. Basically they just wanted to have a human presence up at the base overnight. In case of a fire, or equipment failure, and to deter vandals. If anything happened, my brief was to call either emergency services or one of the other numbers they gave me."

"It was your full-time job?"

"I had a day job as well. But my wife and I were having a baby at the time—our daughter—and there was strike action looming at the pulp mill where I worked, and I didn't know if my day job would last. We were so worried about income. I was young—twenty-seven—figured I could handle the double shifts. They hired me the day of my interview. Mostly I stayed in the watchman's hut, drinking coffee, trying to stay awake, listening to the radio." He uses a handkerchief to dab spittle from the corners of his mouth, then gives a sly smile.

"To be honest, sometimes I sneaked a few tots of brandy into my coffee and caught up on sleep. I stayed on with Hemlock after I was laid off from the pulp mill in '82. They were grateful I was on scene when the lodge fire broke out in '80. If I hadn't been there to call it in, the whole place would have gone up in an inferno. I basically stayed on in one capacity or another until my retirement."

"I know this is going to sound offbeat, but I'd like to ask you about the sightings you mentioned to others."

"The lady ghost?"

Jane smiles. "Yes. The lady ghost. I imagine you've heard the news about the discovery of human remains under the old chapel?"

"Oh, God, yeah. Made me think of the ghost first thing. Is it a woman's body that was found?"

"We're still in the process of identifying the decedent. I was hoping you could tell me about your sightings? And do you know if anyone else has spoken about similar experiences?"

He looks out the window. It offers a view of a creeper growing up a cracked wall, a few dying shrubs at the base.

"I guess it was about two years after I started—so probably '76—that I first saw something. Or rather, I heard something. It woke me. I'd dozed off and, well, maybe I'd already had a few nips. Sounded like shovels hitting stony ground. I got my flashlight, went out. It was really dark. Fog thick like soup moving around with the downdrafts from the mountain as the temperature dropped." He thinks for a while, still staring out of the window, his head jerking. He faces Jane.

"The fog bounced back the beam of my flashlight and it spooked me. I could hear the breeze in the forest, moving like a soft river through the treetops. Branches swayed like slow-moving arms." He shivers slightly at the memory.

"What then?"

"I heard the sound of shovels again. Metal hitting rocks, stones. I saw the light then. A soft glow over the chapel."

"Over it? Like above the top of the cross?"

"Hard to tell the way the mist was bouncing light around. And I thought I heard voices."

"Two people? More? Male? Female?"

"I can't be sure. Then I saw the hovering light move."

"Did you go up to the chapel to investigate?"

He rubs his brow. "Like I said, I was working two shifts a day at that time. Basically 24-7 for weeks, grabbing sleep on the job when I could. I probably began drinking a bit more some nights. It was weird and lonely up there, all alone in the dark wilderness, and besides, the chapel wasn't Hemlock property, and not really part of my job description. Then, some months later, I heard a rumor about a missing girl, and someone said maybe it was her ghost, and the story kinda grew from there."

Jane makes a note in her notebook. "Did you ever see lights or a ghost again?"

"Like I said, it was spooky up there. After that incident I'd gotten it into my head somehow that someone was buried up there, or died up there. I did often hear weird noises coming from the woods. I reckon it could have been the screech owl or some creatures hunting and being killed or something like that, but I enjoyed telling the stories. It spooked some of the younger employees, and I guess they told their own versions afterward. Maybe they even elaborated a little each time."

*Where there is smoke there's fire.*

"So you reckon it was 1976 that you heard the digging and saw a light in the fog near the chapel?"

"Yeah, that would be about right. It would have been the Labour Day weekend."

She looks up from her notebook. "That's very specific."

"Well, I know that it was two years after I started work at Hemlock because '76 was the first Labour Day weekend that I worked on the mountain. And it's stuck in my mind because my wife and I had a flaming fight about it—her parents were flying over from Europe, and they were only going to be in town a few days before going on to join a cruise, and she wanted me to spend time with them."

Jane makes another note.

"Around the time that you heard the digging, did you notice anything else unusual on the mountain? For example, was there any person out of the ordinary in the area in the days preceding the incident, or the days after? Any vehicles or other events that stood out?"

He closes his eyes as though taking himself back in time. He sits with his eyes shut for so long Jane wonders if he's fallen asleep.

His eyes suddenly flare open. "No. But it's hard to say because at that time there were contractors and lots of vans and trucks and other vehicles coming and going to dig a trench for the utility lines being installed from the lodge to the chapel. They also installed a pump into the crawl space beneath the old A-frame—they were having issues with damp."

Jane's pulse quickens as she notes this in her pad.

Glucklich says, “And they put fans in for the summer. Heaters for the winter. All operated with hydro from the new lines. There was a concrete truck up there, too, to pour a floor for the basement. And that’s another reason I remember it was the Labour Day period, because most of those big construction vehicles were left up there for the weekend while work stopped and everything went so quiet.”

“Mr. Glucklich, do you recall any particular contractors? Any logos on the vehicles that you remember? The concrete truck perhaps?”

He thinks awhile. “I know the logo on the trucks was something familiar, but I can’t recall the name of the company. I do remember the concrete mixer, though. It was one of those bright red and yellow ones—the turning barrel part was yellow, with a black logo on the side that has a triangle. You still see them everywhere across the Lower Mainland. It’s, like, one of the biggest outfits.”

“Diamond Pacific Concrete?”

“Yeah, that’s it.”

Jane notes the company name. Glucklich goes dead quiet. Something appears to be dawning in his watery eyes.

“What is it?” she asks.

He leans forward, hands still trembling. “Is—is that when it happened? Is that what I heard? Was it her body being buried in the basement of the old skiers’ chapel?”

# JANE

Jane's mother calls while she is driving back to the detachment. She lets it kick to voice mail and phones Yusra via Bluetooth instead.

"We can narrow down the cross-referencing timeline further," she tells Yusra. "Retired Hemlock night watchman Hugo Glucklich claims he heard digging at the chapel during the night over the Labour Day weekend in '76."

"That's quite the recall," Yusra says. "Reliable?"

"Apparently his memory is anchored to a major fight he had with his wife over that Labour Day weekend. Glucklich says the digging noises occurred around the time the chapel was being connected to utilities and a basement floor and pump were installed."

"Maybe the night digging was being done by contractors?"

Jane takes a highway off-ramp. "Apparently construction halted over the Labour Day weekend. He remembers the concrete work being handled by Diamond Pacific Concrete, so there might still be records around that we can confirm. Get Tank or Melissa on Diamond Pacific; meanwhile you try narrowing the missing persons database cross-referencing to between August and September '76. Focus on the periods leading up to, and shortly after, that Labour Day weekend. And let's run a background check on Glucklich. Maybe it was him doing the digging, and he's throwing up a smokescreen."

Jane stops at a red light. She spies the familiar sign of a fast-food chain across the intersection. As the light turns green, before she can engage her brain, she crosses through the intersection and swerves into the parking lot. She enters the line of cars waiting to access the drive-through window.

*Mistake.*

It's going to cost her time, but two more vehicles have already pulled in behind her and she's sandwiched in the line inching toward the takeout window.

"You think Glucklich himself could be a potential person of interest?" Yusra asks.

"He'd have been thirty years old in '76." She inches her vehicle forward slightly as the car in front of her moves ahead. "He was married and expecting his first child, working two jobs, and by his own admission, drinking on his night shift." She moves forward a little more, and her gaze goes to the digital menu board. Her stomach grumbles with hunger driven by her growing baby. "He was also alone up there. Labour Day weekend could have been extra deserted. There was equipment around, shovels presumably. Maybe his ghost story was a form of projection, a way of telling people he was a part of something involving a dead girl while still trying to keep it hidden. The human mind can play strange games." She's almost at the ordering post. "I'll see you in about fifteen. Thanks, Yusra." She signs off, moves her car forward, and powers the driver's-side window down.

The voice coming out of the speaker box says, "Welcome to Harvey's. What can I get for you today?"

Jane leans her head out of her window and orders meal number six. The cheeseburger and fries with a cola.

"Anything else?"

She wavers. "Make the fries a double." Jane feels an instant stab of guilt and says, "And make that cola a diet?"

The cashier repeats the order and instructs Jane to go to the next window.

As Jane proceeds, she tells herself she should probably cut out the artificial sweetener. The chemicals can't be great for her baby. Another twinge of guilt pings through her, followed by an alien sense of being controlled. Her mind and body are being usurped by the little human in her tummy—this tiny creature that is half-Matt.

When she reaches the window, she quickly flips down her visor. Matt smiles at her from his photo. Emotion shimmers. Jane gives a rueful smile back. She still has a part of him with her. Right now. Inside her vehicle. Inside her very body.

For that she is grateful.

# HUGO

Hugo Glucklich feels an electric thrill. He hasn't felt this kind of shivery delight for years. Not since his Peeping Tom days. He *loves* that he's involved now as a potential witness to a heinous deed done in the dark and fog up on the mountain under the cross of Jesus. The lady detective's visit and questions make Hugo feel valued. He still has some purpose in life. And right now, he craves more. He's not going to pass up milking this. He's not dead yet. He can still move himself around. But for how long? So few joys left in life.

*Carpe diem.*

Hugo rolls his chair over to the small table where he keeps the remote for his little television. He struggles against his tremors to click it on and select the local news channel. CBCN-TV airs news and talk shows about local-interest stuff all day long, but for a developing news event like this chapel case, they will often break in with updates.

It's not long before an update appears.

Angela Sheldrick is back on his screen. She wears a snug fuchsia sweater. Her hair blows lightly in the breeze. Hugo adores the way she looks. He turns up the volume and listens intently, clamping his hands down hard over the armrests in an attempt to control his shaking. Angela's report is basically a repeat of last night. Hugo was hoping for something fresh. At the end of the segment, Angela looks into his room, into Hugo's very soul, with her big eyes, and she promises Hugo there will be more breaking news to come, and that she will keep him informed. She then asks anyone who knows anything—no thing is too small, and someone always knows something—to please call her tip line, or text a comment via the website or app. They can remain anonymous if they wish, she says, or she'll call them back if they leave a name and phone number.

The website address and telephone number flash across the bottom of the screen. Hugo strains to reach a pen and paper, and fumbles to write them down.

He wonders if he might possibly end up on TV if he calls Angela. Maybe she'll do a reenactment with him sitting in a replica of his old hut on Hemlock. They will film him rolling his chair out of the hut, or using his walker if he's up to it, and the cameras will focus on him peering into the thick fog with his flashlight as one of those big studio fans swirls the fog around and sinister music plays. People love to watch that kind of thing. Hugo sure does. He finds his phone. He tries several times to punch in the right numbers, getting frustrated with himself and his debilitating illness. He gets it right.

It rings.

Hugo feels even more exhilarated. Better than sex. Or at least what he remembers of it. Angela Sheldrick's sultry recorded voice answers and asks him to leave a message.

He hesitates, suddenly overcome with nerves, and when Hugo is nervous, he stutters. "I kn-know when she was b-buried," he says. "In 19-1976. I h-heard them b-burying her. I was up there. I—I heard the digging in the night."

Hugo leaves his number for Angela to call him back.

# JANE

Jane parks outside the RCMP station across from the hospital and takes another bite of her cheeseburger, getting sauce on her chin. She curses, peers into the rearview mirror, wipes her face as she hurriedly chews. She wraps her burger, tucks it back into the bag, grabs her crossbody, and balancing it all with her food and drink, she clambers out of her vehicle and hip-closes the door.

As she goes through the entrance, she notices two media vans double-parked across the street. She makes for the incident room, intending to aim for the small glassed-in office at the rear where she can quickly finish her burger while calling her superior at HQ to update him on the case details before Sheldrick or the media crews outside lob more unsubstantiated, sensation-mongering information out to the public.

But as she enters their bullpen, Yusra's head jerks up from her computer, and Tank, who is bent over Melissa's shoulder looking at her monitor, stands sharply erect.

Jane stills. Their faces tell her they've got something.

"What is it?"

"Come take a look," Yusra says.

Jane feels a spurt of new adrenaline. She hurries over, clutching her takeout bag and drink, hungry to finish her meal. She sees what is on the screen, and all thoughts of hunger vanish. Slowly, she sets her food and drink down on a desk.

Yusra points. "It's her. It *has* to be her."

Jane stares.

A pretty young blonde stares back.

Big, clear hazel eyes. Fresh skin. A slight smile, like she has a secret. Her hair is honey blonde, parted in the middle, and hangs in a shining fall below her shoulders. She wears a pale-blue sweater and little silver cross earrings.

"Feed it up onto the smart screen," Jane says quietly.

Yusra does. The girl's image fills a large monitor mounted on the wall next to their crime scene board. Jane slowly seats herself on a chair facing the monitor. She reads the details of the missing person report.

Case reference 20149561314

Missing from North Vancouver, British Columbia
This case has **1** Missing Person
This case has **1** Associated Persons

Annalise Grace Jansen was last seen around 11:15 p.m. Friday, September 3, 1976, walking home to her Linden Street residence from a school friend's party. She never arrived home and was reported missing the night of Monday, September 6. Miss Jansen might have left Vancouver of her own accord in the company of Darryl John Hendricks (18) in a 1972 model orange-and-white Volkswagen bus, license plate # 9137CR. Neither Mr. Hendricks nor Miss Jansen have been seen since. Miss Jansen's disappearance is deemed out of character and foul play cannot be excluded.

Yusra clicks open the gallery tab at the top of the file. It shows several more photos of Annalise Jansen. One of them has been age enhanced.

Missing since: September 3, 1976
Year of Birth: 1961
Age at Disappearance: 15
Gender: Female
Bio Group: White
Eye Color: Hazel
Hair: Blonde, Long
Teeth: Good. No fillings
Height: 5'4" / 162 cm
Weight: ~100 lbs / 45.3 kg
Build: Slender
Complexion: Light/Fair, slightly freckled

Jane says, "Show us the 'wearing/features' tab."
Yusra clicks on the next tab.

Shoes: Brown synthetic leather boots with wedge platform heels. DeeZee Inc. brand.
Purse: Purple backpack possibly containing travel effects, wallet, a favorite sock monkey, and a journal.
Shirt: Thin jersey sweater, pale blue.
Skirt: Knee length, tan.
Coat/Jacket: Unknown
Pants:
Scar: Left rib cage
Items on person: A small leather change purse embossed with a dogwood flower attached to a house key for her Linden Street residence.
Watch: Silver color Omega
Jewelry: Silver color stud earrings in the shape of a cross. A St. Christopher surfer pendant with the inscription: R + A inside a heart shape. One braided friendship bracelet, multicolor.

"Go back to the gallery," Jane says.

Yusra brings up the photos of Annalise Grace Jansen again. There are five in total, including the age enhancement, which is dated 2004. This tells Jane someone took another run at the file nineteen years ago. If Annalise were alive now, she'd be sixty-two going on sixty-three. A year younger than Jane's mother. If Annalise Jansen had carried her baby to term, her child would be older than Jane is. If she'd had more children later, they could conceivably have been Jane's contemporaries. Possibly they would have grown up here on the North Shore like Jane had. They might even have attended her school. Might have had their own children. Whole lives that could have been lived if Annalise's had not ended.

The images, their impact, is sobering.

Jane swallows and asks, "Is there a link to that associated missing person, Darryl Hendricks?"

Yusra pulls it up, and it feeds through to the smart screen.

Case reference 20149567914

Missing from North Vancouver, British Columbia
This case has **1** Missing Person
This case has **1** Associated Persons

Missing since: September 3, 1976
Year of Birth: 1958
Age at Disappearance: 18
Gender: Male
Bio Group: Black
Eye Color: Brown
Hair: Black, curly. Afro style.
Teeth: Good.
Height: 5'9" / 175.25 cm
Weight: 144 lbs / 65.3 kg

Build: Slender / muscled
Complexion: Dark

Yusra opens up the next tab. It shows that Darryl Hendricks was last seen wearing tan, lace-up work-style boots, Levi's jeans, and a brown leather waistcoat over a check-patterned button-down shirt. He was also likely wearing a platinum-plated silver medallion around his neck, a gift from his aunt, with an inscription that reads *Wees die verandering wat jy wil sien in die wêreld.* The file shows that the wording is Afrikaans. The translation: *Be the change you want to see in the world.*

Hendricks's photo gallery shows a teen turning from awkward into a striking young man. Thin build. High cheekbones. Intense brown eyes. Big smile. There's another image of Darryl Hendricks standing beside an orange-and-white VW bus with what looks like the iconic Rocky Mountains of Lake Louise in the background. The license plate is visible.

Both case files have the same contact referral details: North Vancouver RCMP. There is no case officer noted. It's been a long time. The cases have gone very cold, and the lead investigator could be long dead.

She clears her throat. "We'll need DNA or dental confirmation, but it looks like we found our girl." Jane turns to her team. Their faces show emotion. "Let's see what we can do to get Annalise home," she says. "Let's find out how she got two lethal blows to her head. And let's find out who Darryl Hendricks is. Because clearly Annalise did not leave Vancouver with him as suggested in this file—she was under that chapel." She points to the screen. "Could Hendricks be responsible for her death? Where did he go, and why?"

# JANE

As Jane and her team regard the images on the smart screen, Duncan blows into the bullpen carrying a glass container of boiled eggs and a green smoothie.

"Did you guys see the breaking news?" he demands. He points his smoothie at the window. "That Sheldrick woman is on air right now saying the chapel victim is a young woman who was pregnant and her fetus has been saponified and paternal DNA is possible."

*"What?"* Jane says.

Duncan suddenly becomes aware of the images on the screen. He goes quiet. His features change. "Is that *her*?"

No one responds. Jane grabs her phone and finds the CBCN-TV app. She clicks on the BREAKING NEWS icon and mirrors the stream up onto the smart screen.

They all stare as the news comes up live.

Angela Sheldrick sits at a glass table with a CBCN-TV anchor. Behind the pair, a backdrop shows an image of the SHU forensic institute building. Angela is speaking and they pick her up midsentence: "—also on the case is forensic psychologist and criminal profiler Dr. Noah Gautier. Many will remember him for his involvement as a young officer in the Robert Pickton case locally, and later in other infamous serial killer investigations across North America."

Jane's jaw drops. She fixates on the screen, which is now split, one side showing an image of Noah and Ella conversing with their heads bent close over a cafeteria table.

The anchor says, "Pickton is the pig farmer from Port Coquitlam who was charged with twenty-seven counts of first-degree murder?"

"That's right. He's in his seventies now and wasn't convicted of all charges, but no one yet knows just how many women fell prey to him in the Greater Vancouver area."

"Fuck," Melissa says softly. "What in the hell is she doing?"

Tank says, "Boss, is this true—is Gautier looking into our chapel case?"

Jane is too enraged to speak.

Angela says, "We tried to catch up with Drs. Gautier and Quinn at the SHU campus earlier today." The footage shifts to an image of Ella and Noah striding through the glass-encased causeway toward the institute doors. Angela's voice comes on air.

"Dr. Quinn! Dr. Quinn!"

They watch as Ella in her white lab coat turns to face the camera. So does Noah.

Angela reaches them. "Dr. Quinn, I'm Angela Sheldrick from—"

"From CBCN-TV. I have no comment. And if you wish to film on campus, you need to file a request with SHU admin."

"But you do have the human remains from Hemlock at your lab?"

The footage cuts to Ella and Noah turning their backs and disappearing through the institute doors, then segues back to the pair in the studio. The anchor says, "And you also have some other breaking information?"

"Correct. The remains found on Hemlock are believed to belong to a young woman, possibly between the ages of twelve and sixteen. According to someone close to the investigation, the victim might have died in the midseventies from blunt force trauma. She was wearing boots with platform heels at the time, and was found with a house key." Angela turns to look directly into the camera, right into the incident room, right at Jane and her team. "And she was about three months pregnant."

Jane closes her eyes, trying to stay calm. High blood pressure is not good for her baby.

"What else do we know?" the anchor asks. "Anything that can add context?"

"Well, thanks to a call to our tip line from Hugo Glucklich, a security guard who used to work night shifts on Hemlock Mountain—it's conceivable the young woman's body was buried under the chapel over the Labour Day weekend of September 1976. Glucklich, now in his late seventies, spoke to me earlier via phone."

Jane surges to her feet. "How did Sheldrick get that? That pregnancy was holdback evidence. How—" Her phone rings. It's her superior. She lets it flip to voice mail. He's likely gotten wind of this news, learning from a sensationalist reporter things Jane has not yet confirmed, or even raised with him. He asked to be kept up to date, no doubt to also keep a check on her state of mind. This is not going to bode well. More worrisome to Jane is Annalise Jansen's next of kin hearing this on TV and joining the dots themselves. She needs to deal with that first.

"Yusra, locate Annalise Jansen's next of kin before CBCN gets wind of our victim's possible ID and reaches her family before we do. Pull out all stops. Bring in additional personnel and resources if you need them. If her parents are still alive, they might not even know their daughter was pregnant. I also need details on Darryl Hendricks and his next of kin. I want to connect with them, too, before anything else gets out there. Tank, the Jansen-Hendricks cases were handled by this detachment. I want the name of the lead investigator at the time. Find out if they're still around, and if there are any other officers alive who might have been involved in the search for Jansen and Hendricks. Melissa, dig up all the old news articles you can find on the circumstances around their disappearances. Who was questioned? Why were they questioned? Are they still alive? What was Jansen's connection to Hendricks? Why was an assumption made that she might have left town with him? Get me anything and everything you can find." As she barks the orders, Jane marches to her glassed-in office. She shuts the door behind her and phones Dr. Ella Quinn.

As the call connects Jane opens her mouth but Ella speaks first.

"That woman should not have been on campus, Sergeant. She clearly eavesdropped on our private conversation over lunch, and her reporting was unethical. Granted, talking about sensitive material in a public venue is inexcusable, but Noah and I had no reason to suspect the couple in the next booth. We spoke quietly—I have no idea how she even picked up as much as she did. Please accept my deepest apologies."

"This could jeopardize the case," Jane snaps. "Derail our entire investigation and cost us a prosecution down the line if we ever try to hold someone accountable."

"I'm sorry. This has never happened in my professional life. Ever. We were ambushed."

*We.*

Jane closes her eyes and inhales, fighting to calm herself. "Why were you even discussing the case with Noah? What's his interest?"

*Is he lying to me about being here only for a guest lecture?*

"He's just a friend, Jane. A friend who expressed a casual and professional curiosity in the case we'd brought in. We had lunch together. We talked professional interests."

Jane counts backward, focusing on breathing deeply. Her mother's words coil through her brain.

*This is not just about you anymore. You have a little person to think of.*

She releases her breath. "Call me stat if anything comes up." She terminates the call and phones her boss. But before he picks up, Yusra opens her door.

"We got them!" she says. "Her parents are both still alive. Still living in exactly the same house from which Annalise went missing. Her sister, too—Faith Jansen Blackburn. She was nine when her older sister vanished."

Jane kills the call before her boss can answer. "Any other siblings?"

"Negative. This is her immediate family unit. I've forwarded their address to your phone."

"Hendricks?"

"Still working on it."

Jane pushes to her feet and heads back into the bullpen, pressing her hand to the small of her back to alleviate an ache. She grabs her coat from where she left it beside her half-eaten cheeseburger meal. As she shrugs into her coat, Melissa hands her a folder.

"I've printed out the first couple of online articles I found on Jansen's disappearance," Melissa says. "I've forwarded digital copies to your phone as well. This got big press forty-seven years ago. Search parties, missing poster campaigns, candlelight vigils. I'll keep digging."

Jane takes the folder. "Thanks. Duncan, you're with me on death knock duty. Pick up a DNA collection kit and the relevant release documents on your way out. We'll need samples from the family for confirmation of ID. Yusra, inform our media liaison to stand by for an official statement—the phones are going to start ringing off the hook thanks to Sheldrick. Let's go."

As Jane and Duncan depart the RCMP premises, Jane sees the media crews outside have swelled in rank. A ticking-clock sense of urgency starts to wind tighter in her chest as she drives. There's no wrestling this back into the bag now. She needs to reach those parents before Sheldrick and this horde do.

# KNOX

Retired Police Chief Knox Raymond is in Lone Butte Hunting Supplies, a tiny log cabin of a store near his campsite on a crystal-clear trout lake in the BC interior. It's his favorite time of year, and Knox is in his element. Many of the higher-elevation lakes have now iced off, and the trout are fat and feisty. He and other members of a Lower Mainland fishing club have left wives at home and migrated north with their campers to fish, camp, and enjoy guy time in the wilderness. They do this every spring when the bugs hatch, and before it gets too hot and the trout dive down deep where it's cool.

"Anything else for ya, sir?" asks the woman in the lumberjack shirt behind the counter. At her rear are shelves displaying boxes of ammo, cans of bear spray, and an array of exquisite hunting knives. A small television set is mounted on the wall near her cash register. It's tuned to a news channel, but muted.

"Yeah, I'll take some of that burnt-orange woolly bugger marabou." Knox leans over the counter to better study the fly-tying materials. He points. "And two bags of those green ringneck pheasant tails over there. And a bag of the grizzly hen saddles. Oh, and some white and red tungsten beads, plus that gold thread there."

As the clerk gathers up the materials, Knox's gaze is snared by familiar movement on the small television set. He looks up, and energy ripples through him as he realizes what caught his eye—an image of the exterior of the North Vancouver RCMP detachment buildings. His pulse quickens.

"Can you turn that up?" he asks the clerk.

She bumps up the volume.

Knox watches and listens intently.

"The remains of the young woman between the ages of twelve and sixteen were found buried under concrete in the basement of the old A-frame skiers' chapel on Hemlock Mountain. RCMP will neither confirm nor deny any of the other details being reported by CBCN-TV. Nor will they confirm that a fetus has been *saponified*, preserved in her body in a way that could make it possible to obtain paternal DNA—"

Knox's heart starts to race and his skin goes hot.

*Is it her? After all these years?*

The footage switches back to the studio, where a host has an "expert" guest.

"Dr. Jakowski, as a forensic anthropologist, do you think DNA from the fetus can be obtained, and the father of the young woman's baby identified?"

"They should absolutely be able to get paternal DNA from a saponified fetus, yes. But unless the father's DNA profile is already stored in one of the national law enforcement databases—as in, if he's committed a crime that authorizes the storage of his DNA, or his DNA was collected at a crime scene—it will be more complicated. It's possible that investigators might have already identified potential suspects, and they can ask those persons of interest to volunteer samples. If they refuse—which is well within their rights—investigators would need to demonstrate probable cause in order to obtain a DNA warrant."

"What about all of this genealogy detective work that we see hitting headlines lately, using the DNA of a perpetrator's family to crack old cases?" asks the host. "Could investigators track the baby's father through his relatives using familial DNA?"

"Absolutely. Canadian police currently partner with labs, like Othram, a Texas-based outfit that leverages forensic genealogy to solve historic cases. This lab recently helped crack a cold case involving the unsolved murders of two women in Toronto in 1983. The same methodology could be applied in the instance of the chapel body."

The host says, "And of course we all know about the high-profile Golden State Killer case solved using forensic genealogy and, more recently, the use of familial DNA to arrest and charge a criminology student in Idaho with the killing of the four university students."

"Correct. The refinement of DNA testing and new scientific developments have changed the shape of cold cases long thought unsolvable, and these chapel bones with a fetus mummified like this . . . she's been waiting almost fifty years for a chance to finally tell her secret using new science."

"Biding her time in the soil like a silent witness," the host says.

"Or not so silent," replies the forensic anthropologist, "given she is now finally able to speak."

"The unquiet bones." The host laughs.

Knox feels dizzy. A memory sears through his brain.

*The missing posters plastered all over the neighborhood. Him knocking on doors, helping canvass neighbors and residents across North Vancouver, asking if anyone had seen her walking home that night. Asking if they'd noticed anything unusual near her house—maybe a car, or a person waiting in the shadows. Or in the woods at the end of her street.*

"How do you want to pay for those?"

Knox's attention whips back to the store clerk. He's confused for a moment. "Excuse me?"

"Your fly-tying materials." The woman in the lumberjack shirt jerks her chin to the amount owed showing on the small screen facing him. "Debit, credit, cash?"

"Ah, yeah—yeah thanks. Visa." He fumbles in the back pocket of his jeans for his wallet as he glances at the television again. The news coverage has shifted to the war in Ukraine.

"You feeling okay, sir? You looked like you were going to faint there for a minute. Can I get you some water or something?"

"I'm fine." Knox hurriedly pays for his purchase, gathers up his bags, and rapidly exits the log building. He makes for his truck feeling spacey.

He climbs in and starts the engine.

He sits for a while, engine running, as he digests what he just saw and waits for the interior to warm and the fog to clear from the windshield. His mind folds in on itself as he struggles to process the news she might finally have been found, after all these years, and that there's a preserved fetus.

It's just a matter of time, he thinks, before he gets a call. He needs to get his story straight. And his head.

He leans forward, puts his truck in gear. As he begins to drive, a plan starts to formulate.

He'll approach the new cops on the case himself, tell them he worked on the investigation all those years ago. He'll offer assistance. He must appear confident, helpful, and give them enough information to ensure they look elsewhere. They must not even begin to consider him as a candidate for a DNA sample. Or Knox could be in trouble.

# JANE

Jane follows GPS directions to the Linden Street home of Helen and Kurt Jansen—Annalise Jansen's parents—while Duncan sits in the passenger seat scanning the handful of articles Melissa printed out.

"Want me to read these to you word for word?" he asks.

"CliffsNotes version." She takes the ramp off the highway and turns into a quieter, leafy subdivision.

"Okay, Annalise Jansen was fifteen years old—a few weeks shy of her sixteenth birthday—when she went missing Friday, September 3, 1976. Last known person to see her alive was her best friend since kindergarten, Mary Metcalfe," Duncan says. "The two teens, both students of Shoreview High, lived a few blocks apart. They were walking home from a party higher up the mountain. Metcalfe and Jansen parted company outside Metcalfe's house at around eleven fifteen p.m."

"So she never made it those few blocks farther to her house?"

"Apparently not." Duncan scans more of the text. "Jansen and Metcalfe were at the party with a close-knit group of friends from Shoreview High, including a guy named Robbie Davine, sixteen, who was Jansen's steady boyfriend. The party was a last hurrah before the start of the new school year."

"Davine didn't walk his girlfriend home?"

Duncan scans another story. "Seems not. The party was crashed by a horde of older kids who'd been at Ambleside Beach earlier that night. Cops were called. Several officers attended, broke up the gathering, and the crowd dispersed. While Jansen and Metcalfe walked home, the rest of their group went to find more booze to continue their revelry in a nearby woodland park."

Jane follows directions onto Linden Street. "So her boyfriend went to party elsewhere?"

"That's what these reports say."

"Who else was in the friend group?" Jane stops at an intersection, glances at Duncan.

"Two girls, Cara Constantine, sixteen, and Jill Wainwright, also sixteen. The boys were Davine, his best friend, Claude Betancourt, sixteen—Betancourt was also Metcalfe's boyfriend—Rocco Jones, sixteen, and with them that night was Rocco's older brother, Zane Jones, twenty-two."

She pulls through the intersection, shoots him another glance. "Twenty-two is a bit old to be hanging with fifteen- or sixteen-year-olds."

He purses his lips as he continues to scan the articles.

"Says here Metcalfe was witnessed by a neighbor across the street from her house arguing and physically pushing Jansen at around eleven fifteen p.m. that night before they parted company."

"And Metcalfe was also the last one to see her alive?"

"Correct. Says here Metcalfe claims while they were walking home there was a guy with a black helmet on a motorbike who appeared to be following them home after the party."

"Does it say what the girls argued about?"

"Not in these stories. Jansen was reported missing by her parents on Monday night."

"That's a while to wait—Friday to Monday?"

"Apparently Jansen told her folks she was going to be sleeping over at Metcalfe's house that weekend. It was only on Monday when Helen Jansen phoned Metcalfe's mother that they realized it was a lie."

"Wouldn't be the first teen to pull that one. Any mention in there about a pregnancy?"

"None."

"Was her boyfriend questioned?"

"All her friends were questioned, particularly the six, and especially Metcalfe and Davine. Seems the cops took a real hard look at the boyfriend, but he denies seeing his girlfriend once she'd left the party with Metcalfe. The media dubbed the close-knit group of friends the Shoreview Six."

The GPS announces they're nearing the address. Duncan glances up sharply. Jane senses his tension.

"You ever done a death knock?"

He shakes his head.

"Let me do the talking. It's easier for the surviving members to focus on one person," Jane says. "You observe. No detail or reaction is too small. Note it all down. Be alert for shock symptoms or signs of medical distress. It happens."

"Right." He inhales deeply as Jane nears the bottom of the cul-de-sac, which is abutted by dense woods.

"Those articles say anything about Darryl Hendricks?"

He flips a page. Then another.

"The more recent one mentions Darryl Hendricks was Jansen's math tutor, and that the two were friendly. When it was learned Hendricks also vanished that weekend, rumors started circulating that Jansen had left town with Hendricks, either forcibly or voluntarily, and several witnesses—including the Shoreview Six—claimed to have seen Jansen and Hendricks being intimate on more than one occasion prior to their disappearances."

"She was cheating on her boyfriend?"

"According to the witnesses."

"I'd have been really pissed if I was Robbie Davine."

"Also says here that the lead investigator at the time was a Sergeant Chuck Harrison."

"Good. Contact Tank, let him know. See if he's making headway locating the old case files."

"Oh, it says here Darryl's parents, Mimi and Ahmed Hendricks, reported their son missing the Sunday before school started September 7.

Apparently the last time he was seen was also at that party. His VW bus was gone, too. The Hendrickses owned a food store and small bistro called Cape Winds."

Jane's attention shoots to Duncan. "That's *them*? I know that place. It's still around. It started out as all South African Cape Malay food. My dad used to get takeout there, and my mom still does. He got me and my mom addicted to their bobotie and samoosas."

"Samosas," he corrects.

She slows outside the address. "*Samoosas.* They're different—made in the Cape Malay style. Christ, I can't believe that's their son. Contact Yusra, let her know if she doesn't already. It'll help her locate contact deets." As Jane parks on the side of the road, she makes a mental note to ask her mother if she remembers this story about the Cape Winds family. Her mom would have been seventeen at the time Jansen and young Hendricks vanished. This in turn reminds Jane that her mother has now phoned several times, and she's let all the calls go to voice mail.

Jane stares at the Linden Street house, mentally running through what to say to parents who have been missing their child for almost fifty years. She asks again, quietly, "And you saw no mention in there about a pregnancy?"

"Nothing." Duncan's gaze is also fixed on the dilapidated little house. It seems stuck in time. Sitting on a dead-end street that terminates in a roundabout. In limbo—like the family—while the rest of the neighborhood seems to have grown and matured and undergone various transformations around them.

Jane is only beginning to understand just how deeply a wound can slice into the life of someone whose loved one drops out of sight and sound, and how permeant that wound could be, how long one might have to wait, and wait, and wait for a resolution that never comes.

"Let's do this." She reaches for the door handle. "Let's give this family some peace."

# THE SHOREVIEW SIX

## Bob

Bob is tasting wine with his son, Trev, and his daughter-in-law, Hazel, while his grandkids play on the lawn outside. Their winemaker pours a grassy pinot gris that Hazel would like to debut on the bistro wine list this season. She sips and takes notes. Trev is meanwhile entranced by the winemaker's technical explanation of the underlying fermentation process and timing. But Bob's mind is elsewhere as he stares absently at the ocean view out the window.

"What do you think, Bob?" Hazel asks.

He snaps back with a jolt of anxiety. "Ah, nice. I like it. Which one was this again?"

She eyes him.

"Really, whichever one it is, I think it'll be a great addition to the wine list."

Hazel makes a notation on her pad. Bob is desperate to sneak a peek at his mobile, to scroll Twitter accounts in search of breaking news on the human remains. He's beyond impatient to find something, anything, that will allay his swirling fears that the "Shoreview Six" will be dragged into the hot spot again, forty-seven years after the nightmare. He needs to believe it's all going to be okay. That this is somebody from the sixties and it's not going to bring up all the other associated stuff. But, if this does go sideways, if their secret is exposed, it'll finish him and his family. It'll kill their wine farm dream. It will tank Trev and Hazel and their children, and Bob's daughter and her husband on the mainland. Even the law firm he helped build will take a massive PR hit.

His phone buzzes and he almost leaps out of his skin. He shoots a quick look at his screen and sees it's a call from Rocco.

*Rocco would be the first to know.*

Trev throws Bob a warning look. Hazel scowls. She abhors people checking phones in company. It's rude, she always says, like you'd rather be somewhere else, like you're telling present company that someone absent is more important.

"Dad," Trev says softly. His eyes say, *Put the fucking thing away. That's why you retired. That's why we all moved out here, to be away from the rat race and constant intrusion and stress.*

"I, ah, I really do need to take this. Sorry, guys. Old client. Something massive has come up. I'll catch up with you later." He hurriedly exits the tasting room. The low-angled sun hits his eyes, and he blinks as he connects the call.

"What's up?" Bob moves quickly down a gravel path toward a small picnic area among arbutus trees. The leaves rustle in the breeze. He glances back, making sure he's out of earshot. "Anything new?"

"It's her. It's fucking her, Bob. Shit. What do we do?"

He stops dead in his tracks. "What do you mean?"

"Our reporter just aired a segment. Media everywhere is jumping on it. Some night watchman on Hemlock heard digging one night at the chapel. He remembers it was the Labour Day weekend, '76. I've already seen Twitter accounts saying it has to be her. Annalise. It's going to go viral."

He swallows, feels sick.

A memory swims up and slides him back into a time everyone called him Robbie.

*He's with Annalise in the back seat of Rocco's brother's car. They're at the Odeon Drive-In in North Van. It's warm. The summer of 1976.* The Omen *is showing, but Robbie and Annalise have barely seen a thing—he's kissing her. Their tongues tangle and his heart races and his skin is hot. She smells so good. Cherry pop lip gloss, vanilla body lotion. He tentatively inches his hand beneath her shirt and he feels skin so warm, so silky smooth. She moans a little, doesn't object. It excites him. He kisses her deeper as he presses his groin hard against her pelvis and edges her into a reclining position on the seat. He cups her breast. She suddenly goes stiff, stops kissing him back. He tries again, his mouth still pressing hard on hers. She begins to struggle wildly, shaking her head, moaning against his mouth. Robbie doesn't want to believe this is happening, that she's suddenly resisting. He tries again but she struggles even harder. He pulls away, frustrated. Hot. All his friends have done it with their girlfriends. He hasn't. He loves Annalise. He's been afraid to move too fast. He's young but his love is so big he feels she is the one, and will always be the one, so this hurts. Really hurts.*

*"What's wrong?" he asks quietly.*

*She shakes her head as she struggles into a sitting position and rearranges her shirt. She turns her head away, and her hair screens her profile from him. But he thinks he glimpsed tears.*

*"Annalise?" He reaches for her face, turns her toward him. Surprise rams through Robbie. Her eyes glisten in reflected lights as tears shine down her cheeks.*

*"What's the matter? Is it me? Did I do something?"*

*She shakes her head.*

*"What is it, then?"*

*She says nothing. It's like she can't speak.*

*Robbie leans back in the car seat. Confused. A little afraid. He bought matching pendants on chains—one for him, one for her—silver St. Christopher surfer necklaces like they wear in California. For good luck in the ocean, and for chasing waves. It's part of a culture Robbie grew up in before his family relocated to Canada when he was twelve. Surfers give these to their girlfriends as a sign of going steady. He's had the backs of the medallions engraved with R + A inside a heart. He brought them with tonight hoping to have sex, hoping to make a promise with her to go steady. Damn it, he's going to do it.*

*He digs into his pocket, takes out the pendants. He hooks one around his neck. Then he unclasps the chain of the second pendant.*

*"Shh, don't say anything," he whispers as he puts it around her neck.*

*Her hand goes to the pendant. "What's this?"*

*"A St. Christopher surfer medallion," he says. "St. Christopher is like the patron saint of travel, and he keeps people safe, especially those at sea." He wavers, then adds, "People exchange these when they go steady. I want us to go steady, Annalise. Will you be my girlfriend?"*

*Tears stream afresh and silently down her cheeks. Robbie is confused. He doesn't know what to do, or say.*

*"Is that okay?" he asks. "You do want to go steady, right?"*

*She sniffs, wipes her nose, and says, "What does that mean, exactly, Robbie?"*

*"You know. We do everything together. We're exclusive. We walk to school together, sit in the cafeteria together at lunch. We do homework together, go out on weekends . . ." His voice fades.*

*She fiddles with the pendant, uncertainty in her eyes.*

◆ ◆ ◆

"Bob? Are you hearing me?"

He snaps back into the present at the sound of Rocco's voice.

"It's all just speculation at this point," he says. "It doesn't mean—"

"That's not all, Bob. Angela is also reporting the victim is definitely a female and she was pregnant. The fetus has been saponified or something, preserved. They'll get paternal DNA from it."

Shock punches him in the gut. Blood drains from his head. Suddenly there's no way back. No way out. If this is Annalise, it will open a Pandora's box of other, more terrifying questions. Fear, black and cold and brittle, fills his chest, suffocating him. *Breathe, breathe.*

Before Bob's next words are out of his mouth, he knows they are ridiculous, desperate. "Kill this story. You're the boss—stop her. Stop this Sheldrick woman."

"You know I can't. It's flown the coop. I told you, it's already going viral. If this is confirmed to be her, those homicide cops are coming back for us. All six of us. They'll reopen the '76 investigation. They'll try to reinterview all of us again, and this time there's DNA from a fetus. They'll ask for *our* DNA samples." A pause. "They'll ask *you*, Bob. They'll ask for your DNA first."

Rocco says it like a threat. A twinge of anger stirs. It brings questions of Bob's own.

"We need to talk," Rocco says. "All of us six. In person and stat. Someplace where no one can hear or see us. We've got to get ahead of this and make sure everyone is still on board with the same story, that our pledge stands." A pause. "We need to trust each other, Bob. Right?"

"Yeah, sure. We do."

But suddenly he doesn't trust anyone.

Because one thing Bob sure as hell does know—*he* did not make his girlfriend pregnant.

If not him, who did?

# HELEN

Helen Jansen assists her husband, Kurt, back into the living room. He's extra unsteady on his feet today as she guides him toward his habitual recliner in front of the television set. There's a game show on, the sound playing softly because as much as television babysits Kurt, it agitates Helen to have it on all day.

"There you go, sit." She steadies his elbow while he lowers himself shakily into the chair and lands with a grunt. She gently places a light throw over his lap. "The painkillers will kick in soon."

She waits for her husband to settle. She's beyond exhausted. Her own health is poor, and she doesn't know how much longer she can do this. It does help to have Faith back home, but she needs a longer-term solution. She feels as though a clock is winding down on their days left in this house, but she's also utterly terrified to leave it.

Her mind goes to the news she heard about a grisly discovery under the small chapel on Hemlock Mountain. How the body was wearing boots. Her gaze lowers to Kurt's liver-spotted hands, his knuckles misshapen with arthritis. His left hand is still pink and slightly inflamed from the hot-water burn. Her husband was once so powerful. Capable. Her eyes mist with complex emotions. The discovery of a body somewhere always rattles her, but this is different. She's sure it's Annalise this time. She wants to share her deepest fears with her husband, but he's gone in so many ways. First it was the prostate cancer diagnosis, followed by surgery and then hormone treatment to lower his androgen levels, effectively castrating her once powerful guy. Then he was hit by a stroke that has locked him inside his head somewhere. And now there seems to be an additional, creeping cognitive decline. While it has all felled Kurt, it has also granted him escape—a relief—in a way that Helen has craved. But perhaps it's not an escape at all, she wonders as she regards him, but an imprisonment, because she can never really tell if the memory of it all is still in there, trapped with him inside his head.

"Kurt?" she whispers.

He doesn't respond. He's now transfixed by the game show on TV.

*"Kurt."*

His eyes dart toward her. He doesn't attempt to speak, yet something almost electrical and tangible surfaces briefly in the air between them.

"I think they found her, Kurt," Helen whispers.

He turns away and stares at the flickering TV again. Helen lowers herself heavily to the ottoman at his side. "I know I've said it before, but this time I *know* it's her."

"F-found w-ho?" he manages to ask in a slow, slurred way.

"Annalise."

He frowns, seems confused. Then whatever he was thinking appears to flee his brain. "Is there almond t-tart left?"

She sighs. She feels so alone, so isolated, after all these years in her own kind of prison—locked behind the bars of grief. But now, the knock she has been both awaiting and fearing for almost fifty years might finally come. She really needs it to be over now. Closure. Resolution. Whatever form it takes, it's time. She needs the relief—she's desperate for rest.

Helen goes to the kitchen to get almond tart. As she carries a slice back to the living room with a fresh mug of tea—lukewarm for his safety—Helen notices a dark-gray sedan parked on the street outside their house. She tenses, watches from behind the drapes. The car just sits there, idling. Two people inside. A man and a woman.

And she knows—just knows—this is it. They've come about Annalise.

It's the beginning of the end.

She almost begins to cry in anticipation of the pending emotional release.

# FAITH

Faith is in the basement laundry tossing her parents' clothes into the washing machine. The laundry window is propped open to allow dryer air to escape because the vent is not working. That's how she hears the vehicle coming to a stop outside their house. She peers out the narrow window, which is just above ground level.

Through the shrubs she can see a gray car parked in the street, engine running. There's a man and a woman inside. The man has deep-red hair and a neat beard. The woman's shiny brown hair is tied back in a jaunty ponytail.

Faith is certain it's the detectives. The cops must have identified the chapel body, and now they've found the Jansen house because they are so damn easy to find. Exact same address as forty-seven years ago. Even the same bedroom waiting for Annalise as she left it.

Faith has anticipated this moment since she was nine. She's always felt that when it came, it would somehow set her free. Everything about her life—all the bad luck and stupid choices she's made over the years—can be traced back to that weekend her sister vanished in 1976. From that moment everything in Faith's world became about Annalise, the girl who wasn't there, yet always was. The ghost who made Faith invisible.

The driver and passenger doors swing open simultaneously. Faith braces. She watches as the woman climbs out awkwardly. She wears a black car coat and short boots and she looks pregnant. The man is tall, very pale-skinned. He's dressed in an expensive-looking suit, which

Faith thinks is unusual for a detective. His deep-red facial hair is impeccably groomed. It was only about three years ago that she read something about RCMP officers being allowed to grow facial hair. But it has to be under a certain length, unless the beard is grown for operational requirements, like undercover work, or because of religious reasons. She fixates on this obscure memory detail as a way of blunting what's coming down the garden path toward them.

The woman regards the Jansen house for a moment, as if assessing, preparing. The man comes around the car to the woman's side. He says something to her. The woman nods. With their mouths set in grim lines, they start up the path.

Faith wishes she'd burned the diary already.

# JANE

Jane rings the doorbell while Duncan stands stiff and stoic at her side. Wind whispers through spring leaves. She rings again, and when there's no answer, she knocks loudly. Duncan shifts weight uneasily from one foot to the other. Jane sees movement behind the textured glass panel down the side of the door, but still no one answers. She exchanges a glance with Duncan, knocks again.

The door opens. A crack. A pale face peers out. It belongs to a woman in her mid to late sixties. Jane expected Annalise's mother to look older.

She asks, "Is this the residence of Helen and Kurt Jansen?"

The woman opens the door wider. "I'm Faith. Helen and Kurt are my mother and father."

Jane absorbs this information. If Faith was nine when Annalise went missing, life has been rough on her—she appears much older than fifty-six.

"I'm Sergeant Jane Munro, and this is my partner, Corporal Duncan Murtagh." They show their IDs. "Can we come in and have a word with you and your parents, Faith? We have something important to tell you."

"Is this about Annalise?"

"Can we come in?"

Faith hesitates, then says quietly, "My father had a stroke some time ago, and now he has dementia. Some days are better than others. I'm not sure how much he's absorbed from the news, but he's not having a good day today." She pauses again. Emotion fills her eyes, which are bloodshot. "I've seen the news."

Jane inwardly curses Sheldrick. She also sees how this woman at the door both wants to let them in and doesn't. She's clearly afraid of the news but also wants to hear it. Jane is familiar with this conflict—she's done her share of death knocks. "Is it okay if we come in and talk to you and your parents about it?"

"This is going to kill my mom. I'd rather not—"

"We do need to speak to her, Faith."

Faith steps back and allows Jane and Duncan to enter.

In the living room, a frail, elderly man sits in a recliner facing a TV showing a *Jeopardy!* rerun. He's tall but shrunken into himself. Gray hair, lackluster complexion, slack skin around the jaw.

"Dad, we have company," Faith says loudly.

Kurt Jansen glances briefly their way, frowns, then returns his attention to his show. Jane notices his hands tightly clutching his armrests. His left hand is pink and swollen.

"I'll go get my mom," Faith says.

She leaves. The father keeps staring at his silent game show as Jane and Duncan enter the living room. They exchange another glance, and quietly survey the room while they wait.

A school portrait of Annalise hangs prominently on one wall. Framed photographs cluster along the fireplace mantel. Jane goes closer to study them. Most feature Annalise. There is only one that captures Annalise with her younger sister standing in front of a green sedan circa the seventies.

"Detectives," Faith says as she reenters the living room, "this is my mom, Helen."

A woman in her early eighties stands awkwardly in the entrance wearing an apron. She fiddles nervously with arthritic hands.

"Mom, this is Sergeant Munro and Corporal Murtagh. They have some news for us."

The mother swallows. She appears frozen to the floor. Eyes bright.

Faith says, "Why don't you sit down, Detectives? Can I bring you some coffee, tea, or water, or anything?"

"No, thank you." Jane seats herself on a sofa. Duncan also declines refreshments and sits in an armchair near Jane. He opens his notebook. Helen still doesn't move. Jane can hear a dryer clunking downstairs—a belt buckle or something thudding around in the drum. She can smell the fabric softener and the unique scent of heated textiles coming from the laundry.

Duncan clicks his pen in and out.

Helen finally sits gingerly on the edge of a chair. Faith remains standing between her father and mother.

"Is it Annalise?" Helen asks, voice quavering. "Did—did you find my girl?"

Jane leans forward, which is awkward around her tummy. "I don't know how much you've seen on the news, Mrs. Jansen, but human remains were found beneath the old skiers' chapel on Hemlock Mountain, and we have reason to believe it might be your daughter, Annalise Grace Jansen."

Helen sucks in air sharply. She presses her hand to her mouth, her eyes wide.

Jane allows her a moment for the news to sink in.

"Are you sure it's her?" the mother asks in a small voice.

"We'll need a DNA sample from either you or your husband to help make a formal identification, but we do believe it will be confirmed to be your daughter, and we wanted to talk to you as soon as we could, given the breaking news around this case. I am so sorry, Mrs. Jansen."

Helen stares numbly into the space between Jane and Duncan. Faith rubs her mother's back. Kurt Jansen's attention remains fixed on his television show; however, Jane glimpses the wetness of tears glinting in the creases of his wrinkles. He understands something of what is happening, she realizes.

Jane says, "I do need to inform you that this discovery is also now part of an active homicide investigation, and—"

"She was *murdered*?" Helen's voice comes out hoarse, whispery.

"There's evidence she sustained two blunt force blows to her skull that likely killed her. This, and the fact she was found where she was, is enough to warrant an investigation." Jane pauses. "Mrs. Jansen, we must also inform you that your daughter, Annalise, was pregnant."

Helen drops her face into her hands and begins to quietly sob, her shoulders heaving. Faith slowly takes a seat beside her mother and tries to comfort her. Kurt Jansen doesn't move a muscle, but his gnarled fingers are white as they clench the armrests.

"Did you know that your daughter was pregnant when you reported her missing, Mrs. Jansen?" Jane asks.

She glances up. Her face is red and tear-streaked. She shakes her head.

"We didn't know," Faith says, her complexion pale. "Are you sure?"

"The forensic team is certain, yes. About three months pregnant."

The mother dissolves into tears again, moaning and rocking as she cries.

Duncan fidgets with his pen. It's a heavy moment. These people are utterly broken. All the years of waiting for an answer have not dulled their pain, and the news appears to cut them just as sharply now as it might have forty-seven years ago.

"Do you have any idea who the father might be?" Jane asks.

Helen Jansen hiccups a sob. "No. No, I don't know. Only Robbie maybe? He—he was her steady boyfriend."

"Robbie Davine," Faith offers.

"Were there any other boys in Annalise's life who might have fathered a child with her?" Jane asks.

Helen shakes her head.

Faith says, "Maybe Darryl Hendricks? He was her math tutor. He was around here a lot. And my sister used to sometimes go to his place to study, and people reported seeing them intimate. He disappeared that weekend, too, and everyone thought he took her."

Duncan makes notes.

Faith hesitates, as though debating whether to tell Jane something more. "She—ah—she also did speak once about a guy who used to come into the Donut Diner, where she worked over the summer and on weekends during school." She flushes slightly. "I was young, so I don't recall a lot, apart from what I read later, but I remember thinking there was something fishy about him. Like, stalkery. Mom, did she talk to you about it? Did she say he seemed dangerous or something?"

Helen shakes her head. "Our Annalise changed so much in those few months before she disappeared. She became very closed about everything. She seemed . . . self-destructive, even." Her voice cracks with emotion and longing. "There hasn't been one single day, not one hour, not one minute, not one second, in forty-seven years that I haven't missed my baby girl. I *need* to see her. I need to know she really has come home. Can I please see her?"

The image of the strangely distended torso and the disembodied skull filters into Jane's brain. Gently, she says, "We'll see what we can work out, but at the moment the remains are still being processed as part of an ongoing investigation, and we must first do a formal identification."

"Why was she there? Why that chapel? Who did this?" Faith asks.

"We'll investigate all these questions and answer them to the very best of our ability," Jane says. "But our first step must be to formally identify her. Mrs. Jansen, if you or your husband will provide us written consent to collect a DNA sample—either via a swab or a very small amount of blood—we can take those now, and once the forensic lab has also collected samples from the decedent and come up with a profile, we can then compare them for a familial match."

Helen wipes her eyes with a shaky hand and glances uncertainly at her husband.

"It's voluntary, of course," Jane says. "And the DNA Identification Act governs how we are permitted to use the samples. How it works is any DNA profiles submitted by family members will be entered into what is called the Relatives of Missing Persons Index. It's part of the

National DNA Data Bank. A DNA profile submitted by a blood relative by law may only be compared to the DNA profile of a missing person or unidentified human remains. It cannot be compared to DNA profiles from convicted offenders, or from crime scenes, and it cannot be sent for international comparison. And of course, if DNA comparisons happen to reveal information that's different from what people know about their family members, this information will not be revealed unless it's pertinent to the investigation. There'll be no reprisal or discrimination if you choose not to." Jane glances at Faith. "We could also use a sample from a sibling."

"No, no, of course," Helen says. "I—I can provide a sample. Kurt is not fully capable of understanding what he would be signing or doing. I have power of attorney for him now. When do you want to do it?"

"We can do it right after we ask a couple of more questions about your daughter and the weekend she went missing, if that's okay?"

"Of course. Yes." She smooths her apron as she attempts to gather herself.

# THE SHOREVIEW SIX

## Jill

Jill and Cara sip cocktails as they watch Isaias, Jill's husband, making an Eritrean-inspired dinner in the stunning outdoor kitchen of their $13 million waterfront home near Eagle Harbour. Heaters beam down from the patio roof and take the nip off the spring evening. A fire crackles in the stone fireplace, and soft jazz pipes in through speakers. The infinity pool glows a luminous turquoise, and lights twinkle across the sound. Zara and her boyfriend share a bottle of wine in the hot tub adjacent to the pool.

Wine has been a heavy constant in Jill and Cara's day since their argument over their early lunch. After Cara's unsettling outburst, the old friends pledged to pretend it never happened, and to just drink a lot and enjoy the rest of their "weekend" together before Cara heads back to Somersby Island. This has basically been the women's MO since that fateful fall of 1976. Have fun, move on, ignore the poison that lurks down deep in all of them, because, honestly, they wouldn't cope if they let it all sink fully in.

But this time something in Jill can't quite let it go.

She watches Cara talking to Isaias, laughing, sipping her drink, appearing so at ease in spite of the ugliness glimpsed over lunch. Isaias of course is being his charming self, regaling Cara with a story about work as he cooks. The scents of spices are rich in the air.

Jill wonders if what Cara said is true. Could she really have built her relationship, her family, her charity work, her entire adult life, out of guilt? Shame? Or remorse? Could she actually have been trying to atone in some subconscious way by falling for Isaias all those years ago? What about her association with Danielle and Cape Winds Foods & Catering? And her work with refugees who mostly came from Africa? Was this Jill's buried way of trying to allay deep-seated fears she was possibly a racist?

No, Jill thinks. Not true. Can't be. She's not racist. Never was. Never will be.

Isaias comes over with a bottle of wine. "Top up?"

She forces a smile, nods. His eyes hold hers for a moment longer than necessary. He's reading something. He's detected the undercurrent between her and Cara. Isaias breaks his gaze and fills her glass. Her husband is perceptive, shrewd. Jill knows he'll broach this later, when they're alone, and tension bands across her chest. She takes a big gulp of wine and casts her mind back, searching her memory for signs of truth in Cara's accusations.

Jill met Isaias in Paris during her gap year of travel. Isaias Osman—dynamic, brilliant, sexy, sensual, entrepreneurial—had at the time been a refugee fresh from Eritrea. Despite his hardships, he'd found connections and thrown himself headlong into the clothing manufacturing business in France. He became a self-made success story, opening a trendy Parisian boutique, and now he has chains worldwide. Isaias, to Jill, had been the human face and soul of what she sees as the biggest problem of tomorrow: Human migration. Refugees. Displaced populations fleeing wars and famines and persecution and catastrophic geological and weather events. It's this looming problem that is changing the tone of politics and fostering nationalist sentiments around the world. Yet the same thing could happen to any of them, even right here. If California experiences the *big one*, for example, or if fire seasons become too intense, or if the oceans rise a few feet around Florida, masses of North Americans could become migrants of a sort. But what if what

Cara said is truer—that Isaias actually was the human face of her own guilt from that fall of 1976?

Isaias had looked so like Darryl, the eighteen-year-old teen they'd all blamed for Annalise's disappearance. It's suddenly so stark and apparent, and now that Cara has trotted it out, Jill can't *unsee* it. She's suddenly terrified that Isaias will see it, too. On the back of this fresh realization rides a spurt of rage. She's furious with the others in their group of six. This news story—this vague possibility that it's Annalise in that grave—is ripping old scars off the whole sordid thing. If this news floats the past back up, the cops *will* come around. They *will* reopen the investigation. If the truth ends up being exposed, Jill could lose Isaias. And Zara. Her charities would disown her. She'd be vilified. She'd lose everything and her life would be worth nothing. There'd simply be no reason to go on.

She sips, and her gaze shifts to Zara and her boyfriend chatting quietly in the hot tub overlooking the inlet. Zara so like her father. Her boyfriend a young Black man and owner of a prestigious art gallery. The kind of man Darryl never had the chance to become. Her wine chokes in her throat as she tries to swallow this thought. She coughs and her eyes water. Isaias glances her way again. Jill takes a deep breath.

She needs to be careful.

She can never, ever, allow her husband to know the truth of what happened when she was sixteen. She loves Isaias with her whole heart, body, and soul and would truly die if he turned against her.

Cara's cell rings. Jill's pulse rate doubles. She watches Cara check caller ID, then connect the call.

"Bob, hey." Cara glances at Jill. "Yes, we're outside about to have dinner. Isaias is cooking. Jill is—"

Jill sees Cara's face change. Her posture stiffens. Her friend's gaze darts Jill's way, and her eyes say it all: *something bad has happened.*

Cara moves rapidly along the patio and past the pool. She stands near the trees, out of earshot, talking more quietly. Jill feels sick.

Cara returns as Isaias heads back into the house to fetch more wine.

"What is it?" Jill whispers.

"It's all over the place," Cara whispers urgently. "The media and internet are saying the body was buried over Labour Day weekend in '76, and that it's probably Annalise."

Jill sees Isaias through the floor-to-ceiling windows. He's opening the wine. He'll return any minute.

Cara curses. She looks really scared now. "That's not all, Jill. She was pregnant."

Jill's jaw drops. Her mind reels. Isaias steps back onto the patio with the wine.

"What did I miss?" he asks.

"Nothing," Jill says quickly.

"Just some trouble at our bistro on Somersby," Cara offers. "One of our—ah—new hires is going to be a no-show."

"A key position?" Isaias asks.

"Manager," Cara says. "We might need to set back the season opening."

"Oh, you'll find someone," Isaias says. But his eyes are watchful. "It's such a prime spot, a lovely place to spend a summer season. Someone will snap the job up."

He walks over to the hot tub to offer wine to Zara and her boyfriend.

Cara lowers her voice. "We all need to meet. In person. Someplace private. The six of us."

"What do you mean *pregnant*?" Jill is still trying to absorb this shock. "Is it Bob's? Did he know at the time?"

Isaias is coming back.

Cara says quickly, quietly, "Jill, listen to me, focus. We need to meet. Stat."

"Where?"

"Can we do it here?" Cara asks. "Isaias is going on his trip tomorrow, right? You said he'd be away for two nights."

"No, no way. Not here."

"Where else?" she whispers hotly. Isaias comes closer. Cara shoots a glance his way. "He won't find out, Jill. Rocco's apartment is too public. Bob hasn't been able to reach Claude yet, and Claude's house is next to that park where everyone can see who's coming and going. And Mary—it'll be tough just to get Mary to come. *Please.* Your place is so private out here, and we can't do anything that will attract the attention of the media. They're going to be hounding us as it is, any minute."

Jill is almost blind with worry now.

"It's going to be fine," Isaias says.

Jill jerks and spills wine. "What?"

"The staffing issue. At the bistro. It'll work out. I don't doubt it."

Jill tries to swallow.

"Yes, of course," Cara says, exchanging a sharp glance with Jill. "We'll fix it. We'll sort it all out." She gives a false laugh. "Right, Jill?"

"Right," Jill says softly. "We will."

# HELEN

Helen stares at the cop with the pregnant tummy and thinks about her own Annalise being with child. She can't seem to absorb this is happening, so much so she's actually beginning to feel numb and confused. Her brain just can't face this painful truth. If she faces the ugly reality head-on, it could become unbearable. It's easier to allow the ugliness to scurry away and hide somewhere deep inside her own cranial vault. It's been like this for decades now—Helen simultaneously craving news of her daughter and being terrified of it coming. Because finally getting the news, finally having to face the truth, also means all hope is over.

"Can you tell us in your own words about the last time you saw Annalise, Mrs. Jansen?" Sergeant Munro asks.

She sniffs and wipes her nose, struggling to corral her mental faculties. "It was Friday. There was a party up the hill. Annalise, her friend Mary Metcalfe, and the rest of their group went. Annalise told us she was going to sleep over at Mary's. She often slept over, so it seemed normal. The last time I saw her, she was wearing her new boots that she bought with money earned at the Donut Diner. She took her backpack—I presumed it was for her sleepover stuff. Afterward I thought maybe it really was because she planned to run away." Her nose starts running again. Helen pulls a tissue from her pocket and blows her nose. Her hands shake but she can't stop them.

"S-sorry," she says. "I—I never thought this day would come. I so wanted it to come, and I also didn't want to hear that she's really gone. I—I'm just so tired."

"It's okay," Jane says. "It's normal. Are you able to continue with questions? Or would you like a break?"

Helen steals a glance at the red-haired cop with the stern white face. He's taking notes. It makes her nervous to see him committing to paper the things she's saying.

"That's all I know for sure," Helen says quietly. "Annalise left with her backpack to go to Mary's house up the road. It was the last time we ever saw her."

"And when did you realize she was missing?"

"When she didn't come home on Monday evening. School was due to start the following day. That's when we got worried and called the police."

"Can you tell me about Darryl Hendricks?"

"He was Annalise's math tutor."

"Were they intimate?"

Helen is suddenly overwhelmed, and tears begin to stream down her face.

"My mom is exhausted," Faith says. "Her health has been going downhill. I think she might need a break."

Helen shakes her head. "No, no, I want to go on." She blows her nose again. "People said Darryl and Annalise had been seen together. I . . . I thought that was probably what happened—that he took her. I—I've hated him and his family for so long now because of it. I—I don't know what to think anymore. As a mother, you believe you know your own children. You do everything you can to take care of them. Protect them. But sometimes . . . you don't know them at all."

"Do you know where Mary Metcalfe lives now?" the detective asks.

Faith steps in. "She runs that garden center and landscaping business on Marine. Near the Persian Marketplace. It's called the Happy Gardener. You'll find her there. A lot of people blamed Mary, you know?

A witness saw Mary and Annalise fighting outside Mary's house the last time anyone saw her. Mary should not have let Annalise walk the rest of the way alone. Mary was the big, strong one. She was on the wrestling team—did you know that? My sister was diminutive. If Mary had walked Annalise home to her door, she might still be alive."

The woman detective regards Faith, then glances at Kurt. Helen worries she's about to ask Kurt questions. It'll distress him. "Would you like to see her room?" Helen asks quickly.

Both detectives show surprise.

"Annalise's room?" the woman detective asks.

"It's exactly as she left it," Helen explains, getting to her feet. "It's this way." She starts down the passage, leading the police away from Kurt before the stress causes him another episode.

Only the woman detective comes after her. The other officer stays in the living room with Kurt and Faith. Helen keeps an ear out for Kurt as she opens the door to Annalise's room.

The detective steps inside. Her features reveal no emotion. People whose faces she can't read always make Helen edgy. She's not sure what to do now that they're in the room.

The cop goes up to the dresser with the mirror and peers closely at the photos stuck there.

"Are these her friends? The group the media called the Shoreview Six?"

"Yes." Helen comes closer. "That photo was taken on Hemlock." She points to a happy group shot. "It was one of several hikes Annalise did with her friends that summer. That's Robbie Davine there, her boyfriend. They started going steady that summer. And that's Jill Wainwright, Cara Constantine, Mary Metcalfe, and Mary's boyfriend, Claude Betancourt. Claude and Mary broke up after Annalise vanished. I don't think they ever really spoke again."

"Why was that?"

"I don't know," Helen says, staring at the photo. "The stress of it all, I suppose. Mary was blamed for all sorts of things."

"Like not walking home and protecting her friend?"

"Yes."

"And if Mary Metcalfe had walked her friend home, who then would have walked Mary home?" the detective asks quietly as she studies another photo.

"I . . . I don't know." Helen has never thought about this. "Mary was a big girl. Capable," she says in her defense. "She argued with Annalise that night, and people said she was interfering with Annalise's relationship with Robbie. People said she was jealous. She ended up an outcast afterward and never really got over it. Jill and Cara stayed friends, though. Cara ended up marrying Robbie. They found solace in each other's grief, I suppose. They've been together ever since my Annalise vanished." She glances at her daughter's bed with the rag doll she made. Tears flood into her eyes.

"It pained me so much. My daughter—our loss—is what brought Cara and Robbie together. I wanted to be happy for them when I heard they got married, then when I learned they had kids, and when people told me from time to time how successful Robbie had become, and about their wine farm—all that life lived. It made me think of what Annalise could have become. I could have been a grandmother by now. A great-grandmother, even."

"And where was this photo taken of them jumping into water?" the cop asks.

"Blackwater Lake. The water is actually crystal clear, but it's so deep below those cliffs it appears black. It's a caldera lake or something."

"I know of it. Can I take these two photos?" the detective asks.

Helen suddenly feels panicked. It's as though this woman has invaded their home and is now dismantling a cord that affixes Helen to the memories of her daughter.

"I can make copies and return them to you."

She nods.

The detective carefully removes photos from the mirror. As she does, Helen sits heavily down on the bed.

"Was there anything else that Annalise might have taken in her backpack?" the detective asks.

Helen sucks in a shuddery breath. "I noticed afterward that her journal was gone. And her toothbrush and some cosmetics. Along with her favorite s-sock mon-key." Great big shuddering sobs suddenly rack Helen's body as she tries to get out the last words. "Oh, God, I can't endure this again, I can't. I can't. I just can't."

"How about we wrap this up for now," Sergeant Munro says kindly. "I'll take some photos of Annalise's room. Then you can sign the consent forms and we'll take a DNA swab and get it to the lab as soon as possible. We'll also keep working to locate the original case files and go through any witness statements and a timeline of events. We'll reinterview everyone involved if we can locate them. And we'll likely return with more questions once we've done that. Is that okay?"

Helen nods, turns her face away.

"Mrs. Jansen," the detective says softly, "I *will* find whoever caused you this pain." Her voice catches slightly, which surprises Helen. She turns back and meets the detective's gaze. "I will find who took Annalise from you. And I will make it my mission to see they are punished."

"Even forty-seven years later?"

"Someone has caused you a pain that is clearly still very much alive to this day, Mrs. Jansen. For that I will see they are held accountable."

# THE SHOREVIEW SIX

## Claude

Claude Betancourt is coaching a kids' hockey game. The sound of scraping ice, sticks clacking, and pucks thudding against the side boards fills the morning air and combines with music and that particular scent of a rink. The sensations and associated camaraderie have been part of Claude's life since he was a boy. The sport defines him. He was never the smartest kid academically, nor good-looking, but he could play. He could win. He'd almost made the national league until a bad ski injury hobbled him for life and nipped his ice hockey career in the bud, but coaching kids has been his salvation. His three sons were—are—all excellent players. Now it's Claude's grandkids getting into the game, and he lives to pass his passion to other children.

Claude's unassailable belief is that sports—the discipline, challenges, competition, team building, pushing out of comfort zones—shape kids for the future and keep them away from other troubles, like drugs. It elevates character, gives tools to navigate life. Which is why Claude also believes his sport should be accessible to all children, not just those with privileged, rich parents who can afford the gear, time commitment, and travel. Ice hockey in particular is a game of privilege with huge barriers to entry, which is why Claude—who is self-made and didn't take a penny from his wealthy parents, and who was fiercely determined to build his sports apparel lines on his own, for reasons known only to him, or perhaps not even to him—started the Betancourt Foundation in partnership with his wife, Susan Presley Betancourt. Their foundation serves traditionally underrepresented groups in ice hockey, and Claude's goal is to farm champions from diverse backgrounds who would never get the chance to play otherwise.

He grins as he watches one particular tyke, just nine years old and all drive and fire.

"He's going to be a winner," says Claude's son Lachlan, who stands at his side watching the kids.

Claude grins. "When he figures out how to tone it down and think before acting." He's secretly proud of the kid, who hails from a remote northern town.

"Finesse can come later," Lachlan says, moving his chewing gum around his mouth. "He's one to watch—my money's on him. And that little Mohammad, too. Look at him go. Small but all over the place, turning circles around those bigger guys."

Claude's mobile vibrates in his pocket. He checks his caller ID. It's Bob. Again. His old school buddy has left several voice messages since last night, and Claude has yet to return one. "Can you take over, Lach? I better take this call."

Claude steps slightly away from his son and connects the call. "Hey, Bob, what's up?" He nods to one of the kids coming off the ice and makes a thumbs-up. The puck slams against the board.

"Did you see the news?" Bob asks.

"What news?" Claude's focus is back on Mohammad near the net.

"About the body found under the skiers' chapel on Hemlock Mountain?"

Claude laughs. "You know I don't watch the news. Bunch of clickbait and I—"

"Homicide cops are investigating, Claude. The media is reporting the body belongs to a woman buried there in '76 over the Labour Day weekend. Social media is already speculating it's her—Annalise."

Claude goes ice cold. The rink and players fade to the periphery of his focus. "What in the hell are you talking about?" The puck slams into the boards again. He jumps. Kids yell. Music seems to go louder. Claude puts his hand over his exposed ear, trying to hear Bob.

"Annalise Jansen. They're saying it's her."

Claude glances around, then moves away from the bleachers and pushes through a door. It swings shut behind him, cutting the sounds. He's alone in a vestibule area. His heart beats fast. "How do they know it's her?"

"It *is* her, Claude. It's fucking her. The remains still have boots on. And she was pregnant. There's a fetus in there. It's been preserved, saponified or something, and they can get paternal DNA."

Blood drains from Claude's head.

A memory rises from the distant past.

*He's alone behind the pool house with Annalise on the night of the party. Annalise, drunk, is acting reckless. She's coming on to him, leaning in to him, touching his groin, kissing him. He doesn't even try to push her away. He's a guy, for chrissakes. He has a dick, and he's going to explode. She knows what she's getting into—Claude and Annalise have done it before, after she came on to him in the same way at a beach party before the summer vacation started. But she wasn't going fully steady with Robbie then. Now she's his best friend's girl, but what Robbie doesn't know isn't going to hurt him, right? And Annalise is hot.*

*Claude has done it with Mary many times, but Mary is not attractive. Nothing like Annalise. Mary is big in all ways—tall, overweight, lumbering. Her skin is prone to outbreaks. She's a wrestling champ, and this sits uncomfortably with Claude. He gets mocked about it, about being dominated by his girl. But she's always up for sex, and that's all that matters to Claude right now when it comes to girlfriends. He told his mates he doesn't have to look at her body when the lights are out. And Mary seems pretty desperate to have a boyfriend. This is how she keeps one—by opening her legs. Claude actually feels he's doing "Mary Mary Quite Contrary" a favor. Him being the school hockey star and all.*

*But now, here's Annalise. Golden, blonde, beautiful Annalise, who is like Skipper Barbie with her lean, tanned limbs. Like Jan Brady in* The Brady Bunch. *Like Farrah Fawcett married to the Six Million Dollar Man . . . He starts to kiss her back, hard, urgently, and Annalise moves rhythmically against his erection, sticking her tongue right into his mouth, moaning. Claude's brain focuses on only the sensations now. He even forgets she's his best friend's girl. He forgets she's fifteen.*

*Annalise undoes his jeans' zipper, slides her hand into his pants. The thumping music from the speakers in the main house fades from his consciousness as he guides her to a lounger behind a hedgerow at the far end of the pool, out of sight of the house, where silhouetted figures in the windows writhe to the beats of The Doors under crazily flashing mirrored lights of a disco ball. He doesn't worry about her boots. He slides his hands under her skirt, finds her panties.*

*It's fast, desperate, and Claude comes almost as soon as he enters her. She doesn't seem to mind. She sort of laughs it off afterward as she straightens her skirt. But her laugh seems hollow. That's when Claude becomes aware of someone watching them. A shadow standing in the trees . . .*

His brain suddenly feels like molasses. Another memory slams into him. *The sound of a tire iron hitting a human head.* He's going to throw up.

"It's not her," he insists. "It can't be. Annalise wasn't pregnant." He pauses. "Was she?"

"She sure as hell never told me," Bob says.

"Look, it probably means nothing," Claude says quickly. "Christ, Bob, you're a criminal lawyer. You know that—"

"White-collar crime, bud. Not this."

Claude fires a glance at the rink through the thick plexiglass windows. The game is over. The kids are coming off the ice. Lachlan glances his way. Tension punches through Claude. He turns his back to the rink, lowers his voice. "What I'm saying is, I'll stand by you. We all will. If they ask for your DNA or anyone's DNA, everyone refuses, and then they get none. They can't force samples without a warrant, right? I mean, I've watched enough crime TV to know this much."

Bob is silent on the other end.

Panic licks through Claude. His friend can't know that he slept with Annalise, can he? Surely Bob would not have remained quiet all these years if he knew. Something else hits him. Motive. The cops will be looking at whoever the father of that fetus is as a potential killer. Claude suddenly feels sixteen again. Lost. Afraid. He steals another look at Lachlan through the glass. Claude's son is laughing with his own son. They're surrounded by hockey kids amped by the game. He thinks of his wife. His life. This cannot happen. Not now. Not when they all have so much at stake, so much more to lose.

Yet another memory slices through him.

*Dragging the deadweight of a body. The smell of blood and urine. The stickiness of blood on his hands.*

Claude leans against the wall. He's going to be sick.

"We need to meet," Bob says. "The six of us. Eight p.m. Jill's place at Eagle Harbour."

"I can't. We've got a barbecue planned for—"

"Grandpop?" Claude jerks and spins around at the sound of the little voice. His grandson has come through the door on his skates.

"Hey—hey, buddy . . . ah, Bob, I—I gotta go. I'll call later."

"There's no *later*. I've been trying to reach you since yesterday. The media will be on us like flies on carrion in a hot second, let alone the cops. Make it happen. Eight sharp. We need a game plan. A united front. We've got to get ahead of this before it controls us. Contact Mary. She has to be there, too."

"There's no way she'll come. She—"

"Fetch her yourself if necessary."

The line goes dead.

Claude closes his eyes. His head pounds. What he did to Mary as a teen still cuts him every time he drives past her garden shop. And it wasn't just him. They *all* used her. They all threw her under the bus. Claude hates himself for what happened to Mary after Annalise was declared missing.

Mary is going to be the weak link.

# JANE

Jane and Duncan pull into a parking space outside Cape Winds Foods & Catering in the new industrial complex near the water in North Vancouver. They called ahead and Darryl Hendricks's father and younger sister, Danielle, are expecting them. Jane figures if they can obtain a DNA sample from the Hendricks family, they can deliver it to the lab at the same time as the sample they secured from Helen Jansen.

The logo on the storefront shows the iconic shape of Table Mountain in Cape Town, South Africa, along with the colors of the post-apartheid South African flag.

Jane and Duncan enter the store and are greeted by the fragrant scent of spices, including coriander and curry, that are the legacy of Cape Malay dishes inspired by Indonesian and Dutch cuisine, among other cultures. Shelves are stocked with imported wares from southern Africa, and expats with varying accents browse the shelves and stock their baskets with apricot jams, rusks, chutneys, pickle mixes, biltong, dried sausage, boerewors, and spice blends for Jane's favorite bobotie dish.

They approach a woman behind a cake counter displaying malva puddings, koeksisters, brandy tarts, and melkterts. Jane shows her ID.

"Sergeant Jane Munro and Corporal Duncan Murtagh to see Ahmed and Danielle Hendricks."

The woman peers at the IDs, then examines their faces. "Hold on one minute." She disappears through a door at the rear. A moment later she reappears and says, "Come this way, please."

She takes them into a warehouse and food manufacturing area and shows Jane and Duncan into a glassed-in office. A brown-skinned and white-haired senior man wearing a kopiah and an embroidered caftan sits with his back to them. He listens to a talk show on a radio. On the desk beside him, a big orange cat preens itself.

"Mr. Hendricks," the woman says loudly. "These are the officers here to see you."

The man turns to face them. He is deeply wrinkled, and the irises of his eyes are milky white.

"Good grief, I'm not deaf yet, Cecelia. Just blind. No need to yell." His accent is thick Cape Afrikaans.

"I'm Sergeant Jane Munro," Jane says. "And I'm with my partner here, Corporal Duncan Murtagh."

"Good to meet you, Mr. Hendricks," Duncan says.

Hendricks wags his hand in the direction of a sofa covered in old magazines and cat hair. "Sit, sit." He says to Cecelia, "Go fetch Danielle."

The woman leaves, and Duncan clears away some of the junk on the sofa. He and Jane take seats. Jane glances at the wall covered with charts, schedules, a giant calendar, images of menu items, photos of an event the company must have catered, pictures of people holding glasses of wine. Taking prominence at the top center of it all is a striking photograph of a young man with a large Afro hairstyle. He wears a leather vest over his T-shirt and a chain with a medallion around his neck. His smile is huge, infectious. Jane nudges Duncan and tilts her chin toward the image.

He nods.

An attractive woman comes hurrying into the glass office. Very slender, stylish. Late forties or early fifties.

"Detectives," she says a little breathlessly as she enters. "I'm Danielle. I see you've already met my father, Ahmed. Is this about Darryl?" she asks. "We heard the news about the chapel discovery, and the talk is that it's Annalise Jansen, which means everyone is going to bring up my brother again."

"And not in the kindest of ways," Ahmed adds. "Are you people coming here to blame my boy again?"

Carefully, Jane says, "We still need to make a formal ID of the chapel remains, but it is likely that it's Annalise Jansen. Which means we are reopening the investigation into both Annalise's and Darryl's cases, and we'd like to learn a little more about your son, Mr. Hendricks. We'd like to hear in your own words what you might recall about the lead-up to Darryl going missing."

Danielle places her hand gently on her father's shoulder as she seats herself on the edge of the desk beside him. "Let's hear them out, Pops." She meets Jane's gaze, then Duncan's. "My brother's disappearance is a cloud that still hangs heavily over our family. I was only five when he disappeared, but it impacted my childhood greatly. It made my mother sick. I'm convinced the stress fed her cancer and killed her before her time. I just hope this time around there is a fair and equal investigation."

"That's our intention," Jane says. "And anything that will better help understand Darryl, and his relationship to Annalise, will assist us in doing that."

Danielle nods. Her father just stares blindly at them.

Duncan opens his notebook and clicks his pen.

"Can you tell us about Darryl's relationship with Annalise?" Jane asks.

Ahmed says, "Darryl was her math tutor. And they were good friends."

"Intimate?" Jane asks.

"As in girlfriend/boyfriend, no," he says.

"Did Darryl have a girlfriend?"

"No," says Ahmed.

"Are you certain, Mr. Hendricks?"

Danielle interjects. "Look, I know witnesses claim to have seen my brother being intimate with the missing girl, but my mother never believed it. And then some years ago, I met Jill Osman when she asked us to cater one of her events, and she admitted to me she never saw it."

"Osman?"

"Jill Wainwright Osman. She was one of the Shoreview Six," Danielle says. "She told me herself she didn't believe my brother and Annalise were intimate, either."

"So you and Jill Wainwright Osman discussed the incident in your pasts?"

"When we first started working together, Jill broached the topic, yes. She said she needed to air the fact out of the gate that she once knew my brother, and she knew of my family through Annalise Jansen's disappearance. She told me Annalise was a close friend, and Jill confessed she did tell police at the time that she saw them being intimate, and she told them she believed Darryl had either run away with Annalise or perhaps hurt her, then fled, but the truth was she never did actually see them being close herself, and she regretted saying what she had."

Duncan writes fast in his notebook. Jane makes a mental note to check Jill's statement when they locate it.

"After that we never spoke about it again," Danielle says.

"So, Jill wanted it all out in the open, even though she might have misled investigators?" Jane prompts, her interest in Jill Wainwright Osman now piqued.

"I think she has a lot of regrets about that time."

Jane and Duncan exchange a quick glance.

"Have you had contact with any of the others?" Duncan asks.

"You mean of the Shoreview Six? Just Cara, Jill's friend."

"Cara Constantine?" Duncan asks.

"It's Davine now. She married Bob."

"Bob, as in Robbie?" Duncan asks.

"Yeah. By the time he left school, he was apparently going by Bob. He became a top criminal defense lawyer but is recently retired. He and Cara bought a vineyard estate with a small restaurant on Somersby Island and have just moved there full time. We're using their wines for Jill's new charity event."

Duncan writes this down.

Jane says, "Mr. Hendricks, can you tell us when you and your wife first realized Darryl might be missing?"

"Well, he went to that party. He was seen there. He drove his VW bus to the party. But the next morning he wasn't home. This was unusual. Darryl would always let us know if he wasn't going to be home. Mimi—my wife—wanted to go to the police right away, but I said we should wait, and that maybe he'd show up. He was eighteen. It was the last weekend of the summer holidays. But as the day wore into evening, that's when I started to worry. I went down to the reggae club where Darryl often hung out with friends. The Marley Joint. It was down near the water. All high-rise condos now. One of Darryl's good mates worked there, and he told me Darryl was supposed to show up after the party, but didn't. Another one of Darryl's friends said they thought they'd seen his VW van parked in the driveway next to the old tire place near the club. The owners of the tire place knew Darryl and said he could always park there when he went to the club—there was usually no one there after hours, so the space was available. But his Volkswagen wasn't there. Other patrons from the club said they heard there was some kind of a fight near the tire place. By the time I went to look, it was raining heavily. I found no signs of a fight, no blood anywhere. No Volkswagen. But the tire people said two of the lug wrenches they left next to a stack of old tires in their private driveway were missing. Mimi and I went straight to the police station and filed a missing persons report."

"So that was Sunday morning that you reported him missing?" Duncan asks, looking up from his notes.

"Yes, Sunday morning. A whole day before Mr. and Mrs. Jansen told the police their girl was gone, but do you think they worried about Darryl? Everyone was suddenly panicked about the pretty blonde fifteen-year-old. Next thing we know, they're blaming our boy. And they're issuing bulletins across the country and over the border, not because he's gone, but because they think he took Annalise Jansen."

"What else can you tell us about your son, Mr. Hendricks?" Jane asks. "What would you like us to know about him?"

"There's two main things you must know about my boy. He was smart. And kind. Darryl was always very, very kind. To everyone. He was also a bit of an outsider as far as the kids at Shoreview High went, but I believe that's because he was brown and most of the kids at Shoreview were rich and white. I wanted to send him to the other school, where some of the kids from the Jamaican community went, but Mimi insisted he attend the other one. She thought his prospects would be better there. She said Canada was all about fairness, and that's why we immigrated here, and we should not shy away from mixing with whomever we wanted. Well, she didn't say that after Darryl went missing, now did she?" He leans forward and stares sightlessly at Jane and Duncan.

"I want the world to know my Darryl did not hurt that girl. Darryl wouldn't hurt a fly." He points a misshapen, arthritic finger at them. "I want you to bring justice for my boy."

Duncan clears his throat. "In Darryl's missing persons file, it mentioned he was wearing a pendant, or a medallion, with an inscription."

"Yes. A present sent from my sister in Cape Town for his eighteenth birthday. It was a special gift—silver disc with a platinum coating. The inscription was in Afrikaans. *Wees die verandering wat jy wil sien in die wêreld.* Which means: 'Be the change you want to see in the world.'"

"And that's Darryl in that photo on the wall?" Duncan asks.

"Yes," Danielle says. "His last school photo."

"And the medallion with the inscription is the one he's wearing in the photo?" Jane asks.

"It is," Ahmed says. "I like having his photo here. I can feel him looking in on us. He's with us always"—he makes a fist and bangs it against his chest—"right here, in our hearts."

Jane gets up and takes a closer look at the photo. "What's the image on the front of the medallion?"

"That's the shape of Table Mountain," the old man says. "Same as in our company logo. It's where we come from, our Hendricks family. A place called District Six on the flanks of that mountain. It was once a thriving multiracial community in the heart of our mother city, Cape Town. But in '66 it was declared a whites-only area. The apartheid government swept in and forcibly removed more than sixty thousand people, pulling apart homes, communities, schools, places of worship, families. The evictees were resettled across the Cape Flats, conveniently far away from the white city. People had to catch crowded trains and ride for hours into town every day to service the whites. Me and Mimi came to Canada before that happened, but my sister, Darryl's aunt, her family was evicted. Their home was demolished to rubble. That medallion was so Darryl would remember his roots."

"But he was born here?" Duncan asks.

"Doesn't matter where you are born, son," the old man says. "You still have the roots of your family." His white eyes stare fiercely over Duncan's head.

Jane reseats herself. "If you've been following the news, you'll have heard that there is evidence that the chapel body was pregnant at the time of her death. Is there any feasible chance the baby could be Darryl's?"

The old man snorts. "You people hear nothing, do you? Why don't you go do your DNA tests on that fetus and see for yourselves. You police need to finally find the truth. Go find where my boy went, and then I will finally be able to die and rest." He turns to his daughter. "Then you can bury me, Danni. I will go to Mimi."

"This brings me to our next question, Mr. Hendricks," Jane says. "We don't have a DNA sample for Darryl on file. Would either you or Danielle consent to provide us with a sample so—"

"So you check if he made that girl pregnant?"

"So we have it on file if we do find him," Jane says gently. "And yes, to rule out paternity."

Ahmed Hendricks falls silent.

Danielle says quietly, "Of course we'll provide samples. Won't we, Dad?"

He nods. But he suddenly looks tired. This has drained the old guy.

"Mr. Hendricks," Jane says softly, "would you happen to have contact details for any of Darryl's old friends from the reggae club that you mentioned? Anyone who might have heard about that fight? Or contact details for anyone who worked at the old tire place?"

He presses his lips together, thinking, then shakes his head. "That club is long demolished. Just new condo high-rises there now. Everything gentrified and expensive. Not like it used to be. The tire place was called Dan-Tires. Owner was Dan—I don't remember his last name."

Danielle says, "Darryl's friend who worked the bar at the Marley Joint is still around. I ran into him about a year ago. He's in his late sixties now and owns a furniture store in North Van." She pauses as she tries to recall the name of the store. "The Mexican Warehouse, that's it. He imports goods from Mexico. Jevaun Francis."

Duncan notes the name.

Jane circles back. "And contact details for Jill Osman?"

Danielle reaches for her mobile and looks up the contact. She reads out a phone number that Duncan records. "She lives in a big waterfront place near Eagle Harbour."

"So, did Jill Osman approach you for catering services out of the blue?" Jane asks.

Danielle nods.

"Bit of a coincidence or not?" Duncan asks.

"You mean a coincidence that she knew my brother and was one of the six? I don't think so. The North Shore has changed and grown so much in the last decades, but back then, at the core, it was like a small town, a community where people knew each other. Everyone who still lives on the North Shore from that time is connected in some way within at least six degrees of separation. Besides, we're one of the few local catering services that fit her mandate."

"Which is?" Jane asks.

"Fusion food, and supporting companies staffed or created by refugees, mostly from Africa," Danielle says. "Jill volunteers exclusively for charities that assist refugees in transitioning to new lives here."

"And she lied to police about your brother?" Jane says quietly.

Danielle holds Jane's gaze, and swallows.

# THE SHOREVIEW SIX

## Mary

Mary is having a late brunch with her daughter, Heather, at a tiny hipster joint in Kitsilano near Heather's house. They sit at a counter of thick butcher block facing out the window. They can see the beach. People walking dogs. Wind blowing up whitecaps. Gulls wheeling. Big foreign tankers skulking in the bay. The North Shore Mountains on the other side of the water stretch northward into wilderness and are still capped with snow.

Heather is alive with excitement. "The board chair said I'm basically a shoo-in now. I can't *believe* this job and the adoption coming together all at once." Her eyes shine, and Mary is struck by how beautiful her child is, and how she would do anything as a mother to keep her baby happy and to protect her.

"It's like I've been waiting for years, and suddenly it's all happening. I am so thrilled, Mom. So thrilled it doesn't feel right. I'm finally in a really good place, and I'm kind of afraid it's too good to be true. Like, I'm terrified something will jinx it now."

Mary sips her cappuccino, nods, and turns her attention to the ocean. She's afraid, too, that things could go sideways. Heather's life has not been an easy one, and it's mostly Mary's fault. Her daughter turned four when Mary hit forty and smashed head-on into a life crisis. As her milestone birthday landed, she was besieged by a mortifying sense that her entire existence was built on falsehoods. Lies. Especially lies to herself about herself. Mary was either going to crash and burn like a comet hitting Earth's atmosphere, or she needed to speak truth to herself, and about herself. And that's what she did. She finally confessed to her husband she was gay. Mary and her husband struggled through five more years of marriage for Heather's sake. They wanted to provide a stable environment at least until she was a little older. When Heather turned nine, they finally separated, then divorced. Heather was shuttled between two homes.

The separation was amicable enough, and Heather eventually grew to understand why it happened. But divorce is never easy on kids, no matter the reasons. Heather struggled in many different ways. Mary has since done whatever she can to make up for it.

Her goal now is to stand by Heather as her daughter becomes a single, working mom. Mary is nearing retirement anyway. She has an amazing staff she's trained to run the garden center in her absence. Plus she has a big bucket list of her own travel dreams. Like her daughter, Mary was finally allowing herself to believe she'd reached a good place.

Then came the news of the chapel body.

It dragged dark memories with it, triggering unhealthy feelings.

Mary's thoughts turn to Annalise and the gang of six. If the body belongs to Annalise, even more shocking than her being found beneath the chapel is that she was pregnant when she vanished.

"You're far away today, Mom. Everything okay?"

"Of course." She quickly reaches for her coffee. "How are the nanny interviews going?"

"I'm down to a short list of three. Just having references cross-checked."

Mary's phone buzzes and shudders along the wooden counter near her half-eaten plate of eggs benny. Her nerves twitch. She stares at her phone. It buzzes again, jerking slightly farther across the counter. One more buzzing session and it will topple over the counter edge and fall to the floor. She feels Heather watching her. She can't seem to move, or answer it.

"Aren't you going to get that?" Heather asks.

In slow, syrupy motion, Mary reaches for her mobile. Part of her has been expecting this. A call. Or a knock. The media. Cops. She looks at the caller ID. It's an unknown number. A cloud of doom settles over her.

She glances at Heather, then connects the call.

"Hello?" she says cautiously.

"Mary? It's Claude. Claude Betancourt."

Her heart kicks. For a moment Mary is lost for words. She turns to her daughter. "Hon, I—I think I need to take this."

She heads out of the bistro and stands on the sidewalk in the breeze.

"What do you want, Claude?"

"How are you?"

*"How am I?"* After all these years, all the crap, never apologizing, and *these* are the words that come out of his mouth?

Claude clears his throat. "Look, this isn't easy. I—you've seen the news?"

She doesn't respond. Her brain is wheeling. She expected the police, or a reporter, but not Claude. She isn't sure how to deal with this. A memory washes into her brain.

*It's 3:35 a.m. on Saturday, September 4, 1976, and Mary is tossing and turning in her bed in her moonlit upstairs bedroom. Her adrenaline is amped. She has been unable to sleep since she got home after her fight in the street with Annalise. She tosses off her covers, feeling hot. Agitated. Scared. Profoundly hurt. Shamed. Humiliated. How could her friend have done and said what she had, and still laughed in Mary's face about it?*

*Annalise's words snake through her brain.*

"I know why you're with Claude, Mary. I know why you do it with him all the time. You're a lesbian, that's why. You're gay and you are too scared to admit it. And you think if everyone knows you're having sex with Claude Betancourt, they won't see the truth. Even Claude says so."

*Tears burn afresh in her eyes. She fists her hands in her sheets.*

"I don't need your friendship, Scaredy Mary. I'm moving on. In fact, I might even just leave town. Real soon. Get out of this shithole dump. And you know who I fucked at the party? It was Claude."

*Mary is so enraged, so furious, she could kill.*

*A ticking noise sounds on her windowpane. Her mind goes still. She listens. No more noise comes. It must be the wind picking up, knocking a branch against her window. She checks the clock again. It's 3:43 a.m. The minutes are crawling by in slow motion.*

*The tick against her windowpane sounds again, followed by a louder clocking sound. Mary tenses. Someone is throwing stones at her window. She gets out of bed and goes cautiously on bare feet to the window. She peers down into the moonlit backyard. Trees sway in the wind, moving shadows across the lawn, but she sees something. Surprise rustles through her. It's Claude. Standing there in a partial puddle of silver moonlight.*

*She opens her window and whispers down to him, "What do you want?"*

*He puts his finger to his lips. Then he makes a motion to show he's going to climb up into her window.*

*"No!"*

*He starts climbing.*

*Panic licks through Mary. "Stop, Claude!" she hisses. But he's already partway up the trellis. Panic washes into horror. Her parents. They'll kill her if they find out she let a boy into her bedroom at night. Not only that, Claude, her boyfriend, just screwed her best friend at the party and said awful things that undermine Mary's self-worth and self-identity and everything she's trying to hold on to.*

*As he climbs in through her window and thumps onto the floor, the stink of him hits her. Sweat. Acrid. Weird. Mixed with soap and shampoo.*

*An unspecified fear curdles through her belly. She takes a step backward. "Do you know what time it is?"*

*He sits on her bed. His face is pale and strangely gaunt in the moonlight. His knuckles are raw, bloody. It startles her. But his clothes are clean, and he's definitely had a shower.*

*"What happened to your hands?" she whispers.*

*"We got in a fight," he says quietly.*

*"Who?"*

*"Me and Robbie. I fought with Robbie."*

*Shock ripples through Mary. She knows they were both drunk, maybe a little high on the mushrooms Rocco brought to the party. "Why did you fight? Was it about Annalise?"*

*He drags his hands over his hair, which sticks up, still damp. He then rubs his face hard. "It was. Apparently she made up some story about having sex with me, and Robbie got wind of it and came at me before I even knew what was going down."*

*Mary swallows and stares at him. Could Annalise have lied to her and made it all up? Is Claude lying now?*

*"Did you?"*

*"Did I what?"*

*"Screw Annalise?"*

*"God, no, Mary. She's acting freaking weird. She has been for weeks. None of us know what's gotten into her."*

*Mary sits slowly on the bed beside Claude. She's desperate to believe his story.*

*"She did have sex with someone at the party," Mary says very quietly. She glances at her bedroom door. Her parents are at the far end of the hall upstairs. She's worried they will hear.*

*His gaze locks on hers. "Why do you say that?"*

*"Darryl told me. He said he saw it. He said I should take Annalise home and that she was going to get herself in trouble and that she was drunk. That's why I persuaded her to walk home with me instead of going with you guys to drink even more." She hesitates. "Annalise told me it was you who fucked her."*

*He curses and rubs his raw hands over his face again. As he moves his hair, Mary notices a fresh gash on the side of his temple, almost at his hairline. It's quite a big cut. It might need stitches. A sick, unarticulated feeling begins to swirl and rise up from her unconsciousness. It brings fear.*

*"It's not true," he says. "I finally managed to convince Robbie it was all lies. Because why the fuck would I do that?" He rubs his knees. Nothing about him wants to stay still. Mary realizes his hands are shaking. His eyes begin to glisten with tears. The empath in her is suddenly at war with her drive for self-preservation. She's always been too trusting, a people pleaser. It's a big fault of hers. She'll do almost anything to keep others happy, things that end up being really bad for her.*

*"Why would Annalise lie to me?" Mary asks cautiously.*

*"I don't know. Robbie finally admitted that she's been on a total self-destructive streak and sending him mixed messages. Drinking too much." His glance darts toward Mary. "She's been getting intimate with her tutor."*

*"Darryl? No way."*

*"Yes way. The math tutor dude. The Jamaican."*

*"He's not Jamaican, Claude. He's Canadian. His parents are from Cape Town in South Africa."*

*"Yeah, well, he hangs out with those guys from the Jamaican reggae club down at the docks. He might as well be one."*

*"Annalise would've told me if she was seeing Darryl in that way."*

*"Would she? Would she, really?"*

*Mary looks away, emotions high, heart hammering. She doesn't know anything about her best friend anymore. She thought she understood Annalise. They've basically been friends their entire lives, and they used to share all their secrets. But earlier this year, Annalise started growing progressively more closed. She even mentioned something about a "dangerously sexy" guy at the Donut Diner, and when Mary asked why he was dangerous, Annalise just laughed and said he wore a wedding band. She said that maybe he carried a gun. But Mary isn't sure she can trust Claude, either. She doesn't know who to believe.*

*"Can I stay here, until daybreak?" he asks.*

*"No way. My dad will—"*

*"Please, Mary. I'll be quiet. Totally quiet. I'll leave as soon as it starts getting light."*

*"But why?"*

*"I just need you to say you were with me tonight." Tears slide down his face, and some part of her heart responds. "No matter who asks, okay? Promise me you'll say that. Tell them I came here around twelve thirty. After the rest of us went to get liquor and went to the woods for a very short while. Then they dropped me off here."*

*"Is Robbie okay?"*

*"Better off than me."*

*"Did anyone else get hurt in the fight?"*

*"It was just Robbie and me."*

*"So why do you need me to lie about where you were?"*

*"Because the argument started when we were in the car."*

*"Whose car?"*

*"Rocco's brother's car. I was driving along Marine Drive when Robbie lunged for me."*

*"Why were you driving? Where was Zane?"*

*"He had his bike. I swerved and we swiped a VW Bug parked on the side of the road. I—I didn't stop, Mary. We'd been drinking, and you know I don't have my full license yet. I still need to drive with a fully licensed adult."*

*"Was anyone inside the punch buggy?"*

*"No. It was empty. Just parked in the street at night."*

*"You're sure?"*

*"Yes, I'm sure. Christ. We checked—"*

*"You said you didn't stop."*

*"I mean, we checked briefly, saw no one, then we drove off quickly. Promise me? Please? I will owe you so big."*

◆ ◆ ◆

"Mary? Are you there?" The voice coming from her phone startles her back into the present.

She clears her throat. "I'm here." She walks quickly toward her car parked near the curb, beeps her lock, climbs in, shuts the door. No one can hear her conversation in here.

"We need to meet," Claude says. "All six of us."

"I have nothing to say to you guys." *I never want to see any of you again in my life.*

"The cops will come, Mary. They'll reopen the investigation, reinterview us all."

"So? I'll talk to the cops. I have nothing to hide." She's been thinking about this since the news first broke about human remains. If this is indeed confirmed to be Annalise, the best she can do for Heather's sake is come clean, and fast. Own the truth—that she lied for Claude. It will reveal he never had an alibi. But that's his problem, not hers. She was young and stupid. And now she's not. Yes, she argued with her best friend in the street that night, but she would never, ever hurt her. She loved Annalise. Deeply. In all sorts of ways. And she supposes that was part of the problem.

"We all need to be on the same page, Mary. We need the same narrative. It has to be the exact same story we told back then. Because if cracks or contradictions show up now, the homicide cops *will* dig deeper. Harder. Media scrutiny will be intense. It's not like pre-internet days."

She hears the edge of desperation entering his voice. But Mary has learned who she is now. She's learned to stand her ground. To stand strong.

"Whose baby is it, Claude? Is it yours?"

"Christ, no. I told you, that was a lie. Besides, if the fetus is three months old, it didn't happen at the party."

"I guess the DNA will reveal all, eh?"

"Mary, if this goes sideways—"

"I won't lie for you, Claude. Not now. When you asked me to cover for you, I didn't know Annalise was going to turn up missing. Maybe you did it. Maybe Robbie did it. Maybe—"

"Maybe *you* did it, Mary! Just like some people thought you did back then. *You* fought with her on the street. *You* were seen pushing her physically, screaming at her. Have you considered that your lie gives *you* an alibi, too? Have you considered that maybe I will tell the police it was you who asked *me* to lie about being in your room to cover *your* ass?"

She goes cold. Her brain reels as she tries to imagine how this could play out. She glances at the bistro where Heather is sitting and probably wondering where her mother went. Any moment Heather will come out looking.

"If you pull the plug, Mary, you no longer have an alibi."

"I don't need one."

"Are you so sure? Look, let's just meet and all talk about this. Calmly. I don't want to face this any more than you do. And I'm sorry—truly sorry—for what happened between me and you, but I also know that Annalise mentioned to Robbie you might swing both ways. She told him you were desperate to appear 'normal' and that's probably why you had such easy sex with me. As a cover. If the cops find this out, it's possible motive, Mary. If Annalise threatened to tell everyone at school, and you fought about it—"

"Fuck you," she whispers hotly, her hand tightening around her phone. "Fuck you and your fucking lies, Claude."

"The cops will be interested."

"It's all lies." Emotion stings into her eyes.

"You know what it is? It's really, really bad press. And you know what else? If the media runs with it, if it all goes viral on social media, I guarantee this will cost Heather that big job I heard she's up for at Brockton House. There are only two things that matter to the Brockton House parent council. Prestige and reputation. Even a whiff of a scandal, and she's done."

"This has *nothing* to do with Heather."

"Doesn't it, then?"

She closes her eyes, tries to breathe.

"I swear, I don't want to spread these things about you. But I need to protect my family. And so do you. Don't force me, Mary. I'll pick you up at the garden center at seven thirty tonight. Be there."

The call goes dead.

# JANE

When Jane and Duncan swing by the SHU forensic institute and drop off the DNA samples, Ella calls them into her lab.

"Since you're here, I have something I think you'll want to see in person," she says as they follow her to one of the evidence-processing tables.

The tone between Jane and Ella is still cool. Jane remains frustrated that the news of the pregnancy was spilled, and Ella is clearly irritated herself. As Jane walks behind Ella, she glances reflexively up toward the observation gallery. No Noah. She notices Duncan noticing her looking. Again, Jane is struck by how her partner remains ever vigilant, silently cataloging everyone and everything around him.

"This is what we've cleaned up and processed thus far," says Ella. She points to a small metal tray. "These were found in the soil around her body—silver-colored stud earrings in the shape of crosses. We're guessing they're real silver, or at least plated with silver given their condition. We'll know for sure once they're tested."

"Those are featured in one of the photos in her missing persons file," Duncan says, glancing at Jane. "And mentioned as some of the items she was last seen wearing."

Jane leans closer and studies them. "Did you notice any other religious artifacts in the Jansen home?" she asks Duncan.

"Nothing that comes to mind. You thinking she wore these crosses for religious purposes? That there could be a link somehow to the chapel, her faith?"

"I don't know," she says quietly. "But it's hard not to notice the symbolism—whether intended or not—of Annalise Jansen being a young, unmarried mother buried beneath a church that prominently features a stained glass panel of a Madonna and child."

"And what's that over there?" Duncan points to another tray that holds a snaking, thin piece of metal several feet long.

"A zipper," Ella says.

"Freaking long zipper." His gaze shoots to Ella. "What needs a zipper that long?" Duncan asks.

"Duvet cover," Jane says softly. "I recently bought one, and I like mine with zippers."

Duncan's attention returns to the tray. He frowns. "You think she was rolled up in a duvet?"

Ella says, "It would be consistent with some of the very tiny feather fragments we found encased in some of the adipocere. We'll be doing additional testing to see what kind of bird they might come from."

"Maybe goose or duck down if they're from a duvet," Jane surmises. "Anything else trapped in the adipocere?"

"We haven't cut into it yet, but we've been picking off trace from the exterior. We also found what could be animal hair of some kind. And we've recovered some textile fiber, possibly from some kind of carpet. My guess so far is nylon—maybe automotive. Again, we'll be doing tests. The fibers can potentially be run against some textile databases. The FBI, for example, has been developing a Forensic Automotive Carpet Fiber Identification Database. We might get lucky, but it's going to be challenging to find a match to historical fibers from the midseventies."

"We could always start with carpeting for a VW bus," Duncan notes.

"A bus from the seventies could have been custom kitted with any kind of carpet," Jane counters.

Ella says, "We've also cleaned up the medallion we found alongside her body. It's in the tray here." She shows them over to another artifact. "If you look at the monitor above the table, you can see we've enlarged the image of the design on the front, and the inscription on the back."

"The St. Christopher surfers' medallion mentioned in the file," Jane says.

They all stare at the engraved heart shape on the back, the letters in the middle of the heart.

*R + A.*

"Robbie and Annalise," Jane says quietly. She glances up at Duncan. "We need to speak to this Robbie-Bob Davine. Ella, is this what you thought we should see in person?"

"I know how you like the best saved for last," Ella says, but this time she doesn't smile. There's definitely lingering animosity between her and Jane.

She shows them another tray. Inside is a metal brooch about an inch in diameter.

"This is what I thought you might find especially intriguing."

"A metal pin?" Duncan asks. "Was she wearing this?"

"Look closer," Ella says.

Jane leans in. Her pulse quickens instantly. Her gaze shoots to Ella. "Have you got an enlarged image of this?"

Ella pulls one up on the screen.

Jane stares at a pin with a frontal view of a buffalo head in the center. The buffalo is ringed by leaves along with legible words that read MAINTIENS LE DROIT. On top of the leaves is a crown. At the bottom of the pin is a curving ribbon design that shows the words ROYAL CANADIAN MOUNTED POLICE.

"What in the hell?" Duncan whispers. "That's an RCMP pin. That's the RCMP crest and motto on there."

"Badge," Jane says very quietly. "It's technically not a crest. The design is registered as a badge. *Maintiens Le Droit*—it means *maintain the right*. Or *uphold the right*. It's been the motto and symbol of the RCMP dating back to the 1800s, when the force was still known as the North-West Mounted Police."

"What in the hell was she doing with that?" Duncan asks. "Wearing it? Or did it come off someone she was struggling with?"

Jane doesn't answer. She is fixated on the image of the police badge.

# THE SHOREVIEW SIX

## MARY

Mary sits uncomfortably in the passenger seat of Claude's hefty SUV. Silence between her and Claude is thick, tangible. Lights from oncoming cars slide alternating bands of shadow and light over his face and arms as he grips the wheel. She hasn't seen her old boyfriend for many years, and the powerful-looking man he has become is both a complete stranger to her and so discomfitingly familiar.

He turns the SUV down a narrow and dark street that curves among towering conifers. It takes them toward an exclusive enclave on the rocky shore near the yacht club. Homes in this glossy pocket of suburbia fetch upward of $11–20 million. They enter a driveway between two stone pillars softly illuminated with discreet lighting. As they reach the circular parking area in front of a glass and concrete home, Mary notices a black Escalade parked in front of the house. Claude's headlights pan over a Davine Estate sticker on the rear of the Escalade. Bob and Cara are already here. Mary tries to swallow against the ball of tension tightening her throat.

As he turns off the engine, she asks quietly, "What really happened that night, Claude?"

She knows the reason for this gathering is for the six to close ranks and to get their lies straight. But Mary has a different goal. She plans to prod and provoke and seek gaps that she might be able to leverage in order to save herself and Heather. She owes it to her daughter. Heather's good fortune is all still so fragile. It just teeters in the balance.

"Save it for the group." He reaches for the door handle.

"There's the group's story, and there's ours," Mary says softly. "The lie I told was for you, Claude. It was between you and me. Not the group. Tell me where you really were that night. Give me a reason to stick to the story you asked me to tell."

He breathes in deeply and stares at the lit house waiting for them, his hand still on the door handle, his jaw tight. He's scared, thinks Mary. This realization feeds a dark and secret place in her. It stirs a hunger for revenge. The bad part of Mary suddenly wants to punish Claude and the others for everything that went wrong in her life after that night. They did awful things. Surely they should not get away unpunished for the rest of their lives? Surely justice must be meted out in some form, eventually? Or perhaps it's already been doled out in silent and subversive ways that have changed each and every one of them since that night forty-seven years ago.

"Did you guys kill her?"

Claude's gaze flashes to her. "How dare you even ask that?"

"Somebody did. Her body has been buried since that weekend. Something happened that night with you guys. And to Darryl, too. Because if Annalise has been buried up on Hemlock all this time, Darryl sure didn't run off with her. So where is he?"

"Maybe he did it, Mary. Maybe Darryl killed her, hid her body, and fled. Maybe it's *why* he fled. Like they always said."

"Maybe *you* did it."

"You know I didn't."

"Do I? I have no idea where you were before you threw stones at my window."

"Your neighbor saw you shove her that night. You were yelling at each other in the street. *You* were the last one to see her alive."

"I'd never hurt her. I loved her."

"Right. Must have freaked her out, learning you loved her in that way?"

"It wasn't my knuckles and hands that were bloodied, Claude," she snaps. "You'd had a shower before coming to my house, and changed your clothes. I don't believe you fought with Robbie at all. Tell me what happened."

Before he can respond, the front door of the house swings open wide. Standing in the square of yellow light is Bob, not Jill. As though Bob Davine owns this place, not the Osmans. He waves at them to hurry on in.

Mary and Claude exit the SUV. She walks slightly behind Claude. Just as they begin to climb the stairs to the door, she says, very softly, "I know you slept with her more than once, Claude. Annalise told me herself. And you know what else she told me? She never had sex with Robbie."

Claude freezes on the stairs. He doesn't move for a few seconds, then spins sharply to face her. His pugnacious face is pale and his eyes huge and angry in the darkness. Fear prickles through Mary, but she stands her ground.

She whispers, "The question is, does Robbie know you slept with his girlfriend? Because I sure as hell bet he never found that out, did he?"

Claude opens his mouth, but Bob calls down to them, "Claude, hey. Mary. Come on up, come on in." He stands back, holding the door open wide to usher them inside.

They enter a large hallway. Mary can see through to a cavernous open-plan living room and kitchen area. Floor-to-ceiling windows run the ocean-facing length of the house. Beyond them, the lights of an infinity pool glow a luminous blue-green. Beyond the pool is the inky black sound.

"What can I get you guys to drink?" Bob asks, as though they're here for a good ol' social reunion after all these years.

"Bourbon," Claude says crisply as he and Mary take off their jackets. "Make it at least four fingers."

"Beer," Mary says. "Bottle or can is fine."

As Bob repairs to the kitchen, Mary hangs her coat on a hook, then sits on a bench to remove her shoes. Claude doesn't bother with his shoes. He tracks whatever dirt they carry into the living room.

On socked feet, Mary follows Claude into the expansive living area.

Sitting on a long and low sectional are Jill, Cara, and Rocco. Each holds a drink. All stare at her. She hasn't seen their faces in ages, and she feels a sharp clutch in her stomach. Although they've all chronologically aged and are technically seniors, it's as though they've all been transported through a weird wormhole and are suddenly back in 1976 and they're all sixteen, despite the wrinkles. And she's the outcast again.

Perhaps a part of each one of them has always been locked in the autumn of 1976. In the amber of time. A limbo—or prison—for their lies. Neither heaven nor hell. All waiting in one way or another for that knock to come on their doors. Waiting for justice to finally find them. Fearing it.

"Mary," Jill says. "Thank you for coming." Her face is tight like her voice. Her features are etched with stress in spite of the obvious Botox, lip filler, and whatever other tucks she's splurged on. Mary wonders if Jill has ever told her husband anything about that night. Or whether Isaias Osman is completely unaware that nearly fifty years back in his wife's past, her friend vanished and their group came under intense police and media scrutiny. Mary nods at Jill, then Cara, and Rocco, who says nothing.

Cara perches awkwardly on the edge of the sofa clutching a flute of Prosecco. The Prosecco bottle is on the table in an ice bucket. Rocco's face is ruddy, his eyes bleary. He seems loose limbed and possibly quite inebriated.

Bob returns with drinks.

"How's the gardening business?" Bob asks with a forced conviviality as he shoves a cold beer into Mary's hands. She glances at the bottle. It's some bougie craft thing with a ridiculous name and label.

"Fine. How's the white-collar crime and wine business?"

His mouth flattens. Bob hands Claude the bourbon, clears his throat, reaches to pick up his own glass, and raises it to the group.

"Well, cheers. Here's to the reunion of the Shoreview Six."

"Ha ha, cheers." Claude takes a huge swallow of his bourbon. "We spent effing years shaking that moniker. Let's pray the media doesn't drag that one up again."

"Here's to Annalise." Mary raises her beer. "And a very belated congrats to my dear old missing friend on her pregnancy. Ain't that just something?" She sips. "Oh, and here's to the father of her baby, too." She raises her bottle again.

Silence, ominous, hums between them all.

Mary tilts her beer back and swallows deeply.

Cara leans farther forward. "Look, I'll just say it. We don't know what happened to Annalise, okay? Or to Darryl, for that matter. But we need a strategy to manage—"

"Is that a fact, Cara?" Mary asks. "Because I'm not getting it. If none of us know what happened, then it has nothing to do with us. Why the stress? Why the concern about a strategy?"

Cara pins her gaze on Mary. The look in her eyes is murderous. It simmers with threat.

Mary takes a seat. "I told one little lie that night, Cara. That's my crime. And once I told it, I was swept along with the rest of it all and was too scared to take it back. But none of you guys ever came clean with me, so please feel free now to convince me why I shouldn't just go to the cops and tell my truth this time around."

The others exchange quick glances. Tension thickens. Wind blows outside and ripples the calm surface of the pool. Trees wave and move shadows across the porch. Mary swallows more beer. She's shaking inside, beneath her bravado. Her old group, in all their wealth and accumulated power over the years, scares her. How far might they go to keep a secret that could cut everything out from under every one of them?

*Did they kill?*

*Would they kill again to guard the truth?*

"Maybe you did it, Mary," Cara counters coolly. "Maybe you're the one who never came clean with *us*. But innocent or not, we all told a certain story forty-seven years ago. We just need to stick to that exact same story in order to make this go away simply. None of us wants to be dragged into this kind of limelight, and any inconsistencies will just increase police and media scrutiny. That means there will be negative fallout for *all* of us. We all have so much more to lose now than when we were sixteen, right? We have extended families, children, in-laws, grandchildren, businesses." Cara glances at Jill. "Charities." She turns her gaze on Claude. "Spouses, foundations, reputations. All of it could be damaged, destroyed." Cara places her hand on Bob's thigh. "And no one has to volunteer DNA samples," she says.

"Why not?" Mary asks.

"Jesus, Mary. Are you going to be a problem here?" Rocco snaps.

"Someone made her pregnant," Mary says.

"Probably Darryl," Jill fires back.

"Well, the DNA will reveal that, then, won't it? But as far as I know, my best friend told me pretty much everything, and she never told me she slept with Darryl." Mary keeps her eyes on Bob as she speaks.

Bob shifts uncomfortably on the sofa. But so does Claude. And interestingly, Rocco, too. Cara presses her hand even more firmly on her husband's thigh. Proprietary. Protective. A bodyguard not to be crossed.

Claude takes another hard swig of bourbon. "I'm with Cara. If none of us volunteers a DNA sample, then Bob doesn't look bad when he's asked. And they *will* ask him."

"Yeah, they'll definitely go at him first for a sample," Mary says, turning to Claude. His gaze locks with hers, and she knows he's thinking of what she said on the stairs outside. His face looks thunderous, and fear unfurls deeper in Mary.

Rocco's focus drops to his lap. He doesn't look good.

"Then they'll have to come with a warrant if they want Bob's DNA." Cara reaches for the Prosecco bottle and refills her glass.

She's very afraid, thinks Mary.

Cara holds the bottle up toward Jill, who nods. Cara tops Jill's flute up as well. Jill is beginning to look flushed. Cara's features, on the other hand, seem to harden—Cara, who always got what she wanted. And Mary figures Cara always wanted Robbie. Ever since he arrived at school from California. Cara just had to find a way to wrest him from pretty, popular, clever, fun, sweet, kind Annalise Jansen. A sinister and ugly little idea cracks open deep inside Mary. It spills a toxic thought out.

*No. It's not possible. Surely? Could Cara have initiated something to hurt Annalise in order to get Robbie?*

"But they could do that—come with a warrant," Jill counters. "They'd have probable cause for Robbie, wouldn't they?"

"Whose side are you on, Jill?" Cara asks.

"I'm just playing devil's advocate, okay? Because we need to think of contingencies. If this, then that. Damage control. And Mary's right. They *will* go after Robbie again. It's always the boyfriend, right? Annalise's pregnancy is going to speak to motive—at least that's how this new team of investigators will see it." Her hand shoots up to halt Bob as he opens his mouth to counter her. "It's not what *I* am saying, Bob. It's what you always hear on the news when a woman goes missing. It's always the husband, or the boyfriend, like ninety-nine percent of the time. And the cops did press you hard when she first went missing. Now they'll come back with almost five decades of newly refined forensic science at their disposal. Plus they have her body, which they didn't the first time. And a fetus. Plus it's not just any cops—it's *homicide* detectives this time around."

Claude says, "Just to dial back a little here, there's been no formal identification of the body yet. The police haven't actually confirmed it's Annalise."

"Yet," says Rocco. "But there'sh no doubt in anyone's mind it'sh her. Thoshe boots. That timing over Labour Day weekend. What are the odds itsh some other girl?" His words are becoming alarmingly more and more slurred.

"Well, Bob has an alibi for that night," Cara says. "After the guys got more liquor and we went to the woodland park for a short while, he slept over at my place."

"And why would he do that?" Mary asks. "I mean, he was going steady with Annalise."

"Because Annalise went home without him and was behaving weird." Cara turns to her husband. "Wasn't she, Bob? She was making up stories and—well, Bob thought it was probably going to be over between them anyway."

"Is that so, Bob?" Mary asks.

He doesn't respond.

"Claude and Mary also have alibis," Jill says. She glances at Rocco.

Rocco inhales and looks even more red-faced and flustered. "I—I was with my brother."

"Who happens to be dead," Mary says.

"Jesus, Mary," Jill snaps. "How cruel do you want to be? Zane was a huge loss to Roc."

"I know I lied about Claude's alibi," Mary says. "Claude asked me to cover because he claims he fought with Robbie and he hit another car while driving drunk without a full license. I have no idea where he really was between when Annalise and I left the party and he climbed in my window with bloodied knuckles."

Silence swallows the group. Outside the wind blows harder. The lights across the water wink and vanish and reappear as branches sway.

Quietly, Mary adds, "Perhaps Claude was still with you guys—Rocco, Cara, Robbie, Jill."

Jill says, "I went home to my parents' house. Cara told me she was with Robbie, and that Rocco and Zane were in their garden suite at their parents' place. If Claude wasn't with you, Mary, I don't know where he was. But that means no one knows where *you* were, either."

"Is that what this is going to come down to?" Claude says. "You're going to throw me under the bus, Mary?"

Rocco lurches forward, grabs the tequila bottle in front of him, sloshes a few shots into his glass, swallows it all, and pours more. "Well, I agree with Claude." He holds his glass toward Claude. "No one volunteersh DNA samples. All for one. One for all. Shircle the wagons around Bob."

"You're not supposed to use that wagon term." Jill's voice is brittle, clipped.

"Whatever." He raises his glass. "Beshides, Bob has the legal balls and financial resources to fight any damn warrant for hish DNA."

The group's attention is now turned on Rocco.

"Beshides, jusht because someone made her pregnant, what'sh the big deal? Doesn't mean they also killed her and buried her on that mountain in the dark."

Bob leans forward, a suspicious look entering his features. "What are you implying?"

"Nothing, jusht what I said."

"Being the father of her baby totally goes to motive," Mary says. "If the fetus isn't Bob's, for example, and he found out she got pregnant by cheating on him, well, that might just enrage a jealous guy like Bob."

"Fuck you, Mary," Cara snaps.

"Well, Cara, you wanted Robbie-Bob so badly—what if *you* learned Annalise was pregnant with Bob's kid? It would mean your chances with him were over. Maybe you took it into your hands to do something about it?"

Bob surges to his feet, grabs the Scotch bottle, pours calmly, and says quietly, "I'm going to volunteer my DNA." He glances at Claude.

*Something is dawning on Bob,* Mary thinks. *He knows he didn't sleep with Annalise. Is that why he called them all together? To ferret out if it was one of his close friends from school?*

Maybe it's not just Mary who's attending the gathering to hunt for leverage. She glances around the room. Maybe that's what they're *all* doing. This reunion is not going to coalesce them. It's going to blow them apart.

"I don't think that's a good idea, Bob," Claude says. "What if the DNA *is* yours?"

"Maybe I'll roll that dice," he says quietly as he reseats himself beside his wife. His eyes are clear, sharp. He sips his drink, his gaze still fixed on Claude.

Bob Davine is morphing into the criminal defense shark, playing his judge and jury. Rattling their cages. Lights seem to dim and flicker suddenly. It unsettles them all visibly. Something fundamental has shifted. Bob's gaze moves slowly to Rocco.

"A bit like Russian roulette, eh, Roc?" Bob makes a gun shape with his hand and points to his temple. "I spin the barrel—" He pulls an imaginary trigger. "Click," he says. "I'm not the father. Or—" He rolls the imaginary barrel again, aims, pulls the trigger. "Or boom. It's my little saponified fetus. But as you said, it doesn't make me the killer, does it, Roc?" His gaze sweeps the group. "Does it, guys?"

Mary is uber tense now. Her gaze flicks to the doors. She becomes acutely aware of all exits. What exactly is Bob doing?

Cara looks really rattled now. "Bob, I honestly think it's better if you don't—"

He halts her with a firm hand on her arm while eyeing the other two men in the room. And Mary is now certain. Annalise told her the truth. She never did have sex with Bob.

It's not his baby and Bob knows it.

Mary leans forward and says quietly, "I do have one question. *Did* you ever sleep with Annalise, Bob?"

# JANE

It's evening, and Melissa is ordering pizza for the team while Jane pins up copies of the photos she borrowed from Annalise Jansen's bedroom: the group of happy teens gathered at the swimming hole, and on Hemlock in 1976, smiles back from the crime board. Above these two images are two larger photos: one of Annalise Jansen and one of Darryl Hendricks.

Jane also pins up the photos she shot herself of Annalise Jansen's room. She follows these with an image of Hugo Glucklich supplied by Hemlock management, and photos sourced online of Bob Davine and Cara Constantine Davine at their wine farm; Jill Wainwright Osman with her husband, Isaias Osman, at a charity event; Mary Metcalfe in a news story about hanging baskets; and Claude Betancourt and his wife, Susan Presley Betancourt, at a hockey benefit.

To one side of the board, she adds photos of the artifacts found with the remains in the shallow grave on Hemlock, including the boots, earrings, change purse, coins, key, long zipper, and RCMP brooch.

"Okay, everyone, listen up." Jane turns to face her team and points to the current photos of the Shoreview Six. "We now have contact details for five of the Shoreview Six, but are still in the process of locating Rocco Jones. One fact of note that has come to light is that Zane Jones, Rocco's older brother, was killed in a bike accident in late 1978. So, obviously no contact details for him. We also now have in hand copies of the original Jansen and Hendricks missing persons files, including witness statements and investigators' notes. Thanks to Tank for securing these. Tank, can you walk us through the high notes? And let's see if we can fit in puzzle pieces as we go, particularly this new one." She taps the image of the RCMP pin.

Tank goes up to the crime scene board. Adjacent to the board, he's pinned up a large map of the pertinent areas of North Vancouver.

"The lead investigator at the time was Sergeant Chuck Harrison," he says. "We made contact with his wife earlier today and learned from her that Sergeant Harrison passed three years ago. She told us it was her husband who requested the age-progression imagery of Annalise Jansen in 2004. Mrs. Harrison said it was one of her husband's big career regrets that his team *never solved that one*."

Tank circles an area on the map with a red marker. "The central event—the party—occurred here at a private residence near the Upper Levels Highway on the night of Friday, September 3, 1976. Rose Tuttle, sixteen, hosted the event while her parents were away. Annalise Jansen attended the party along with her tight-knit group of school friends, all students at Shoreview High. Darryl Hendricks was also at the party." Tank points to their images as he mentions them.

"The party was crashed by a group of older teens around nine forty-five p.m., including Zane Jones, the twenty-two-year-old brother of Rocco Jones. According to statements of those interviewed, the event quickly got out of hand. North Van RCMP responded to a call for assistance made from the residence by Rose Tuttle at 10:17 p.m."

Jane asks, "Any record of which officers responded?"

Tank checks his notes. "Four uniformed officers. Constables Bing, Simon, Raymond, and Corporal Jackson."

Jane's gaze goes to the image of the RCMP badge recovered from the grave. "Okay, Melissa, let's see if we can locate any of those responding officers for additional context."

"On it," Melissa says, taking notes.

Tank says, "Upon RCMP arrival, the party attendants dispersed. Metcalfe and Jansen splintered off from the rest of their friend group and walked home together along this route." He draws a zigzag between blocks and makes a line down to the bottom of Linden Street.

"According to Metcalfe's statement, she saw a biker on a black bike and wearing a black helmet at these locations along their walk." Tank makes small Xs on the route. "Metcalfe believed the biker could have been following her and Jansen." He reads from his notes. "Her words were, 'He made me nervous. I couldn't identify him or the bike. Just all in black. Annalise didn't seem worried. It was almost like she knew him or found it amusing that the bike might be following us.'"

Tank makes another X on the map. "Metcalfe and Jansen had an argument here, across the road from Metcalfe's residence. We have a statement from a neighbor who said he heard and then saw Metcalfe and Jansen arguing on the sidewalk at around eleven fifteen p.m." Tank reads from his notes. "'They were yelling, and the noise woke me. I looked out the window and saw them kind of shoving each other. I recognized Mary and Annalise and knew they were friends and figured it was just drunken Friday night teen stuff and went back to bed, so I didn't see anything that happened after that.'" Tank turns a page.

"This account is consistent with Metcalfe's own statement. She said she arrived home at around eleven fifteen p.m. Metcalfe said she was angry with her friend and did not watch Jansen walking the two extra blocks alone to her residence in the cul-de-sac. She said there were two streetlights out of order at the time, so 'it was pretty dark down there.'" Tank circles the Jansen residence on Linden Street.

He consults his notes.

"Witnesses in this house here, across the cul-de-sac from the Jansen residence"—he circles a property at the bottom of the cul-de-sac, next to the park trailhead—"an elderly married couple named Elise and Will Janyk, stated they were letting their poodle out before going to bed when Elise Janyk, who was in the front garden with her dog, saw a girl she thought was Annalise Jansen running across the cul-de-sac toward a metallic-brown sedan parked on the other side of the cul-de-sac at the trailhead into the woods." He makes an X on the map.

Yusra asks, "Elise Janyk couldn't say for certain it was their neighbor Annalise?"

"Apparently she wasn't paying much attention. It was late Friday night. Teens were often out in the street late on Fridays, especially during the summer vacation, and often tipsy. She also said two streetlights were not working, so it was unusually dark. It was only after they heard that Jansen was missing that Elise Janyk recalled seeing the girl, and reported it."

Yusra says, "So she didn't see the car registration?"

Tank shakes his head. "Negative. Nor did she recall the make or model other than it was a metallic-brown four-door sedan. She stated she thinks the girl bent into the driver's-side window, as though to talk with the driver. Elise Janyk then took her poodle indoors, and before shutting the door, she glanced over again. She said, 'A hand came out of the window and grabbed her arm. The girl seemed to resist, and pull back, which momentarily piqued my interest, but then I heard her laugh. She was released and she ran around to the passenger side and got in the car. I shut the door and went to bed.'"

Tank looks up. "When the Janyks woke Saturday morning, the sedan was gone. It was only on Tuesday that they learned Annalise Jansen was missing. They were devastated." He reads again from Elise Janyk's statement. "'They are the nicest, kindest family, and have helped us with so many things over the years, like cleaning the gutters, taking stuff to the trash, mowing the lawn, taking our senior poodle to the vet after he had a seizure. I really wish we had reported what we saw earlier, but at the time there seemed no cause for alarm.'"

Jane says, "Dr. Quinn mentioned finding possible automotive fibers in the adipocere. If we can identify the make and model of that metallic-brown sedan, it could be a start point for cross-referencing forensic automotive carpet fiber databases."

Melissa says, "If it was Annalise Jansen getting into that sedan, it appears she knew the driver and was willing to go of her own accord."

Yusra asks, "So what about the rest of her friends? Where did they say they went after the party?"

Jane says, "Darryl Hendricks apparently left to meet up with friends at the Marley reggae club, according to his father, Ahmed Hendricks, who spoke with some of his son's friends at the club. We have a name for one of them. Duncan is following up tomorrow."

Tank says, "According the file statements, Robbie Davine, Rocco Jones, Claude Betancourt, Cara Constantine, and Jill Wainwright left the party in Zane Jones's vehicle, with Zane driving." He glances up. "And here's an interesting point—Zane Jones owned a 1973 metallic-brown Dodge Dart Custom."

Tank pins up an image of a vintage brown Dodge Dart Custom sedan. He taps it. "Four-door sedan. A very common make and color at the time. But the five teens claim to have driven nowhere near Annalise Jansen's house that night. In fact, their statements, taken separately, are almost identical."

"Coordinated?" asks Melissa.

"It sure was a red flag to the investigators at the time, according to their notes," says Tank. "Which is why they kept pressing the teens, but they never managed to poke holes in the stories." He checks his notes. "The four boys—Davine, the Jones brothers, and Betancourt—apparently dropped the two girls, Wainwright and Constantine, off at Wainwright's house so the girls could change into warmer clothes for the woods. The boys meanwhile drove down to a motel near the quay to buy more liquor from an off-sales outlet over here." He makes a red X with his marker near the water. "Now here's a curious fact." He faces them. "Davine, Betancourt, and the two Jones brothers admitted to using a fake ID in the name of a Leon Springer to purchase liquor, and it was Betancourt who did the buying."

Jane asks, "Why did Zane Jones not do the buying? He was the one of legal age, at twenty-two?"

Tank shakes his head. "Don't know. All it says here is that Zane Jones was said to be driving, and Betancourt went into the off-sales to make the purchase with the fraudulent ID. The retailer later confirmed it was Betancourt who came in with the Leon Springer ID. The other inconsistency in these files is that two party attendants claim they saw Zane Jones arrive at the party, and leave on his bike."

Yusra says, "So maybe Zane was not in the Dodge Dart at all. Could it have been Zane Jones who followed Jansen and Metcalfe on their walk home?"

Jane says, "Possibly. And the reason the kids lied about Zane driving was because at the time, given their ages, they would not have been licensed to drive without a fully licensed adult in the vehicle."

Duncan says, "It sure would explain why Zane wasn't on hand to buy their liquor then, and why Claude went in with a fake ID."

Tank says, "And maybe that's why they actually came clean about the Leon Springer ID—because they knew the retail clerk could—or would—confirm this with police."

Yusra asks, "Did investigators at the time question Zane Jones about this inconsistency?"

"Yes. It seems he stuck with the same story as the rest of them: The boys returned to pick up the girls from the Wainwright home. They all then drove to the woods here." Tank makes another X on his map. "They claim to have stayed there drinking, and they claimed Zane remained sober so he could drive. They all claim they left the woods in the Dodge Dart at around midnight. They dropped Jill Wainwright at home first. They then drove Betancourt to Mary Metcalfe's house. He claims to have arrived at Metcalfe's around twelve thirty a.m. Metcalfe confirms this, and that he climbed into her window and stayed the night. Robbie Davine and Cara Constantine were both dropped off by the Jones brothers at Constantine's house, where they say they spent the night together."

Jane says, "Even though Davine was dating Jansen, he spent the night with Constantine?"

"Fishy, right?" says Melissa.

Tank says, "Then Rocco and Zane Jones apparently went home. Their parents were not there. The boys shared a separate dwelling in the garden, apart from the main house."

Jane goes to the board and taps the red X made by Tank. "The motel off-sales here is right near the reggae club, which used to be there." She makes another mark. "It's basically a block away. And the old tire place, where there was a report of a fight, and where Darryl Hendricks used to park his VW van whenever he went to the Marley Joint, is here, also barely a block away." She circles the area. "It puts those boys bang in the neighborhood at the same time as Hendricks after the party."

"Interesting," says Melissa. "But what about the brown sedan at the Linden Street cul-de-sac? Is it conceivable—from the timing of the liquor purchase—that the boys could have driven their brown Dodge to the bottom of Linden Street?"

Tank checks his notes. "Liquor purchase was apparently made at 10:47 p.m. So yes, it's conceivable the boys could have driven to Linden Street and been at the cul-de-sac by eleven fifteen p.m., when Metcalfe last saw Jansen alive."

"Did Metcalfe say what she and Jansen were arguing about?" asks Jane.

Tank says, "Metcalfe claims Jansen got angry with her when Metcalfe accused Jansen of being drunk and acting promiscuous at the party."

Jane crooks up her brows. "And what did Robbie Davine think about his girlfriend being promiscuous at the party?"

"Davine claims he didn't notice anything." Tank consults his notes again. "He stated that, 'Annalise just said she wanted to walk home early with Mary to discuss the events of the night, which included the guys coming up from Ambleside to crash Rose's party.'"

Yusra says, "I think it's time for us to have a good go at Davine."

"Agreed," Jane says. "What did the boys tell investigators when asked about what happened to Darryl Hendricks?"

Tank says, "Apparently both Constantine and Wainwright stated they saw Hendricks on previous occasions being intimate with Jansen. They felt Hendricks might have done something to Jansen, or they ran away together."

Duncan says, "But Danielle Hendricks, Darryl's little sister, who now caters for Jill Wainwright Osman's charity events, told us that Jill apologized to her for lying to officers about this, and said she regretted having done so."

Yusra says, "I'd sure like to hear Jill Osman's side of the story now, and ask her why she lied."

"We'll bring them in," Jane says, "as soon as we get official identification of the body. Meanwhile we keep fleshing out a picture of what transpired. Anything else pertinent in the files, Tank?"

"Investigators did at the time take into evidence clothing that Robbie Davine claims he wore to the party, and to the woods. But between these events and the time Jansen was actually reported missing by her parents, laundry had been done and his clothes had been through a wash. We also no longer have that clothing in evidence." He checks his notes. "Investigators did report that Betancourt's hands were cut and bruised, and he had a gash on his head. Davine's hands were also cut and bruised. The boys explained this by saying they'd had a bit of a drunken brawl with each other in the woods over some slight that neither seemed to remember." Tank glances up. "An extensive canvass of the neighborhoods surrounding the Jansen residence also revealed no additional witnesses. Nothing else unusual was reported that night. It seems that in the end, the investigators leaned fully into the hypothesis that Hendricks either hurt Jansen and fled, or he abducted her, or Jansen departed town with Hendricks willingly." He pauses.

"According to these files, no one had pregnancy on the radar, and nowhere is an RCMP pin mentioned as part of her belongings."

Duncan says, "Those DNA results, when they do come in, could provide some definite investigative direction and possible motive."

"What about Hugo Glucklich?" Melissa asks with a tilt of her chin to his photo on the board.

Jane nods. "I want him brought in and officially questioned again." She points at the board. "Glucklich was up there alone at night, had access to all that equipment, plus he was around at the time the chapel floor was laid. He also appears to have an overly keen interest in involving himself in this case, plus we know from the photos from Jansen's bedroom that the kids were all up there over the summer of '76. Was there a chance Annalise Jansen encountered a young Hugo Glucklich that summer? Could he have developed an interest in her? Stalked her later?" She checks her watch, suddenly exhausted. "Okay, let's call it a night, guys. Get some rest. We'll brief again at seven thirty a.m. Tomorrow we go after the concrete company for any records around that basement flooring. I'm also interested in what employees and other tradesmen were involved in the chapel work that summer. And I'd like to speak to those RCMP officers who busted up the party September 3, 1976, if any are still around. I want Rocco Jones located, and background checks run on our Shoreview Six."

# THE SHOREVIEW SIX

## MARY

Mary waits for Bob to reply to her question about whether he ever slept with Annalise. It's so quiet inside they can hear the ticking of a clock down the hall. Pressure builds in the room.

Jill laughs shrilly, then quickly falls silent. It has an unnerving effect.

"Of course he slept with Annalise," Claude says. "He told us all he did."

"Ah, but *did* you, Bob?" Mary asks. "Or did you just say it in order to look macho because all the other guys were doing it?"

He watches her, reading her. He leans forward suddenly, his gaze pinning hers. Predatory. "Here's the thing, Mary," Bob says quietly. "It doesn't matter. Maybe I did. Maybe I didn't. But if I refuse to volunteer my DNA, I look guilty either way. I come across to the police and the media as though I have something to hide. And believe me, the media—a bunch of clickbait cowboys—is going to attack us like rabid dogs seeking to tear down privilege in some desperate act of self-congratulatory schadenfreude." He sits back. "But if my DNA profile comes back as not a paternal match, then we'll all have to ask, If not mine, whose? I'd like to know."

"I have another question," she says.

"You said one," Rocco slurs. "Why does she get to ask all the questions?"

"Let her ask her question," Jill says.

"They called us the Shoreview Six, but it was really the Shoreview Five, wasn't it? I never actually *belonged* to your group. I was just a tag-along because I was Annalise's friend. I don't know what happened that night, but I think you all do. And the only reason you all pressured me to come here tonight is because Claude still needs his alibi for all this to work. But I'm done. I'm not going to play along anymore unless you tell me what the game is. What happened after the party?"

Another heavy blanket of silence weighs down on them. Again, Mary hears the metronomic *ticktock ticktock* of the clock down the hall.

"Cara, did you really see Darryl making out with Annalise?" she asks.

"Of course."

"When, how, where?"

Cara doesn't reply.

Mary faces Jill. "How about you, Jill? You told police you saw Darryl and Annalise being intimate. *Did* you?"

Jill's face flushes deep red. Her gaze darts to Cara.

"Cara told you to lie, didn't she, Jill?" Mary says, picking up on the cues. "Cara never actually saw them together, did you, Cara? Yet all of you—each and every one of you—lied about Darryl and Annalise being intimate? Why? So you could blame Darryl for what happened to my best friend? Is that it? Where is Darryl? What happened to him?"

"Mary! Just shut the fuck up, okay?" Cara snaps, all edges now.

Bob glowers at his wife.

"Or what?" Mary demands. Her heart gallops. Her fear is peaking. She's overstepped. She's poked a hornet's nest and enraged them, and she doesn't know what they might do now—what they are capable of. But she's unable to stop herself from pushing all the way.

"It doesn't the fuck matter what happened that night." Cara grabs her Prosecco bottle. "We just need to get our stories straight. And there's one thing I can tell you: we all lied." Her gaze flicks to Bob. "Maybe even to each other. And the other thing I know—obstructing justice, obstructing a police officer, obstructing an investigation, committing perjury or otherwise interfering with the proper administration of justice—these are serious criminal offenses." She fills her glass with bubbly wine almost to the rim. "A conviction could mean prison time. The consequences would be life altering for any one of us."

She sits back with her glass in hand. "So how about we all just stick to our pact, huh? We were at the party. All of us together. Rocco's brother, Zane, told a huge crowd at Ambleside Beach there was an event up the mountain. They crashed. The hostess—Rose Tuttle—called the cops when she got scared. The cops arrived. The crowd scattered. We—"

"For fuck's sake!" Rocco surges to his feet. He's drenched with sweat. Mary can smell the fear on him. Sour and acrid. "I can't take this anymore. Tell Mary!" He points at her. "Tell *me*! I want to know what I did that night. I need to know what I did that I can't remember—what you guys are supposedly protecting me from. Did I do it—did I kill Annalise, too?"

It hits Mary like a load of bricks.

*Rocco thinks he killed Darryl.*

"Just tell me," Roc pleads. "Please. I'm dying here."

Mary says very quietly, "Go on. Tell him. What did you all lead Roc to believe he did while he was blackout drunk? Because blackouts happened to Roc all the time, didn't they? He'd do shit during a night of drinking and wouldn't recall any of it in the morning. Did you use this? Did you blame *him* for something you guys did? What in the hell *did* you all do that night?"

Rocco flops back onto the sofa, drops his face into his hands. He moans as he rocks his body. "I killed him. I killed Darryl. I woke up Saturday morning in our garden cottage all covered in blood and bruised and they said I did it, and I remember parts of it. I do. They said they tried to stop me from beating him but couldn't. They said I flipped out on the booze and mushrooms and went berserkers, bludgeoned him to death with a tire iron, and they couldn't stop me because I tried to attack them, too. They said they would cover for me. Protect me. Lie for me. We made a pact. I was so scared. I didn't know what I had done, what I was capable of." He sits upright, stares at his open hands, as though searching for ancient bloodstains. "I still don't know what I am capable of."

Aghast, Mary stares at Rocco. Blood drains from her head. "Is *that* what he believed all these years? You guys messed with his head like that?"

Cara surges to her feet. "It's not like that. It's—"

A bang sounds at the front door. Everyone spins around. The door opens, and a man carrying a travel bag enters. Jill sucks her breath in sharply. She leaps to her feet, her complexion ghost white.

"Isaias! What—what are you doing here? I . . . I thought you were coming back tomorrow night."

He stands there. Dark. Handsome in his long wool coat. He regards his wife. His gaze goes to the rest of the group seated on the sectional in his living room. He sets his keys down quietly on the side table in the hall.

"You didn't tell me you were having company, Jill."

"I—ah . . ." Her voice fades.

"Cara." He nods. "Bob." His attention goes to Mary, Rocco, then Claude. "Jill, are you going to introduce me to your other friends?"

# JANE

"I can't stay. I—I just thought I'd quickly stop by on my way home," Jane says to her mother, who stands holding the door open to Jane's childhood home in North Vancouver. It's late, cold, and Jane feels beat. She didn't really mean to come by at all, but as she was passing a few blocks away, she sort of turned on autopilot into her old neighborhood. And now she's here. Possibly she was driven by guilt for not returning her mom's earlier calls. Or maybe it's some deeper need she's really just too tired to even begin to articulate to herself.

Her mother wears a painting smock over a sweatshirt and jeans. Her smock is smeared with slashes and splotches of acrylic paint. Jane knows it's acrylic. Her mom always paints with bright acrylics in her basement studio.

"Come in. The chapel case must have you busy."

"Yeah. I'm sorry I didn't return your calls."

She takes Jane's coat and hangs it up. "I have a pot of Bolognese on the stove."

"Not really hungry," Jane says.

"You need to eat. Come into the kitchen. We can talk there." She ushers Jane through.

"You must remember the disappearance of Annalise Jansen?" Jane asks as she follows her mom through the living room. "She was just a year younger than you and lived barely blocks away from where you used to live as a kid."

"I do remember the missing girl. And the boy, Darryl. They weren't at my school, though. Darryl was the son of Ahmed and Mimi Hendricks of Cape Winds."

"So you recall their names?" Jane sits on a stool at the kitchen island while her mom stubbornly dishes up some pasta and homemade Bolognese. The scent is heavenly, and the kitchen is full of color. A bunch of daffodils fills a vase near the sink, arranged in her mom's haphazardly easy fashion.

"The whole community was rocked by their disappearances," she says as she grates a hard block of parmesan over the top of the dish—just like Matt always did. "Parents were scared there was some kind of predator around. Doors were locked. Daughters were told not to walk home alone. I never thought Darryl did it." She puts a plate in front of Jane.

Jane feels a spurt of love, of belonging, of *home*. Despite her declarations of not being hungry, she realizes she's suddenly starving. As she digs her fork into the food and starts twirling pasta onto it, she glances at the photo of her dad on the wall in the adjacent dining room. It hangs surrounded by her mom's vibrant artwork. Jane thinks of loved ones they've all lost in one way or another. She thinks of the Jansens and the Hendrickses, of the tiny baby growing in Annalise's tummy and now being prodded by scientists in a lab. Of the Madonna and child stained glass window in the chapel. She glances at her mom, and for a moment Jane sees not her mother but a strong single woman, a widow who lost a law enforcement husband to senseless violence, and who fought her hardest and damnedest to raise a stubborn daughter on her own, and for a moment it's like a mirror of life being held up to Jane's face. She's going to be a mother, like Helen Jansen, like Mimi Hendricks, like her own mom. Suddenly Jane is overwhelmed and emotion rushes up, clogging her sinuses, tightening her throat, and making her eyes burn. She lowers her fork.

*Just pregnancy hormones,* she tells herself. *And need for decent sleep.*

"Eat, Jane. I know you're busy with a case, but you still need to eat. Not just anything. Protein. The right macro and micronutrients. You have a responsibility now, whether you like it or not."

Jane gives a wry smile and scoops the forkful of pasta and sauce into her mouth. "Enough already. You're like a stuck record, Mom. You've gotten even more bossy—how's that possible?" she says as she chews.

"It builds up," she says as she opens the fridge and takes out a bottle of wine. "With you and your father both gone, I have no release." She grins as she pours two very small glasses of white wine. She gives Jane one and takes a seat at the counter with her own.

"I probably shouldn't," Jane says, nodding to the glass.

"It'll be fine. I had wine now and then when I was pregnant with you. You turned out all right, didn't you?"

"Well, I don't know about that."

Her mother sips, sets her glass down. "I think the community blamed Darryl Hendricks because it was easy. When people don't have answers, they try to make them up, fill the gaps in the brain. And because Darryl was gone, too, it made sense to them. I really don't know how his parents coped."

"I don't think his mother did cope."

She nods solemnly, sips her wine.

"Is there anything else you recall about it all?" Jane asks as she gathers up another forkful of pasta.

"Well, I do remember the news of Annalise's disappearance being everywhere for a while. Posters of her on the lampposts and in store windows and at the post office. Vigils with candles were held in the park near her house. I remember her parents pleading on television and in the newspaper for information, and calling for her to come home if she was out there somewhere, listening. It was all over the news that she was a 'good' girl, smart, friendly. Everyone liked her at school, from the jocks to the nerds to the rocker-wild types. She worked part-time at the Donut Diner—that place that was down on Marine. We used to go there. Really good donuts and milkshakes."

"Do you remember anyone who might've worked with Annalise at the diner?"

"You could ask Beth Haverton. She used to be Beth Blaylock back then. She was the manager over that summer before Annalise went missing."

"Is she still around? Do you know?"

Her mother gives a light laugh. "Beth? I think she'll be around until she's at least a hundred and nine. She's in her mid to late seventies now and did the Kona Ironman last year. Won her age category, too. She also swims at Dundarave every morning, rain or shine, summer or winter, all year round, with the Dundarave Dippers."

Jane takes a sip of her wine. Everything in her body is starting to feel better. "This is good, Mom. Thanks."

Her mother nods and watches her. Jane can see her thinking, taking her mind back in time.

"There was even talk at the time that her disappearance might be linked to a serial killer. There were other women who went missing, too, mostly in the city, but I don't think that investigative angle really went anywhere."

Jane thinks of Noah. Maybe he is lying to her. Maybe he thinks this is linked to an old serial case.

"And why do you think Darryl didn't do her harm? Did you ever meet him?"

She shakes her head. "Saw him around once or twice at the shop. Good-looking guy. I guess I don't really know what I believed back then, Jane. I mean, we think we know people, but we can never really be sure, can we? Your father drove that home to me. His job showed me that villains are more often than not very ordinary people who, for whatever reason, end up doing a bad thing. They're seldom twirling mustaches, wearing black hats, and scheming to take over the world with clever cat and mouse mind games. They're your neighbor, some kid's father, your friend from school, your boss, your boyfriend, the guy who works at the garage, the mailman, a schoolteacher. Sometimes good people just do very bad things."

Jane glances at the framed photo of her dad again. There's another on the mantel beside it, showing him in his police uniform, and next to that is a photograph of her mother accepting a folded flag as a piper played "Amazing Grace" and a gun salute cracked into the air. Jane remembers the day of the memorial clearly. She's there in the photo, too, sitting in a chair next to her mom's. It was that day the fierce little girl in Jane vowed to become an officer herself one day and catch bad guys who hurt good people like her dad. But her mom is right. It's seemingly good people who most often do the terrible things. It was a homeless veteran with mental health issues and a machete who killed her father when he tried to help him move out of the way of traffic. The man's family didn't think of him as bad, just sick. The system let them all down, and sometimes "bad" really does depend on whose point of view you are in.

"I also remember some officers coming down our street," her mother is saying. Jane jerks herself back to the present. "They were knocking on doors, canvassing our neighborhood, asking if we'd seen anything."

"Your old street?"

"Yes. I opened the door. It was two RCMP officers in uniform. Young guys. I remember because one of them was really handsome with amazing green eyes—he actually went on to become the West Vancouver police chief many years later. I caught an interview being done with him on TV when he was promoted, and he mentioned to the interviewer that he'd worked the Annalise Jansen case. He said the case impacted him greatly because it was never solved, and some of those unsolved cases get under an officer's skin and never, ever leave. He said he'd personally canvassed door-to-door as a rookie, searching for witnesses, and that's when I realized it was him. Same bright-green eyes that seemed to hold a naughty secret."

She lowers her fork, stares at her mom. The image of the RCMP brooch filters into her mind. "*Which* WVPD chief?"

"Knox Raymond."

# THE SHOREVIEW SIX

## Mary

Mary and Claude simmer in silence as he drives her home. The sword of Damocles has finally dropped and sliced through bonds that have held their pact together over decades. Isaias kicked them all out before they were done, and now the Shoreview Six are scattering away from the Osman mansion like bits of debris from an exploding star in space. No gravity can stop things now. No one knows where all the broken pieces will land or what will be damaged in the fallout. The sense of impending doom is thick.

She glances at Claude, still struggling to process the horrifying notion that her friends might have killed Darryl and allowed Rocco to believe he'd done it solo. She's now terrified she'll also learn they killed her best friend and got her to help cover it up by lying to police. No amount of lawyering is going to convince cops or a jury that Mary didn't know what she was doing, that she wasn't complicit. What proof can she possibly present now? It'll be their word against hers. She could go down simply by association and obstructing justice.

Before they left the Osman house, Claude at least put Rocco into a cab, and while they waited for the taxi to arrive, Mary sat alone in the darkened interior of the SUV, watching Claude and Rocco talking intimately and out of earshot in dim light near the shrubs. Above them, inside the lighted kitchen window of the Osman house, she saw Jill and

Isaias arguing, gesticulating wildly, pointing at each other—actors in some illuminated shadow theater. She also saw Cara and Bob bitterly arguing in their Escalade before the interior light faded off and they backed out of the driveway and sped back to their "perfect life" on the Davine wine farm on Somersby Island.

Mary swallows. Very quietly, she says, "Is it true? Is Darryl dead? Was he killed the night Annalise went missing?"

Claude presses his foot down harder on the gas, drives faster. He doesn't reply.

"Is this what I covered for? I gave you an alibi for *murder*?"

He curses, swerves sharply into the next lane, guns the gas, and overtakes a long, swaying semitruck hurtling down the dark highway.

"Claude!"

"He's dead, okay? There, I said it. He died that night. Happy now?"

The contents of her stomach drop like a cold stone to her bowels. She gags. Her eyes water. "Why?" she whispers. "*Why* was he killed? What happened?"

"What you don't know can't hurt you, Mary. So shut the hell up with the questions, all right?"

"It *can* hurt me. I refuse to lie for you again. Unless you tell me what really happened, I'm going to go to the police myself tomorrow. I will confess you begged me to cover for you."

"Oh, that's rich. Are you threatening me, Mary?"

"Damn right I am."

He shoots her a murderous look. Mary recoils inwardly. Carefully, she slips her hand into her jacket pocket, feels for her cell phone, ready to call 911. "Tell me, Claude. I swear I'll do it—I'll go to the cops. What happened to Darryl? Where is his body?"

Claude overtakes several more cars at even higher speed. They barrel toward a bend in the highway. Mary grabs the door handle, braces as they lean around the corner. Her heart gallops. Sweat prickles across her lip. She shoots another glance at Claude, and shock ripples through her. A sheen of tears covers his cheeks. Light from oncoming vehicles shines off it.

"Claude?"

"It happened because of a lie," he says, still not slowing down. His voice is hoarse. "After the party, Cara told Robbie she saw Darryl having sex with Annalise near the pool. I knew it was a lie because it was *me* having sex with Annalise by the pool. Afterward, when Annalise was pulling her skirt straight, I saw her—Cara—standing in the shadows watching us. I think Darryl might have seen us, too. I couldn't call Cara on her lie because she had me over a barrel and knew it. Robbie freaking lost it when she told him. He was already high on the 'shrooms and drink. And when Robbie, me, and Rocco drove down to this motel off-sales near the docks to get more booze, we saw Darryl's orange-and-white VW bus pulling into a lane beside that old tire place. Robbie insisted we follow him. I didn't argue. I was scared. I was prepared to blame Darryl rather than kill the deep friendship between me and Robbie. I was fucking weak, okay? And pretty high. We parked him in, got out, dragged Darryl out of his van. Robbie and I picked up some lug wrenches lying there and started to 'teach him a lesson.'" Claude swipes tears from his face. "It got out of hand. He—he didn't make it."

"*You* killed him? The three of you?"

"Me and Robbie. Rocco was so out of it, he basically swung once and fell over. We put Darryl and Rocco in the back of the Volkswagen. I drove the van. Robbie drove Zane's Dodge, and we got rid of the VW bus and Darryl's body, then Robbie and I took Rocco home in the Dodge and put him to bed. In the morning he woke covered in the blood, and we—we went to see him and basically allowed him to think he'd done it, and that we'd gotten rid of the body and VW bus for him, in order to protect him. We didn't tell him where we put Darryl because Rocco was so goddamned unreliable, he'd probably let it spill in one of his inebriated rages."

"You were framing him?"

"We didn't want to go down for murder, Mary. And he was a loose cannon. It was better for him to think he did it and that he owed us—then maybe we could be more certain he'd stay quiet out of fear for himself." He swipes moisture from his face again and finally slows his speed a little.

"You still would've gone down for—"

His gaze flares to her. "D'you think people act rationally when they kill someone? Especially if they didn't mean to? Do you have any idea the kind of terror that comes with something like that? When your hands are full of all that blood and you don't know what to do?"

She swallows, feeling sick. She's going to throw up. "What did you do with Darryl's body?" she asks. Her voice comes out thick. "And his van? Where did you hide them?"

Claude's jaw stiffens. His hands tighten on the wheel. He looks dead ahead as he drives and says nothing.

"Claude, I swear, I'm going to tell—"

"Think of your family, Mary. Think of your daughter."

"And you think of *your* family, Betancourt. If you don't tell me where you put him and exactly what I'm lying for, I won't lie. Don't think you can drag me into this mess this far and not do me the courtesy of letting me know exactly what kind of a mess I'm in."

He inhales deeply. A vein bulges on his temple. "Blackwater Lake," he says quietly, finally.

"What?"

"That's where Darryl is. Inside his VW bus. In the deep water below the jumping cliffs."

She stares at his profile. Her vision narrows. She feels dizzy.

He glances at her. "And if you confess to the cops, Mary, if you tell them any of this, there'll be no way you can prove you weren't part of it."

"Where was Zane all this time?"

"I don't know. On his bike, I guess. We all told the cops he was with us because we didn't have full licenses and needed to say someone who wasn't drinking was driving. Zane agreed."

She glances out the window. The world of suburbia speeds by. The city lights in the distance twinkle over the water. Very quietly, she says,

"What about Annalise? Why does Roc also think he killed Annalise? Did you guys hurt her, too?" Her voice chokes on a wave of emotion. She struggles to compose herself, clears her throat, turns to him, and says, "Was it you guys in the brown car that the cops asked us about? Was it you waiting in the shadows on the cul-de-sac near her house in Zane's car?"

He doesn't reply. Desperation—horror—rises in Mary's gut, and she can't tamp down the panic swelling with it.

"Did you kill Annalise?" she demands. *"Tell me!"*

He suddenly swerves the SUV onto the shoulder of the highway and slams on the brakes. The SUV skids over small bits of gravel, and the tires screech as they come to a stop on the verge.

"Get out."

Her body goes tight. "What?"

"I said get out of my car."

"We're on the highway."

He lurches across her body, opens the passenger side door, and throws it wide. "Get the hell out of my car."

"Claude—"

"Now!" He undoes her seatbelt. "Go." He shoves her out of the seat.

She half falls and stumbles out of the SUV onto the highway shoulder.

He yanks the door shut. There's a shriek of rubber as he swerves back into the traffic and speeds away. Mary is shaking. She stares after the taillights. And she knows. Her days are numbered.

*If they killed once, they could kill again to keep their terrible secret.*

What can she do now, to save her own family?

# THE SHOREVIEW SIX

## Cara

Cara and Bob pull into a motel parking lot near the ferry terminal in Tsawwassen so they can be in the ferry line first thing in the morning for their trip back to Somersby Island. The last vessel of the day already left just after 5:00 p.m.

Cara stares at the profile of the low-cost motel. Paint peels from the clapboard walls. The neon sign is missing a letter and flickers as though in some tropey horror movie. Wind howls off the nearby sea and scatters paper and other litter across the surface of the cracked parking lot. Sitting inside the lit reception area is a balding man hunched over and eating a burger as he watches a television set.

She feels ill. She and Bob would ordinarily not be caught dead staying in a place like this, but they don't want to be seen. This is what they've been reduced to—secretive beings scuttling about in the darkness because no one can know that the six of them gathered in West Van. It might be overkill, but they're both really afraid, and Bob, being a lawyer, is already second-guessing interrogation from police and possibly even prosecutors who might ask if the group gathered again to coordinate stories.

He rubs his face. "Is it true, Cara?" he asks.

"Is what true?" But she already knows what he wants.

A cat darts across the parking lot, body held low, as though it's hunting something.

"*Did* you see Annalise and Darryl kissing weeks before the party? Did you actually see him screwing my girl at the party?"

*My girl.*

Cara swallows. Her body is tense. It's all cracking apart. Nearly fifty years later, when she thought it was all finally, totally gone, that the horrible past wasn't even a part of her anymore, that it had happened to some other young person, not her, they're here, in front of this seedy motel with a broken sign, probing the old lies.

"Was it a lie, Cara?"

She looks at him. His face is dark, thunderous. She doesn't even really recognize him as her husband.

"I'm sorry," she whispers.

*"Sorry?"*

She glances down at her hands in her lap.

"Sorry!" He slams his hand on the steering wheel. "What the fuck? Why? Why did you lie to me?"

Tears fill Cara's eyes. "I just wanted you to dump Annalise," she says softly. "I loved you, Bob. I loved you so much. I wanted you for me."

Bob goes dead quiet, dead still. She steals a glance at him. He stares at her like he doesn't know her at all, like she's some piece of shit that has been curiously stuck to his shoe all these years and he never noticed it until now.

"Sorry? Do you know what happened because of your lie, Cara?"

Tears spill from her eyes and stream down her face.

"Do you know what you made us all do?"

A sudden shot of anger sparks through her veins. "I didn't *make* you do anything, Bob. I didn't *make* you hunt down Darryl and beat him with tire irons. I didn't *make* you kill him, and I didn't *make* you and your friend drive his VW up to Blackwater and push him in his van off the cliffs."

"You could have stopped us. If you'd said it was a lie."

"I wasn't in the car with you three boys, now was I? You dropped me and Jill off at Jill's house so we could get changed before going to the woods—remember? By the time you came back and told me what happened, it was all over. There was nothing I could say that would bring Darryl back, was there?" She swipes her tears away. "I helped you by giving you an alibi, Bob. And I convinced Jill to stick with the story, too. I didn't even ask you later what you guys did to Annalise."

"I did not hurt Annalise."

"Whatever. I don't want to know."

"I never slept with Annalise, either. What Mary said was true."

Her gaze shoots back to her husband. Her heart starts to hammer. She stares at him. Seconds tick by. Very quietly, she asks, "Why did you never sleep with her?"

He breaks her gaze, rubs his knee, then inhales deeply. "Because I loved her, Cara. Because Annalise was nervous about doing it, and I didn't want to push her. I wanted her trust. I . . . I thought maybe she was the one. That I could be with her forever."

Emotion burns into Cara's throat. It twists with an irrational jealousy. She can't help what comes out of her mouth next.

"Well, I'm glad she's dead."

Her husband stares at her, jaw open. "You didn't mean that?"

"I did. And you don't know the half of it. Because while she didn't want to screw you, I *did* see her fucking someone else at the party by the pool house. And it wasn't Darryl, it was Claude."

"You conniving bitch," he whispers. "Why should I believe a thing you say now?"

"Don't then. You can believe the DNA. Because Claude slept with her more than once. He had sex with her before the summer vacation, too." A bitter little seed cracks open inside Cara. It oozes out hatred and hurtfulness, and it feeds into her veins. "I think she slept with Rocco, too. She was fucking around with everyone but you. Maybe *that's* why you killed her. Maybe that's what I will tell the cops."

"You'd destroy everything we have."

"And what do we really have now?" Cara reaches for the handle and shoves open the car door. She exits, slams it shut, and marches to the motel entrance. Sea wind tears at her hair. She'll get a room for one. If she's irreparably lost Bob's love and trust, should she dare risk throwing him under the bus to at least save her own skin and the rest of her family?

What about Rocco? Is it time to use the old backup plan—land all the blame squarely on him, silence him for good?

Sometimes big problems require big sacrifices. She just has to figure which sacrifice to make.

# THE SHOREVIEW SIX

## Jill

Jill sits on the sofa as Isaias paces relentlessly in front of her. She's exhausted from explaining to her husband what happened.

"So that's everything?" he asks her.

She nods.

"The whole truth?"

"The whole truth, I promise. Isaias, please. Please don't hate me."

He sits. Finally. Her husband is clearly devastated. He drops his face into his hands.

Jill doesn't know if their marriage can survive this. She tried at first to deflect, argue, rationalize, blame. But he wore her down simply by fixing her with his kind, dark eyes. More than anything Jill is rocked by the rawness of his shock. His disappointment in her. And it makes what she did feel all the more real and terrible and heinous.

Isaias sits like that for what feels like a slow, viscous age. He then gets abruptly up, fetches his laptop from his briefcase still at the door, and sits and opens it on the coffee table. Quietly he reads through article after article on the old missing persons cases.

He lifts his head, regards her. The pain she sees in his features cuts physically into her heart.

He holds his hand toward the laptop, palm up. "You're telling me you knew all the time what happened to that missing boy, Darryl?"

"I knew from Cara. Robbie—Bob—told Cara what happened. He needed to talk, to off-load on someone. He arrived at her house with blood on him, shaking. He couldn't hide it from her. And Cara told me because she needed me to know how serious it was so I would lie for them."

"You lied to the police—you said the boys picked you and Cara up after you'd changed clothing, but they never did come to get you? You never did go with them to drink in the woods."

"No," she whispers. He stares at her. Jill wishes she could read what's going on in her husband's brain, but she can only imagine.

"And you told the police you'd seen Darryl kissing Annalise?"

She swallows. "Cara saw them. I—I believed her at the time, Isaias."

"Believing her is one thing. Telling the police you witnessed it with your own eyes is another."

"I regret it. I am so sorry. I didn't know until later Annalise was gone, too. By then I was too afraid to change the story."

Slowly, quietly, as though he's trying to process it by speaking it out loud, he says, "You knew Darryl had been beaten to death even while his mother and father and baby sister were looking for him, hurting, broken, devastated? You knew where he was the whole time, while law enforcement officers hunted him down like some kidnapper or potential murderer and his family was being shamed by the community? And you couldn't spare them this pain?"

"I was sixteen, Isaias, and—"

"Why, Jill? Why was it so easy for you to blame the brown boy? Because he was an 'other'? Because it was convenient? Because you were willing to sacrifice him and his family for some white boys?"

"It's not about race, Isaias. It's—"

"What's it about then?" he demands. "You *knew* he was dead, for chrissakes. You knew where his parents could find him. You knew you could save their reputation. This story here"—he holds his hand toward his laptop—"it says his mother died brokenhearted. Their business suffered."

"I'm sorry."

He stares at her. Like she's an alien. And maybe she is. Wind ripples the water outside on their beautiful pool overlooking the sound. Clouds scud across the moon. Jill feels the foundation of her world silently shifting, sliding away. She doesn't even understand herself who or what she is, or how she came to be involved in this. But once she was in as a kid, she honestly didn't know how to stop, how to get out. And she so badly needed to belong to this group of friends at the time, too. The need to belong is a basic survival instinct more powerful than logic. Biologically it can override the most rational of thinking. To be cut out of the herd represents danger on some unconscious biological level that drove her teen brain. It's how people get sucked into cults and become progressively more isolated from outside influences. That's what happened with their group of six.

Isaias shakes his head and repeats again what she told him. "And they pushed his van over the cliff at Blackwater Lake with his body inside?"

She nods.

"Was he even dead when they did that?"

Tears begin to stream down her face. When she speaks again her voice is thick, hoarse. "I only know what Cara told me they said. You don't plan things like this, Isaias. They just happen. And then you're stuck. It's not like movies or TV. Someone dies and it's messy and confusing and everyone panics and tells a version of the truth or not. And then the police come around and you're scared and locked in."

"Did they kill the girl, too?"

She begins to sob.

Isaias returns his attention to his laptop screen. Jill sees him click on a photo of Darryl Hendricks. He enlarges it so that Darryl fills his monitor. The teen looks handsome. Striking bone structure, large Afro hairstyle. Infectious smile. It's his school photo. He's dressed in his customary leather vest over a T-shirt. Jill can see the chain with the medallion around his neck. His smile is huge.

Isaias reads out loud the inscription the police described to the newspapers: "Be the change you want to see in the world."

She watches as her husband's eyes fill with emotion. Jill knows what Isaias is seeing—a boy who looks so very much like the young Isaias she spotted that night in a bar in Paris during her gap year. Even though she hadn't articulated it to herself at the time, she can see it so clearly now since Cara raised it. Isaias was a Darryl. A Darryl she could still save. And love. And nurture. And keep alive. And in so doing Isaias became the man who might help her atone, who allowed her to justify the rest of her life, who allowed her to exist without crippling guilt. This raw, unconscious impulse—she realizes now—is what probably drove young Jill through the pulsing throngs in the bar that night to single him out. It's why she smiled her best smile at him, touched his arm, and offered to buy him a drink.

And there's not one doubt in Jill's mind right now that Isaias can see it, too. He can see the uncanny resemblance between young Darryl and himself as a young man.

"And all this time you guys let Rocco, an innocent man, think he'd done this? You thought if things went sideways, he could take the fall and you'd all sail through?"

"Rocco wasn't so completely innocent."

"More innocent than you." Isaias comes to his feet. He fetches his coat. He finds his keys.

"Wh-where are you going?"

He stops moving but refuses to look at her. With his back turned to her, he says, "When I come back tomorrow, Jill, I want you gone. I want you out of this house."

"Please, Isaias, please talk to me. Try to understand—"

He exits the front door. It shuts behind him with a thud that sounds like death.

Her marriage, life as she knows it, is over.

She knows her husband, too. He's a man of morals and justice. Isaias will want to go straight to the cops. The question is, will he? She stares at the door, and the sudden hollowness of the house swallows her.

Whether it comes from the law or not, retribution has already found her.

It's found each and every one of them.

# JANE

Jane sits on the sofa in front of the gas fireplace at her mom's house going through the case notes in her laptop, paying extra attention to the sequence of events around the party. Rain falls softly outside, and the cat is curled by her side. Her mother—who is downstairs painting in her studio—persuaded Jane to stay the night, and she's glad she conceded. With her full belly and wrapped in the comfort of a home infused with warmth, love, and good memories, she has a fresh edge to her energy.

She studies a photo of Annalise. Something is niggling Jane. It's the police brooch found with Annalise's body. What connection might the young teen have had with an RCMP officer back in the day? Was the pin a memento? A gift? Did Annalise somehow acquire it herself for some reason?

Jane lifts her head and stares at the flames in the fireplace, thinking of what her mother told her about the young green-eyed officer who knocked on her door, asking if anyone had seen the missing girl. Her mind shifts to the officers who attended the party nuisance call on Friday, September 3, 1976. Jane scrolls quickly through her notes. She doesn't have their names. Tank mentioned them, but she can't recall them.

She reaches for her mobile and calls Tank. It goes straight to voice mail. Frustration bites Jane. She checks her watch. It's not *that* late. She tries again. Once more the call flips directly to voice mail. Jane tries

Duncan next. His memory recall is phenomenal, so much so that it's his party trick.

Duncan picks up on the third ring. Jane can hear the clank and thud of weights and background music, voices. He's at the gym.

"Hey, you got a minute?" she asks.

"Not really. What's up?" He's breathing hard. She imagines him wiping sweat from his pale brow with a neat towel designed specifically for this purpose.

"Sorry to bug you—"

"No you're not."

She smiles to herself. "Okay, I'm not. I tried Tank first, but he's not picking up."

"Because he's not an idiot like me."

"Tank probably has a life."

Duncan gives a snort. "I have a life." She can hear he's moving to a quieter area.

"Can you talk?"

"I can now. What is it?"

"Something came up in conversation with my mom tonight—the name of a young officer who did a canvass around her neighborhood when she was a teen. She lived in the same area as the Jansens at the time. And it got me thinking—do you recall the names of the officers who responded to the party call, the ones Tank mentioned?"

"Oh, you mock my process, and now you want to access my ace memory?"

"Okay, Murtagh, you win. You're brilliant. Green smoothies, keto, perfect recall. Got it. Do your party-trick magic for me, will you? Can you remember their names?"

He gives a small laugh, then goes quiet.

"You still there?"

"Please, a moment of time. Genius at work." There's another lull. Jane hears gym music pulsing faintly in the background. "I remember Tank saying there were four uniforms who responded—one corporal, three constables." He pauses. "He mentioned only their last names. One of them was Bing. I remember that because it's quirky, made me think Bing Crosby. One was called Simon, as in Paul Simon. The other was Jackson, as in Michael—see the music theme here? It's how it works. You anchor everything you're absorbing to a particular narrative or theme, then you just need to recall the narrative or the theme, and it serves as a prompt to dig out the names."

"Right. Got it. Musicians. Like, *all* of them?"

"The last one was an odd one out. Or at least I thought so at first. Raymond. Couldn't think of a musician with the last name Raymond, until it hit me—"

"Usher Raymond IV."

"See? Even you can do it."

"Christ," she whispers. "Raymond. I think he was also there at the party that night. That's what's been bugging me—a subliminal memory of the name connection."

"Care to elucidate now that you've stopped me from crushing my PB on bench press tonight?"

"Knox Raymond. He canvassed the neighborhood, knocked on my mom's door, and it sounds like he also responded to the party."

"Knox—you mean, as in *Chief* Knox Raymond, who recently retired from the West Van PD?"

"We have a link, Murtagh. Someone alive who might be able to give us some context from the old investigation."

Jane thanks Duncan, then calls the WVPD detachment. There should be someone on duty who can furnish her with retired Chief Knox Raymond's contact details.

Twenty minutes later she's on a call with Knox Raymond's wife, Meghan.

"Knox is out of town," she tells Jane. "Fishing up north. That old Jansen case really got under his skin—one they never solved. He was so young at the time, too. We were expecting our first child when he helped work that one."

"Can I reach him via mobile?"

"He's not always in cellular range while in the backcountry, but you can try. You might get lucky. I know he'll be more than happy to help." Meghan Raymond gives Jane the number.

"It really was such a tragic story," Meghan adds. "I remember Knox telling me he saw the girl several times before—she apparently worked part-time at the Donut Diner on Marine, back in the day."

A prickle of goose bumps creeps over Jane's skin. Faith Jansen's words rise in her mind.

*She also did speak once about a guy who used to come into the Donut Diner, where she worked over the summer . . . I don't recall a lot, apart from what I read later, but I remember thinking there was something fishy about him. Like, stalkery. Mom, did she talk to you about it? Did she say he seemed dangerous or something?*

Jane thinks of the police brooch. She clears her throat. "Did your husband often frequent the donut place?"

"What cop didn't?" Meghan laughs. "Best donuts in town. He used to bring me some occasionally. I craved sweet stuff when I was pregnant."

After thanking Meghan Raymond, Jane immediately calls Knox Raymond's cell. An automated message tells her the cell user is likely not in range. She leaves a message saying that she's looking for help on the old case and she understands he might be able to provide her team with some valuable context.

Jane returns her attention to her laptop and starts searching for any information she can find on retired WVPD Chief Knox Raymond. About a half hour later, she encounters something in the digitized online archives of the old *North Shore Gazette* that turns her blood cold.

It's a small article with a photo announcing the birth of a baby girl to local officer Knox Raymond and his wife, Meghan, in October 1976. This would mean Raymond's wife would have been around eight months pregnant at the time of Annalise Jansen's disappearance in early September of that same year.

With the article of congratulations is a photo of Knox and his wife holding a tiny baby in front of a metallic-brown sedan.

Jane's phone rings. Her heart kicks. She grabs it.

"Munro here."

"Sergeant Munro? This is Knox Raymond. You called?"

# ANGELA

Angela Sheldrick is working into the night in her newsroom cubicle. There's just a skeleton crew left in the office to take breaking news calls. The fluorescent lights have been dimmed. The sound of a janitor's vacuum whines from one of the editors' glassed-in offices. Even Mason departed at a normal hour today, which is highly unusual. Angela had hoped to corner him again.

She's pissed with him for stalling on her proposal. Even though she and Rahoul broke this story, other media outlets with more money and staff have already gained ground ahead of her. She's also bummed by the hate mail and social media comments that are calling her out for being disrespectful, a clickbait c**t, unethical, a life wrecker, a cheap excuse for and shame to real journalism.

This era of instant feedback sucks.

She scrubs her fingers through her hair feeling exasperated and, yes, hurt. She went to journalism school. She knows what good, old-school reporting looks like. She consumed books and stories about female correspondents such as Martha Gellhorn, Ida B. Wells, Marie Colvin. She still idolizes Christiane Amanpour. It's not her fault the landscape changed under the surge of the electronic revolution and social media and fake news. The only way to snare short attention spans these days is with shock value. Isn't it? Should she be taking a hard, cold look in the mirror and rethinking what she wants out of a career and life?

Angela prefers to not look too hard into any mirror—she might see the damaged little girl and swirling dark secrets of her own past if she does.

She inhales deeply, shuts down the ugly emails, and returns her focus to research. Since there's been no real information coming from the cops, she's devoted her time this evening to reading old news stories and collecting whatever new information she can find on the Shoreview Six. She's got a sense of who they have become now, and where they live—apart from Rocco Jones. He remains a cipher to Angela. She can't easily find any current references to him.

She sits back and chews her pen, her mind fixating on Rocco as she keeps an eye on the little icon on her computer screen that will show her if a new tip or voice message comes in.

"Hey," Rahoul says behind her.

Angela jumps. "Crap, you spooked me. Why do you sneak up like that?"

"I didn't 'sneak,' Angela." He dumps a bag of takeout on her desk. *"Thank you, Rahoul, for getting me takeout,"* he says.

"Thank you, Rahoul, for bringing me takeout." She grabs the bag, opens it. The smell that comes out is divine. "Beef chow mein?"

"Yep." He sets his camera gear on his desk, which is an arm's length from hers in their tiny shared space. He shrugs out of his jacket, hangs it over the back of his chair, sits, puts his booted feet up on the desk, and opens his own container of food.

"Extra hot sauce?"

He gives her the side-eye.

She grins and jabs her chopsticks into the carton.

"Annalise Jansen's old group of friends still live in the region," she says, delivering noodles to her mouth. She chews. "Apart from Rocco Jones, who I have yet to locate."

"What's your next step?" Rahoul asks, poking his chopsticks into his carton.

"Interview them." She takes another mouthful of chow mein, considering how she might tackle this in a way to stand out from the crowd.

Maybe she could go deeper, try more of a sophisticated approach. Maybe that's why they haven't green-lighted her proposal—she hasn't demonstrated the depth and nuanced layers she knows she's capable of.

Her work mobile rings on her desk. She glances up. It's the phone to which calls are being forwarded from the dedicated tip line. She quickly sets down her food carton and grabs her phone.

"Angela Sheldrick."

"You still interested in tips about the chapel body?"

Angela's heart kicks. She can't tell whether the caller is male or female—the voice has been altered by some kind of voice distortion app. She makes a motion to Rahoul and quickly hits the RECORD button. She puts her phone on speaker.

Rahoul stops chewing. He watches her face intently as she listens to the caller.

"I am interested," she says. "Do you have some information on the case?"

"I do."

Angela still can't discern whether the voice is male or female. "And you wish to remain anonymous?"

"I do."

"What would you like to share with us?" She glances at Rahoul. His dark eyes are wide.

"They lied."

"Who lied?"

"The Shoreview Six. They all lied."

"What did they lie about?"

"Alibis."

"Which alibis? When?"

"I'm sending you something. Check your inbox."

The call goes dead.

Angela sees the red button icon on her desktop screen blinking to indicate a new message. She hurriedly opens it.

A scanned copy of a news article fills her screen. Dated July 1982 from a paper in Bakersfield, California. She reads the headline.

> CANADIAN ARRESTED IN VIOLENT LIQUOR STORE ATTACK

Her heart beats faster as she begins to read.

> The inebriated and tire iron–wielding suspect in the Tammy Vale Liquor Store break-and-enter was arrested in a Walmart parking lot Friday morning, where he was camping in his vehicle. Rocco Jones, originally of Vancouver, Canada, stands charged with—

"What in the hell?" Rahoul whispers as he peers over her shoulder. He points at the article. "There's your Rocco Jones. Wherever he is now, he has a US criminal record from the eighties?"

"And a history of violence," Angela says quietly. Her body hums with adrenaline. "Someone knows," she says softly. "Someone always knows. It's like I said, Rahoul—time changes circumstances and people, and they finally want to speak about old and cold cases. We need to run with this." She points at her screen. "I need to verify this. We—"

As she speaks, a second email with an attachment pops into her inbox.

> Check attached Vital Statistics records for official name change of Rocco Jones to Mason Gordon.

With the email is an image of a BC Vital Statistics name-change certificate. Rocco Adam Jones applied for—and was granted—a change of name to Mason Adam Gordon in 1991.

Angela blinks. Her world narrows as she stares at the image. Slowly she looks up and meets Rahoul's gaze.

"Fuck me," he whispers.

"This is huge. We need to speak to Mason," she says. "On camera. Now. Grab your coat."

"In person? We don't even know where he is right now. Shouldn't we tell the higher-ups about this first?"

"If I tell them, or call him, he gets a heads-up. We need his shock at being discovered captured live on camera. If he's not home, we stake out his apartment until he is."

# THE SHOREVIEW SIX

## Bob

Bob doesn't follow Cara into the motel reception area. He lets her go find a room alone. He sits for a while, replaying and obsessing over the evening's events at the Osman mansion. His mind turns to Cara's lie and what that did to him as a teen. He thinks about all the beautiful possibilities that could have been with Annalise. He still vividly recalls the satiny feel of her skin, the scent of her hair, of her cherry pop lip gloss. Yes, she was his first love, and he was smitten during the lustful, hormone-filled days of his early teens, but he did believe he loved her with a depth that could last forever. Those summer months of 1976, filled with lake swimming and hiking and beach fires, had unspooled before them both like a golden carpet promising endless potential, possibilities. He'd been poised that summer for life to go one way. It changed in an instant. Instead, his life had spiraled another way. Because of Cara's lie, he'd ended up with Cara. With this.

And now?

He doesn't know the answer to that.

He also can't understand why Annalise was ready to go steady with him yet not sleep with him, especially if it's true that she had sex repeatedly with his friends. It's confusing. It hurts. Even now.

All Bob knows for certain is that someone else—possibly one of his close friends—made his girlfriend pregnant behind his back. And a desire to pin the murder on whoever that was burns fierce and furious. The other thing Bob knows for certain is he needs a drink. Right now. Many drinks. Maybe once he mutes the sharp edges of his anger and growing fear, he'll be able to formulate a concise plan of action.

Bob locks the Escalade and walks across the cracked and littered motel parking lot to the adjacent pub.

He orders doubles, drinks fast and hard while listening to the honky-tonk of the old jukebox as he watches blue-collar types in their more advanced years playing pool or sitting alone at tables, morosely hunched over beers and whiskies. He's reminded of that Springsteen song about glory days that are gone, and he suddenly feels overwhelmingly sad. A woman with overdyed hair perches atop a high stool at the bar. Bob reckons she's a sex worker, and a cheap one at that. Her pleather skirt is too short, too tight, her stockinged thighs are dimpled, and her stilettos look painful. She laughs loudly and flirts with the barman in a muscle shirt who polishes beer glasses with hands and arms covered in tats. The whole bar smells of life gone sour and stale. The lighting is bad. Outside the window he can see the flickering of the motel's pink neon sign reflected in a parking lot puddle. As he stares drunkenly at the moving color, he notices a black SUV drive past the window.

*My Escalade?*

Bob lurches off his barstool and stumbles to the window. He sees the vehicle stop at the end of the road. Taillights flare red. It turns, and is gone.

He stares after it.

*Cara?*

He can't even be sure it was his vehicle. He leaves his drink and walks out into the windy parking lot to check. The air smells like brine and is tinged with a manure fertilizer stink from the nearby Delta farms. His SUV is gone. Cara has taken it, and he has no idea where she has gone. Or if she'll ever come back.

Bob inhales deeply, trying to use the chill air to clear his head. Is this what it all boils down to? His marriage over? What about the rest of his life's work? Kids? Grandkids? Their farm? The wines and the bistro? All their dreams? He stares at the empty spot in the lot where he left the Escalade. Seconds pass. Bob needs another drink. He glances at the seedy pub, makes a decision, and pulls out his phone to call a cab. He'll go into the city. He'll drink at the sort of establishment where he belongs. There's a club near his old work, just around the corner from where Rocco said he has a new apartment. Bob will go there. Perhaps he'll bump into a familiar and friendly face. At least there will be better hookers.

Maybe he'll even go see Rocco. A plan suddenly begins to hatch in Bob's legal eagle head.

## Mary

Mary walks along the dark verge of the highway, staying as far away from the whizzing traffic as she can. It's dark. The drivers won't see her. Pedestrians are not legally permitted on the highway. She's terrified of being hit and killed and is having trouble processing that Claude even did this to her, left her, a sixty-three-year-old woman, like this, to walk alone in the dark on the verge of the Upper Levels Highway. But he's just proved what he's capable of, and she's even more afraid of what he'll do next. Perhaps she should not have so overtly threatened him. She needs a plan—something, anything—before Claude or the rest of them act first and she ends up being thrown to the wolves. Or worse, before Heather loses everything she dreamed of because her mother fucked up again. A last-ditch, desperate option begins to present itself as Mary walks, keeping an eye out for the yellow taxi she has called.

*How bad would it really be for Rocco to take the complete fall?*

He's such a washed-up mess already. That damage has been done. Would it matter if laying the blame for the murders on him meant saving everyone else, but mostly Heather? The instant this notion enters her head, she feels ill that it even came from her own mind. But it's been seeded, and she can't let it go.

*The things we do, for our children—to keep them safe, to atone for our own childhood sins, when inside our aging bodies we're all really just still frightened and bullied children ourselves . . .*

## Claude

When Claude sets his keys down in the hall, he spies his wife, kids, and grandkids playing a game in the living room. A cozy gas fire flickers in the hearth. The atmosphere is warm, content. Happy even. Claude feels as though his heart is going to snap clean in two. He'll lose them, all of them. Tonight was the beginning of the end of it all. Justice has finally come calling.

Or perhaps Lady Justice has been dogging him all these years, and part of Claude has always recognized her presence in his life, lurking near his shoulder, watching, waiting for her chance to move, to catch him up, or biding her time until he somehow snared himself in the muddle of his past, like he has now. Perhaps it was this lifelong awareness of her constant and watchful presence that has driven Claude to work harder, to be better, to build a business himself from the ground up, against all odds, while refusing to take a single penny from his wealthy and sports-famous parents. Perhaps this is why he's given all his spare time, his whole heart, to teach kids his sport of privilege. Perhaps it's all been a way to say to her: *Justice, look, see, I* can *be good. I'm not at the core a bad person. I help children. I give my time, my money, my love.*

But all Claude has really done is stave off what he's always known deep down is inevitable: That one day there would come the hard, cold knock at his door. He'd open it, and she'd be standing there holding her scales, hiding behind her blindfold, not seeing all the atonement work he's been doing. And she'd ask him to pay.

"Hey, hon," his wife says as she gets up and comes to him in the hallway. She leans up and kisses him. Her eyes meet his. An earnestness shapes her features as her gaze searches his face. She places her hand on his arm. "Is everything okay?"

"Yeah." He shrugs out of his jacket. He feels like crying.

"Did you manage to sort out the problem with the supply chain?"

This was the excuse Claude gave her for not being able to attend the family barbecue tonight. He nods. "Sorta. How'd dinner go?"

"I saved you some barbecue. Want me to warm it up?"

"Go back to your game," he says softly. "I'll warm up my food."

In the kitchen, as Claude watches his plate go round and round in the microwave, something firms inside him. He can't give this up. He *cannot* yield yet. He needs to keep fighting to the end. Claude Betancourt has never been a quitter.

## Isaias

Isaias finds a parking spot on the street near the North Van police station near the hospital. He sits watching the hulking concrete building in the dark. Marked cruisers come and go. Officers converse on the sidewalk and beside their vehicles. A fire engine leaves the adjacent fire hall and puts on sirens. Red lights flash into the darkness as the wails of the sirens rise.

His initial gut impulse was to come straight here and put this right. To tell the RCMP where they can find Darryl Hendricks's VW bus and his body so the Hendricks family can finally bring their boy home after all these lost years. So Rocco Jones might be freed from the mental prison destroying him. So Bob and Cara Davine and Claude Betancourt and Mary Metcalfe can be punished for their heinous acts and cover-ups. But this means Jill will certainly be swept up in it all, too. And she really should be. But Isaias has always loved his wife deeply, and the shock of it all is registering slowly, the implications sinking in. Isaias looks upward out of his car window and catches glimpses of police officers moving in a lit office area upstairs.

Another siren wails, the sound rising and falling as it grows louder and louder, approaching the hospital across the street. Ambulance. Cops. Firefighters. Society looking after its people.

He rubs his brow. He surely cannot return to his sham of a marriage, can he? Not now that he knows what Jill is, and what she's done. Now that he knows how easily she allowed friends to control her, and how quickly she allowed a community to blame the brown boy, the "other," the son of refugees whom she purports to help. Are her charities all guilt-driven, too?

Should she be forgiven?

What does forgiveness really mean?

And how can he forgive when she is *still* too gutless to go to Darryl's family and tell them the truth, or to come here to talk to the cops herself? When she doesn't have the courage to bring peace to Darryl's parents because it will upend her nice privileged life and friendships and so-called charity work?

And she still hasn't told him what they did to Annalise Jansen.

He has to tell the cops. But first Isaias wants to do something. He leans forward and starts his engine.

## Rocco

Rocco nurses a fat whiskey in his sparsely furnished, post-third-divorce unit on the twenty-second floor of a high-rise in a swanky and newly redeveloped area of the city. His massive picture windows afford him a view over False Creek and into countless other windows that give glimpses into a myriad of little apartment-box lives. Human beings living atop one another like termites in a colony. All different yet all the same in some way.

When the cab dropped him off, he stumbled straight through the main doors of his building, rode the elevator up, stepped out of the car, crossed the hall, let himself into his own box, and aimed directly for his drinks cabinet, his sole goal to dull the edges of panic consuming his brain. He takes another big swallow as he squints and tries to mentally rehash the sequence of events at the Osman mansion. Supposedly they gathered to unite, but something darker transpired. They were, in essence, all looking for a sacrificial scapegoat to appease the clamoring law enforcement gods, a sacrifice that would make everything go away for them. They'd all looked at him. Then Mary seeded in his brain a poison pill.

He sips again.

Could she be right?

What if he *didn't* actually kill Darryl? What if he's actually been innocent all these years? He takes a bigger gulp. This idea threatens Rocco in an unexpected and profoundly terrifying way, because everything Rocco is, everything he's become and done in his adult life, every pathetic mistake, every drunken mishap or arrest, every mindless binge, every failed marriage and lost job and AA meeting and outburst of violence, or rehab stint—he can trace it all back to his fundamental belief that he beat to death a boy from his school. That he's an awful and evil person. An unworthy piece of pathetic shit. And he truly doesn't deserve a single good thing in life.

Now he has doubts. He has sinister whispering questions.

What if he isn't evil?

What if his best friends were never friends at all?

What if they really did set him up all those years ago to take the fall if things went sideways, and—given that they are, in fact, going sideways now—they're ready to do it again? Are they going to seal his fate and somehow blame the deaths all on him?

He frowns to himself, sips again. He *does* remember striking someone. He does recall the feel of a metal bar in his fist, and the thud and give of flesh, and the sound of crunching bone. He recalls the smell of blood. He even remembers excitement curdled with horror at what he was doing to another human being. Or did he manufacture these memories with his own nightmarish brain? Were these memories even real, or had they been fictions planted by Robbie and Claude?

Or could it be remotely possible he *had* actually killed Annalise, and the guys didn't tell him about that part?

He feels sick. Worse than usual. Every molecule of his body craves the truth, and he fears it with his entire soul.

He finishes his drink and pushes himself awkwardly to his feet. He aims himself toward the drinks cabinet to fetch the bottle for some more. He stumbles a little on his way and catches himself, bracing his hand on the cabinet. He waits a moment for the world to stop spinning, then grabs the bottle and shuffles back to the sofa. He sits down heavily and refills his glass.

As Rocco raises the glass to his lips, a noise sounds. He stops his hand midair, listens.

It sounds again. For a moment he's confused. Then he realizes it's the buzzer on his security panel. Someone is ringing his apartment from the entrance downstairs, and the sound is completely foreign to him because no one has yet come to visit him in this new place.

The buzzer buzzes again. Insistent.

Indecision immobilizes him.

He can't face anyone now. He decides to ignore it. Rocco swallows the rest of his second drink and pours another. He half passes out, wakes, drinks some more, and feels himself fading out again. The sound of the buzzer again jolts him conscious. Had he passed out at all?

Rocco mutters to himself as he pushes his weight up from the sofa. He stumbles toward the security panel on the wall next to the door but suddenly veers sideways and bumps a small table. A glass ashtray crashes to the floor and shatters. He blinks. The whole world sways. He's had far too much to drink to be walking.

He holds on to the dining table, steadying himself, then pins his gaze on the door. He takes a breath, and lurch-walks toward it. He bumps up against the wall, steadies himself, and squints at the buttons on the panel, trying to recall which ones to push. He presses one and the small monitor comes to life. Rocco frowns and tries to pull into focus the shape of the face looking into the camera from downstairs. The features slowly take form. His heart begins to race as he sees who it is.

"Rocco? We need to talk," comes the voice from the panel. "This will change everything. Please, let me in."

He stares as his brain struggles to process what's happening. But part of him knows. This is it—the end. This is his Ebenezer moment complete with a visit from the Ghost of his past. The time for his reckoning is nigh. But unlike Ebenezer Scrooge, Rocco does not see himself attaining redemption. Not from this Ghost.

# ANGELA

Angela and Rahoul ring the buzzer to Mason's apartment yet again. It's fully dark, and the city lights are blurred by a soft drizzle that has begun to fall.

"You should have called him first," Rahoul says.

"And tip him off?" She presses again. Still no answer. She gives an exasperated sigh and checks her watch.

"What do you want to do?"

She glances across the street. "We could wait in that coffee shop over there and watch the building to see when he comes home."

"What if he drives straight into the underground and goes up from the parking levels?"

"He's been using a cab for weeks. Probably because he drinks all the time. I reckon he's perpetually inebriated and just topping up his blood alcohol levels. My bet is a cab will drop him out front. Come."

She starts to cross the street just as a loud *thud* sounds to her left. Angela startles, stops, spins around.

A woman starts to scream, and scream, and scream.

"Shit!" Rahoul says and starts running down the sidewalk.

Angela is confused. "Rahoul?" She sees him stop where people are suddenly gathering farther up the sidewalk outside a clothing boutique. Angela runs up to join him. He turns to face her.

His brown face is pale, almost sickly green in the reflected lights from the windows of the nearby store. "Someone . . . fell."

"What?"

"Someone came down. From—" Rahoul points upward. "From one of the units up there. He hit the roof of that parked car and bounced right off onto the sidewalk there."

The gathering crowd is thickening. Voices rise. The woman stops screaming. In the distance Angela can hear the rise and fall of sirens. Adrenaline surges into her blood.

"Start filming," she says quickly as she begins to shoulder her way into the crowd collecting around a person lying in the rain on the sidewalk.

She pushes through, motioning for Rahoul to hurry. As someone steps out of her way, Angela is suddenly afforded a view of the man lying on the paving. Dark, shiny blood pools around his head. His limbs lie at impossible angles. Her brain takes a second to catch up with what her body already knows, and for a second Angela is rendered immobile, speechless. The sirens grow louder, louder, coming closer. The sound of them echoes down the canyons of glass skyscrapers as the rain begins to fall harder on the crowd, and on the man splayed on the pavement.

It's Mason.

And he looks very dead.

"He jumped." A woman points as a Vancouver Police Department officer comes up to her. "From up there. Up near the top. I saw him come down." Someone starts crying. Another man crouches down at Mason's side, feeling for a pulse at his neck. Yet another holds his limp hand.

A black-and-white VPD cruiser swerves to a dramatic stop across the street, blocking traffic. Two officers exit the cruiser and hurry over. More sirens sound. A fire truck arrives and parks behind the cruiser, followed by an ambulance.

Rahoul keeps filming, capturing it all. But Angela still can't move. Mason Gordon, a.k.a. Rocco Jones, is dead.

# JANE

The morning has dawned clear and bright after the nighttime rain, and the world sparkles as Jane drives to see Beth Haverton, the old manager from the Donut Diner, where Annalise Jansen worked part-time in 1976. Jane feels refreshed after her night with her mom in her old home. It was the best kind of nourishment she could hope for. She's also energized by her contact with Knox Raymond. He told Jane on the phone that her timing was fortuitous—he was actually on his way back from the interior expressly to come see her and to volunteer his input. He said he should arrive at the station later this morning. Jane is saving her questions for a face-to-face, where she can closely observe the old chief's reactions and possible tells.

She turns off Marine at the West Vancouver recreation center and slows her vehicle as she peers at the street addresses looking for the community facility where Haverton lives.

Jane finds the address, parks, and enters the lounge area of the community living facility. A woman in her senior years gets up from a chair and waves her over.

She offers her hand as Jane approaches. "Beth Haverton." Her grip is firm. Bold. Her body is wiry and her complexion tanned even this early in the season. "So nice to meet you, Sergeant. You look like your mom."

Jane laughs. "I wish, but I have my dad's genes."

Beth smiles. "More of a good blend then. Take a seat."

They both sit in the comfortable armchairs at a window overlooking a vegetable garden and lily pond. Beth might be seventy-nine, but she could easily be in her sixties and she could probably outrun, out-lift, and out-bike Jane even in prepregnancy days.

"This is nice," Jane says of the facility.

"It's not a seniors' home, just so you know," Beth offers with a grin. "It's a community-living concept. We have couples, singles, some young families, some middle-aged, and a smattering of goldens. There's a large community kitchen and dining area if anyone wants to share or have company. We have this communal lounge, a media room, the edible garden—we all have tending duties. It took some dreaming and years to get it up and running, but I like to think it's a model for more like this in the future. We look after each other. We're available to pool resources like child care, pet sitting, dog walking. It works."

Jane thinks of her mom's words.

*It takes a community—a village, a clan—to raise a child. It's not an unusual arrangement.*

Her mother suggested again last night that Jane move into half the house. The idea is beginning to take a small root inside her mind.

"Have you seen or heard the news about the remains discovered under the old skiers' chapel on Hemlock?"

"I've heard the chatter."

Jane shows her the photo of Annalise Jansen. "Do you remember her?"

Beth studies it. "Yes, I remember her well." She glances up. "Annalise. Is it her body?"

"Not confirmed, but I was hoping you might be able to tell me a little bit about what you remember of her working at the Donut Diner when you were manager?"

She nods. "Annalise worked there part-time in the year leading up to her going missing." Beth hesitates. "It was an awful affair, and frankly—it sounds strange to say, and I know sounds like victim blaming—there was something about Annalise that had it coming. Or rather, I should say, the news didn't surprise me that much."

"What do you mean?"

"The way she was carrying on."

"Explain."

She glances out the window, casting her mind back. "Annalise flirted with a much older married guy. Or at least I presumed he was married from the wedding band he wore. And the reason I mention this is because it got to a point where I was worried about her and called her on it."

"Who was the guy?"

"I don't recall if I ever learned his name, but he had a real lust thing going on for her. It became a bit of a game for him, I think. She was interested, and he was working it, and the more he worked it, the more she seemed to fall for it. In the end he was coming into the diner, like, five times a week, different times of day, and I think this is what gave me the notion that he had some kind of shift work."

"Any idea what kind of work?"

She shakes her head.

"Can you describe him?"

"He was tall. Not as much good-looking as he was built, powerful. He had a real presence and these enigmatic, sparkling green eyes—I remember that about him. I could see why Annalise fell for him. Sometimes he parked his car right outside the diner windows and watched her awhile before coming in. I could see she knew he was parked out there, observing. She'd smile to herself. I think it really flattered her. To be admired like that. But I called her aside after he left one day. I told her to be careful."

"Why?" Jane asks as she recalls her mother's description of the young Knox Raymond who came to her door: *handsome with amazing green eyes.*

Beth inhales deeply. "It was the way he watched her. The same calculating way a predator observes prey. And there was that wedding band on his ring finger. He always paid cash, too. Never left anything with his name on it."

"How did Annalise respond when you warned her to be careful?"

"She laughed. She said something to the effect, danger is not so obvious. It's the danger you can't see coming that you should really fear."

"How old would you say he was?"

"Mid to late twenties."

"Can you describe the car he parked outside the diner window?"

"Brown with a bit of a metallic sheen. One of those four-door Dodge sedans that were really popular at the time. I remember because my dad had one."

"Ms. Haverton, did the RCMP ever question you in connection with her disappearance?"

"Me? No. And please, call me Beth."

Jane nods. "So you never told them about this man?"

"Well, I did. The cops didn't come to me at the diner, though. I actually went into the station to tell them about this guy. There was a young female constable who listened and took some notes, but I don't know if the information was actually relayed to anyone who mattered. The police had also at that time become very focused on her boyfriend, Robbie Davine, and the rest of the Shoreview Six, and then they totally went with the theory that a young Black guy—her tutor—either ran off with her or did something bad to her and fled. I think it stopped them looking anywhere else at that point."

Jane reaches for her phone and pulls up one of the photos she found online and saved last night.

"Do you recognize this man?"

Beth reaches for the colorful glasses dangling around her neck. She perches them on her nose and leans forward, peering closer.

"My goodness." Her glance flicks up. "Yes. That's him. This is the guy from the diner. Is that . . . his wife and baby?"

"Are you certain this is the man?"

"As certain as I can be."

Adrenaline crackles through Jane's veins. "Thank you, Beth. You've been a great help."

On her way back to her car, she calls Melissa.

"Knox Raymond is now a priority," she says as she beeps her lock and climbs into her car. "I want interview room C available for when he comes in. I want him relaxed and thinking he's there totally of his own volition to assist."

# FAITH

It's a fresh new day, and Faith's parents have left the house for some scheduled medical tests. She helped guide her father into the car, but her mother insisted on doing the driving herself today. It's a fine line—this wanting to help, but not taking away her autonomy. And her mother is adrift again since the cops came, and while awaiting an official ID on the remains. So Faith let her mom do it. Hopefully it will distract her and provide her with something she can control. The hospital is only a few blocks away, and should her mom need help suddenly, Faith can always get an Uber to go to them, and then drive them home.

The morning also dawned cool, which is good. It gives Faith an excuse to make a fire. No one will question smoke coming out the chimney.

Faith gets down on her hands and knees, opens the grate and fireplace damper, then crumples newspaper into balls. Carefully she stacks kindling on top of the paper balls, then adds a few bigger split pieces of cedar to the kindling. She uses a lighter she found in the kitchen junk drawer, and she sets the pile alight. The flames whoosh to life and the fire begins to crackle. Heat is instant against her face. She leans back in a kneeling position, her hands on her thighs, watching. She wants to ensure the journal pages burn properly, and that there is no evidence left. In case the cops come by, it needs to appear as though she just had a regular fire going.

As she watches the orange flames crackle and spark, her minds slides back in time.

To a camping trip. With her big sister and her parents. It was supposed to be a nice family experience. A dark kind of stringy blackness and noise begins to scribble over the images trying to form in Faith's head—like a child's angry drawing with black crayon over a picture, erasing the memories before they can even be properly seen. It happens every time Faith tries to recall things from her childhood. A bad feeling creeps up her throat as snatches of sound and slices of images struggle to cut into her mind.

Angry parents. Yelling. Crumpled, empty beer cans. A plastic camping wineglass tipped over. A puddle of sour-smelling red wine on the picnic table, dripping through the slats. Ants beneath the table. Annalise arguing, being dramatic, storming furiously off from the campsite. Heading down a little path into a big forest of dark-green trees. Vanishing. A clutch of fear. Faith remembers the trees were so tall they hid even the sky and blocked out all light. A raven cawing on a dead snag. She frowns. When exactly was this trip? How old was she? Seven? Eight? Had her sister always been a petulant prima donna like that?

As she watches the flames dance and feels the warmth of the fire on her face, she tries to sink deeper into the memory.

Calling voices. Yelling. Different voices. Men. Women. *Annaleeeese, Annaleeese* . . . blasts of a survival whistle, clapping of hands to scare bears, someone mentioning a cougar in the area, and a sow with cubs. *Annaleeeese* . . . other campers helping, their calls echoing in the faraway canyon and bouncing back from the hills nearby, the haunting calls of the loons. *Annnaaaaleeeeese* . . . *Annnaaleeeese* . . .

Faith recalls clamping her hands tightly over her ears, shaking her head back and forth to make it all go away, her eyes scrunched tight. Her big sister gone—this couldn't be happening.

Then scribbles and dots cover it all up again like angry static.

She doesn't recall what happened next. She only remembers a bad, dark, dark feeling.

Frustration bites.

She did ask her mother some time ago what her snatches of memory were all about. Her mom just laughed and said Annalise had been sulking, again, and she stomped off into the woods that day and got lost. They found her before nightfall, and she was afraid and very sorry.

Faith has many gaps like this in her childhood memories. She spoke to the therapist who counseled her after her spousal abuse and divorce. Faith told the therapist she feared something was in fact really wrong with her. The therapist said memory gaps were a thing for women in her situation. Part of her years of trauma. She said Faith had been through a lot with her husband, and she should just try and relax, stop worrying, focus on her health and getting strong, and it might all come back.

But Faith worried. And the worst part was that Faith felt she knew all the answers even as her mind hid them for her.

She shakes herself, closes the fire grate, and goes downstairs to fetch the journal. She has decided she won't burn the backpack and the sock monkey. That will make a terrible smell and mess. She'll have to take those to the dump later, when she gets the car back.

She carries Annalise's journal upstairs, gets back onto her knees, and almost throws the whole book onto the blaze at once, but pauses. It might be better to rip out the pages in chunks and burn it in bits. The cover is coated with a padded plastic, and that will melt and cause a weird stink, too. Maybe even a toxic one. She doesn't want her mother detecting anything strange. She can always get rid of the cover with the sock monkey and backpack later.

She opens the grate and starts ripping out pages, feeding them one by one into the flames, watching them brown and curl, then quickly shrivel into translucent bits of filament that crumble into ash. As she feeds a bunch more pages into the fire, a strange and powerful feeling rises inside Faith's chest. Her face grows hotter from the flames.

*You're doing the right thing. This is for the best. The pregnant cop is going to come and tell us it's definitely Annalise's remains, but this has to end now. Here. Forever. For all their sakes.*

Then she sees something on the page in her hand. Faith stills.

Slowly she rereads the final two pages in her sister's journal—the words Annalise wrote the day before she never came home.

# KNOX

Knox sits on a chair in the North Van RCMP detachment reception area while the civilian assistant behind bullet-resistant glass goes to call Sergeant Jane Munro. His plan of attack after hearing about the remains discovery on TV was to hit this head-on—drive home and come at the investigators before they come at him. But Munro reached out to him first last night, and it's thrown him.

He did some research, though, and he knows a bit more about Munro now. He connected with an old contact from the Integrated Homicide Investigations Team based out of Surrey, and learned she's a sharp investigator with an excellent close rate and also a stickler for ethics. However, she's also apparently suffering from a degree of PTSD since her fiancé vanished in the mountains. Her mental stress manifested in an outburst at work that came close to costing the IHIT a case. She was subsequently transferred to a cold case unit of essentially one as a disciplinary measure, but she landed this corker of a chapel body case out of the gate.

Annalise Jansen's case.

Knox has not heard of any formal confirmation yet that it's Annalise, but he knows it has to be her.

His plan is to offer Munro assistance in a way that will direct things away from himself. He wants to ensure nothing comes up that will warrant her asking him for a DNA sample. He also basically just wants in.

He's desperate to know what's happening behind the scenes. He needs to be part of the thrill again.

A side door opens, and a pregnant woman in comfortable slacks and a blazer steps out. Her shiny brown hair is neatly tied back. Her cheeks are pink and her eyes bright. She offers him a smile as she comes forward.

"Chief Knox Raymond?"

Knox is momentarily taken aback. For all the talk of stress, Sergeant Jane Munro radiates energy. Mental health clearly can be an invisible demon. She offers her hand and he shakes it. Her grip is small but like a vise. This tells him Munro feels she has something to prove. It also reminds him to be cautious. It's easy to mistake appearances like hers as friendliness and to be thrown off guard.

"Thank you for coming in," she says. "We're grateful to find someone alive who was involved in the investigation."

Knox gives a big smile. "Well, I was just a rookie at the time. My involvement was minimal, but I thought I might be able to offer some context, or perhaps answer questions you might have."

"Your timing is perfect. Shall we talk somewhere more private?"

Before he can even answer, she starts toward the side door and opens it with her access card. She motions him in.

"This way, please."

She leads him down a corridor and opens a door to an interview room. She shows Knox in.

He removes his fishing cap. The room is clearly one of the casual, more friendly ones used to question children or those who might require a nonthreatening environment.

"Take a seat." She holds her hand out to the sofa. Knox sits. He notices the CCTV camera up on the ceiling and wonders if anyone is watching.

"I haven't seen news of a formal identification," he says. "Is it definitely her—Annalise Jansen?"

She regards him in silence for a moment. The unease that started after her call last night deepens in him.

"I saw speculation online that it was her," Knox tries to explain, but regrets his words the instant they come out of his mouth. He's fallen straight into the silence trap, trying to fill empty space because of his own guilt.

"We're pretty certain it's her," she says. "Familial DNA will tell us more in a day or two."

"What about Darryl Hendricks?" he asks. "Any new developments with him?"

"Not yet."

A knock sounds on the door and it opens. A tall, redheaded guy with very pale skin steps in. He hands Munro a blue folder. She takes it, sets it on the coffee table in front of her.

"Anything else, boss?" the redhead asks.

"I'll let you know. Stand by."

The redhead glances briefly in Knox's direction, then steps out of the room. The door closes quietly behind him. Knox is instantly leery. He's a veteran. He did his time in interrogations and he's reading the room, sensing an underlying adversarial tone. Munro did not bother to introduce her colleague, and this does not bode well, either.

His gaze flicks to the camera, and anger begins to bud low in his gut. He was a police chief. He held power over people like Munro and the redhead. He doesn't deserve to be treated like scum by some pregnant woman with PTSD who's been demoted to cold cases.

"So what can you tell us off the top of your head about the cases?" she asks. "What stands out in your memory? Anything you feel we should know that might be missing from the case documentation?"

Knox moistens his lips and leans back, casually hooking an arm across the back of the sofa, taking up space, using his body language to project false confidence.

"Well, at the time the initial working theory was that Annalise Jansen left town with Darryl Hendricks, either voluntarily or she was abducted by him," Knox says. "Or Hendricks did something to her and then fled."

She smiles slightly. "We can rule out the abduction scenario now since her remains are still here. What was your take on Hendricks? Did he have motive or capacity to do Jansen harm in your opinion?" Her gaze locks on his. Knox senses a calculating mind behind those deceptively warm eyes.

"Like I said, I was just a rookie and not really privy to the team thinking. My job was to pound the pavement going door-to-door looking for additional witnesses. Unfortunately there was a delay of a few days between when Jansen disappeared to when her parents reported her absence, so we lost some really valuable time. Same with Hendricks."

Munro nods, reaches for the folder on the table, opens it, and scans a page. "From the file it seems no additional witnesses were located as a result of the canvassing?" She poses it like a question.

"No. The only witnesses were a guy who lived across the street from Mary Metcalfe who saw Metcalfe and Jansen arguing on their way home, plus a married couple who lived in the last house on the cul-de-sac, on the boundary of the woods."

"The Janyks?"

"I—ah, yes, I think that was their name."

"They claim they saw a metallic-brown sedan and a woman they thought might be Annalise Jansen approaching it?"

Knox feels a tightening of tension. "That sounds about right, yes."

"Did anyone mention at the time that Jansen was pregnant? Did the possibility ever come up?"

Knox's pulse increases further. He's careful how he responds. "Negative. It was a shocker when I saw that on the news. A true shocker."

"Knowing this now—that she was about three months pregnant at the time she went missing—how might you have approached the '76 investigation differently? I mean, if it were you handling it at the time?"

He blows out some air, buying a moment to take his pulse rate down. This is his chance to deflect. "You know, I actually thought about that on the drive into town. I think I definitely would've looked a lot harder at the boyfriend, Robbie Davine. Possibly the other guys in her circle, too. She was a pretty girl. And there were rumors among some of the partygoers that Jansen was flirting with several guys at the event, and she was fairly intoxicated. Some believed she might have even gotten it off with one of the other guys that night. I'd look for domestic violence–type motives on the part of her boyfriend: jealousy, revenge, vindictiveness."

"So why did the team pull their focus back from Davine?"

He gives a shrug. "Again, I was just a lackey at the time. But I know the investigators became very focused on Hendricks when they learned he was missing, too, and he was also last seen at that party. Perhaps the flirting-jealousy thing just took a back seat."

Munro holds his gaze. "Any particular guy in the friend circle you'd look at, apart from the boyfriend?"

Knox feels hot. And thirsty. He's a bit hungover, he realizes. There's not much air in this room, either. He tugs at his collar slightly. "Well, her friend, Metcalfe, did say there was a guy on a bike with a black helmet who seemed to be following them home that night. She couldn't name the bike model, but said it was black with chrome. Rocco Jones's older brother, Zane Jones, rode a bike that matched the description. Odd siblings, those two. Absent parents. Tons of cash. Wild boys."

Munro returns her attention to the folder. "But the Shoreview Six stated Zane Jones drove them in his vehicle that night?"

"I can tell you there was a lot of chatter about those kids lying about that. Their stories were suspiciously identical. Maybe Zane wasn't driving. Maybe they lied because they were underage and over the limit."

"So you figure Zane Jones might *not* have been with them? He could have been on that bike?"

"Could be. And he can't speak for himself now. He was killed a year or two later in a bike accident on the Sea to Sky. He was also known to have an eye for Annalise Jansen."

"That's not in the files."

"Like I said, the team fixated on Hendricks. Tunnel vision can be the death of an investigation."

She glances down, reads more. "Zane's vehicle was a—"

"Metallic-brown Dodge Dart Custom '73."

She glances up. "Good memory, chief."

"Some cases stick. Especially ones that are never closed. They burrow under the skin, you know?"

"I know." Munro rubs her chin as she studies the contents of the folder. She turns a page. "Says here that the vehicle seen parked at the end of the cul-de-sac was also a metallic-brown four-door sedan." She meets his gaze. "Any possibility it could have been members of the Shoreview Six waiting for Annalise Jansen to arrive home?"

"There was some speculation about that, yes. But the witnesses—the Janyks—apparently didn't pay attention to what the make and model of the vehicle was that they saw parked near the woods. Just said it was an 'ordinary' brown sedan. And the Shoreview kids denied being there."

Munro frowns at something in the files, and Knox is seized by an uncomfortable sensation that her file folder is a prop, that she already has all the information stored in her head and she's playing him. She glances up. "Did *you* witness Jansen drunk and being flirtatious at the party?"

His breathing catches. *She knows.* She's known the whole damn time he was one of the officers who responded to the nuisance call that night.

Knox clears his throat and speaks slowly, calmly. "I witnessed it myself, yes—her being drunk. I was one of the units who responded to the call that night."

"And was she flirtatious? I mean, with you specifically?"

His gaze locks hard on hers. Silence swells. The room grows warmer. Panic begins to tickle low in his belly.

"She was," he says finally. "With all the officers. Several of the girls were. It happens. Badge bunnies. Girls who've had too much to drink and come on to the cops who arrest them."

"Chief Knox, had you actually met Annalise Jansen prior to that party on the night of September 3, 1976?"

"Excuse me?"

"Had you seen her around town? I mean, it's not a huge place—especially in the seventies. You lived locally, no?"

This is when Knox realizes Sergeant Munro has done background research specifically on him. His only option now is to hew as closely to the truth as he can; otherwise it could go very badly for him indeed.

Acutely conscious of the camera, he clears his throat. "I lived maybe five klicks away from the Jansen home as the crow flies. It was our first house. My wife and I bought it early in '76 with a loan from my in-laws. We were at the time expecting our first child. So, yes, I had seen the young teen around the neighborhood."

"Hard to miss a girl like Annalise, I imagine. As you said, she was very pretty."

He says nothing.

"Did you ever frequent the Donut Diner on Marine, Chief Knox?"

Blood drains from Knox's head. *Stay calm, stay cool.* "We all did. Donuts. Cops. Diners." He laughs, but it rings hollow to his own ears.

"Right." She smiles again. "My dad was also a cop. RCMP. The Donut Diner was located on Marine even during his time. Big car dealership down there now."

"The place has changed remarkably over the decades." Knox's heart thumps hard against his ribs. In his mind he can suddenly see pretty, blonde Annalise with her lean, tanned limbs coming up to his table in the diner. He sees how her breasts pushed against her apron with the donut logo. How she smiled and seductively side-eyed him as she poured his bottomless cup of coffee. How those big, clear eyes invited him to try. How he'd softly hummed that Hot Chocolate song about miracles and sexy things and it would make her blush. How she called him Mr. HC, after Hot Chocolate, the group who made the song famous. Knox moistens his lips, says nothing more.

Munro takes a photo from the folder. She hesitates, then sets it on the coffee table and slides it toward him. "This was one of the items found in the shallow grave with Annalise Jansen's remains. Jansen might have been wearing it when she sustained two fatal blows to her head, or it could have come off someone else, perhaps her assailant, in a struggle."

"You have evidence she was killed by two blows?"

"There's evidence, yes. Obviously there remains a chance the trauma was the result of an accident, but given the manner in which she went missing, and where she ended up . . ." Her voice fades as she waits for Knox to look at the image.

He picks it up and slowly glances down. He studies it.

His gut churns. Knox keeps his gaze fixed on the image, fighting to show no reaction because he knows she's watching closely for one.

*I've walked into an effing trap of my own making. But given what she seems to know, she'd have come for me anyway.*

"An RCMP badge?" he says quietly. "*This* was with her remains?"

She nods. "With some textile attached to the pin. We'll be getting analysis on the textile remnants, of course, but this item was not listed on her missing persons file. Did it ever come up with the task force?"

"Not to my knowledge."

"Any idea why she was wearing it?"

"No idea."

Her gaze lasers his. "Or where she got it?"

"No."

She reaches for the photo, slips it back into the file. "So how often did you visit the Donut Diner?"

"What?"

"Once a month? Once a week? Several times per week?"

He swallows. "I can't recall."

"The old manager, Beth Haverton, thinks she remembers you coming in up to five times a week at one point."

His heart begins to pound fast and angry against his ribs. "I might have. How would she even recall it was me, though? I don't think I ever introduced myself."

"Your green eyes." She smiles slightly. "My mother remembers them, too, from when you knocked on her door during the canvassing."

"I personally stood out in your mother's memory like that? I must have been *that* good-looking if she remembered me."

"Apparently you were. She said she recalled you specifically after she saw an interview with you on TV when you were appointed WVPD chief, and you mentioned having worked on the Jansen case as a young RCMP officer, and canvassing neighborhoods." Munro pauses. "*Same bright-green eyes,* she said."

"Well, well." He stares at her. This he had not anticipated—not even close. "Where are we going with this, Sergeant?"

"So you were aware Annalise Jansen worked there?"

"She served me a couple of times."

Munro regards him in silence for a few beats, and Knox feels heat creep into his face. "Is this what you meant when you said you'd seen Annalise around the neighborhood?"

He says nothing.

"Did you request to be seated in her section in the diner, Chief Raymond?"

"I'm not appreciating your insinuations here."

"Is that a yes or a no?"

He glowers at her in silence.

"Did you occasionally park your car outside the diner window and watch Annalise Jansen working inside before entering the diner?"

Knox's anger suddenly turns white hot. "I have no idea what you are talking about."

She meets his eyes. "What kind of vehicle did you drive at the time?"

"What's that got to do with anything?"

She removes another image from her folder, slides it toward him. Knox picks it up. It's a printed copy of a small story that appeared in the local newspaper in 1976 congratulating him—a local police officer—and his wife on their new baby girl.

"Is that your car in the photo of you and your wife, Meghan Raymond, holding your new baby?"

"It was a very common model at the time. Yes, it was ours."

"What is the model?"

He feels the camera up on the ceiling burning into him. He feels people listening. Quietly, he says, "A Dodge Dart Custom."

"Metallic brown. Four-door sedan."

"That's right."

"Just like the one parked at the end of the cul-de-sac near the Jansen home on the night of September 3, 1976?"

"I told you—it was a very, very common make of car in the seventies."

"What time did your shift end on September 3, 1976, Chief Raymond?"

"I have no idea."

"Did you clock out right after the party callout?"

He surges to his feet and yanks his cap back onto his head. "We're done here, Sergeant. I'm not liking your tone." He starts for the door.

"Will you be staying in town, Chief Raymond?"

He spins to face her and says, voice low, "I cut my fishing trip short and drove all the way back down here of my own volition to offer my assistance, and I'm treated like this—this interrogation? If you want to talk to me again, contact my lawyer." He reaches for the door handle.

"Before you go, sir"—she comes to her feet—"would you be willing to provide a DNA sample? Just for elimination purposes."

"You want my DNA? You get yourself a fucking warrant." Knox lets himself out of the interview room and marches for the exit, blood boiling.

This was a mistake.

A big fucking mistake.

He thought he could play the woman. But she played him all the way, like a fucking fiddle.

He needs to get out of Dodge. The sooner the better.

# ANGELA

Angela sits with Rahoul in the editing booth. They came into the office super early this morning, both feeling drained after being questioned by VPD officers last night. The VPD asked to see their raw footage of Mason lying dead and broken on the sidewalk amid the gathering crowd, and Angela and Rahoul watch this footage again now.

The faces of the people gathered around Mason—or Rocco Jones—are sheened with blue light that shines from the adjacent boutique window. Other snippets show red and blue flashes from the emergency vehicles reflecting in street puddles and glinting off droplets of rain. Angela forgot it had started to rain. She feels spacey as she studies footage that captures half-naked mannequins in the store window. The juxtaposition gives the whole scene a horror-ish, noir tone. She rubs her arms.

"I like that—we should keep that." Rahoul points to a frame that features a homeless person passed out and covered with pieces of cardboard near Mason's broken body. "I like the irony," he says. "The fall of man—Mason Gordon, a.k.a. Rocco Jones, and this nameless person."

Angela inhales. "I hate it."

"What?"

She gets up, paces. She has not been able to shake the queasiness curdling in her stomach. One minute Mason was the bane of her life. Now he's gone. Angela feels it's partly her fault.

"You think he jumped after he saw us buzzing to get in?" she asks. "Maybe he jumped because he knew I'd expose him on TV. And he thought it was over."

"He could've been pushed, Angela."

"I heard one of the VPD cops say he left a note."

"Could've been a ruse. Plenty of murderers have left fake suicide notes."

She runs her hands through her hair. She can't breathe.

"You okay, Ange?"

She pivots and strides toward the exit. "Just need some air."

She leaves the studio and goes down in the elevator, trying to avoid glancing at her own reflection in the mirrors, but she can't help it, and looks. She sees a woman she doesn't quite recognize anymore. Someone hard. Someone who has lost empathy in her hunt for clicks, for viewers, for fast-food feels. Angela can't quite articulate it to herself, but hearing Mason's body land on a car as he came down from his apartment on the twenty-second floor has cracked something open inside her. For the first time she sees in herself what those people who send her hate mail see.

*Disrespectful, a clickbait c**t, unethical, a life wrecker, a cheap excuse for and shame to real journalism.*

She steps out into the morning air and starts walking fast, faster, faster, trying to physically process what she witnessed, seeking to exorcise this self-blame that has taken hold in her head. She is *not* responsible for Mason Gordon's death.

If her news director had allowed her to go to air last night, she'd be over it already. But the CBCN-TV legal team ordered her to hold off. They insist on all Mason's next of kin being properly notified. CBCN-TV wants to be "respectful." Mason was an employee, and management needs to cover their own asses. They were apparently aware Mason might be having some mental health issues, and there's a record on file that his superior recently discussed this with HR. The station wants to ensure "all the legal bases are covered."

So there goes her scoop anyway.

Perhaps she's actually relieved.

Perhaps she should've told the VPD cops last night that Mason Gordon was once Rocco Adam Jones and a person of interest in a cold case investigation on the North Shore.

As she walks she begins to breathe harder, deeper, better, and her brain clears a little. She begins to mull over the situation in fresh context. She's pretty certain the VPD has no idea yet that Sergeant Jane Munro might have an interest in Mason Gordon. The VPD and RCMP operate in different jurisdictions. It could take some time for Munro's team to actually learn that a man who fell from a building in downtown Vancouver is in fact one of the Shoreview Six, and is now dead. And he may have jumped—or not.

An idea begins to hatch in Angela's brain. She stops near a city dog park bench and reaches for her phone.

# JANE

"Wow," Duncan says quietly as Jane enters the incident room.

"Did you all catch it on the camera feed?" she asks.

Duncan and the others nod.

"Sure has taken a new and interesting turn," Tank says.

Melissa says, "But how does it connect with the Shoreview Six? Or does it?"

"One thing we know for sure," Yusra says, "they were all at the party—Annalise Jansen, Darryl Hendricks, the Shoreview Six, plus Knox Raymond. That's a nexus. And each one of them had some prior relationship to Annalise, who—likely by the end of that night or shortly thereafter—ended up dead. I'm more than curious to see the results of the fetus DNA profile now."

"No kidding," Duncan says. "But if we want to compare it to the chief's DNA, we need something solid to secure a warrant, because he's not going down easy."

Jane nods. "And whoever made Jansen pregnant—it did not happen at the party, but around three months prior."

"Possibly news of the pregnancy came out that night, at the party?" Yusra says. "It would go to motive. My bet is Knox Raymond is shit-scared about what that DNA is going to reveal. What do you think his game is, coming in like this? Heading it off? Trying to appear helpful so we look somewhere else?"

"Possibly intent to redirect the investigative narrative." Jane's thoughts turn to Noah Gautier. Noah would probably remind her that a certain kind of human predator needs to return to the scene of a crime, often trying to insert themselves into the investigation. Or into news around the case, like Hugo Glucklich did. Or perhaps like Knox Raymond just did.

A phone on a desk buzzes and Melissa picks up. She nods and holds up the receiver.

"A call for you, Sergeant. A woman who apparently has new information on the Annalise Jansen case. She wants to speak directly to you."

Jane heads into her glassed-in office and picks up the call.

"Munro."

"Sergeant, this is Angela Sheldrick from CBCN-TV, and before you hang up, my cameraman and I were on scene last night when a guy fell—or was pushed—from a twenty-second-story apartment in downtown Vancouver. VPD responded. His name has not yet been released, and notification of next of kin is still pending, so we have not aired the news, but I thought it would be of interest to you that the man was our CBCN-TV program director, Mason Gordon. Thirty years ago, Mason officially changed his name. He was Rocco Jones, one of the Shoreview Six." She pauses. "He has a criminal record, a history of substance abuse and violence. And now he's dead."

# JANE

Jane and Duncan are shown into Mason Gordon's, a.k.a. Rocco Jones's, apartment by VPD Detective Aaron Bates. When Jane contacted the VPD after Angela Sheldrick's surprising call, she was connected to Bates, who told her it appeared to be a suicide and that the occupant left a note.

"This is how the unit looked when first responders arrived," Bates says. "Nothing stood out as foul play. But since you told me Gordon is a person of interest in your chapel case—" He glances at her. "Possibly you'll want to take the lead on this?"

"Where was the note found?" Jane asks, focusing on her first impressions before negotiating jurisdictional issues.

Bates points to a long coffee table in front of a sofa that faces the windows and the sliding glass door. "On the table there."

A whiskey glass on the table contains some amber liquid. Beside the glass stands an empty bottle of Macallan twelve-year single malt, and a toppled bottle of liquid Benadryl. There's a pen, a pad of lined paper. A red tie lies in a crumpled heap on the sofa cushion.

"Benadryl cocktails?" Duncan says quietly.

Jane's gaze goes to the sliding glass door that leads to a small balcony. The wood floor in front of the door is puddled with water.

"We found the slider open wide, drapes blowing," Bates says. "The floor is wet from where the rain came in. That chair outside on the deck was on its side like that. He could have stepped up on the chair, used it to launch himself over the railing, knocking the chair over in the process."

"Or someone strong could have helped him along," Duncan muses.

Jane turns to face the apartment door that leads back into the hallway. A suit jacket and a coat hang on hooks near the door. A pair of dress shoes, tan, lie on the floor near the door.

"He fell without a jacket?" she asks.

"Affirmative. And no shoes," Bates says. "His tie is on the sofa there. Management at CBCN-TV said Gordon left work around six p.m. yesterday. Apparently unusual for him. He'd taken to staying very late on a regular basis, and occasionally sleeping in his office. The neighbors on either side of his unit say they heard him arriving home around ten p.m. last night. He was knocking about, making noise like he was drunk. Both neighbors said this was not unusual. Gordon routinely came home unstable on his feet."

"So he cabbed? Or took an Uber?" Duncan asks. "I'm presuming he didn't drive in that state?"

Bates says, "CBCN-TV said Gordon habitually cabbed. He stopped driving around the same time management started noticing his drinking and became concerned about his mental health. They'd noticed a corresponding deterioration in his work, mistakes, and he was also drinking on the job. They said it's not unusual for management to have a nip or two in the station culture, but usually only after hours. Occasionally with clients. But indications were that Gordon had begun working over the limit, and they'd scheduled an appointment with HR to strategize how best to approach him about taking some time off to perhaps seek treatment."

"So he'd been informed about their concern?" Jane asks, thinking this could be a motivating factor in Rocco Jones taking his life, if that was indeed what happened here. Or perhaps all the news about the chapel body possibly belonging to his old school friend Annalise rattled old guilt.

"Not yet, according to CBCN-TV."

"Okay, so he leaves the station around six p.m., arrives home around ten p.m. Any idea where he went in the interim?" she asks.

Bates shakes his head. "Maybe somewhere to drink. We've made contact with his most recent ex-wife, who says this would not be out of character."

"Where's the note now?" Jane asks.

"Being processed." Bates hands her an iPad. "This is an image of the note. Ex-wife confirms it looks like his writing, especially when inebriated."

Jane studies the image. The note is messily handwritten on what appears to be the lined paper from the pad still on the table. She reads the words.

*His VW bus and body is in Blackwater Lake. Below the cliffs.*

*Can't live with the burden of their deaths any longer. It's eaten me up. Time to end. There can be no way forward for me. Karma has come to collect. I'm sorry.*

*Goodbye.*

*Rocco Jones—Mason Gordon*

Jane hands the iPad to Duncan to read.

"'His VW bus'?" Duncan glances at Jane. "Does he mean Darryl Hendricks?"

"Sounds like."

"Where's Blackwater?" Duncan asks.

"Where that photo of the kids we have on the crime board was taken. It's a caldera lake near Furry Creek, accessed via a logging road. People go up to the cliffs to rope swing, jump, dive, swim. At the highest point the cliffs are probably about forty feet above the water. If someone drove or pushed a vehicle off those cliffs, it would go down super deep. The cliff shadows and depth of the lake make the water appear black, and it would likely be impossible to see a vehicle at the bottom of the lake. Perhaps not even from the air above."

"'Can't live with the burden of their deaths'—is that a confession?" Duncan asks. "He killed both Darryl Hendricks and Annalise Jansen?"

Jane thinks out loud. "Okay, let's play this through: Rocco Jones comes home from someplace he went after work. Perhaps a pub. He stumbles out of the elevator, dropping his keys et cetera in the hallway outside his unit, knocking about and making enough noise for the neighbors to notice he's arriving. He enters his unit, kicks off his shoes by the door there, removes his coat, jacket. Yanks his tie loose, tosses it on the sofa, goes to the drinks cabinet there. He grabs a glass and that bottle of Macallan, brings it to the sofa, sits. Maybe he mixes a Benadryl cocktail for some kind of max numbing effect. He gets morose. Decides to end it all. Writes the note. Drinks more to take the edge off, opens the sliding door, goes outside on socked feet into the rain. Climbs on that chair. And jumps?"

"That was our initial thinking," Bates says. "His ex also felt this was a likely scenario. She said Mason—she did not know him as Rocco Jones—had addiction issues even when they first married, and he was prone to occasional violent outbursts, which he often couldn't remember due to his blackout drinking. She believed there was some trauma in his past that fueled his destructive behavior patterns."

"What kind of trauma?" Jane asks.

"She didn't know, and Gordon never confessed to anything when she prompted him."

Duncan says, "Maybe he was screwed up by whatever he did on the night of September 3, 1976."

"You mentioned this was your initial thinking," Jane says. "What are your subsequent thoughts? What changed?"

"What you've told us, for one. Plus we found a second whiskey glass in the sink," Bates says. "It was rinsed. Our thinking was it could have been Mason Gordon's from sometime earlier, but then we checked his video intercom panel."

"Someone *else* was here—inside his unit?" Jane asks.

"Come take a look." Bates leads Jane and Duncan to a panel mounted on the wall next to the door. "This apartment complex was constructed a few years ago, and every unit was fitted with one of these video intercom systems that links to a panel with a camera at the main entrance downstairs. The individual systems each have video-recording functionality. They record the last five interactions—audio and video—depending on the duration of each interaction, before beginning to overwrite the oldest ones." He glances at Jane. "Mason Gordon was buzzed twice after he came home at ten p.m. Two separate visits. Take a look."

Anticipation ripples through Jane as Bates uses a gloved finger to press a button on the panel. The most recent call begins to replay.

A slightly fish-eyed image of Angela Sheldrick appears on the small screen. Behind her Jane can see her cameraman, Rahoul Basra. She hears Angela's voice.

"Mason? Are you there, Mason? We need to talk. I know about the criminal record in Bakersfield. I know you changed your name from Rocco Jones and that you're one of the Shoreview Six. I need to go to air with this, but I want to give you an opportunity to give your side of the story." Silence. Jane sees Angela turn to face Rahoul. She says something quietly to him, then presses the intercom button.

"Mason? Rocco? Are you there? Can we come in? We need to talk."

Jane exchanges a fast glance with Duncan. Her own call with Angela plays through her mind.

◆ ◆ ◆

*"He was Rocco Jones, one of the Shoreview Six. He has a criminal record, a history of substance abuse and violence . . . I was at his apartment, trying to give him an opportunity to talk. When he didn't let us in, we left the*

*complex to go wait across the street. That's when his body came down. I think he might have jumped because of me." A long pause. "I also have to wonder if there's a chance he was pushed. Rahoul—my cameraman—and I have been questioned by the VPD. I—we didn't at the time admit we knew Mason was Rocco Jones and one of the Shoreview Six. I was hoping for a scoop."*

*"And now?"*

*"They'll find out eventually, but I want you to know stat—I figured time might be critical." Another pause, as though she's wavering. "I'm sorry for jumping the gun earlier. With the eavesdropping. I—I'd like to work with you properly on this."*

*"I don't 'work with' media, Ms. Sheldrick."*

*"I—I didn't have to call you, Sergeant. I'm not looking for gratitude. I just wouldn't mind being looped in when and if you have information to share that comes out of this."*

◆ ◆ ◆

"He didn't let those two in," Jane says. "Angela said he didn't respond." She turns to Bates. "Who visited Gordon prior to Sheldrick and Basra?"

"Unidentified as yet. But digital records from the security system show Mason Gordon did let the other caller in." Bates presses PLAY with his gloved finger.

Jane stares as the features of the caller take shape on the monitor. Her pulse quickens—she's seen that face before, but where? She listens to the audio.

"Rocco? Are you there, Rocco? Let me in. I have something to share with you. Something that will change everything."

"Are you thinking what I'm thinking?" Duncan asks.

Jane's mind shoots to an image pinned up on their crime board. Very quietly, she says, "Isaias Osman. Jill Wainwright Osman's husband. He was here, and Rocco let him in."

# JANE

Jane sits across from Isaias Osman at a table in an interview room at the North Van detachment. Duncan sits at her side. The rest of the team—including Jane's superior, who has now been looped in—watches the interview via camera feed on a monitor in the incident room. Meanwhile, an RCMP search and dive team has been dispatched to Blackwater Lake about an hour's drive north.

Isaias was picked up at his residence near Eagle Harbour at 12:35 p.m. He was found home alone and came voluntarily to the station.

"Mr. Osman, you do understand this interview is being recorded?" Jane asks.

Isaias nods. "I also know I have right to legal counsel, but for the record, I'm here of my own free will. I have nothing to hide. And before you start with the detailed timeline questions, yes, I went to visit Rocco Jones last night. I buzzed for entry a couple of times before he answered. He then let me in."

"You were captured on his security camera saying"—Jane reads from the transcript in front of her—"*Rocco? Are you there, Rocco? Let me in. I have something to share with you. Something that will change everything.*" She looks up, meets his gaze. "Did you know Rocco Jones was Mason Gordon?"

"Not until earlier that evening, when my wife told me their old school friend was one of the Shoreview Six and he'd changed his name after being arrested, going into rehab, and trying to clean up."

"Why did your wife tell you this last night?"

He swallows and casts his gaze down at the table for a moment. He breathes in deeply, then looks up.

"This is hard for me. But I need to do the right thing. Yesterday I arrived home around nine p.m. My business trip was canceled, so my arrival was unexpected. I thought I'd surprise my wife, Jill. But I found her with guests—I surprised her, all right." He pauses. "It was the Shoreview Six. They gathered at my house to get their stories straight about that night in 1976. The group dispersed as soon as I arrived. Jill broke down when I confronted her about what was going on, and she told me everything. She hoped if she was entirely honest and forthcoming, she might save our marriage, but . . ." His voice fades as he takes a moment to compose himself. His eyes shine with emotion. "My wife is not who I thought she was, Detectives. I knew nothing of her past, or her lies. Or what kind of a person she was. I can now see how our entire relationship was founded on her guilt. I—I just don't think there's a way back from here."

Jane says, "You say your wife told you 'everything' that happened that night in '76?"

He nods. "Yes."

"You believe it's the truth?" asks Duncan.

"I do. I really do. She has no reason left to lie to me. She put her fate into my hands. She knew I'd come straight here."

"Yet you didn't, Mr. Osman," Jane says. "You went to the apartment of Rocco Jones, who is now dead."

He says nothing.

Duncan says, "What did you mean when you said you wanted to tell Rocco something that *would change everything*?"

"The hard truth. For forty-seven years, the rest of the group has allowed Rocco to believe he alone was responsible for murdering a fellow student."

"Darryl Hendricks? Or Annalise Jansen?"

"Darryl. Rocco believed he'd killed him. But the truth is, while he swung once at Darryl with a tire iron, he was apparently so drunk he fell over and passed out. He couldn't remember anything from that point, and he certainly didn't know who actually killed anyone, or where any bodies were taken."

"So out of the goodness of your heart, you wanted to make him feel better?" Duncan asks. "How nice."

A small flicker of anger ignites in Isaias Osman's eyes. "He deserved the truth. We all do. Telling him was part of my own processing, too. There are a few things you need to know about me, Detectives. I'm a religious man, and an honest man. My entire life is built on my moral compass, my empathy. When I fled Eritrea as a refugee, it was the kindness of others that helped me survive. Not only survive, but thrive, and my gratitude, my vow, has been to use that as my true north going forward. Perhaps you can't fathom a man like me, Detectives, but that's your problem, not mine. I wanted to free Rocco from his pain, and I also needed to talk to him, to ask him for more context. I . . . it was a lot to absorb. It didn't feel real hearing all that from just my wife, and I did drive here first, to the station, but I had trouble coming in. I was still digesting the news. I figured talking to Rocco would help."

"But now he's dead."

"I didn't kill him. He was alive and in his apartment when I left."

"Did he offer you a drink?" Jane asks.

"A whiskey, Macallan, yes. I had a small one. He was quite drunk."

"What was he drinking?"

"Same. Whiskey."

"Any medications visible?"

"I didn't see any."

"You say Rocco didn't know anything about bodies being taken anywhere, yet he left a note claiming he did."

"If he did, it was because I told him what my wife told me, that Darryl's VW with his body inside was pushed into Blackwater Lake."

"But if Rocco didn't kill them, why might his note imply he was responsible?" Jane asks. "For more than one death."

"I don't know what his note said, or why. I only know that when I walked into his apartment, he appeared terrified, as though he was seeing a ghost. I realized later why—I looked a lot like Darryl when I was younger. I imagine if Darryl was lucky enough to have lived this long, we'd look similar still. When I left Rocco, he appeared utterly heartbroken, filled with remorse, emotional. I thought some of that was the drink. And he still blamed himself. He said the fact that he'd swung at Darryl hasn't changed, and if he hadn't swung, the others might have dialed back. Perhaps the false narrative drummed into his head by the others was so hardwired into his brain he didn't know how to go forward. Or perhaps it was his addiction fueled by his lifelong guilt that ultimately took him over the balcony. Or a mix of it all."

"You didn't come to the police station after you left the apartment, either," Duncan says.

"I wanted to see my wife one more time before I did. I thought she might not have left home yet, but she had. I had a bourbon, went to sleep. I was trying to call her hotel when your people showed up."

Jane says, "Okay, let's start at the beginning, Mr. Osman. What did your wife, Jill Wainwright Osman, say happened on Friday night, September 3, 1976?"

He moistens his lips, glances at the camera. "After the police arrived, they all left the party—Robbie Davine, Claude Betancourt, Rocco Jones, Jill, and Cara Constantine."

"No Zane?" Duncan asks.

"She didn't mention Zane was with them. She said Claude was driving Zane's car. The boys dropped the girls off at Cara's house to change for the woods. They then went down near the quay to buy booze. After they bought liquor from a motel off-sales, they saw Darryl Hendricks's orange-and-white bus turning into a laneway beside a tire shop. They parked him in, and jumped him when he got out of his vehicle. Rocco picked up a lug wrench, swung, and then fell over, knocking his own head and passing out. Darryl landed Robbie some good defensive punches. Apparently this triggered Claude, who grabbed a second lug wrench and started beating Darryl around the head and torso with it. Robbie gathered himself and laid in, too, using the wrench Rocco had dropped. Darryl went down. The two boys kept beating him until they realized he was not breathing and no longer responsive." He reaches for the paper cup of water in front of him, swallows deeply. His hands are shaking.

"And this is what your wife told you?"

"Yes. It's what she learned from Cara later that night in '76. Cara had heard it all from Robbie when he came to her house after."

"What happened next?" asks Jane.

"Robbie and Claude panicked. They bundled unconscious Rocco and the dead and bleeding Darryl into the back of Darryl's VW bus. Claude got into the VW driver's seat. Robbie got into the Dodge. And they drove north. They went to Blackwater Lake, a place they knew well, near Furry Creek. They figured if they pushed the VW off the road at the top of the cliffs, it would go down deep. At Blackwater they put Rocco in the Dodge, then they pushed the van off the edge with Darryl's body inside. They drove Rocco back to his place, dumped him in his bed, then showered and changed—Rocco lived in a garden cottage with his brother, Zane, who only returned home the next morning. Robbie and Claude then made a plan. They drove to Mary's place in the Dodge and dropped Claude off at her house, where Claude persuaded Mary to be his alibi. Robbie drove to Cara's place and did the same. Cara, who always wanted Robbie to herself, obliged easily. The next day Cara convinced Jill to stay consistent with their stories. Jill said she couldn't unless she knew exactly why. So Cara, who was pretty stressed at the time, told her what Robbie said they'd done."

"And why did Robbie tell Cara everything?" Jane asks.

"Apparently murder is no simple matter, Detectives. The kids were in a state of panic. They needed to talk it through. Cara helped Robbie streamline and memorize the story." He pauses. "The six made a pledge. And they've stuck to it for forty-seven years."

"Why did they jump Darryl?" Jane asks.

"Cara had told them all that Darryl was messing around with Annalise and that Darryl had sex with her near the pool on the night of the party."

"Did they?"

"I don't know. But the boys believed Cara's story—they wanted to teach Darryl a lesson."

"Some lesson," says Duncan.

"It got out of hand."

Jane regards Isaias Osman. He seems genuine. She glances at Duncan. She can see he believes Isaias, too.

"Mr. Osman," she says, "what about Annalise Jansen? What happened to her?"

"My wife said she didn't know, and I believe her. If those boys went back to do something to Annalise, they didn't tell anyone about it."

Jane excuses herself from the room while Duncan gets Isaias to write out and sign a statement. She heads to where the rest of her team and her superior have been watching the feed. Her superior gives a small nod. "Good job, Sergeant."

"Teamwork," she says.

He nods curtly, but Jane can see that she's passed some unspoken test in his mind. For now. And the relief is both bitter and sweet.

Jane asks Tank to check on the dive team's status, and she dispatches a Gulf Island unit to go by boat to Somersby Island to pick up Bob and Cara Davine on their wine farm. She tasks another RCMP unit to pick up Jill Osman at the hotel where Isaias said his wife is staying. She dispatches a third unit to the residence of Claude Betancourt, and a fourth to pick up Mary Metcalfe at the Happy Gardener on Marine Drive. She's rounding them all up for questioning.

As this is happening, Tank gets off the call he placed to the dive team. He shoots his fist high into the air, and his eyes are on fire. "They found it! A submerged van! Underwater remote control cameras show footage of human remains—a skeleton—inside the back."

The news punches Jane hard in the gut. Her first thought is of old Ahmed Hendricks. She grabs her coat off the back of a chair.

"Melissa, inform the coroner's office. Yusra, contact the Hendricks family before the media gets wind of this." She pauses, swallowing a wave of emotion. "Let Ahmed know we think we have found his son. Let Danielle know we might be bringing her brother home." She pauses. "Good job, everyone."

# THE SHOREVIEW SIX

## Jill

Jill sits at a table in the hotel restaurant and stares out windows overlooking the pool and the Burrard Inlet beyond. Clouds have muscled in and block views of her beloved North Shore Mountains. A soft rain pocks the pool's surface. She's not focused on anything in particular, can't even really think. Her bags are packed and ready at her feet. She knows Isaias so well. It's just a matter of time before the weight of what she told him will drive him to inform the police where they can find Darryl's body. He won't be able to be complicit in lies to cover a murder. He'll want her to face the truth, too, and accept whatever consequences must come. Her husband is all about honesty, owning one's actions.

She should have done this forty-seven years ago—told the truth. It would have gone so differently for everyone if she hadn't allowed herself to be persuaded by Cara—by her own *need* to belong to the group. Darryl's family would have had answers. Police might have been able to quickly find Annalise, giving the Jansens immediate resolution. Everyone could have properly grieved and laid their loved ones to rest. And Jill does believe Robbie and Claude did something heinous to Annalise. Annalise of course never ran away with Darryl, because he's dead and deep in Blackwater Lake. She could have told the whole world that Darryl had not abducted their friend, or harmed her. The boys were so amped on the mushrooms and drink and rage, Jill is pretty sure they drove to Annalise's house and waited for her there, and they had motive—Cara had told them Annalise was cheating on Robbie.

That need to belong as a teen is so powerful, Jill thinks. It's wired into human biology. To be cast out from a herd in the wild is to be rendered vulnerable, weak. You become the victim for circling prey. Being inside her group, being part of a pledge, knowing a dark secret about life and death that only the six of them shared—it defined Jill and empowered her.

She thinks of Zara and tears fill her eyes. She's tried several times to call her daughter, but Zara has not picked up. She imagines Isaias would have contacted Zara by now and told her.

Out of the corner of her eye, Jill catches a movement. She turns slightly and notices the waitress talking to two RCMP officers in uniform. The waitress points in Jill's direction. Jill tenses and turns back to stare out the window as the two officers come through the tables toward her.

"Mrs. Jill Osman?"

She glances up. The officer who spoke is tall, dark skinned, bearded, and wears a turban. With him is a shorter, blonde woman with her hair tied back tightly.

Jill reaches down and clasps her hand around the handle of her bag. "I've been waiting for you to come."

Some buried part of Jill has been waiting forty-seven years.

## Claude

Claude is trying to coach a kids' game. Parents and friends cheer and whoop as the puck slams into the net. He can't focus. He's worried about Mary and what she'll do. He should never have dumped her on the highway like that, but it was a gut-fear response, a raw need to dump this whole thing out of his life and just drive away. He *has* to believe she'll play it safe, keep her mouth shut. It's in her interest to protect the status quo because Mary and her daughter have plenty to lose—a top job, maybe even an approval for adoption. It's the paternal DNA results coming down the pike that really make Claude sweat. If police find a way to compel a sample from him, he could be done. Another goal is scored. The crowd goes nuts.

One of the dads comes up to Claude and slaps him on the shoulder. "Coach, we owe this to you!"

Emotion surges through Claude's body. He almost begins to tremble. These parents, these kids, his family, this hockey community—they respect him. Love him. All Claude has ever wanted is respect and love.

He sees them coming behind the plexiglass that surrounds the rink—three RCMP officers in uniform. They speak to the rink attendant, who looks Claude's way and points.

His world narrows. The noise of the hockey game fades to a dull roar inside his brain. He glances at the exits as every molecule in his body screams to flee. But where would he go? He can see two police cruisers outside, waiting.

Justice has come. Finally. Annalise and her bones have spoken.

She didn't have to tell a whole story, just enough to begin to unravel them all in a manner that forced them to bring the cops to their own doors. The rest of the truth will leak out now, one way or another.

## Mary

Mary tends seedlings in the greenhouse at her garden center. The tiny plants feed her soul as she nourishes them. The atmosphere created by the soft mist from the irrigation pipes is warm and smells of soil and greenery. At least she has this. She picks up a tray of baby basil plants, and her mind returns to her episode with Claude. She's thankful she found a cab driver who agreed to pick her up on the side of the highway. She was going to ask him to drive her directly to the police station, where she planned to give the rest of them up. Then another despicable part of herself contemplated the possibility of getting rid of Rocco. Because if he died and took all the blame with him, maybe they'd all be spared somehow. In the end Mary did nothing but go home. She hates herself for all this. She's a loser who has always defaulted to inaction because it seemed safer. She did nothing to confront Claude all those years ago, did nothing to challenge the group, did nothing to stand up for herself about being gay. All she did was slide into a marriage with Heather's father because it was easier than any form of self-confrontation. And look where it's gotten them all. If she's learned anything, it's that honesty—while difficult—has merit.

Maybe she will confess everything to Heather, yet Mary still remains terrified of disappointing her daughter in this way.

"Mom?"

She startles and drops her tray of basil plants. It explodes into a pile of soil and broken delicate green things at her dirty boots. Heather stares at her. Her daughter's features look wrong. She's gone white. Her eyes are big dark holes in her face.

"Heather? What—what is it? You spooked me."

"Some police officers out front want to speak to you," she says.

Mary regards her daughter as her heart begins to thump. She feels the greenhouse walls closing in. The temperature rises. She can't breathe with the mist and dank smell of soil. The roof is lowering.

"What do they want, Mom?"

Tears fill Mary's eyes. She glances away. They've come. There is no place to run or hide anymore.

It's over.

Even though her brain doesn't articulate it, her body suddenly relaxes—she doesn't have to lie anymore. A memory flashes through her brain. Annalise and her laughing over milkshakes at the White Spot at Park Royal. They had both turned twelve—a period of golden memories before hormones, puberty, boys, and peer pressure changed it all. An era when their friendship was pure as the sun and the moon.

The emotion spills from her eyes.

"I'm sorry, Heather," she whispers. "I'm so sorry."

# Bob

Bob sucks in air with every third stroke of his arm as he plows his body through the ocean swells along the rocky shore near his island home. He wears no wetsuit, just his bathing suit. He needs the burn of the cold on his bare skin. Pain and perpetual motion are all that's keeping him going right now as he swims back and forth between his dock and the rocky point. His lungs burn. His muscles ache. He's running out of breath. But he can't slow the pace, cannot stop. Cara never did return to the motel last night. He half wondered if she'd gone to see Rocco. Even he had thought about going to visit Roc. If the guy and his loose mouth disappeared, maybe they could all still hold this lie together.

After Bob returned to the motel last night, he tossed and turned until early dawn, when he was able to rent a car and catch the first ferry home to Somersby. Cara wasn't on the island, either. He's tried calling her cell, but she's not answering. It's not out of love that Bob is desperate to reach her—it's fear. He's growing paranoid, fretting that even his wife might fold on him to save her own skin.

He reaches the rocky point, turns around, and begins a sprint back to the dock, punching through the water, gasping in huge breaths and getting salt water in his mouth with each turn of his head. He hates Cara suddenly, with a hot and furious passion. He doesn't care if he never sees her again as long as she doesn't turn on him. Something switched in Bob when he learned she'd lied about Annalise being with Darryl.

He swims even harder, driven, desperate to escape the horror of what he did after her lie, because of her lie. Because of stupid teen hormones and drink and drugs and peer pressure. Because of his own fragile ego. Because of a pathological need for approval and his old need for Annalise's love. He detests his traitorous friends, too. One of them slept with Annalise—he's now certain of it. Either Claude or Rocco.

DNA will tell. But if the cops find out who, the whole pack of cards might come tumbling down.

He swims even harder. He's feeling dizzy. He can see it in hindsight now: how Annalise changed. She was so sweet, kind, happy, pure, vivacious, but something dark and self-destructive had awakened in her earlier that year. Was it the pregnancy? Was this why she had rebuffed his advances? But why did she sleep with others? He still doesn't understand it. He's almost at the dock. Annalise's face suddenly swims in front of him—a vision just out of his reach. Smiling at him. Her hair fans about her head, long and blonde and undulating with the swells. She holds her hand out to him, luring him to come deeper, colder, darker.

*Come, Robbie, come. We can be together. Like we were meant to be.*

In his mind's eye he sees Darryl's van going over the cliff, sinking down down down into the dark cold of Blackwater Lake, ripples and silver bubbles rising slowly to the surface. Bob is Robbie again. He's also sinking. He can't breathe. He thrashes harder, trying to stay afloat. An errant wave hits his mouth. He begins to choke. The waves are getting higher, a storm front closing in. He nears his dock. His goggles are fogged. He reaches blindly to take hold of the wooden slats, and he sees blurry boots next to his fingers. He struggles to keep his hold on the dock as he pushes his goggles up onto his brow. He squints upward. The boots belong to a large man backlit by the sky. There's a second man with him. Yellow stripes run up the sides of their pants. RCMP uniforms.

"Robert Davine?"

He swallows, vulnerable in his bathing trunks with his skin raw and pink with cold. He feels small. Frightened.

"Can you get out of the water, please, sir? We need you to come with us."

He sees Annalise's sweet smile again as she reaches out. *Come, Robbie, come. It's time now.*

## Cara

Cara is at YVR airport when she hears her name being broadcast over the intercom system, authorities calling for her to go to a nearby counter. She's been on standby for a flight to Athens since she drove here from the motel last night. She's just secured one via Frankfurt, and boarding is about to begin.

*You conniving bitch. Why should I believe a thing you say now?*

She and Bob can never resume their perfect life now. After she first considered flipping on him, her next instinct was to flee.

If she can escape the country while the shit hits the fan, she can at least buy time to think, to hire an ace legal team, to come up with a solid strategy once she sees where the chips are falling. After all, *she* didn't kill anyone. Bob and Claude did. And one thing Cara knows is she's *not* going down with them.

Her extended family has relatives on a tiny Greek island near Lesbos. She'll lie low there. The island doesn't even have Wi-Fi. She hears her name over the intercom again: "Cara Davine, please report to the nearest Air Canada agent."

Panic licks through her gut. They're coming for her. No time to wait for the flight. She gathers up her bags. If she escapes the airport quickly, she can catch the SkyTrain, then maybe a bus or ferry to the US. She can fly out from there. But as she starts toward the doors, she sees two airport security guards and two RCMP officers hurrying toward her. She freezes. Her inner voice goes into overdrive.

*It'll be fine. You are Cara Constantine Davine. You get what you want. You always win. You've got this. It's Bob's fault. You are victim to your husband's lies. Just a victim.*

# JANE

It's 4:57 p.m., and the sky is low and dark with clouds and rain. Jane stands with Duncan at the Blackwater cliff edge in the same location the photo of Annalise and her six friends from Shoreview High was shot over the summer of 1976. Jane is bundled in her coat against the chill wind. Rainwater drips from the bill of her cap and from the trees of the surrounding forest. Somewhere, unseen behind clouds, a chopper thuds.

Slightly lower down the rock face to their right is a large staging area where a crane and flatbed truck have been brought in via the logging road. Jane can see Darb, the coroner, down there speaking to technicians who have fed cables to the divers below. The team has now hooked the cables to the submerged VW bus and is starting to raise it. Generator-powered light towers have been brought in to ward off the creeping dark. Dr. Ella Quinn and her crew are on standby at the institute to examine the skeletal remains once they've been brought up. Excitement and tension simmer in Jane.

"Looks as though they'll have the Volkswagen on land before dark," Duncan says quietly as he steps backward, farther away from the edge.

"Yeah." Jane turns to look at him. His face is paler than usual. "Not a fan of heights?"

He shoves his hands deeper into his coat pockets and shakes his head.

Someone yells from the staging area and the cables begin to turn. The world seems to fall silent as the cliff-top crane starts to winch up the waterlogged Volkswagen bus.

Farther away, maybe five hundred meters down the logging road, a barricade restricts access to the lake. When Jane and Duncan arrived at the barricade, media crews were beginning to gather behind the sawhorses, curious about the activity. Jane saw Angela and Rahoul among the group. Parked near them in a warm car is Darryl Hendricks's father, Ahmed, with his daughter, Danielle. Ahmed insisted on being near. He told Jane he wants his boy to have family present to welcome him back when he's brought up from his watery resting place—if indeed it is Darryl in the van. Meanwhile the five remaining Shoreview Six members have all been brought in and are being held at the station to await questioning. All have lawyered up significantly.

"Seems we might have a handle on what happened to Darryl Hendricks now," Duncan says. "But what about Annalise?"

Jane takes a step backward to join him. She speaks as she watches the cables. "Hopefully the Shoreview bunch give something up during interrogations."

"I want to know who was in that brown sedan parked at the end of the cul-de-sac when Annalise came home, because my money is still on Knox Raymond." Wind gusts rain at them.

"Maybe Claude Betancourt, Robbie Davine, and Rocco Jones lied to the two girls and some or all of them went back for Annalise and called her over to their car," Jane says quietly. She glances up at Duncan. His gray eyes match the sky. "The DNA results will hopefully give us some additional investigative angles, because things are still not adding up."

"Any word from Dr. Quinn on timeline?"

"She said sometime today if we're lucky." Jane checks her watch. "But I'm doubtful—it's gone past five p.m. now."

Another yell comes from below, followed by excited calls and a flurry of movement. Jane sees lights emerging under the water now. The divers are coming up. Suddenly the roof of the VW breaks the surface. Chills run down Jane's body. Orders are barked as more of the bus appears. Water gushes in silvery streams out of the windows and the open passenger door.

"Holy shit," Duncan whispers as the VW spins slowly as it's drawn higher into the air. "Orange and white. From this angle you would never think it has been down there for forty-seven years."

The crane arms swings the van slowly toward the cliff.

"Let's go take a look," Jane says.

They move quickly along a twisting and rocky path through the trees to the lower staging area. By the time Jane and Duncan get down, the VW bus has been lowered onto a flatbed truck and the cables have been dismantled. A suited-up forensic ident team is moving in, documenting everything with cameras.

One of the white-suited techs calls Jane and Duncan over. He points through the open sliding door of the van and shines his flashlight in. Crumpled on the floor is a skeleton, still clothed, jaw open wide, full set of teeth. A cocktail of elation and poignancy fills Jane, and she stares at the remains of what she believes they will prove to be Darryl Hendricks, after all these years.

"Looks like a leather vest," Jane says quietly.

"And there's this." The tech points carefully with a gloved finger to a piece of metal partially exposed under the fabric. It's attached to a chain.

*The medallion.*

"It's still so silver," Duncan says.

"Platinum tarnishes far less easily than silver and some other metals, especially in very cold, freshwater conditions like this," the tech says.

"Is that a tire iron?" Jane asks, pointing to a metal bar near the skeleton.

"It appears so," says the tech.

"Could be one of the murder weapons," Duncan says. "Especially if it has the tire shop logo or any blood trace."

Another tech shoots photos in the front of the van. He stops suddenly, then calls to Jane, "Sergeant, take a look at this." The tech carefully holds up a laminated card with a gloved hand. "Stuck between the driver's seat cushions. It could have come out of the driver's pocket. It's an ID card, and the name is still legible. Leon Springer."

Jane exchanges a hot look with Duncan. She says, "What was the name on that fraudulent ID Claude Betancourt used to purchase liquor near the docks?"

"Leon Springer," he says quietly.

She blows out a chestful of air. "We're going to be able to put those boys inside this vehicle," she says. "Especially if there's additional trace on that card and tire iron."

# JANE

The Hendrickses' vehicle is stippled with rain and the windows fogged because the engine is running to keep the occupants warm. Jane raps gently on the passenger window. Both car doors open simultaneously. Danielle and Ahmed Hendricks—hungry for news—both get out despite the rain and look eagerly toward her. Ahmed's milky white eyes see nothing, but Jane feels as though he sees everything right now.

"It's him," Ahmed says. "I feel it. Is it him, Sergeant? Have you found our Darryl?"

"We still need to match DNA or dental records in order to make a formal identification, but it is his VW bus. The registration is still visible. And there's a leather waistcoat and a medallion on the remains that match the description of what Darryl was last seen wearing before he disappeared."

"It's him," Danielle says, coming quickly around the car to be at her old father's side. She touches his arm, and Jane notices she's trembling.

*"Wees die verandering wat jy wil sien in die wêreld,"* Ahmed murmurs in Afrikaans. "Be the change you want to see in the world." Tears pool in his eyes.

Jane swallows the emotion surging in her chest. She feels Ahmed Hendricks—or Darryl himself—is speaking the words of the inscription directly to her.

*If you want resolution, if you want answers, if you seek closure, bring closure to others. Be the change.*

Ahmed turns to his daughter. "We can bury him now, Danni. With Mimi. We have him back." He wipes his face. "After all these years he's come home. His reputation is clean again. Thank you, Sergeant. Thank you from the bottom of my soul."

Tears rise in Jane's eyes, and she's grateful the rain hides them. Her thoughts turn to the therapist's words uttered in the church basement.

*In the context of ambiguous loss, "closure" is a myth . . . We should not be forced to chase closure. What we need to find are ways to coexist with our complex feelings, and to always remember that our reactions are completely normal. They're not a sign of personal weakness.*

Words be damned. It's not a myth. It's real and raw and she can see it right here and now in the faces of Ahmed and Danielle Hendricks. Closure makes a difference to those who find it. Jane is not going to give up trying for herself.

"Can I have it—the medallion?" asks Ahmed.

"Right now it's evidence, Mr. Hendricks, and it needs to be processed," Jane says. "Everything must be done carefully, and properly, especially if we want everything to stick when we bring charges and prosecute. And there will be trials. But when we are done, yes."

"Who did this?" Danielle asks. "Will someone be punished for what they did to Darryl, to us, to our family?"

"It's my job to see that happens. And yes, I believe we will be able to charge the people responsible."

"But who was responsible?" Danielle presses. "Was it the Shoreview kids? Did Jill Osman have anything to do with this? What was her role? Why did she come to me with her business—to atone?"

"Again, we need to proceed with due care, and as soon as we officially charge the perpetrators, you'll be among the first to know." She glances at Darryl's father. "I promise."

"What of Annalise?" Ahmed asks.

Jane's phone rings. She glances at the screen, sees it's Dr. Ella Quinn from the lab. Anticipation bites. This could mean the DNA results are in.

"Excuse me, please—I need to take this. I'm going to send a family liaison officer over to take good care of both of you, and to help walk you through the next steps."

She steps away and connects the call. "Ella? What have you got?"

"A couple of things. First, the DNA from the traces of animal hair found with the down feathers in the adipocere—it's from a white poodle."

*"Poodle?"*

"A purebred poodle, yes."

Jane mentally runs through the known case facts, trying to pinpoint where a poodle came up. It hits her—the witnesses at the bottom of the cul-de-sac—the Janyks owned a poodle.

"We also got a match via the FBI databases on the fiber trace. It was on file because a similar vehicle was used in a high-profile crime in Kentucky in the seventies. The trace matches automotive carpet fibers from a 1972 model Plymouth Valiant, a popular four-door sedan at the time."

*Not a Dodge Dart Custom.*

"And we have a familial DNA match with the mother, Helen Jansen. We can confirm our Jane Doe is her daughter Annalise Jansen."

Jane's heart beats faster. "What about the fetus? Have you got a fetal DNA profile for us to work with?"

"Well, I can tell you the father is not one of those boys."

Surprise rustles through Jane. "How can you tell? We haven't yet got samples from any of them."

"Unless one of those boys is her blood brother, you're not going to need samples."

"What do you mean?"

"We have a case of consanguinity. The father of Annalise Jansen's baby is a first-degree blood relative to Annalise Jansen."

Jane feels dizzy. She steps under a large conifer to shelter from rain, which is coming down harder. Her brain reels. "Walk me through this."

Ella says, "I'll forward the reports, and also go through them with you in detail, but in a nutshell, normally we'd expect to see a fetal genome with a high degree of heterozygosity, indicating that the baby received half their genes from a mother who was biologically unrelated to the baby's father, from whom they received the other half. In this case, large blocks of DNA showed an absence of heterozygosity on multiple chromosomes, accounting for about a quarter of the genome, suggesting the fetus is the offspring of first-degree relatives."

"Incestuous paternity?" Jane says quietly.

"Does Annalise Jansen have brothers?" Ella asks.

"Not to our knowledge." Jane feels ill as her mind goes to Kurt Jansen in his recliner, and the strange Linden Street house locked in time, and Helen Jansen and her divorced daughter, Faith Blackburn, living in the basement. Jane's conversation with Beth Haverton from the Donut Diner replays in her mind.

*How did Annalise respond when you warned her to be careful?*

*She laughed. She said something to the effect, danger is not so obvious. It's the danger you can't see coming that you should really fear.*

There was danger for Annalise in her own home, inside the walls of that little Linden Street house on the cul-de-sac by the woods. The danger was not lurking outside in the world; it was closer than anyone saw. *That* was the danger Annalise feared.

Her own father.

# ANGELA

Angela and Rahoul are among the media entourage collecting behind the police barricades that block the logging road up to Blackwater Lake. They came because of emergency services chatter on their scanner and reports earlier of a circling helicopter thudding behind the clouds.

Angela knows there's currently a large police presence up at the lake along with a dive team, and the coroner's vehicle has been spotted. A truck, crane, and other equipment have been brought in, but no one gathered behind the barricades seems to have a clear idea of what is going on.

Suddenly she spies Sergeant Jane Munro and her partner walking rapidly down the logging road toward the barricade. Adrenaline pumps into her blood.

The pair come through the sawhorses and make for a row of unmarked vehicles parked farther down the logging road.

"Look, it's her," she whispers to Rahoul. "This *has* to have something to do with the chapel case—otherwise why is she here? Come with me, but stay calm. Don't alert the others."

They catch up to Jane Munro and Duncan Murtagh as the pair are about to enter an unmarked vehicle.

Sergeant Munro tenses as she sees them approaching, but she stops short of getting into the car.

"Sergeant?" Angela speaks quickly as she reaches the sergeant, wanting to get her words in before attracting the other journalists' attention.

"Is the lake search related to the Annalise Jansen case? Did you find anything? What are you looking for?"

Corporal Duncan Murtagh gets into the driver's seat and shuts the door, but Jane stands with her hand on her door and regards Angela, and Angela knows the detective is thinking about her phone call tip about Mason Gordon being Rocco Jones.

The detective glances away for a moment, looking in the direction of the forest, as if considering options.

"Off the record?" she asks.

Angela angles her head. "C'mon, Sarge. I need—"

Jane begins to get into the passenger seat.

"Okay, okay, off the record."

Her gaze pins Angela's.

"I promise," Angela says softly. "I'll honor my word. I want to do this right."

"You'll need to confirm anything with our media liaison—and this information will likely be released later today. We found an orange-and-white Volkswagen van with a registration from the seventies in the lake. It contains human remains."

Angela stares as her pulse quickens.

Rahoul says very quietly, "Do you want the camera running, Ange?"

Angela shakes her head. "No. She said it's off the record." She asks Jane quietly, "Darryl Hendricks?"

"That's all I can say at this point."

Angela knows Jane Munro is giving her a heads-up. It's a good-karma payback for her call about Mason-Rocco. This will be her scoop, but this time she really is going to handle it differently.

"What about Annalise Jansen?" Angela asks. "Have you made any formal identification yet?"

"We have a DNA match. We should be able to release information to the public shortly."

Angela takes this as a yes. The chapel remains belong to Annalise Jansen.

"What about her baby—do you have a DNA profile for the fetus?"

"Yes."

"Is it Bob Davine's? Did he provide a sample?"

"That's all I can say." The detective gets into the passenger seat. Her partner already has the engine running.

"What about Mason?" Angela calls out. "Did he jump or was there foul play?"

"That's all." She starts to pull the door closed.

"Sergeant Munro, thank you."

The detective hesitates. "Thank you, Angela." The door shuts, and the car begins to reverse as the detective pulls her seatbelt across her body.

Angela stares after the car as it does a three-point turn and bumps down the logging road into the mist. She knows what Jane Munro meant—a thank-you for the heads-up. She feels both good and irritated, because Angela knows she can be better. She *knows* she's capable of presenting deeper, more complex, and nuanced pieces of journalism if she just corrals her impatience, tamps down her edgy need to always be first, and allows herself to be vulnerable. The vulnerability bit scares her. As the police vehicle disappears with a last flare of red taillights into the mist, Angela realizes just how much she hides from her true self.

"And now?" asks Rahoul.

"I think we go stake out the Jansens' house on Linden Street. If I'm reading between the lines correctly, the cops are not able or willing to release information to the public until they've informed Annalise Jansen's parents of the DNA match. So that's where they'll be going. And if it's Darryl Hendricks's body and van they found in the lake, something in Mason-Rocco's apartment must have led them here." She glances at Rahoul. "I'm betting our colleagues here won't make the connection between this lake search and the Jansen case for a while, and I don't think we'll get much more here tonight, but the Linden Street house—that could yield some footage, maybe even an interview with the parents."

# JANE

Jane stares out the car window, watching the black water of Howe Sound slide by as Duncan drives the Sea to Sky on their way back to the Jansens' Linden Street house. Windscreen wipers clack.

"That house has been their prison," she says. "The Jansen family—trapped by their own making. Appearing to yearn for resolution, but surely, also dreading it might actually come."

Duncan inhales deeply, eyes focused on the twisting curves of the road, his hands tight on the wheel. Jane can see he's as rattled by this ugly development as she is.

"And what's with the poodle?" he asks after a few moments in silence.

"Only poodle that's come up is Elise Janyk's. She stated she was letting their poodle out before going to bed when she saw a girl she thought was Annalise Jansen running across the cul-de-sac toward that metallic-brown sedan."

He shoots her a quick glance. "So their poodle's hair somehow got on Annalise before or after she was killed?"

Jane purses her mouth, thinking. "Do you recall what Tank read out from Elise Janyk's statement?"

"Something like, the Jansens are the nicest, kindest family, and have helped with chores over the years, like cleaning the gutters, mowing the lawn"—he fires Jane another glance—"and taking their old poodle to the vet."

Jane rubs her brow, thinking, and it suddenly strikes her hard—a memory of one of the photos on the Jansens' fireplace mantel. "That photo on the Jansens' mantel—the only one that showed both Annalise and Faith as kids. The girls were standing in front of a green sedan, and if I am not mistaken, it was—"

"Shit—a Plymouth Valiant."

Jane hurriedly gets out her phone and scrolls through the photos she shot of Annalise Jansen's bedroom. She comes to the one with the Raggedy Ann doll on the bed.

"There's just a throw on Annalise's bed," she says. "No duvet. If that family really did leave her room exactly as it was, where is her duvet, or blankets?"

"You're thinking the long zipper and the feather trace found with her remains?"

"Maybe she was wrapped in her own duvet and transported in her own family car." As she speaks, Jane places a call to the rest of her team still at the detachment. She listens to the phone ring as she waits for someone to pick up.

Duncan says, "Making your own kid pregnant sure gives motive to get rid of her, along with the 'evidence.' And the chapel location, under that Madonna and child stained glass, the way she was laid out in the grave with care—it all begins to make more sense. And Annalise was wearing those earrings in the shape of crosses. There had to have been some religious element to the Jansens' lives."

Tank picks up the call.

"Hey, Tank, did we ever find out what Kurt Jansen did for a living?" Jane asks.

"He was a contractor. Building trades."

"Anything in the files about which company he worked for?"

Tank is silent for a moment as he scans the digitized case files. "Nothing I can see so far."

"See if you can find out if he ever worked for one of the companies contracted for renovation work on Hemlock over that summer of '76."

"On it."

Jane ends the call. They're approaching North Vancouver. Within moments they will be at Linden Street, bringing closure to the Jansen family.

But not in the way anyone hoped.

# JANE

Jane and Duncan face Helen and Kurt Jansen in their living room. Helen has helped her husband onto the sofa beside her. She's white-faced and holds his hand. Kurt stares intently at Jane and Duncan but has not said a word. Jane has no idea how aware he is of the situation, or whether he might be using his health as an avoidance tactic to some degree.

Faith sits on a chair to her mother's left.

"You—you have news about Annalise?" Helen says.

"We do," Jane says. "We can now confirm via DNA that the remains found buried beneath the skiers' chapel on Hemlock belong to your daughter Annalise."

Helen swallows and her eyes water. Faith sits stiff and dead silent.

"Mr. Jansen, does—or did—Annalise have any brothers?" Jane directs her question to Kurt. She sees a flicker in his eyes. He glances at his wife.

Helen says, "We just had the girls." Her voice begins to tremble. "Why do you ask?"

Faith continues to stare intently at her hands in her lap.

"That photo on your mantel with the green sedan—was that your car?"

Kurt's eyes shift slightly toward the mantel. Helen says, "Our Plymouth Valiant. Yes."

"Do you know what model it was?" Duncan asks.

A panicked look darts through Helen's eyes. She turns to Kurt. "When did we get the Plymouth?"

He just stares at her.

She faces Jane. "I—uh—I think it was four or five years before Annalise was taken."

*Taken.*

Duncan makes a note in his book.

"Did your family ever own a poodle?" Jane asks.

"What does this have to do with my sister?" Faith asks suddenly.

"There were traces of poodle hair on Annalise's remains, along with down feathers from a goose. Did you own one?" Jane asks again.

"No," Helen says. "The only poodles around here belonged to Elise and Will at the end of our cul-de-sac. When one died, they'd just get another. They were never without dogs, but we never had any dogs."

"Mr. Jansen"—Jane again addresses Kurt directly—"did you ever transport one of the Janyks' poodles to the vet in your Plymouth? To help them out, perhaps?"

"Mom," Faith says in a loud voice. "Don't answer their questions. They can't make you. Not without a lawyer. Tell them to leave."

Tears pool in Helen's eyes, and she swipes them away. "I don't want a lawyer. I just want this to end. I've waited so many years for them to learn what happened, and to come and find us. Yes, Kurt transported a white poodle in the back of the Plymouth late in the summer of '76. I . . . I . . . it's all my fault. I could have stopped it. I . . ." She breaks down into body-shuddering sobs.

A knot of tension tightens in Jane's stomach. She takes a steady breath. She wants to be careful to pace her questions.

"Mom," Faith snaps. "Stop it. Please, stop. I don't want to hear." Her eyes are like saucers suddenly. Her gaze flares to Jane. Fear twists her features. "I—I don't know what happened back then. I just know my sister vanished, and I don't want to hear what happened. I can't. Mom, please, stop. It's not your fault."

Kurt glowers at Jane and Duncan, but Jane sees tears welling in his eyes.

"What exactly could you have stopped, Mrs. Jansen?" Jane asks gently.

Helen can't seem to hear. She continues sobbing, her body shuddering like a rag doll that has been gripped by the shoulders and is being shaken by an invisible force. The sound that emanates from her is inhuman.

Faith lurches to her feet. "You need to see something," she says quickly. "I need to get it from downstairs."

Jane makes eye contact with Duncan. He nods and comes to his feet.

"I'll go with you, Faith," he says.

Jane sits with the sobbing Helen and silent Kurt, thinking that Faith is trying to create a distraction. Or the woman just couldn't sit still a moment longer and listen to what her father might have done to her sister.

Faith returns with Duncan a few moments later. She trembles as she thrusts two pieces of paper at Jane.

"It's not my mother's fault. It's his. These are from my sister's journal—the diary. It never did leave this house, and neither did my sister's backpack or sock monkey. I was at a sleepover when Annalise vanished, and I was too little, or too protected, to understand what was really going on before she disappeared. I only found the journal and other items a few years ago, when I was clearing out the basement so I could move in after my divorce." She pauses, trying to gather herself. "When I was little, I was so jealous of Annalise. She was my parents' special one. She always got little gifts and attention I never got. I hated her sometimes. I envied the love my father seemed to shower on her." She inhales a shuddery breath. "Now I know. From those two pages. And I was safe in this house because of my big sister. Annalise." Faith swipes away a tear. "She used to call me Pop Tart. She wanted to leave this house but wrote in her diary she was worried that her leaving might expose Pop Tart—me. And now I understand." She glances at her immobile father. "Annalise didn't want him to hurt me, too."

"Where's the rest of the journal?" Jane asks.

"I burned it."

"When? Why?" Jane asks.

"Just—just recently." She glances again at her father, whose hands are pressed hard on his thighs. Her mother sobs and moans.

"I burned it so my mom would be spared this. You people coming here and forcing her to hear these things. I burned the diary so it would all end, so my sister's ghost and everything awful associated with her memory would go up the chimney in smoke. I thought, What good could come of exposing our sordid family truths now? What my dad did to my sister was not my mom's fault—she was a victim. And he never touched me in the end. When Annalise went, everything changed. Then my dad got sick and impotent. And now he's locked in his own skull along with his regrets. I know he remembers. I know he feels sorry. I can read it all in his eyes even if he can't express it. So outing the truth wouldn't touch him any more or less. But it would pain and humiliate my mother, destroy her, and it sure wouldn't bring my sister back. So what good, Detectives, what good can it do?"

Jane closes her eyes briefly and inhales. She thinks of Ahmed and Denise Hendricks and how badly they needed the truth outed. She thinks of the aunt who sent Darryl the pendant with the inscription, and of how fundamentally they all needed to have the family name cleared, how badly Ahmed wanted to prove to the world that his Darryl was a good boy and he would never, ever, have hurt Annalise Jansen. She thinks of the justice still barreling down the pike for the Shoreview Six. She thinks about the missing gaps—questions she still has about how this is all connected, and who was in the brown car at the end of the cul-de-sac.

"We're going to need to bring you all in for formal questioning," Jane says. "But tell me, Faith, if you wanted it all gone, why did you save these two pages?"

"I—I was going to put them into the flames, too. But I just couldn't kill that last little sound of her voice. She wouldn't let me. And maybe this is why." Faith nods at the papers in Jane's hands. "Maybe she needed you to hear her words. So that she might yet have her final say."

"Or maybe *you* needed to have her words heard, Faith?"

She breaks eye contact and stares at the carpet a moment. Softly, she says, "Some part of me, maybe. The part that doesn't know how she actually died. The part of me that also is afraid to hear."

Jane turns to Helen, who has gone quiet. "Did you read your daughter's journal, Mrs. Jansen? Do you know what was in it?"

She nods. "I hid it because of what was in it, and I didn't want the police finding and reading it when we reported Annalise missing." She glances at her youngest daughter. "I didn't know you found it, Faith. I didn't know you knew about your father. I'm so sorry. I failed both of you. I should have protected you both, and instead I tried so desperately to act like it never existed."

"Mr. Jansen"—Jane directs her words to Kurt again—"did you know your daughter was pregnant with your child?"

He closes his eyes. His head trembles on his neck. Tears escape under his lashes, but he doesn't—or can't—utter a word.

"We knew," Helen says in a thin voice. "We both knew."

Duncan takes fast notes in his book.

Jane asks, "Mr. Jansen, did you kill your daughter before wrapping her up in her duvet and transporting her in your Plymouth?"

"I did it." Helen begins to sob again. "I—I killed my beautiful girl and the baby she was carrying, and I am so sorry. So, so sorry. She's dead because she made me so angry that I lost my control and struck her head with a baseball bat and she went down and hit the back of her head on the stone coffee table and she never woke up again and—and we didn't know what to do next."

# ANNALISE

## HATEHIMHATEHIMWANTTOKILLHIM

**My mom won't believe me. She refuses to hear the truth about HIM. The Monster. I don't know who to talk to now so I am writing it down here.**
**He started when I was too little to understand it was not love. Not normal. He was always so kind and caring. He always brought me little presents and put his finger to his lips: Shhh Annalise, don't tell Mom. She'll be jealous. It's between us because you're my special little one, okay honey? The best little girl in the whole wide world. Daddy and Anna have a secret. A special secret. Right, Annakins?**
**He'd come into my room at night and I'd force my mind to go far away to a safe fairytale place until it was over. And then he would kiss me on my brow and stroke my hair and tell me there would be a chocolate milkshake that weekend, ice cream, a new soccer ball, a skateboard, a doll, a new pair of those yellow corduroy pants I wanted, new Adidas sneakers like all the cool kids at school were wearing.**
**When I showed up at school in my corduroys and sneakers the other kids smiled and said I was cool, and there were girls who were jealous because they liked my hair and said I could carry it all off better**

**than anyone, and I was so pretty, and it made me proud. But also I began to feel dirty. And dirtier and dirtier. I learned other fathers didn't do this. Something was wrong with me, with us, our family and it would be the worst thing ever if the kids at school found out.**

**I began to feel sick a lot. I tried to tell Contrary a few times, but I always chickened out. Once a secret is told it's no longer a secret because someone else knows. And when that happens you no longer control the truth. You can no longer guard it for yourself.**

**A few years ago, in the kitchen, when he was at work on a job out of town, I found the courage to tell my mom what he'd been doing to me. I cried and sobbed and said I needed her help.**

**She turned her back on me and carried on washing the dishes. She said nothing. Nothing at all. I said, "Mom, please, talk to me."**

**"Go to your room, Annalise."**

**"Why?"**

**She spun around and her face was red and she was so angry and said, "Don't ever speak such nonsense again. I will wash your mouth with soap, you ugly little girl. You have an imagination that is disgusting, dangerous. Your family will disown you if you repeat that utter rubbish. You evil, evil little girl. Go. Now. Your room. At once."**

**And that's when I hated her, too. My mom was supposed to protect us. I began to worry if something happened to me, or if I ran away, Pop Tart would become the next target. Right now I'm the only thing that stands between her and Monster.**

**The other day I almost told Contrary again, but couldn't. Instead, I got a little mean, and I know that I've begun to push her away, push everyone away.**
**HATEMYSELFHATEMYSELFHATEHIMHATEHER**
**Then I missed my period.**
**I missed another.**
**I grew terrified the whole world would start to see my dirty, evil secret. See I was a disgusting, filthy girl. They'd know what I did with my father.**
**I had to make it seem possible the baby could be someone else's until I figured out what to do with it. If I had sex with as many guys as I could, and quickly, all in a row, they'd never know whose it was. It helps to get drunk first. I've been getting drunk a lot. It makes me nice and numb for a little while.**
**I also met HC. He showed me something else—how sex has power over men like him and the danger is intoxicating and reckless and I don't know why but I keep egging him on and he gave me that police brooch which is so cool and I wear it like a secret. Like a weapon. In everyone's face yet none of them know what we do in his car. I did it with Mullet and Puck a few times, too, but never with Smurf. I care for him. Maybe I love him. Maybe I can't do with it him because when I have sex I always think of Monster, and my feelings for Smurf are clean and I don't want to ruin them. I really don't want Smurf to learn my secret but he'll see my tummy soon. They all will. It's getting bigger. Time is running out.**
**And then there's CW. I tried to come on to him, too. But CW saw something was going on in me, some desperation, self-destruction. He's kind and so very smart and I think he might become a great**

**psychologist one day. When he came to tutor me he began to sense things in my house and with my parents weren't kosher. I think they realized he saw it, too, because they became uneasy and distrustful of having him around. CW tried to talk to me about what was going on with my parents, and I was drunk again and broke down and told him and cried. It was the first time I spilled the secret but it was getting so big inside me I couldn't actually hold it in any longer. He said he would protect my secret and maybe he could help. The people who work at the reggae club he goes to—his friends—know someone across the border who can make this awful thing of HIS go away, make it ALL go away. He said I could start over again. I asked him why he would help me like this and he said we need to become the change we want to see in the world. I trust him. I think I have no choice but to go with him in his VW. Just for a little while.**

**When it's over I will return and take Pop Tart and we'll never come back again.**

# HELEN

Helen sits at a table in a police interrogation room across from Sergeant Jane Munro and Corporal Duncan Murtagh as the sergeant reads out loud the final words written in Annalise's journal.

She closes her eyes as she forces herself to listen. Alone. Kurt has escaped. He's been admitted to the hospital—he had another stroke because of all the tension caused by the cops coming to the house. He's stable but his long-term prognosis is not good. If he ever gets well enough, he'll need to go into an assisted living facility.

She's been told that a forensic psychologist will need to assess Kurt's cognitive ability so police and prosecutors can decide how best to proceed with him. She knows this interview is being recorded. She knows she's being watched through that camera up near the ceiling. She's declined legal counsel.

She could use one of the free lawyers. She could fight back, blame it solely on Kurt, lie, try to bury it all down inside a hidden compartment in her mind again, but Helen knows all too well how that can fester toxic ooze into her body. She feels old and beyond exhausted now and is almost relieved to finally be getting this off her chest. She wants it to end. She *wants* to take whatever punishment she deserves. She might even be able to sleep properly again. Helen has not slept through the night since she struck Annalise. She's probably even more guilty than Kurt. She's not sick like he was. In Helen's mind, Kurt was born that way. His own parents made him that way. He couldn't help being ill in his mind—that's the way she always tried to justify it.

*But me? I didn't have the courage to stop him, to dismantle my marriage, walk away with my children and no marketable job skills. I didn't have the guts to face my neighbors and show them how dysfunctional our perfect little Linden Street family actually was. I am weak. Selfish. A pathetic excuse for a mother. I didn't help my baby because I didn't want to face all the consequences. It terrified me. It's now time to put myself in God's hands.*

When Sergeant Munro finishes speaking Annalise's words out loud into the room, where they hang in the air around Helen and point accusing fingers, the sergeant looks up. She looks right into Helen's eyes and soul.

"Who are these people that your daughter mentions in this journal, Mrs. Jansen—Puck, Smurf, Mullet, CW?"

Helen rubs her mouth. "I—I believe Puck is Claude, the hockey player. Smurf is Robbie, the surfer and because it rhymes with *surf*. Mullet is Rocco. And CW stands for Cape Winds, because clearly he's Darryl."

"How do you know this?"

"I read her journal many times, and sat and thought and figured it all out."

"After you told investigators it was missing?"

She nods.

Corporal Murtagh says, "Can you speak out loud for the recording, Mrs. Jansen?"

"Yes, after I lied that it was gone with her backpack and sock monkey. We—I—wanted to make it appear as though she ran away."

"Is this true—Annalise tried to ask for your help?"

Helen says quietly, "It's all true."

Corporal Duncan Murtagh says, "So what exactly did happen on the night of September 3 in 1976, Mrs. Jansen?"

She reaches for a cup of water on the table and sips, but she spills because her hands are shaking so hard. "Annalise went to that party. She was going to come home that night."

"She never claimed she was going to sleep over?" Sergeant Munro asks.

"No. I lied. I woke around 11:25 p.m. that night, when I heard the Janyks' poodle yipping. I got up to go to the bathroom and I looked out of the window. I saw our Annalise running to a brown car at the end of the cul-de-sac. She bent into the window and spoke to someone inside, then tried to leave. Whoever was in the car reached out, grabbed her hand. She tugged, then she laughed, ran around the car, and got into the other side."

"The passenger side?" Sergeant Munro asks.

"Yes. I watched awhile. The car was bumping. I knew what she was doing in there. I went back to bed and lay there wide awake. I heard the door downstairs open and close as Annalise tried to sneak back inside. She bumped the hall table, and something clattered to the floor."

"Where was your husband at this time?" Sergeant Munro asks.

"Sleeping. I suddenly got irrationally angry. I can't explain exactly why. I went downstairs and called Annalise out for being drunk and a slut. I could smell the booze on her. I could smell sex. And that's when she started screaming at me that she was not a slut, and it was *his* fault and my fault because she tried to explain years ago what Kurt was doing to her. She yelled that the whole world would know just how sick our family was now because my husband—her father—had made her pregnant." Helen pauses. Her whole body trembles as the terrible memory rises like a fire in her chest.

"A-Annalise lifted up her sweater to show me her tummy, and I—I cracked. It was like the two parts I tried to keep on opposite sides of a wall both crashed through, and I reached out and struck her with the back of my hand. So hard."

She falls quiet.

"Was this the first time you learned your daughter was pregnant?" Sergeant Munro asks softly.

Tears burn in Helen's eyes. "I—I suppose I had a feeling and was terrified it was true. And then she confirmed my worst nightmare—she made it real. I couldn't bear that Kurt had actually done this to her, to me, to us all. I—I couldn't hide from it anymore. Annalise shoved me back, which just blinded me with rage. It's like she suddenly represented this horrible thing my husband had done, and I wasn't thinking, and I grabbed the bat near the door and . . . I swung it."

"What happened then?" Sergeant Munro asks.

"I swung so hard. She was already unstable on her feet, so she wheeled sideways, stumbling, trying to correct her balance. She caught her foot under the rug and she smashed down hard."

"Smashed down?" the woman cop asks.

Helen presses her fingers to her temple. "I hit with the bat here. Behind her temple. When she went down, the back of her head smacked the stone coffee table. Kurt made it years before, during his stone masonry hobby phase."

The detectives both watch her keenly. She feels the others watching via the camera feed somewhere. She clears her throat. "She just lay there. Unmoving. Bleeding. I went numb."

"Where was your husband at this time, Mrs. Jansen?" asks the redheaded cop.

She rubs her brow, feeling a bit dizzy now. "I realized Kurt was standing at the bottom of the stairs—he'd seen the last bit of what happened."

"What was his reaction?" Sergeant Munro asks.

"He was shocked. Horrified. Even though he'd been hurting Annalise her whole life, he really did love her, I think."

The woman detective doesn't blink. Helen can see her judging.

"What happened next?" the redhead asks.

"We didn't know what to do. I told Kurt she was pregnant and that's why I lost it. He just started to cry. I said we needed to bury her. Soon, before anyone found out. Someplace nice where she could be with God. I—I was still trying to protect him. And Faith. I was still trying to hold our dysfunctional family together. I said we could pretend she never returned home from the party."

"And who was in the brown car that night?" Sergeant Munro asks.

"I don't know. I never found out. The car was gone when I looked out the window again. We worried about the fact the driver saw Annalise coming home, but no one ever came forward to counter our story. I began to think they might be afraid because they were doing something that night they shouldn't have been doing. But all this time we've known someone out there must surely know we were lying."

She reaches for her water, takes another wobbly sip, clears her throat. "I was hysterical. I couldn't believe what I'd done. But we couldn't turn the clock back."

"Where was Faith?"

"At a sleepover, thank God. Faith never knew what really happened, I need you to understand that, Detectives. She might have learned some years ago through the journal about her sister's abuse, but she never asked what actually happened in the end. Faith is not strong. She finds it easier to not ask things, to not know, because it's safer. Maybe she perceived something of the abuse over the years and has been messed up by it all, too. Maybe it's why she married a horrible, abusive man and couldn't leave him for such a long time."

Sergeant Munro says, "So you decided to bury Annalise?"

"At the chapel. Kurt had been working up there—he was employed by Diamond Pacific Concrete at the time and was going to be laying the floor in the basement after the long weekend. He's so good with his hands. Always so kind. Sometimes I still can't believe it all went so wrong."

"So the chapel basement was convenient?" Sergeant Munro asks.

"I'd been up there before and seen that beautiful stained glass. The Madonna and child. I thought—" Her voice breaks and tears flood her eyes. "I thought the Madonna could watch over my baby, and her own child, Kurt's child." Tears spill down her face. Her voice grows thick. "It's so beautiful and peaceful up there, too. Kurt knew the Labour Day weekend would be dead quiet there, especially at night, and there was equipment, shovels on hand. He knew the ground had been prepped. He figured if we could just get her into the ground and smooth it all over, then he himself would direct the pouring of the concrete and would seal her in and she would be safe."

"Or *you* would be safe," Corporal Murtagh says coolly.

She glances down at her hands.

"When did you actually first suspect what your husband was doing to your eldest daughter, Mrs. Jansen?" Sergeant Munro asks.

Very quietly she says, "I'm not sure. I really—I blocked it all out so hard. I suppose part of me knew something was going on from when she was little, and I could also never really believe it."

"And when Annalise confronted you—"

"I couldn't. I just couldn't bear to face it, or her. I wanted her—it—gone." She wipes away tears. "Annalise became two things that day. In one part of my brain, she was my beautiful teenage daughter. In another part she was this evil thing that threatened our lives. I would never have killed my child on purpose. I think at that moment, when she showed me her tummy with Kurt's baby inside, she simply became that evil monster that threatened us all, and I struck out at it. I have been so sorry about it every second, every minute, every hour, every day, week, month, year, ever since." She pauses, wipes more tears. "And I have waited for you to come."

# JANE

The mood in the incident room is somber after the Crown prosecutorial team leaves. This kind of closure is not what Jane and her team expected. And there remains work ahead: interviews with each of the remaining Shoreview Six, legal wrangling with the phalanx of criminal lawyers representing the individual parties, assessing how competent Kurt Jansen is and whether he can be interrogated, charged, and potentially stand trial. They still don't have proof that Chief Knox Raymond was inside the brown car that night, or that the married cop had sex with a fifteen-year-old, or that he had firsthand knowledge Annalise Jansen did, in fact, return home that night.

"I get what people mean when they say they both want news but also fear news," Yusra says. "Because no one wants to learn a mother killed her child, or did not save a daughter from sexual abuse inside her own home."

"We need to bring Knox Raymond in," Jane says. "My theory is he saw Annalise at the party when he attended to bust it up. He already had a relationship with her and was stalking her at the Donut Diner. He also drove a metallic-brown Dodge Dart Custom sedan. I reckon he and Annalise spoke at the party, and he said he'd meet her later at the bottom of the cul-de-sac when he knocked off his shift."

"It would explain why no one ever came forward and said they saw her going home," Melissa says. "A married RCMP officer with a baby on the way banging a fifteen-year-old schoolkid who's gone missing—that's a real bad look."

"He was probably also shit-scared they'd finger him for the crime," Duncan says.

"Maybe we can shake something loose when we interrogate him formally. But one thing that's evident to me"—she points to their crime scene board—"is none of this would have happened had it not been for Kurt Jansen abusing his daughter and making her pregnant. Everything spun out in a web over the years from there. Annalise's drinking and drunkenness on the night of the party, her promiscuity, her trying to obscure the fact her dad was the sole sperm donor by sleeping around, the resulting jealousy from Robbie Davine, Cara Constantine using the opportunity to secure Robbie for herself by lying about Darryl Hendricks, Helen Jansen's distress and misguided fury in striking and killing her own daughter, Helen and Kurt Jansen burying Annalise under the chapel—it all spirals back to the fact Kurt Jansen was a sick, sick man, and his wife did nothing to stop him."

"The ripple effects of a crime," Duncan says quietly as he stares at the images on the board. "Kurt was the trigger. Lives were destroyed in ripples from there." He glances at the rest of the team. "And now, forty-seven years later, they all finally have some answers."

As Jane observes her team, she feels she can do this. Cold cases. Historic crimes. If this is what it can mean. It fires her purpose. And she'll have a solid team at her back when she gets her next case.

"Thank you, guys," she says quietly. "Work ahead yet. But we've got this. We'll bring justice for Annalise and Darryl. Now go home, you all. Get some good rest tonight."

# KNOX

Knox is three hours north of his home, driving his RV over the twisty and weather-beaten Duffey Lake Road high-elevation pass that is still seeing avalanches at this time of year. He's getting the hell out of Dodge and making his way back into the interior of BC. He wanted to leave earlier, but his wife insisted he help with some maintenance around the house first. He didn't want to make a fuss and arouse her suspicion, so he conceded, but he's been totally wired since he made that idiotic decision to confront Sergeant Jane Munro on her turf. He thought it would be a pushover to manipulate a pregnant woman with PTSD issues.

He was dead wrong. She had him cornered.

He's now on tenterhooks awaiting news—any news—of those fetal DNA results because he's done the calculations. It could be his.

He listens to CBCN-Radio as he drives. As he hits a tricky section of road and begins the steep decline toward the town of Lillooet, the radio host says, "We have a breaking and shocking new development in the Annalise Jansen and Darryl Hendricks cold cases first broken by our affiliate CBCN-TV crime reporter Angela Sheldrick. Angela was outside the home of Kurt and Helen Jansen last night when an RCMP homicide team arrived to break the news to the parents that the remains under the chapel were confirmed to belong to their daughter. But that's just the beginning. We've got Angela Sheldrick on the line now. What can you tell our CBCN listeners?"

Knox's fists tighten around the wheel. Pinprick dots gather in front of his eyes as tension narrows his field of vision. The road drops sharply. He taps the brakes and gears down. A canyon drops off in a sheer cliff to his right. The only thing stopping vehicles from going over into a desertlike abyss of rock and stone is a low concrete median. Several small rocks lie in the road—constant rockfalls are a given for this section.

Angela Sheldrick's voice comes through the speakers. "As we reported last night, human remains suspected to belong to Darryl Hendricks were found in his Volkswagen van, which has been lying submerged in the depths of Blackwater Lake since September 1976. We also have some stunning news from a source familiar with the investigation: The DNA profile for the fetus that Annalise Jansen was carrying has come back as a familial match to her own father, Kurt Jansen, who has since been hospitalized for a stroke. Helen Jansen has also confessed to the RCMP that she killed her daughter by accident in a fight."

Knox's heart races so fast he thinks he's going to pass out. It's not his—the baby is not his. He's free. The road suddenly drops sharply in front of him as his heart soars with relief. But his distraction has upset his focus. He puts his foot on the brake a fraction too late as he approaches a hairpin bend too fast. His rig wobbles and slides slightly on a scattering of loose stones and gravel. He tries to correct by swinging the wheel to the left.

The host asks, "Did we ever find out why Dr. Noah Gautier was involved with the case?"

"He wasn't," Angela says. "That was an error I made in my haste, and I apologize deeply. Dr. Gautier was guest lecturing at SHU, and I should have made that clear. Again, I apologize for any confusion."

"So Annalise's bones have finally spoken," the host says.

A second bend is coming up too fast. Knox hits his brakes harder and turns in the corner. There's a rock in the road. He gasps, tries to swerve, and the movement takes his rig straight into the stone wall. He smashes through and lurches over into the void.

"A candlelight vigil is being planned for when the old skiers' chapel is placed in the alpine. For Annalise, Darryl, and the young woman, Wendy Walker, for whom the chapel was originally built—"

Knox's RV smashes into rocks, bounces out into the air, and plummets down, down, down.

Tears burn into Knox's eyes. He sees Annalise. Her smile. He smells her skin. He can almost taste her again on that last night of her life in the front seat of his Dodge Dart Custom as they had sex, mere weeks before his own baby was born.

He's free. He's finally free from this all.

His RV crashes onto a ledge, bounces, and shatters, and pieces fly as it rolls down the side of the mountain, coming to a stop against a stand of trees, engine steaming. Up high on another ledge, mountain goats look down. Knox's world fades as his light goes out.

# ANGELA

After her on-air segment, Angela makes her way back to her cubicle jonesing for a couple of shots of espresso and a sugar hit. She's amped, but focused and doing due diligence on this story now, hopefully bringing to it the gravitas it deserves in honor of the two teens from the seventies.

The revelations about Annalise's family and the secrecy that enshrouded it all for so many years have rocked Angela more profoundly than she will ever admit. Her own dark family background is shrouded in secrets. A shrink might argue this is what has always fueled Angela's drive to be bigger, better, shinier, larger than life, because if she ever goes too quiet, she is forced to face herself and her past in the mirror. Obfuscating with smoke and mirrors and flash and sensation is her protective armor. People don't look for deeper things in loud Angela.

But this case has tempered her. So has Jane Munro—a class act. In a strange way, the pregnant and grieving sergeant showed Angela that flat-out confrontation and subterfuge are not the only ways to yield information, and that sometimes building bridges rather than burning them can be a prudent long-term strategy.

As she nears her cubicle, she hears her name called from the far end of the room.

"Angela, can we speak to you for a moment? My office?"

It's the CBCN-TV producer.

Rahoul whispers from his seat in the cubicle, "Who's *we*?"

Nerves bite. "No idea," she says quietly.

She smooths down her skirt and blouse as she makes her way to the producer's office two doors down from Mason Gordon's old one. She knocks and enters.

The producer sits at a glass boardroom table with two of the higher-ups Angela has never had occasion to interact with.

"Take a seat." The producer holds out a hand.

She sits. Waits.

"Congratulations on the chapel case, Angela. There's been a new sophistication in your most recent segments. More nuanced, layered. We like the depth, the way you approach from different angles. You've managed to add poignancy to a story that is also sensational. Viewers trust reporting like this. It's not just news, it tells a bigger picture. We'd like to green-light your series concept, if you can continue to bring this kind of tone to a reality-based crime series."

Angela's blood begins to pound. "Did Mason speak to you about it?"

"We found your proposal among his office effects. How would you feel about starting with this case? It has legs yet. There's the in-depth interview you're planning with Ahmed Hendricks to finally clear his son's name and family honor. There will be additional charges coming, the trials—we'd like you to follow it all through in a series. *Someone Always Knows.* As you mentioned in your original concept, this chapel case hits all the notes, right down to the pregnant cop who led the investigation and has brought closure to a community, to the families, but not for herself. We love it."

Angela struggles to hold in a burst of emotion. She didn't need to rush at all. She needed to slow down. Go deeper. See all the sides before her bosses could see for themselves what she had in mind. Her thoughts turn to Darryl. *Be the change you want to see*, his medallion advised, and the words make her feel strangely teary. Forty-seven years after the teen murders, this crime still has impact in unexpected ways. This ripple, this halo effect, is something she wants to honor, and she will use it as the true north on her own compass. Nothing is ever truly over. No case should be deemed forgotten. Sometimes years later, people might want to talk, context changes, and there will be new science, and she herself can play a part, breathing life into the dead, the forgotten, the silent, the missing, fleshing them into living characters who are no longer quiet, or forgotten. Through her, they will speak. They will have their names back. This is her goal, starting with Darryl Hendricks and his family.

She steps out of the office feeling spacey. Rahoul watches her face keenly as she nears their tiny cubicle.

"Well? What did they say?"

She tries to keep a straight face but breaks into a stupid grin and grabs her coat. "Come. Champagne cocktails and dinner are on me tonight."

"You got the show?"

"*We* got the show, Rahoul. *We* did it."

# JANE

The spring evening is glorious as Jane arrives at Dr. Ella Quinn's North Vancouver house with the bottle of pinot gris she and Matt had been saving for when he was supposed to come home last September. It's time to share it, she thinks. She's also brought a bottle of sparkling water for herself, and a potato salad.

Ella's smile is warm when she opens the door. "Thank you for coming, Jane."

Jane offers up her bottles and salad.

"Oh, you shouldn't have—"

"My mother made it," Jane says quickly, taking off her coat.

Ella smiles with a strange look in her eyes, as though she's seeing Jane for the first time.

"I know, right?" Jane says. "Grown woman, homicide cop, and a mother making her food."

"It's a privilege," Ella says, taking Jane's jacket and hanging it on a hook in the hall. "We've got outdoor heaters on the patio, but if you need it, your coat's here. I wish my mom was still around. Lost her in a small plane crash in Kalimantan, Indonesia. Plane went down in the jungle and has never been found. I still miss her terribly."

Jane regards the professor and sees a sudden gleam of emotion in her eyes.

"Was it a long time ago?" she asks.

Ella gives a small, self-deprecating laugh. "Going on ten years now. She was on a dig—old war crimes site, working for the Dutch and Indonesian governments at the time."

"So she was an anthropologist like you."

"Not like me. Ten times better than me. I live to fill her shoes one day."

"I'm sorry for your loss. All I can offer is a personal knowledge that grief is never linear, particularly ambiguous grief like that."

Ella pauses, as if carefully considering her next words. "I heard about your fiancé. I'm sorry, too. It's a difficult road, and no one can ever say the right thing, can they?"

"Hell no. You got that part right." Jane's mind wheels back to group. "They mean well."

"Come on through. Everyone's here."

Jane follows the professor out onto the garden patio, wondering if Ella decided to host this party as an offering of peace, an apology for discussing their case in public. Duncan is already here, beer in hand, talking to the grad student he was making eyes at earlier in the lab. Tank, Yusra, and Melissa are all here, too. So is Darb in her loud and oversize button-down Hawaiian holiday shirt. Darb loves all things Hawaii—her grandfather was of native Hawaiian ancestry. Jane can see Ella's husband, the espionage novelist, chatting with a group near the small pool.

She hesitates, absorbing the pretty scene for a moment, half debating leaving because it suddenly feels like too much. Yet it's also welcoming. The urban garden is lush with spring blooms. The trellis is hung with lanterns. She suddenly catches sight of a tall, dark-haired man holding a glass of red wine and talking with Tank. Jane's heart stalls. She turns and glances toward the exit, ready to bolt.

"Jane?" He comes toward her with his glass.

*Shit. Too late.*

"Noah. Thought you'd left town."

"Look, I just want to get this out of the way. I'm sorry for what happened with that reporter. It should never have occurred."

"Water under the bridge."

"Can I get you something to drink?"

"I'm not sure I'm staying. I was just—"

"Congratulations on closing the case," he says before she can finish speaking.

"Well, we still have a ways to go before it's a wrap. Mostly Annalise did the work, her remains holding on to her evidence for all these years, and then rattling apart the alliance of the six when her presence became known, and showing us the way to Darryl Hendricks."

"Cold cases are kinda special that way."

She holds his gaze and relents to a smile. "Yeah. I think I could get with the program. Bet my superior didn't realize what a favor he was doing me when he relegated me to the unit. What truly fascinates me with this one is how many years that kind of abuse can go on in a family that has such a seemingly normal exterior. And why the child victim never speaks. Or why the spouse of the abuser and other adults in the family stand for it."

He sips his wine. "Maternal response to a child's sexual abuse is critical. A mother's support for a victim can help stop the abuse and mitigate the immediate psychological effects, plus decrease negative long-term outcomes. Without it, adults who were incestuously abused as children end up as adults presenting with a myriad of psychological problems, including sexual dysfunction, periods of promiscuity, depression, intense guilt, substance abuse, marital difficulties. And they risk emotionally or physically abusing their own children, committing incest themselves."

Jane inhales deeply. Noah is ever the shrink, even at a backyard barbecue. But the shoptalk sets her at ease. "Yeah. And who knows what happened to Kurt Jansen as a little boy, and how generational trauma was passed down to him. And Faith—Annalise's little sister—might not have known fully as a child what was going on in her home, but she certainly has some dysfunction in her own life."

"A mother can break the general pattern."

"As long as *she* is not the abuser."

He nods. "Right enough. And as they say, secrecy is a predator's best friend."

Jane ends up relaxing and enjoying the evening with her colleagues, but her longing for Matt grows overwhelming through the evening and she leaves early. She drives to her mother's house.

"Jane?" her mom says as she opens the door. "I thought you were going to be out tonight."

"I was. I—I, ah, just—" Her eyes fill with tears and emotion strangles her voice. "God, I don't know what's going on with me. I'm sorry."

"Come, come inside." Her mother hugs Jane, her arms tight and full with love, and she just holds, and Jane finally, after months, allows herself to sob properly. "Let it out, love. Your body needs you to let it go."

Jane steps back and angrily wipes away her tears. "I'm sorry. I really don't know what overcame me."

"Emotion is not weakness, Jane. Empathy is not soft. It's what makes us most human. Most strong." She pauses. "It's why I loved your father. And you are his daughter. Just as strong. Just as kind. And being a woman doesn't mean you should fight harder to appear cold and professional. We need to change perceptions about what is powerful and strong."

"It's still sure seen as weakness in my job." Jane shrugs out of her coat, and her thoughts turn to Helen Jansen and the Madonna and child image on the stained glass of the chapel. She thinks of Annalise and her baby buried in the dirt, and her own baby growing by the day in her belly. She thinks of Dr. Ella Quinn missing her own mother. "Thanks, Mom," she says.

"For what?"

"For being a great mom. Us daughters are not all so lucky."

"Want some tea?"

She laughs. "Yeah, sounds great. Tea can fix anything, right?" She follows her mother into the kitchen, thinking of Matt again, and how she misses him like a hole in her heart. She tells herself she might never find her own closure, like Annalise and Darryl. That's the nature of ambiguous loss. Or grief limbo. It doesn't always have a happy ending, or any ending.

But Jane has found some solace in working to find closure for others. And she still has a part of Matt living inside her—she needs to hold on to that. She has a responsibility in bringing a new little life into the world, and she'll just have to build family in new ways, while never letting go of hope.

# ABOUT THE AUTHOR

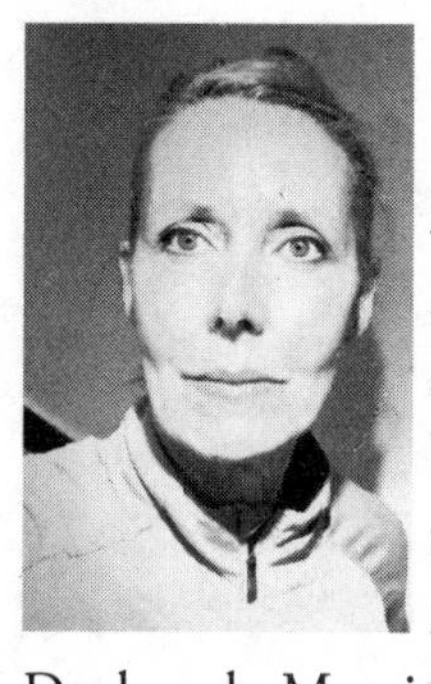

Loreth Anne White is the Amazon Charts, *Washington Post*, and *Bild* bestselling author of *The Maid's Diary*, *The Patient's Secret*, *Beneath Devil's Bridge*, *In the Deep*, *In the Dark*, *The Dark Bones*, and *A Dark Lure*. With more than three million books sold around the world and translations in over twenty languages, she is an ITW Thriller Awards nominee, a three-time RITA finalist, an overall Daphne du Maurier Award winner, an Arthur Ellis Award finalist, and the winner of multiple other industry awards. A recovering journalist who has worked in both South Africa and Canada, she now calls Canada home. She resides in the Pacific Northwest, dividing her time between Vancouver Island, a ski resort in the Coast Mountains, and a rustic lakeside cabin in the Cariboo. When she's not writing or dreaming up plots, you'll find her in the lakes or ocean or on the trails, where she tries—unsuccessfully—to avoid bears. For more information on her books, please visit her website at www.lorethannewhite.com.